DP —

I HOPE YOU ENJOY THE READ. STOP @ CHAPTER 2. LET ME KNOW YOUR THOUGHTS BACK AT PADRIACS.

Expect

Nothing

Less

Upcoming from Warren Strickler

THE BLUEHORSE CHRONICLES

Expect Nothing Less

Warren Strickler

 For information, contact June Muse Publishing, 6165 Blackwater Trail, Atlanta, Ga 30328.

ISBN 978-0-9818461-0-1

FIRST EDITION

I wish to express my sincere gratitude to the following individuals:

My wife, Renee, whose long suffering patience and abiding love informs my every word.

My favorite editor, Jo Ann Strickler, who is nothing like the mother described in this book.

Lynn Shine who helped transform my dream into reality.

Paul Brown for his perseverance, objectivity, and talent in developing artwork, and Adrienne Freeman for her finishing touches.

My friends and family who read and endured my early pages and offered their encouragement and suggestions.

Special thanks to Sonya West, an avid reader and kindred spirit, whose encouragement and support was critical to this project. I hold dear her kindness.

- Warren Strickler

In memory of G. B. Strickler who, for my money, is the smartest man in the world.

…I once was lost but now am found,
Was blind, but now I see…

Amazing Grace – John Newton 1772

I. Only the Young Die Well

There *is* life after death, and I am breathing testimony to this claim of divine insight. My first life was short and long ago but I remember it well; at least I remember the passionate student who was my father until I was five and he was twenty-two. One day he died, and my life took an abrupt turn that carried me along two paths at once. The after-father life, of which my memories are vivid but not as warm, left me with an irresponsible mother and a grandmother who regarded me with contempt. But this new life also blessed me with my soul mate who would become my teacher, the object of my affection, and elemental of the person I am today.

As a Catholic student I was schooled extensively on the subject of sin, of which my immoral mother and cantankerous grandmother constantly reminded me I was possessed, but it's tricky to judge any transgressions of mine prior to the suicide. Before that, in my entire life, I never committed adultery or coveted or killed; in fact I was virtually void of vice – one of the most fastidious of God's creatures. Once, I was convicted of being a thief, but that was a legal judgment not a moral one. Bearing false witness is a toss-up. I never spoke falsely of a fellow man, but my personal standing was based wholly on a fraud that began even before I was born. Still, I was one of the most trustworthy and reliable souls anyone could hope to know. Beyond that, I was optimistic to the point of being unrealistic. That's why the few who knew me were shocked at the news that I took my own life.

My funeral was generic – the kind of service that's held for a non-churchgoer, with a priest who knew nothing about me, a pittance of a crowd, and a mass that cited many religious writings, executed the rites, and mentioned the departed Charlie Lofton's name only twice. After all, what can any priest say about one of God's children who commits the cardinal sin of suicide? As funerals go it was hardly a glowing endorsement of me or my lifestyle, and it broke Gracie's heart that her friend had to suffer such an undignified send-off. Vince looked shaken. Bobby, who was preoccupied with the circumstances of my demise, was holding up well after the initial blow. He felt consoled that at least there were a few others besides him and Eileen who cared enough to attend. These are the people who have been influences in my life, some for the good, and others perhaps not so good, but none of them had more influence on me than Gracie. She took over where my father left off, and while I hated to lose him, I will be forever grateful that I found her.

……..

I knew nothing of Gracie the Sunday before Memorial Day in 1961. Father was studying in the tiny kitchen of our modest apartment when I asked what he was doing. He stood up, wringing his big hands together to say, "I'm reading about a concept called Chaos Theory. It's a school of thought that natural systems in the world seem to be disordered, but there is a mathematical way to…

"Charles, you are speaking to a five year old, you know," Mother interrupted as she squeezed by the kitchen table which was strewn with scribbled notepads and scientific textbooks. "He just recently learned his ABC's. You think you're going to teach him *that stuff?"*

"He's known his ABC's for two years," said Father. Then he said, "No thanks to you," but he said that a little quieter just as Mother made it to the bedroom.

"Have you seen the brooch that Mother gave me?" my mother called from the back of our apartment. "I know I left it right here on the dresser. Buddy, come back here and put your nice clothes on. Your grandparents will be here in just a minute, and we have to be ready. I don't want to catch hell from your grandmother for being late to church again."

"They want to be sure to get there in time to partake of the blood of Christ," Father said under his breath, sneaking a smile at me and tipping his thumb up to his lips in a drinking motion.

"Hello in there," Grandmother cried as she barged in the front door as if she owned the place. She *did* pay the rent so she probably felt she had license. "Is everyone ready?" she said. "Your father is in the car, and he doesn't want to wait." Patience was never one of Grandfather's strengths.

"Be right there, Mother," my mother said. "Buddy, get in here right now and put on your clothes," she shouted through pursed lips while applying her red lipstick. I caught the strong aroma of AquaNet hair spray wafting from her bedroom.

"Charles, you aren't even dressed," Grandmother scowled when she found Father and me sitting at the messy kitchen table. "You'll have to catch the trolley to a later Mass. You can take young Charlie with you then."

"I'm not going to Mass," Father said resolutely.

"What? Not again?" Grandmother complained. "What is wrong with you? It is important that you go to Mass, Charles."

"I'll tell you what's important, Mary," said Father. "It's important that I pass this Thermodynamics course so I can get out of school and get our family out of your hair." That's what my father said, but he meant he wanted to get Mother's family out of our hair.

"Well, surely you can find time to go to church," said Grandmother.

"Mary, you try taking my course load at Georgia Tech, making the grades I make, then work all night for Herb in that hell hole downtown. Meanwhile, take care of Buddy, here, and keep your daughter happy too; then you'll see how much time you can spend for meaningless mumbo jumbo every week." I looked at Grandmother, cowering from the response Father might have provoked, but she was speechless. Herb's hell hole that Father mentioned was the Bottom's Up Lounge, one of the striptease clubs my grandfather and his partners owned on the Peachtree Triangle in Downtown Atlanta. It was the place my father spent six nights a week working as a bouncer.

"What the hell's the hold-up in here?" Grandfather groused through our open apartment door. "I've been waiting in the car for half an hour for you people."

"Oh please," Mother said. "Oh please" frequently framed her remarks when she was dealing with my grandparents. "You haven't been here ten minutes. Buddy, I'm not going to tell you again," she insisted as her high heels clicked onto the kitchen linoleum.

"There is no time for Buddy to get ready now," Grandmother sneered, as her silent anger began to regain verbal momentum. He can stay here with Charles, and they can both go to the devil."

"What? Charles isn't coming?" said Grandfather, tugging Grandmother out of the kitchen toward the car.

"No, he doesn't have time for church. He's more interested in his Thermo-what-ever-you-call-it," Grandmother said sarcastically.

"Well, we've gotta go," said Grandfather impatiently. "Charles, you will have time for the barbeque on Memorial Day, won't you? I got the new grill in, and it's going to be the granddaddy of all cookouts. Everybody will be there, and they'll all want to see you." That was Grandfather, the Boss, speaking to his employee. The "everybody" he mentioned was the five of us and the contingent of cronies he worked with in his adult oriented businesses.

"Yes, I'll be there," said Father as the door shut, and the maelstrom of bitching that invaded our apartment with my grandparents' visits gave way to welcome peace. "Hypocrites," he snickered as he turned back to his books.

"So what *is* Chaos Theory," I said, overjoyed that I had cheated another trip to the boring ceremony my Grandparents insisted we attend each Sunday. I treasured the times I got to spend alone with my father whom I considered the smartest man in the world. I knew Father treasured them, too.

He jumped up again with fascination in his eyes and began espousing his own brand of theology. Father rejected religion; he was dedicated to the mathematical world he studied in college. I did not understand any of the principles involved in his lesson on Chaos Theory, but I will always remember how he finished and what my naive misinterpretation of his conclusion was. It went something like, "…so you see son, there are countless numbers of seemingly insignificant occurrences that constantly combine and magnify to construct the destiny of the world and everyone in it, making it difficult to predict large scale, global events. One butterfly on the other side of the world might flutter its wings in a particular manner, pushing the air in a certain direction. This will set off a chain reaction of events that might affect our weather or determine whether you or I have a good day."

My father's unintentional proclamation of the power of butterflies gave me an inflated regard for the delicate creatures.

"When is Memorial Day?" I asked him.

"Day after tomorrow," said Father. "Why?"

"'Cause I want to go see the butterflies in Grandfather's yard," I said. Our apartment was flanked by a treeless, grassless parking lot ill-suited to sustain any kind of nature other than the occasional ant or cockroach struggling along the asphalt tundra. My grandparents had a house on a big hill surrounded by what was a forest in my way of thinking. It teemed with all kinds of nature, and there would be plenty of butterflies flapping away, creating all kinds of chaos.

My father laughed, realizing my misinterpretation of his lesson, but he just said, "That's fine, Buddy, but first you have to be polite. Let Grandfather show off his new grill and act like you're interested. His cookouts are very important to him – to the point of insanity." When I asked him why, Father looked circumspect and earnestly tried to answer the question. "I don't know about your grandfather, Buddy. Maybe he doesn't have enough to do, and his barbeques make him feel important. They *are* good, and he's got the process honed into some kind of ritual of flame-broiling finesse. He prepares the marinade and the meat before the sun rises. The problem is, he fixes himself a stiff morning toddy at the same time. By the time he places the kindling papers and charcoal just so in the grill, he's usually well into his booze. So his ritual, which he insists requires split second timing, is inevitably performed by everyone else while he barks out his slurred commands that we all ignore. It usually comes off well, but your grandfather ends up passed out in his study, where he always does more sleeping than studying."

Whether or not Father nailed down the reason for Grandfather's obsession, he reminded me what to expect when we arrived before any of the other guests that Tuesday morning. Grandfather greeted us at the door with alcohol on his breath and a hint of unsteadiness in his gait. "Come in, come in," he said shaking Father's hand and accepting a peck on the cheek from Mother. "Come on back; I'll show you my new toy." We followed him through the house past a large pork loin and a beef tenderloin marinating in the kitchen for going on six hours. It was a good bet Grandfather was more infused than the meat. As we stepped out onto the patio, I got my first glimpse of the shiny sable behemoth standing inert, poised for someone to ignite it so it could work its magic. "This is the Craftsman Model 29DS," Grandfather crowed, his chest puffing from pride. "I got it from Sears and Roebuck just last week. It's been on backorder for months. Look at the duel sided grills with the top warming rack and this optional rotisserie", he said as if reading it from the catalog description. "See, it's got a metal hinged top and this underside ignition port." We couldn't see most of the features he was describing because the top was closed. I began to open it when my Grandfather jerked my hand away. "Don't open it, son," he cried. "I've got the newspapers and charcoal soaking in lighter fluid in there; I don't want it to evaporate in the sun." That suited me. The grill was impressive, but I had other things on my mind. I impatiently followed Mother – who was not at all impressed – back through the house on my way out front to find butterflies. Mother took a turn for the bathroom about the time Grandfather snapped the order to Grandmother. "Mary, I'm ready to light the grill. Bring me some matches."

I had just slammed the door when a deafening explosion

knocked me off the porch onto the walkway where glass from shattering windows – along with my entire world – crashed around me.

The police came up with the only plausible explanation at the time when they determined my grandfather used gasoline, not lighter fluid, to start the Craftsman 29DS. The great grill master bought his supplies in bulk, including large metal cans of charcoal lighter similar to standard gasoline can. When Grandfather, doubtlessly drunk, transferred a volatile liquid from a big can into a more manageable size container for grilling, he evidently took it from the lawnmower gas can. He created what investigators called a powerfully efficient bomb, blowing up himself and my father and leaving my Grandmother a paraplegic. The fumes trapped under the metal top exploded when the grill was lit through the handy ignition port – a feature that proved to be a flaw of the Craftsman 29DS grill. In 1961, though, no jury would think of finding Sears negligent for lacking the corporate conscious to put a bold label on its grills warning outdoor chefs of the dangers of loading them with gasoline and putting a match to them. Grandfather's accidental explosion was attributed to his own negligence; there was no litigation and no monetary award. I wondered what butterfly deigned to flap its wings and send the wind of death and uncertainty in my family's direction on that memorable Memorial Day.

II. The Summer of '61

My father never knew his parents who, by circumstances unknown, left him to grow up in an orphanage. My mother was an only child, so when Grandfather committed his reckless act he blew half my family away leaving her alone to care for me and my paralyzed grandmother.

By the time Grandmother came home, helpless and bitter from her hospital convalescence, the funerals had come and gone. Our truncated family was already moved into her foreboding, granite-gray stone castle which, having been repaired, looked in steep morbidity down the ivy clad landscape onto Habersham Road. Years before, Grandfather planted ivy to stop the erosion of his real estate investment. Since then, the hardy vines had flourished and become the front lawn. They created a comfortably familiar aroma for my outdoor escapes from my newly adopted dwelling.

It was a horrifying house that served as a twelve year detention center for me, but the decision to live there was a no-brainer; when Father and Grandfather checked out on the back patio, both sources of family income went with them. We had to leave our apartment to save money and care for Grandmother.

I hated the menacing Victorian immensity of the old place, especially with the aura of death that had so recently cloaked it, but worse than the house was the way our lifestyle deteriorated. Ever since the accident, Mother sat next to Grandmother's bed mixing drinks for both of them, rehashing the same discussion day after day. This made for a volatile concoction of emotions.

"Your grandparents would be tossing in their graves if they knew you took up with those people," my grandmother would say. By "took up" she meant Mother went to work for Grandfather's partners, dancing for tips at The Bottom's Up Lounge.

"Oh please," Mother would say, "*Those people* were Father's partners. You reaped the benefit of what *those people* did all these years."

"The Duttons and the Johnsons were always proper people," Grandmother would protest. They would never allow you to make a tramp of yourself."

Mother, inured to the tramp comment, would predictably say something like, "Gene Dutton ran a speakeasy downtown on Luckie Street during prohibition. He's the one who got Father involved in the business." Then Grandmother would insist that Grandfather was a respected dentist, to which Mother would reply, "Oh please, Father didn't earn a living pulling the teeth of those goons he ran around with. He only worked a couple of days a week."

"Nevertheless, you have no business being involved with that stuff," Grandmother would say, having no other defense.

"Then you tell me how we're going to put food on the table," Mother would say, and Grandmother would dredge up the incident.

"Well if you hadn't, you know..." Grandmother would say, shooting a glance in a random direction, indicating me, whether or not I happened to be there. She was referring to my parent's high school prom when my orphan father, in a single instance of fornication, experienced *his* first Big Bang, implanting what would eventually become me in my mother's teenage womb on the night of their high school prom. Father was a naive sophomore when he attended the dance with Mother, a junior with a little more *experience*. In that moment of adolescent, hormonal bliss, Father secured his future as a shotgun groom and a bouncer in the Bottoms Up Lounge, courtesy of Grandfather and his partners. He became a sort of indentured son-in-law to Grandfather. Nine months later I arrived as a hearty six-and-a-half pound bastard baby boy.

Our sordid social and familial condition was veiled from my callow eyes until years later when Hugh McDowell Jr. floated the revelation in the school lunchroom. Until then, I knew only my mother's storybook version of the unquenchable romance between two teenagers who fell madly in love and chose to get married and start a family just before Mother would leave for almost a year. She went to Europe to "study abroad", as she liked to put it, flavoring her words with a subtly aristocratic flair. It wasn't clear to me just what Mother ever studied, for she never pursued her education once she was back in the states. But she would tell me of the great love she and Father shared and how she missed him when she was in Europe, and what beautiful letters they wrote back and forth to each other. That was when I was too young to remember she was away. It never struck me strange that she would temporarily entrust her newlywed husband and infant son to her parents to experience a single year of meaningless studies overseas.

If things had gone another way my parents' early mistakes would probably have been overcome, and I might have remained ignorant of the harmful truth. With his night job routine and his in-law subsidized apartment Father was getting his college degree. Once Mother returned from her European excursion she was required to stay at home to present a charade of family refinement so as to rear me into a proper young man. In retrospect, if I had grown up to be proper, I would have been the first respectable one in my family.

If it isn't already understood, I should state, unequivocally, that my grandfather was a certifiable alcoholic, and my grandmother was his daily drinking partner. Their influence – genetically, and as role models – on my mother nurtured her alcoholism. Father was never much of a drinker. There was a time I thought I inherited his aversion to booze, but more likely I merely developed an aversion to the destruction it wrought.

After Grandmother's mean spirited remark about the irreversible past mistake Mother would say, "That was a long time ago," as her eyes began to mist. The insipid argument would repeat itself every day in one form or another until it ended in drunken crying sessions and apologies. Afterwards, Grandmother would pass out while Mother retreated to restore her alcohol ravaged face before she left for the club to seduce horny men out of their money.

It was an argument – and a bedroom – I avoided with terrified determination. I withdrew from the turmoil of the house, remaining an amazingly optimistic child in my outdoor sanctuary, but judiciously avoiding butterflies. I resolved to eschew the battle inside and concentrate on growing up to be like my father: confident and upbeat, and most importantly, the smartest man in the world. If the weather was disagreeable, I retired not to the house, but to the garage that sheltered the old Cadillac my grandfather left us. The detached garage was made of the same stone as the house, but it didn't hold two drunk, bickering women. Its imposing granite walls yielded to generous, bright windows that, even during storms, illuminated my private lair clearly enough for me to play. It was a two car garage divided by rusty metal poles that ran down the middle and delineated the parking places. Grandfather's Cadillac was the only car we owned, so the other side accommodated the space I needed to park myself in avoidance of the nasty doings in the house.

When Mother left for work each evening, I waited until Grandmother's tirades ebbed into slumber before I dashed through the main floor, past the daunting master bedroom and up the stairs to protect myself under my bed covers. I woke up early enough each morning to hear the old Cadillac squeaking and groaning its way up our steep driveway, carrying Mother home from a night of denigrating work. My ears followed her routine of checking on my sleeping grandmother before going into the bathroom and preparing for bed. When I was sure that Mother was fast asleep, I got up for the day and returned to the garage while the sun came up and directed its warm morning rays across the southern windows of my lair. Even if the day was cold, the combination of rising sunlight and the heat from the freshly driven car warmed me as the metal of the engine ticked and creaked, indicating it was expanding or contracting as it cooled – I didn't know which, but I was sure Father could have explained it to me in detail.

One day, my first summer living at Grandmother's, I left the sanctuary of the garage to forage behind the house and lose myself in the woods of the backyard. Suddenly, a girl appeared from nowhere. Her abrupt presence startled me for a moment, but I was instantly smitten.

"Who are you?" I asked.

"Annie," she said with a smile that made me love her. "Are you Charlie?"

"Yes. Where did you come from?" I said.

"That house," she said, pointing toward the back edge of our property. In the distance, beyond the lush woods and our vine covered fence, I could make out the back of the big brick house to which I had never given a second thought.

"You live there?" I asked, watching Annie nod her head, making her silky blonde hair bounce around the most beautiful face I had ever seen. "How do you know my name?" I said, imagining she might be some kind of divine creature sent from heaven to deliver me from my new home.

"My mother told me," she said. "She told me your father died, and I should come be your friend. She said I ought to keep you company."

Mrs. Fiona Willingham was in her backyard weeding her garden that Memorial Day morning when the exploding Craftsman 29DS knocked her off her knees. She knew my grandparents only by name before the accident, but she made it her business to find out what happened. She visited us one day shortly after we moved in to bring us a casserole and some groceries. I remembered meeting her, but I had no idea she lived behind us, and I certainly didn't know she was the curator of the seven year old vision who stood before me.

"What is it like when your father dies?" Annie asked.

"I don't know," I said. "It's bad, I guess." When I was five, time crept along at the only pace a child can handle. It had been forever since I had been born, and it seemed like a long time since my father died. It was simply my life's experience. I didn't know anything else.

"My mother's dying," said Annie, flatly. "She thinks I don't know about it, but I do. I heard her and my father talking about it."

I knew how my father died – in one accidental instant. I never heard of anyone dying slowly. "What do you mean?" I said. "Why is she dying?"

"She has cancer," said Annie. "She's had it before, and now she has it again."

"She should go to the doctors," I said. "They can make her better. They made my grandmother better," I said, feeling a twinge of guilt that I wished they hadn't.

"She goes to doctors, but they can't make her better," said Annie. "Cancer is a terrible thing. I don't ever want to get it, because it will kill you just like the bomb that killed your father."

I wanted to tell her it was a grill, not a bomb, but I let it go.

"How did she get cancer?" I said, anxious to find out so I could avoid it.

"I don't know. She just got it," Annie said with a dainty shrug.

"Maybe it was a butterfly," I said.

"A butterfly?" she scoffed, apparently unaware of the havoc the entomological wonders were capable of creating. "What do you mean, a butterfly?" she said.

I proceeded to explain my warped interpretation of my father's explanation of Chaos Theory to my new, fetching friend. When I was finished with my own version of Father's lecture, Annie considered it for a minute and smiled, indicating she liked my idea. The one thing my explanation had in common with Father's was its wordiness. As I was concluding my dissertation, I heard Annie's mother calling from beyond the woods.

"Annie," came the pleasant adult voice through the trees. "Time to come home."

"That's Mama," she said, still smiling about the butterfly theory. "I gotta go."

"Right now?" I said, desperately afraid I would never again see her.

"I've gotta go have lunch," she said, turning away from my eager eyes. She skipped away into the woods hesitating at the fence to look back and giggle. "Steer clear of the bad butterflies," she cried as she disappeared over the fence into her own yard.

I watched, awestruck, as her blonde hair followed her over the fence and out of sight. That was my first meeting with Ann Grace Willingham, and I pined for her the instant the meeting was over. From that moment, I wanted only to see her again.

I went in to make myself a peanut butter sandwich. The familiar clanking of ice against the short cocktail glasses emanating from the open door of my grandmother's ground floor bedroom let me know that Mother was awake and was probably serving the first round of the day. I could hear muted conversation, amicable enough, coming from the master bedroom. I hoped it remained amicable as I quietly went about the business of preparing lunch. Since our move to Grandmother's I had mastered the art of padding around the house in stealth quietness, lest I trigger inquisitive and intrusive comments like, "Is that you Charlie? Come in and say hi to your grandmother and me." By the time I met Annie, my activities around the big house went as unnoticed as the silent growth of the prolific ivy in our front yard. I ate my sandwich and chugged a glass of milk as quickly as possible, then raced to the back yard and camped near the fence, sheepishly praying that I would get another chance with my new acquaintance.

The day came to a disappointing close when my mother called me in as she was leaving for work near sundown. As Mother's car coasted down the driveway, I silently raced past my passed out grandmother, upstairs to bed. Sleep eluded me for too long, but when I finally did nod off, I had my most pleasant dreams since Grandfather's Big Bang. Even the complaining Cadillac couldn't rouse me from the airy images parading through my soothing sleep early the next morning.

Mother had already gone to bed when I awoke, suddenly panicked to see I had let the sun rise high in the morning sky. I leapt from my bed without a sound and threw on my clothes, angry that I may have let an opportunity to catch a glimpse of Annie escape me. It escaped me that I was probably the only kid my age in the city who kept the kind of hours I kept, and it would be awhile before Annie even opened her eyes.

I skipped breakfast and camped myself at the fence that faced Annie's house. An eternity passed, and soon I had to pee, but I refused to leave my post. Finally, her back door opened, and Annie emerged in all her grace and beauty. She skipped up to the fence and greeted me. I felt as if my dogged vigilance paid off when she spoke to me and climbed over the fence. I began to speak back when I realized how desperately I had to pee. It was hard to concentrate on anything except not wetting my pants as tears welled up in my eyes from the pain in my bladder, but I couldn't surrender the moment.

"Are you crying?" Annie said, about the time the warm flood began to run down my legs, creating a dark stain in the crotch of my light brown shorts. By then I was crying from embarrassment, and I ran away in shame, certain that the worst of all butterflies had ruined my life. I fled to the sanctuary of the garage, cursing the human body and its need to perform bodily functions. In the garage I pouted, trying to devise a plan to keep my indiscretion from my mother. All I had to do was hang my wet shorts on a tree limb behind the garage in the sun and sneak into the house for a new outfit, and Mother would be none the wiser. The wet clothes were cold and uncomfortable. I took them off and waited until the right moment to move. My sense of my Mother's whereabouts and my ability to avoid her detection was almost second nature, so at the proper time I crept naked around the garage and tossed my shorts and underwear up on an accessible branch. I had a sixth sense when it came to eluding Mother and Grandmother, but I had not yet gained such an advantage over Annie. As I rounded the corner of the garage and made my way toward the back door, Annie, for the second day in a row startled me with her presence. This time I was exposed to her in all my nakedness. It didn't seem to faze her. I stopped, frozen in my tracks from mortification.

"Were you crying because you wet you pants?" said Annie. "Don't worry about it. I've done that before, but it's been a long time. When you get older like me you don't do that anymore."

Her tone was condescending, but I knew she was trying to make me feel better. Still, I considered myself at a disadvantage, being bare bodied, and I tried to hide myself behind a tree like Adam before God. Then my goddess spoke the words that would change my world and cement our new relationship forever.

"Don't hide behind there," she said. "I want to see you naked. Let's go back in there, and I'll take off my clothes and show you myself." Annie was indicating my garage.

"I'll do it if you will," I said eagerly.

There couldn't have been a more welcome suggestion, and I came out from behind the tree less self conscious. We went into the garage where Annie nonchalantly removed her clothes to reveal something I had never seen, but something I knew I liked. In all my years with my mother, I had no recollection of seeing her unless she was dressed. I knew there was a difference between men and women; now, looking at Annie, I was captivated by the sight. While she didn't live in such a superficially puritanical household as mine, she seemed intrigued by my apparatus as well. When I asked her why she didn't have what I had, she said she had something better. I didn't know why, but I had to agree.

"Mama says this is like my own treasure," Annie said seriously, pointing at the area of my fascination. "She told me some other things, too. I know she's trying to tell me about girl things while she's still here to tell me." Annie's mood became momentarily somber, but I was too engrossed with her body to notice. The analogy of a treasure for what I was looking at seemed perfect to me.

"It looks graceful," I said, having no idea how or when the word "graceful" entered my vocabulary. She seemed to brighten at the idea.

"Yeah, it is graceful," she said, smiling. The little girl who was about to turn eight suddenly looked circumspect as she looked past me into the distance. She seemed transported by our curiosity spawned conversation. Annie may have been only two years older than I was, but she was possessed with twenty years more wisdom. It would take me almost forty years to close that gap.

"Grace is my middle name," she said. "I'm Ann Grace. In fact, that's what I want to be called – Grace."

"You want to be called Grace?" I said.

"Absolutely," she said too seriously for a girl her age. "I don't like my first name; it's too common, but I like Grace, and that's what I want you to call me from now on." It wouldn't take me long to learn that my new friend had an affinity for descriptive monikers.

"Okay," I said, willing to do anything my newfound love asked of me.

"Say it, Charlie; call me Grace," she implored. "I want to hear how it sounds."

"Okay Grace," I said, mystified by the sudden importance this name had taken on for her, although it did seem to fit.

We spent the next few minutes, gawking at each others' bodies, and I got used to calling her Grace – and then Gracie. I share this private, childhood experience of sexual discovery not for gratuitous effect, but rather to say that I became interested in sex at an early age, and lost my enthusiasm for it at an age when most boys can't take their minds off it.

In the muffled distance we heard her mother calling, "Annie." She jumped back into her clothes and before she made her way toward the fence she smiled at me and reminded me, "Steer clear of the bad butterflies."

"Okay Gracie, goodbye," I called as I watched her disappear through the woods. She sounded so grown-up, but then, Gracie would always sound grown-up.

That was the first event of my life in which the garage played a pivotal role. It provided privacy for us for the rest of the summer, and we grew to like each other and count on each other. Actually, I counted on Gracie more than she counted on me; after all, she *was* two years older than I was – and twenty years more mature.

I began to visit Gracie in her yard, and I met her mother and father, who were older than either one of my parents. They were both more like my grandparents, except that they were approachable. I didn't see Mr. Willingham very often. He was a lawyer who kept long hours at work. When I did see him, he was always kind to me in that grandfatherly way. He was an interesting man who seemed to know as much as my father knew. Mrs. Willingham took to me right away, and having a good sense of what life was like at my house, she was happy to have Gracie and me under her own supervision. We would play together in the backyard, and Mrs. Willingham would check on us regularly.

While Gracie was mature for her age, I was bright for mine, and Mrs. Willingham recognized this fact. She was often telling me how smart I was – something I hadn't heard since my father used to say it. She would have me in for lunch, and she was impressed with how independently I went about preparing my own meals. I would climb up to get our glasses out and pour the milk without being asked. Mrs. Willingham would say, "See how Charlie takes the initiative to do things without being told, Annie. You would do well to follow his example."

Gracie would look cross as she complained to her mother, "Mama, it's *Gracie*, not Annie," and she would shoot me a sly, knowing grin. Eventually, she wore her mother down regarding her new name, and she became known as Gracie around her household. With that, just like a caterpillar changing to a butterfly, she began her own metamorphosis, to become Gracie, the wonderful girl who would grace me with her presence and put meaning into my existence.

She was the only thing to salvage that summer of my father's death. I was young and Mother was absent. With Father gone, Gracie became my new father figure, in a feminine way. To me, she was a hero, as my father had been. Like Father, she was a teacher, but while Father slanted more toward the scientific nature of the world, Gracie was a creative creature, always observing and commenting, styling a phrase or assigning insightfully appropriate nicknames to people – or things – whose proper names she deemed inadequately evocative for their exaggerated characteristics. I hung on to her every word.

Gracie's father was not just a lawyer, but a literary agent. I thought he must have read everything that was ever written, and his influence on Gracie had her devouring every book she could get her hands on. Her father gladly provided the fodder for her reading compulsion. The authoritative Gracie set about teaching me to read, and I was a quick study and caught on in a snap. Soon we found ourselves sitting, silently, for hours in her sunny breakfast room reading to ourselves, while Mrs. Willingham went about her daily activities until she became too tired and had to lie down. I would read the books Gracie put aside a couple of years earlier, and as time went on, I had to interrupt Gracie fewer and fewer times to ask her how to pronounce a word or what the word meant. When Mrs. Willingham fell asleep, Gracie and I would take the opportunity to visit my garage where we were completely unsupervised and we could do the one thing I enjoyed more than anything else with my friend and mentor.

It wasn't unusual, when we were on my property, to hear Grandmother's ranting emanate from the windows of her downstairs bedroom. The unpleasantness seemed a normal part of existence for me, and her spiteful words long ago became white noise I didn't even notice. They bothered Gracie, though, and one day she said to me, "Charlie, how does your mother put up with Bloody Mary and her tirades?"

I had to ask her what she meant. Somewhere, she had read about Mary Tudor, and she knew enough to explain that she was a queen of England back in the fifteen hundreds whose reign was marked by hundreds of executions. In Gracie's mind, my grandmother's propensity for persecution along with her predilection for the bottle, rendered the label fit for the infirmed queen who held court in her depressing bedroom with her lone subject – my mother. Mother would always be "the Mary Widow", to Gracie. That was her ironic use of a homophone to refer to the Franz Lehar's operetta, since Mother was neither merry, nor wealthy like the title character of the opera. The whole business of Gracie was fascinating to me, and I absorbed it all, constantly entertained and educated by her slant on the world.

We could never spend much time in my house, because Gracie said it was stifling her. After she "had all she could stand for one afternoon", Gracie insisted we "flee the Rock" as she came to call it – not so much because of the ingredients of the house, but more for the oppressive, prison like nature it held for us. It was another term she picked-up from her reading, and it struck just the right nuance for the weight of the place. When I was with Gracie at her house I felt like a prisoner who was freed, or at least temporarily paroled for a day release program until I had to return to the Rock in the evening.

That was the summer of 1961 – the summer I lost my father and found Gracie and learned to read and discovered the pleasures of the flesh – Gracie's flesh – and it was the summer I will always remember for its deep pain and unbridled joy.

III. The Garage Incident

As the summer of sixty-one came to a close, Mrs. Fiona Willingham came to pay a visit to my mother. In her typically cordial style, she brought along a small gift for Mother as a calling card of sorts. "Let me get right to the point Mrs. Lofton," she said to my mother as she studied her foggy eyes. "I'm sure you have been planning for Charlie to start school, and I wanted you to be aware of some options he might have." If mother was indeed planning for me to go to school, she never said anything about it to me.

"Well, I just figured he'd go to the public school," Mother said. It wasn't clear she even knew which public school I would attend.

"Well, that's fine," Mrs. Willingham said. "I hope you don't mind if I make a suggestion, though."

Nothing could offend Mother, who was clueless when it came to providing for her child. She just looked blankly at Mrs. Willingham and said, "Go ahead."

"I'm sure you've noticed that Charlie is an exceptionally bright boy," Mrs. Willingham proceeded. You and your late husband must have done a wonderful job with him up to now," she said. "In a matter of weeks he has caught up to my daughter's reading level and maybe even surpassed it. I would go so far as to say that he may be a prodigy."

Mother looked puzzled. She had no idea I read books, but she tried to maintain decorum. "We always felt education was important for our son," she said unconvincingly.

"Yes, it is," Mrs. Willingham insisted, giving Mother the sense she had said the right thing. "That's why I want to make sure you know what is available for him. You may know that we send Gracie to St. Mary's and…"

"Oh, we don't have the money for that Mrs. Willingham," my mother interrupted. "I appreciate your concern, but he will do just fine at public school."

"Well, that's just what I wanted to tell you, Mrs. Lofton," Mrs. Willingham pressed. There are options. I know you are a member of the church. St Mary's provides a limited number of scholarships for members who aren't able to afford the steep tuition, providing the students are capable of doing the work. Here in the Buckhead area, there is little need among the members for such financial aid. In fact, the church has to solicit other parishes to give away the scholarships. If Charlie tests as well as I am sure he will, the church would love to have one of their own get the benefit of the financial aid."

Mother looked at me sideways, a little surprised that I might be actually be as smart as her neighbor seemed to think. I looked at Mrs. Willingham. She looked at my mother. There was an instant of embarrassing clarity that my mother knew practically nothing about me. It was so embarrassing that Mother could do nothing other than acquiesce. "How do I go about getting the scholarship for him?" she said.

Mrs. Willingham breathed a satisfied sigh. "I'll talk to Father Baxter and get the necessary paperwork. We don't have much time, but I am sure we can get it worked out. What Mrs. Willingham didn't tell Mother was that she had already brought aptitude tests from the school and had me take them when I was at Gracie's. The basic Math my father had drilled into me since I could talk and Gracie's books combined to impress the administration and faculty of St. Mary's. They considered starting me in second grade, but Mrs. Willingham told mother I should start school with kids my own age. After that it was simply a matter of completing the forms and I became a Catholic student in the fall of 1961.

Since I didn't attended kindergarten, and the farthest I had been from my house without my mother was two backyards away at Gracie's, Mother had the misguided notion I might get homesick being away at school. While Mrs. Willingham was telling me how great school was, and how I was going to be such a good student, Mother was busy assuring me that if I got scared, or didn't like, it I could call her and she would come get me. What she thought I would do instead of go to school I have no idea. No matter, her fears were unfounded. The first day of school I eagerly fixed my breakfast, and while mother slept, I wolfed it down and ran through the two backyards to meet Gracie at the end of her driveway and wait for the bus. After that day, I never wanted school to end. The more time I spent in school meant the less time I spent in the shadow of the Rock.

The nuns who taught us wore the strange habits, and some were less agreeable than others, but they all gave each student a lot of attention, and they cared about our educations. I was so keen to stay ahead, I worked hard and became one of Sister Bella's best students. I was following in the third grader Gracie's footsteps, and I was already grateful to Mrs. Willingham for insisting I go to St. Mary's.

Buckhead is an area in North Atlanta. While we were growing up it was like a conservative, small town unto itself where the gossip mill worked overtime, spilling grains of sensational news gradually, but persistently. The fact of the mother of an honor student at Saint Mary's being an exotic dancer was too salaciously explosive to be contained. As we grew older, and meddlesome mothers were overheard by their sons and daughters tittering about Mary Lofton and her scandalous behavior, I began to catch rumblings at school. It was hard not to notice some of my classmates snickering behind my back, but I ignored them and pretended I didn't know what they were saying.

Hugh McDowell Jr. was in my class at St. Mary's. He was a popular kid who came from a well-to-do family. His father was a local politician on Atlanta's Board of Aldermen who was held in high esteem in our tony part of town. Hugh's friends were of the athletic variety, popular with the girls – the kind of clique to which many of my classmates aspired to belong. I was not athletic at all, and I was happy to let them be while I concentrated on schoolwork. I was determined that high academic achievement was going to be the vehicle to deliver me from the Rock and Bloody Mary, so I kept to myself and to my textbooks of salvation.

Hugh was not content to leave the universe of Saint Mary's in its natural order. He felt an unexplainable obligation to collide his world into mine, and his compulsion created cosmic disturbances for me. He began to make thinly veiled comments like, "Hey Lofton, how's your mother doing?" or "Did your mother bring you to school this morning, or was she not home from work yet?"

Hugh's entourage would hoot with laughter, as if he had divined a hilarious gem requiring more wit than Hugh McDowell was capable of mustering. I just smiled in silence, confident I could outclass Hugh in a verbal joust with a comment such as, "No, Hugh, your philandering father kept her overtime." Gracie was not immune from the rumor epidemic, and I got that item from her. I resisted, confident my riposte would transform the contest from one of words to one of fists, and on that front I was no match for Hugh.

His need to call attention to me was puzzling, since no one else seemed to even notice my presence. Nevertheless, Hugh became my bad butterfly according to Gracie. I would simply say he was my nemesis. When school was out, and I found Gracie, I was under her protection. Gracie was intimidating to everyone at Saint Mary's, including the nuns. When I was with Gracie nobody crossed me, particularly Hugh McDowell. As she put it, "When I'm around, Charlie, nobody'll screw with you." I would have stuck with Gracie forever, but things wouldn't go that way in a world that existed at the whim of Father's chaos theory.

....

Over time, Gracie – the devourer of everything readable – became the student body's authority on everything, including sex. By the time she was in seventh grade, she was counseling the high school students on sexual terminology, and practices. It wasn't just because of her prolific reading, but her parents were also more liberal than most families in our community.

The Willingham's approach created two effects. First, everyone at Saint Mary's – younger and older – sought Gracie for advice when it came to matters of the flesh. Second, although Gracie was the authority, she was never a participant. She was always a little more mature than anyone else, and she didn't waste her time with the boys at Saint Mary's.

By the time I finished fifth grade, Gracie's maturing body was showing gradual signs of its own metamorphosis into a young lady. This made her reluctant to get undressed for me, and made me more desperate for her to do it. One summer day, though, in my perpetual quest I caught her in a mood. We were in her father's study perusing books from his extensive collection when I came across a tantalizing passage from Henry Miller's *Tropic of Capricorn*, where Henry described a torrid encounter with Maxie's sister Rita. When I finished reading it, I looked eagerly at Gracie and said, "Listen to this." I reread the salacious words to Gracie. By the time I finished, Gracie bore a deep sense of desire into me with her soft eyes.

"C'mon," was all she said as she took my hand. We walked outside, through her backyard and climbed the fence on our way to my garage of paradise. We didn't say a word, but we danced in lock step directly to the Cadillac where she opened the back door, pushed me down and lay beside me. We started to kiss, something we had never done, and at that moment I thought I was a man and Gracie would be my lover until the day we would get married.

Perhaps it was my surprise at the rapturous turn of events, or maybe I was just too aroused to be in possession of all my faculties, but my otherwise reliable radar for Mother malfunctioned. In one unpredictable act, Mother burst into the garage door to retrieve the new bottle of Vodka she uncharacteristically forgot to take out of the Cadillac. Gracie stood straight up, her clothes slightly askance. I jumped up and tried to hide the symptom of my excitement. Mother, who was on one of her angry drunks, gasped, and with one hand up to her mouth she brought the other hand across my face with enough force to slap my arousal into oblivion. A tirade of scorn was directed at Gracie who, for once, lost her air of maturity. Terrified and debased, Gracie burst into tears and ran out of the garage bawling.

Mother turned to me, screaming that I was a sinner, and would go straight to hell. I had no interest in what my mother, the embodiment of hypocrisy, had to say to me in that terrible moment; I wanted only to catch up to Gracie to comfort her and make sure she was okay. I ran past my mother, who was still ranting alcohol induced curses at me. Before my eyes could adjust to the summer afternoon sunshine, Gracie had straightened her shorts and shirt and was climbing the fence back into her yard. I called after her, but she ignored my cries and ran into her house.

"Steer clear of the bad butterflies," I whispered out of my mother's earshot. All of a sudden, I thought, in one moment of carelessness, I might have lost that confidential relationship I shared with Gracie. I turned defiantly to my mother, shouted, "Fuck you!", and ran, laughing from the property. My mother was too drunk and out of shape to chase me, and I just sped blindly away from the house until I couldn't run any more. Then I continued to walk. After hours of walking I found myself at Chastain Park where I sat and watched a Pony League baseball game. When the game finally ended, I knew my only option was to begin the long trek back home. Mother would have left for work by the time I got home; I thought I could get in some shuteye and be gone again before she returned. At least that was the plan.

When Mother couldn't find me after a few hours, she called the police, crying frantically that her son was missing. The police, being sober – and not at all frantic – could not be fooled by a ten year old mind deficient in criminal concepts and strategies. I made it about halfway home when a black and white Ford with the red light on top pulled up to my side of the road.

"What's your name, son," the officer asked me.

"Charlie Lofton," I said.

"Come get in the car," said the officer. "Your mother is

worried about you."

I was astonished the incident escalated into a police matter. I got into the car and rode in silence back to The Rock. The policeman reported recovering me over his radio. Soon the powerful cruiser roared effortlessly up my driveway where Mother stood at the top looking pitiful, as only she could. She ran to greet the police car.

"Oh thank you, officer," she said trying to maintain steady speech. "I'm sorry to bother you, but I was so worried I didn't know what else to do."

"Don't worry about it, ma'am," said Officer J. Saler. "Usually, in these situations, the kids aren't gone too long. I *do* see he's got a pretty good welt on the left side of his face, though. It looks like it'll probably turn into a black eye. How'd that happen?"

Mother didn't lie. "Yes, I lost my temper and slapped him," she said in awkward shame. "I know I shouldn't have."

The thoughtful policeman looked at both of us and said, "Let me speak to your son for a moment." He took me out of my mother's hearing range and knelt down in front of me, taking a closer look at my injury, which was not insignificant. He pressed his hand lightly against the swelling. "How does that feel? Does it hurt?" My mother was walking toward us, trying to protest that I was okay. "Please ma'am," the policeman said, "I need you to step back over there."

It had been a few hours, and I had to be honest; I shrugged and shook my head, no.

"Has your mom ever hit you before?" he said. Again I shook my head. "So you want to stay here with your mom?" he said.

I had no idea what my alternatives were, and I said, "Yes sir." I didn't want to go anywhere that would take me away from Gracie.

"Okay then," Officer Saler said, leading me back to my shaken mother. "Here he is, ma'am," he said to her. "I think he's all right, but you need to watch out for that kind of thing. Kids can be a handful, but you have to realize you're a lot stronger than they are, and you can really hurt them if you're not careful. And you son – you need to obey your mother, and don't be running away, scaring her like that." We both nodded like children and Officer J. Saler left us to settle our differences on our own.

Mother took me inside, lecturing me on the sins of sex, insinuating that the older Gracie was not a "proper girl" for me to spend my time with, unaware that I was the instigator of the incident. I noticed Mother had this strange tendency to misinterpret situations. That tendency usually wrought detrimental effects for me. This was such an instance. She promised to find me new friends – boys my own age – with whom I would do the kind of things boys did. I had no desire for other friends, but I judged it pointless to try to explain anything to my mother at the moment.

I was awake the next day before the Cadillac groaned its way up the driveway, and I could hardly wait for my mother to complete her morning ritual and fall asleep. I would have to wait for Gracie to emerge, since she was not the early riser I was, but I settled myself by the fence the way I did that first day I got to know her. I did not want to get that intimate again with her for a long time to come, though; that was the last thing I had on my mind after the fiasco in the garage. Gracie never emerged from her house that day. The next day I waited at the fence again, but Gracie wouldn't come outside.

IV. Two Patio Incidents

The third day after *the garage incident*, when Mother woke up, she called outside for me to come see her. I hated to leave my post at the fence, lest I miss my chance to catch Gracie. I sighed in exasperation, but stomped out of the woods to find Mother in her robe at the back door, looking tired.

"Charlie, you're going to keep away from Annie Willingham's house," she said, lacking the authority to enforce the proclamation. After all the years, Mother was the only one who never acknowledged that Annie was now Gracie, because she never paid enough attention to be clued in to our developments. "That girl is nothing but trouble," she continued. "Tomorrow I'll bring over some boys your own age for you to spend time with. You know your Uncle Vincent and his boy Eddie. Eddie's a year younger than you, but you like him."

"Uncle" Vincent Palomino was a partner of my grandfather's, and the rare recent times I saw him, he was nice to me, but my youthful intuition left me uneasy about him. He used to be at all of Grandfather's notable barbeques, but since the blow-out barbeque of 1961, he had been scarce. He ran the club where Mother danced. I saw his son Eddie only a few times, and I didn't know him well enough to like him. I had no desire to know him better.

"And my friend Candi's son Bobby," Mother pressed on. "You don't know him, but he is a nice kid your age, and you'll like him, too."

Skeletons tend to emerge from closets in unpredictable ways. Bobby Wells was told he was literally a bastard by his own mother, and he unabashedly divulged this article of dirty laundry to Eddie and me early in our relationship, long before my own illegitimate beginnings were revealed to me in a school cafeteria.

I never knew who Bobby's father was, and Bobby was at the same disadvantage. Judging from his features, accented by creamed coffee colored skin, the father must have been a Latin lover of Candi's, but even she probably wasn't sure who he was. When Mother offered to take Bobby off her hands every few days, Candi was glad to have a place to send her ten year old, allowing her more time to pursue her ample parade of paying gentlemen suitors. Besides her job at the club as a dancer, the enterprising Candi, in an entrepreneurial spirit that earned her extra money, ran a cottage industry of her own out of her home during the day. When Bobby was younger she thought her discretion was shielding her son from her illicit activities, but Bobby, like Gracie, was wise beyond his years.

So my mother, in all her misguided wisdom, proposed to introduce Eddie Palomino and Bobby Wells into my social milieu. She did it to introduce me to a culture that would foster my development as a more "normal" kid, as she put it. I only wanted to get back to the fence and catch Gracie. Mother finished what she had to say, and returned to Bloody Mary's room to be bartender. I re-manned my post at the fence, and waited vigilantly until Gracie finally emerged.

In all the time I'd known her, I'd never seen her cry before *the garage incident*, and when I saw her walk out the back door the first thing that came to my mind was how she had looked then – crying as she ran from my hysterical mother. She looked like she wanted to cry again as she strode with her normal sense of purpose toward the boundary that separated a wholesome upbringing from a dysfunctional childhood environment. In my myopic outlook, I thought she was still upset with me.

"Are you okay?" I asked timidly.

"Mom's gotten worse, all of a sudden," said Gracie, holding back the tears that I never wanted her to have to shed again. "I've been at the hospital with her. She's going to have to stay there for a couple of more days. Dad just brought me home," she said, her voice quivering.

The shock of what she told me vanquished the silly, self

absorbed concerns I had only moments before, and I felt selfish for being so rapt in my needy obsession with Gracie. Mrs. Willingham had been sick ever since I met her, and she had survived so long she must have felt she would beat her own bad butterfly. I just fooled myself into believing her situation would go on forever. Perhaps Gracie was duped by that same deceptive hope. Suddenly, it was apparent to Gracie – and through Gracie it was apparent to me – that her mother was not going to be with us much longer. I reached for Gracie and held her tight; I felt closer to her than ever, and I wanted to be strong for the girl who I knew would always be stronger than I was.

....

Gracie spent her days at the hospital and, surprisingly, as Mother promised, I became host to Eddie Palomino and Bobby Wells. My two visitors hit it off well with each other, but their common interests made *me* feel like the guest at my own house. Gracie had been my exclusive partner; she wasn't like other girls in those days. She was never one to play with dolls or have tea parties, but when we were together we were reading, or studying the natural world in our lush yards, or listening to the rock and roll she introduced to me.

Bobby and Eddie had no interest in such cerebral pursuits; they wanted to play catch and, realizing in embarrassment I didn't even have a baseball glove or baseball, I was relegated to watching those two toss the most suitable rock they could find back and forth until they quit in frustration. As days passed, we anticipated my lack of sports oriented supplies so we engaged in other activities – "boys will be boys" activities, as Mother would put it. Gracie was absent from my life while she dealt with her mother's illness. During that stretch, my Uncle Vincent Palomino brought his son and Bobby Wells to my house where I came to know my guests a little better each visit.

While Gracie and I would capture various bugs, and feed

them, and observe them – and Mrs. Willingham would provide reference books that told us about our new subjects – Bobby and Eddie liked to use the creatures as objects of their violence. We threw rocks at birds, and tortured caterpillars and worms with sharpened sticks. We destroyed ant mounds, carrying out an ant massacre as the frantic critters scrambled about, confused by their lack of shelter, struggling in vain to save the queen before they were obliterated. I took part in these alien activities with Gracie and the ant farm that we kept at her house weighing on my guilty conscious.

When we got tired of the carnage at the anthill we moved to my lair in the dank shade of the garage. When the loaded Craftsman 29DS blew-up my loaded grandfather he left behind a few artifacts, some that resided in the garage, none that interested me except for an old telescope I was trying to put back together. When I discovered it, the telescope was a scattered collection of lenses, gears, and rust, and I was having trouble finding some of the parts. Many of the parts I *did* find were in no condition to be reassembled. I gave up on the project, but the parts lay in an organized fashion in the back of the garage.

The day before Mrs. Willingham came home from the hospital, Eddie, Bobby, and I were sharing unsupervised time in my garage. The telescope pieces weren't the first thing to catch Eddie's eye. He went straight to Grandfather's grilling ensemble. That was one set of artifacts I never disturbed. When Eddie started uncovering bags of charcoal, tongs and spatulas, and big and small cans of charcoal starter among other barbeque paraphernalia, a stampede of memories trampled over me. My appreciation for the potential mayhem from such paraphernalia grew my eyes wide.

"I don't think we ought to get into those things," I said, nervously.

My new acquaintances knew nothing of the power of those things to transform healthy, whole people into dead people, but I knew better. Bobby and Eddie were fascinated with the newfound tools of mischief – and mischief was what Eddie

Palomino and Bobby Wells were all about, as Gracie would later put it.

Eddie uncovered a case of *Blue Diamond* matches – the large wooden matches with the blue striking tips were the only proper way to light a barbeque, and grandfather was nothing if not a proper barbeque chef. The twenty or so match boxes were neatly stacked like a complex of drawers. Inside the drawers lay perfectly lined square matches looking like little soldiers with blue heads and a torso, but no limbs. As I moved cautiously toward Eddie's discovery and peered inside, the prone, blue headed soldier-matches feigned a deceivingly benign attitude. I knew they were capable of coming alive to unleash their destructive energy at the slightest hint of friction.

"Matches," Bobby said with salivary excitement. "Lots of 'em," he cried, even more impressed when he realized the enormity of the lode Eddie uncovered.

"Mother told me to leave those alone," I lied. Mother had no idea what the old garage housed, and even if she knew the matches were there she wouldn't have thought to warn me away from them.

"And lighter fluid," Bobby said, ignoring my concerns. The thought of the combination of those four – Bobby and Eddie and matches *and* lighter fluid – had me on the verge of panic. I could sense the bad butterflies swarming all around us.

"Yeah," Eddie said.

"Yeah, yeah," I said, trying to conceal my dread. "Look, this is a telescope my Grandfather had. I've been trying to put the thing together so I can look at the stars and planets at night."

"You can't see 'em without a telescope?" said Eddie.

"Yeah, I can see 'em without a telescope," I said, encouraged that I momentarily diverted Eddie's attention. "I can see 'em a lot better with the telescope, though."

"Have you seen 'em with the telescope?" said Eddie, as Bobby began to fondle the pyrotechnics Grandfather passed down to me and my friends.

"No," I said, keeping a wary eye on Bobby,

"How do you know you can see 'em better with that thing,

then?" Eddie said, as Bobby began to fiddle with some intricate gadget that acted as tongs but looked more like specialized pliers of doom. I was glad he lost interest in the incendiary items, but I was exasperated with Eddie's inane questions.

"Well," I said, in a voice that suddenly sounded too much like Gracie's, "it's a *telescope*. That's what it's for: looking at the stars and planets."

"I know," Eddie said as he chuckled. "I was just fucking with you. Don't get all worked up about it," he said. I wasn't sure Eddie actually did know. In my frustration with Eddie, I lost track of Bobby, until I heard a spark and saw the garage light up momentarily as a *Blue Diamond* soldier flared to life.

"Don't do that," I shouted at Bobby.

"Why?" he taunted. "Are you afraid you're gonna get in trouble with your mama?"

"Yeah – you afraid of mama?" Eddie mocked. They had no idea how unafraid I was of Mother; I was afraid of him playing with fire in an enclosed room with gasoline and other combustible liquids hardly a spark away. It was obvious neither of them was afraid of much of anything – whether they were brave or merely stupid, Eddie and Bobby weren't afraid of fire or fuel, or their new, more timid acquaintance.

When it became clear I wasn't going to talk them out of acting on their arsonists' impulses, I was at least able to get them out of the garage so we could start fires away from the hazardous contents of the stone hut. Eddie carried a box of the wood matches and Bobby brought out a small can of charcoal lighter. He squirted a generous puddle onto the stone patio and Eddie was just about to light it when I screamed, "Wait a minute!" It was such a deafening scream it instantly dropped both of my friends' jaws, while Bobby dropped the can of lighter fluid and Eddie jerked upright, scattering a whole battalion of blue tipped matches into the air.

Grandmother shouted an indiscernible expletive, and Mother called out the window, "Are you boys alright?"

"Yes, Mother, we're fine," I said, embarrassed by the panicked pitch in my voice and the doting pitch of Mother's query from Bloody Mary's chambers. I grabbed the can from Bobby; there was no telling how many small cans Grandfather refilled with gasoline instead of lighter fluid before the Big Bang of '61, and I knew those cans hadn't been touched since the incident.

"What!" Eddie complained, still startled.

I took a good whiff to be sure it was what the label said it was. When I was satisfied the can's contents were, in fact, lighter fluid I said, "Nothing, go ahead." Eddie lit the already evaporating puddle, which erupted in a small rush of flame, delighting my two companions and amplifying my uneasy feeling. Not more than thirty feet from where we stood on that same patio, about four years earlier, was the sight of the much bigger fire. It was a memory I wished Eddie and Bobby hadn't rekindled with their firebug antics.

Bobby found a wayward beetle struggling across the patio and took great delight in dousing the poor bug with the flammable fluid while Eddie struck another match, sending the beetle to a fiery but mercifully quick end. This act was repeated on other various lower life forms, and each time I cringed. It had been one thing to be instantly crushing ants and watching them scurry about, but this was tantamount to sadism. I watched in horror as an earthworm flailed in flames, his flesh crackling and popping like a spit on a barbeque. I couldn't train my mind away from the scene I had come upon four years earlier when I raced to the patio after the ear shattering explosion. The concussion of the blast – along with projectile parts of the Craftsman 29DS – were more than my Father or Grandfather could survive. The awful sight and smell of their seared skin, came back to haunt me as the poor earthworm struggled, consumed by the micro-holocaust. I faded away from the scene, unnoticed by the two torturers, and vomited behind the garage.

After the couple of minutes it took to regain my composure, I rejoined my guests on the patio. To my boundless relief, the torture activity was over, and new, more moronic pursuits were in play.

"Gawd," Eddie was exclaiming, "Lemme see that again." Bobby was just smiling, proud of the response he evoked from Eddie. "Where'd you go?" Eddie said to me, too enthralled to wait for a response. "Watch this. Do it again," he prodded, eyes wide with excitement. Bobby stood before us, possessed with an air of showmanship, and deftly readied a match next to the coarse striking side of the big *Blue Diamond* box. He then proceeded to coat his forearm with charcoal lighter. Wasting no time, he struck a match with dramatic flair and ignited his arm. I gasped as Bobby flung his arm in a throwing motion. The burning liquid flew from his arm, and a puddle of fire burned itself out on the edge of the patio.

"Wow," I involuntarily exclaimed. I had to admit, that was impressive.

Eddie was crying, "Gawd! Did you see that?"

"Are you okay?" I said, intrigued by the audacity of the stunt.

"Sure," said Bobby, offering his arm for both of us to inspect. It was slightly red, but all in all, it appeared no worse for the wear.

"Do it again," Eddie said, overcome by simpleminded stimulation.

"Naw, it does start to get to you after a couple of times," Bobby said, flatly.

"Come on," Eddie whined, "Once more."

"No," Bobby refused. "If you like it so much, you do it," he said, and I could tell it hurt a little more than Bobby admitted. There was no way Eddie was going to light his own arm on fire, and for that my assessment of his intelligence notched a bit higher.

"Watch this," Bobby said, still eager to impress his new friends. He pulled a 20X lens that belonged to the telescope from his pocket. I wondered why it was in his pocket as he lay a match down on the slate of the patio. He pointed the lens toward the sun and directed a piercing beam of light right at the blue tip of the match. For a moment the flint of the match gave off a puff of smoke, and then it erupted into flame. This was something both Eddie and I were more than willing to try for ourselves. That one idea of igniting a match with the magnified power of the sun was one that would serve me poorly many years in the future – but not as poorly as it would serve Eddie. That day on the patio, though, we quickly tired of the new concept.

Having experienced the best in pyrotechnic entertainment in the form of Bobby's burning forearm, we became bored with the patio and retreated back to the garage. I made sure to recoup the lens before Bobby put it back into his pocket. As Eddie began rummaging through more of Grandfather's old gear I breathed an easy sigh, glad the fireworks were over. Bobby was unusually quiet, just sitting there holding his arm, so I thought I would ask the question again.

"Is your arm okay," I said.

"Yeah, I think so," said Bobby. "It *is* starting to hurt, though," he said blowing on his skin, which seemed redder than when we first inspected it. I could hear the pain in his breath, but whether he had fortitude or was simply embarrassed, he wasn't going to complain further about it.

"You better come in the house, and we can put something on it," I said.

"It'll be okay," Bobby said, trying to ignore the pain.

"Come on," I implored, "it'll only take a minute, and it'll feel a whole lot better."

Eddie had an industrial sized barbeque skewer in his grip, and he struck the pose of a fencer. "He said it was okay," he said impatiently as he waved the skewer in my face. "What are you, his mother?"

"Shut up," I said to Eddie for the first of countless times I would speak those words to him. "Come on in and we'll take care of that burn," I said to Bobby, as Eddie struck me on the back of the leg with the whip edge of the skewer. I wanted to whelp in pain, but I took my cue from Bobby's stoutheartedness. Bobby didn't say a word, but he willingly stood and we walked out the garage door to head inside.

We didn't get far before we were greeted by a spectacle of

disastrous proportions. We figured out later that the flaming fluid Bobby cast off of his medium rare arm not only hit the edge of the patio, but some went over the edge and lit the dry underbrush of the ivy covered yard. By the time we discovered the fire, it had overtaken a sizeable patch, and flames were licking at a small dogwood tree as well as some dead vines attached to the house. The stone wall of the house would be fine, but its wooden eave was becoming charred. At that instant, Mother called out from the bedroom window, "Charlie, what's that burning smell…oh my God." I was frozen in panic, and Eddie was running around the house and down the driveway, not to escape the fire, but the fireworks he was sure it would cause.

I could hear Mother calling the fire department as Bloody Mary said, "Land sakes," and then another expletive. Out of nowhere, Bobby appeared with a hose he dragged from the garage. He quickly attached the hose to the spigot on the side of the house being accosted by fire. Mother called outside for me to come in and help her with Grandmother. I ran into the house in a state of shock, reacting mindlessly to what Mother was telling me to do. Even in the dire situation I hesitated momentarily before entering the room I despised so much.

"Come on, Charlie," Mother shouted as she was ripping the sheets off Grandmother, exposing her withered legs. Grandmother's glazed eyes focused disgusted fear in my direction. "Help me lift her into the wheelchair," Mother slurred as she cleared the liquor bottles off the nightstand so as not to disturb them in the moving process. Again, I hesitated, thinking Grandmother's ghostly, vein covered spindles would snap in two if I tried to pick her up by them.

As I started to reach for her, Bobby startled us all by barging into the bedroom and announcing in the voice of a super hero, "Everything's alright now. I put out the fire." I spun around in disbelief. Bloody Mary reached for the sheet and covered herself in old fashioned modesty. Mother looked out the window and smiled.

"Thank God. Thank you, Bobby," said my unpredictable

mother. Bloody Mary snorted and cursed. "I'm glad you were here," Mother said to Bobby, again misinterpreting the situation. It escaped her that if Bobby hadn't been there, there wouldn't have been a fire in the first place. Bloody Mary clanked the ice in her empty drink glass indicating it was time for Bobby and me to leave and Mother to serve her another. The faint sound of a siren crept into the depressing, sepia bathed room, growing louder and closer by the moment.

"Oh my God, the fire department," Mother cried. She shot out of the bedroom door in her threadbare bathrobe. Bobby took one look at me standing dumbstruck before my scary grandmother who just rolled her eyes. He decided his next best move was out the door behind Mother. That left me alone, face to face with Bloody Mary – a predicament I had deftly avoided for quite some time.

Grandmother scowled and said, "I'll swear to you son, if you put your mother's and your brains together on a plate, there'd still be enough room left for a whole serving of smarts."

I was smart enough to know one thing – that was not to argue with a mean old drunk. I just said "Yes ma'am," and ran out the door, less afraid to confront the firemen than Bloody Mary. Outside, three helmet and raincoat clad firefighters were hoofing their way up the driveway, looking like gladiators in full fighting armor. I recalled from the last time they came – way too late to do anything for the victims of the exploding grill – they had to leave the truck at the bottom and pump water up the steep hill from the street.

Mother met them near the top of the driveway with Bobby close behind. "You got a fire here, ma'am?" said the man who appeared to be in charge. His fire hat identified him as Chief of Battalion Four.

"Well we did," my mother replied in an inebriated attempt to seem composed. "This young man put it out, though."

"We better have a look," said the chief as he tipped his helmet and wiped his perspiring forehead with his gloved hand. He followed my mother and Bobby and me, leading the way for his men. We rounded the corner of the house, and it was obvious the head firefighter recognized the place of the disaster four years earlier when he was probably not even a chief; the proof was in his eyes. He almost mentioned it, but he hesitated. He shot Mother and me a couple of covert glances, and I could tell he was calculating the years, subtracting them from our present age, trying to get a fix on the faces. He barked orders to the men.

As I looked at the drenched patio littered with burned remnants, it was easy to see how that one terrible scene came back to this man who probably saw more than his share of terrible scenes. The ivy was wilted. Smoke and steam still rose from below its vines. Half burned leaves and other debris clung to the soaked granite of the Rock like insects on fly paper, and the white paint on the eave was stained with soot.

"How'd this happen?" said the fireman, as he inspected the area. The other men hustled back down the driveway. Mother, trying to steady herself, struck an honestly puzzled look.

"I dunno," she said artlessly.

The fireman looked at Bobby and me. Bobby shrugged, looking so innocent that *I* almost bought into his gesture. I, on the other hand, could feel the heat of the fireman's suspicious eyes. I stood silent for what felt like ten minutes looking alternately at Bobby and the fireman. I couldn't believe Bobby had the nerve to just stand there as if dressed in chrome plated armor, which deflected the fireman's accusing gaze and reflected it onto me. More firefighters arrived and they ran a hose up the driveway. I could hear the reproaching roar of the fire truck's engine as the rpm's raced to pump the water up the precipitous slope. My heart raced like the engine of the truck. Finally, our interrogator's piercing eyes got so white hot – hotter than the fire that brought him there – I could stand it no longer.

"We were fooling around with matches," I confessed. Bobby kicked me, and I said, "Ow!" The busy firemen propelled leaves and debris into the air as they doused the yard with substantially more force than Bobby's garden hose could muster.

"I know," said the fireman, pointing out the collection of half burned matches that washed into the corner where the patio met the side of the house. "Let's take a look at that arm," he said to Bobby who had forgotten about the telltale blister that was beginning to form there. "You're lucky this thing didn't get out of hand and turn out worse than it did. And you in particular son…" he said in my direction, but trailed off, thinking better of bringing up what he knew were painful memories for me. The chief called out for a first aid kit.

Suddenly, to my surprise, Mother interceded on our behalf. "Sir," she said trying to gather herself, "you should give them a break. After all, boys will be boys. This young man saved the house," she said, putting a hand on Bobby's shoulder. "I'm sure they learned their lesson – haven't you boys?"

Bobby nodded with a cherub's innocence. It was such dastardly genius, I felt blameless by association. The chief took pity on me, but turned to Mother, "Well, it's your house, lady. By the way, you might think about keeping a closer eye on these boys. Like you say, boys will be boys, and only the adults can save them from themselves."

Mother took offense at the fireman's advice, and lit into him, informing him that not only did she have to take care of three young boys, but she had an invalid mother she cared for every day. "Perhaps you should walk a mile in a person's shoes before you judge them," she said. The alcohol took over, and Mother began spitting insults at him in an elevated volume.

"Yes ma'am," the fireman said sarcastically, whenever he could fit the phrase in between an alcohol saturated breath. He finished treating Bobby's self inflicted burn and walked over to the side of the house glancing up at the eave. "Rex," he shouted to a man raking the water soaked, uprooted vines in the yard, "come here for a minute." The man dropped his implement and joined his boss, who continued his instructions. "That wood up there looks like it could have some hot spots in there. Go get that axe and take out that section, right there."

Mother stumbled away in a snit, but I was watching as the thud of the axe spun her around. "What are you doing," she screamed, running toward the site of the destruction. Her feet tangled in the loose vines and she landed face down in the muck created by the fire and the water. A fireman bent to pick her up, but she pushed him away, stomping toward the chief, unaware that her bathrobe had flown open and the nightgown underneath was transparently wet, exposing her otherwise naked body. All the firemen stopped what they were doing to gawk as she approached the head fireman, her eyes peeping through the debris that littered her face. "What are you doing?" she repeated when she reached him.

"Well ma'am, the fire was up in this wood," said the chief, pointing to the eave. "You can see where it's burned there. We have to take this section of wood apart to make sure there are no hot spots. If we left the hot spots there, they would just smolder, and reignite, causing more fire. You don't want us to leave your house to burn up do you? We have to take care of your hot spots."

I heard a fireman say, "I'd like to take care of her hot spots," under his breath. I could see Bobby staring in a horny trance at my mother's exposed body parts. I kicked Bobby, but it didn't distract him.

There was nothing Mother could say. She turned and wove a drunken, defeated path back into the house as the fireman resumed chopping the eave. It was then I realized Eddie was missing. "Have you seen Eddie?" I said to Bobby.

"Fuck him," said Bobby, smiling like the fat fox that'd left the henhouse just before the farmer arrived.

"Clark will never be blamed for anything," Gracie would later say of Bobby, to whom, as was her habit, she gave a new name. "He's too good looking and too likeable." She called him Clark for the newspaper reporter of the comics, because she said he was her superhero. That was when she became enthralled by my friend's charms. She tolerated Eddie whom she allowed to remain just Eddie, because she thought him too insignificant to receive a more appropriate name. She tolerated him only because he was always around – except for the afternoon of the second fire at the Rock. That afternoon, Eddie was long gone and nowhere to be found when his father came to get him and Bobby.

Mother was holed up with Bloody Mary and their drinks ever since the firemen tore into her roof and left. Uncle Vince asked us where Eddie was, and Bobby just gave his innocent shrug. Vincent didn't see the damage at the back of the house until he walked around the grounds to find his son. That's when he said, "What the hell happened back here?"

Bobby shrugged and I said, "We had a fire."

"A fire?" said Vince. "Is Eddie okay?"

"Yes. He ran away," I said, as Bobby clammed up and shrugged again.

"Where's your mother, Charlie?" Vince said. Except for the first day he brought Bobby and Eddie over, Mother never greeted him when he dropped off my guests, nor when he picked them up, so it wasn't strange that she wasn't around that day. "You boys get in the car," said Vince, "we'll have to look for him." We did as he told us, and he went inside to find mother. When they emerged from the house, Mother was screaming at Vincent and sloshing a clear drink all over the front porch. We couldn't hear their words with the car windows up and the radio tuned to a rock station. We could see, though, and I saw Vince put his index finger in Mother's face. She slapped it away and Vince raised his hand to her face, but restrained himself. I didn't do anything except worry. Vince began to walk away, then turned to deliver one last salvo that brought tears to Mother's alcohol flushed cheeks. Vince spun back toward the car and headed our way.

"Mom says he can be a bastard," said Bobby, alluding to the fact that Uncle Vince was the boss at Candi Wells's and my mother's "place of business" – a fact too well known by me.

"What was that?" said a livid Vince who opened the car door as Bobby was finishing his comment. Bobby's impudent sense of timing was a little off the mark.

"Nothing," Bobby said, and Vince dropped it; it was the natural way that things seemed to go for Bobby.

"Charlie, go take care of your mother," said Vincent,

impatiently. "Can't you see she's a mess?" I didn't respond; I just got out of the car, and Vince sped down the hill. He and Bobby picked up Eddie as he was walking in the direction of the Rock up Habersham Road. Eddie waited to return to the scene of the crime in the cover of a neighbor's wooded yard until he saw the fire trucks drive by on their departure from the Rock. In a sincere effort to do what I was told, I offered some assistance to Mother who retreated inside and was slumped on the settee in the foyer.

"Oh go away, Charlie," the Mary Widow said through her tears – not at all merry – and then added, "This wouldn't have happened if you would behave yourself." I complied, relieved by her demand. Mother would not go to work that night. Vincent took her off the schedule, right there on the porch in front of Bobby and me. She was distraught. Even with my lack of life experiences I could see Mother was losing a grip on her own life, as Gracie suggested more than once. I was still too young and naïve to know that Mother had discovered a variety of illegal drugs, and was using them on a regular basis.

....

The next day, Mrs. Willingham arrived home looking as weak as a freshly hatched baby sparrow and just as scrawny. In those days, they kept a person in the hospital long enough to recover, even if her recovery was temporary, and it had been almost two weeks since I had seen her. Her deterioration surpassed Bloody Mary's – an injustice since she was blameless for her infirmities.

Gracie looked different too – perhaps not physically, but there was an austerity about her that she never before revealed, even though she had been dealing with her mother's illness for a long time. It was as though she were bracing herself. "Your mother looks horrible," I told her, with the tact of the eleven year old I was about to become.

"Yeah, I know. She's sick," said Gracie, not sarcastically, but with resigned staunchness. "She won't be around much longer." I could see the moisture building in her fetching blue eyes. "She finally gave in, and we talked for a long time, and she told me she knew she was going to die," Gracie said, her voice cracking only slightly.

"How long will she last," I asked, under the naive impression that doctors could predict such a thing with certainty.

"We don't know," Gracie said. "But look at her." That was all she had to say.

For the next two weeks, Mother was suspended from work, and suspended in a virtual catatonic state of alcohol and drug abuse. Mrs. Fiona Willingham lay in *her* personal state of disability, but she remembered my birthday. As decrepit as she had become, her mind was on her interests, and she instructed her only daughter how to prepare for the party that would not be held for me. Two days before my birthday, Mrs. Willingham asked to see me. I was intimidated by what the cancer had done to her, and I didn't want to see her, but a force vague in its manifestation and strong in its compulsion had me at her bedside.

She smiled at me, and somewhere beyond her creased visage, I gleaned a hint of the lovely, vibrant mother of Gracie, the mother I wished was mine. She spoke barely louder than a whisper, but there was strength in her muffled words. "Charlie, it's so nice to get a chance to see you," she said. You're growing up so quickly; you'll be eleven in a couple of days, and I know much better than you how young that is. As grown up as you may think you are, there's a lot to learn in this world Charlie, and you will find out that you'll continue to grow your entire life. As you can see, I'm not going to grow much older. I want you to act extra grown up in one respect; I want you to stick by Gracie and be her best friend for as long as you two are together. I don't mean you can't find someone else to fall in love with when you're older. I mean I want you to be her friend when she needs you. Gracie likes to think she's more mature than just about anyone else, but things will be tough for her and Mr. Willingham in the coming days. I wish I could be there for her, but that's impossible. Her father will be great, but he can't be with her during the day, and he can't go to school with her. Please keep her in mind, Charlie."

"Yes ma'am," was all I said, but I couldn't imagine why she thought she had to tell me such a thing. Gracie and I had been there for each other since we met, and I was sure I would do anything for my friend. "I'm sorry you're so sick," I said.

"Yes, me too, Charlie," she said. "It's not so bad, really; I don't mind the thought of dying. I only wish I could be around long enough to see you and Gracie grow up. But it's just not to be, Charlie."

"I love you," I found myself saying even before the words formed in my mind. I hadn't said those words since I said them to my father. I wanted to say them to Gracie at times in the past, but I never marshaled the courage.

"And I love you," Mrs. Willingham whispered with feint smile. "Now scoot – and you go out there and live a good life, and maybe we'll meet again in another life."

I didn't know why, but when I walked away from the room where Mrs. Willingham would take her last breath, I felt strangely vibrant and fit and willing to carry out her wishes.

The next day, Mrs. Willingham succumbed to the affliction that beleaguered her for so long. Eddie had stopped coming to the Rock since the fire and the subsequent blowup between Vince and Mother, and Bobby could not get there without a ride. I wandered over to Gracie's to offer my companionship. Mr. Willingham answered the door looking as if he had been the victim of a small version of the blast from the Craftsman Model 29DS. His thinning gray hair was frazzled above his reddened eyes and cheeks. His normally starched white shirt and well pressed suit spontaneously assumed a rumpled condition in a sympathetic manifestation of his anguish. His kind, sad eyes looked down upon me and I braced for the words he was about to speak.

"Hello, Charlie," he said, his voice as soft as Mrs. Willingham's had been the day before. "I'm sorry to say that we lost Mrs. Willingham this morning. She was just lying there one minute, and then she just closed her eyes and let go."

Mr. Willingham spoke to me as if I were a friend of his, not like he would speak to an eleven year old. I reached for the hand he unconsciously offered, and we walked inside together. I trembled as we walked through the living room and climbed the stairs to the bedroom I visited just a day earlier. The door was partly open. My breath was so rapid I thought it might somehow suffocate me deader than Mrs. Willingham as we nudged the door to reveal Gracie kneeling at the side of her mother's bed. Her head was buried in the limp, indifferent sheet that covered her mother. When she heard us walk in she turned and ran into both our arms. We all three embraced as time disappeared for us.

The light from the bedroom door softly grew as two paramedics who found their way through the house came in respectfully. They waited while I followed Mr. Willingham and Gracie out to leave them to their task. Back in the kitchen I excused myself, knowing it was time to leave them to their grieving.

After that brief interval of serenity, Gracie's house became a hub of very alive human activity. Friends came by, dropping off casseroles and desserts and offering condolences. By the next day, family members began showing up, and instead of celebrating my eleventh birthday, Gracie mourned the significant day in her mother's life. Some relatives stayed at the house. Others found nearby hotel rooms. There was little opportunity to visit once the process began.

I saw little of Gracie for those next few weeks while friends and family floated in and out, occupying most of her time. I did see Uncle Vincent though. One day he appeared at the Rock in a pick-up truck stocked with some materials and tools. I didn't know how, but Mother and he had ironed out their differences. Mother was back at work, and Vincent was working at the Rock to fix what his son was involved in breaking. He was trying to replace the part of the beam the firemen destroyed while simultaneously extinguishing the fire and stoking the flames of Mother's temper.

I offered to help Uncle Vincent with the repairs, but he brushed me off so I watched from a patio chair, becoming steadily amused as he unsteadily climbed his ladder. He clumsily measured the neat break the firemen left in the soffit. He recorded some figures on his hand with a pen before he trembled back down to the ground where he did more measuring and marking on the fresh wood. After staring at the tools and materials before him long enough for a skilled carpenter to have finished the job, he plugged a circular saw into an orange extension cord, propped a board on a couple of sawhorses, and set about cutting. The pitifully dull blade stuttered at a particularly stubborn section of wood, and Vince grimaced as he bent, shouldering the saw through the obstinate board. The saw finally groaned past the hard stuff and then ripped through the soft wood so fast the board cracked and parted instantly at the cut line, allowing Vince's momentum to propel him forward and off balance. The two supported ends of the newly separated boards leapt off their sawhorses and would have met in the middle if Vince's head hadn't been between them. Vince let out a yowl, letting go of the angry power tool that crashed to the slate rock patio, its spinning blade catching the extension cord on the way down, bisecting it and launching sparks into Vince's face. The saw came to rest on a freshly cracked slate tile as the high pitched whine of the motor fell away.

"Phew!" Vince involuntarily exclaimed, backing away in a stunned daze.

"Land sakes," cried Bloody Mary through her bedroom window before she let fly an expletive.

Mother stumbled outside to investigate the commotion. "What is going on Vincent?" she said, her bleary eyes rolling with disdain.

"Huh?" replied Vince, his ears apparently still ringing from the punishment they received at the hands of the aggressive wooden board.

Oh shit," said Mother, "you broke the stone here." She pointed at the cracked slate, either unaware or unconcerned that

Vince was in pain. "It looks like you're making things worse," she complained. With that, she smacked her lips contemptuously and staggered back inside.

Vince was shaking the bewilderment out of his damaged head and stirring his index finger in his right ear. Both ears were hot pink from the impact of the wood, and his eyes were slightly crossed from the concussion, leaving his expression one of aiming a bow and arrow with one eye closed. He didn't refocus until Mother was back in the house, and I'm not sure he ever comprehended the meaning of her grumbling appearance.

"Well," he said, speaking to me in an effort to gather himself, "I think this board's about right." He picked up the wrong piece for a moment until he realized there was no way it was going to fit the much smaller gap in the beam. Without further comment he put his first choice down and picked up the correct board. He struggled up the ladder, laden with the board and his tools.

Vince's calculations were slightly off, and the board he cut was just a little too long for the dearth of wood under the eave. He aimed his cockeyed brows downward, regarded his saw suspiciously, and, in instantaneous deliberation, considered the length of the board fine as it was. He seemed relieved with his decision. Instead of finding a way to fit his substitute board into the space, he simply tacked it upon of both sides of the space, creating an extra-dimensional support beam. It wasn't pretty, but it was better than what the firemen left behind.

Sitting with his butt wedged in between two rungs he worked a screw driver around the top of a can of white paint. I watched as he banged in frustration, prying and trying to loosen the lid. Suddenly the lid popped into the air like an oversized coin which had been flipped to determine heads or tails. It clanked to the ground splattering paint as it rolled along the patio stones until it spun to a stop, paint side down.

"Shit!" Vince exclaimed.

"Land sakes," shouted Bloody Mary.

Mother reemerged from the Rock, arms folded through her

tacky bathrobe. She took one look at the mess, and retreated back inside without a word. Vince turned his attention away from the ground and began to spread the paint along the wood with a brush. The bright white he was using didn't match the more subtle eggshell hue already on the wood trim, but he just plowed ahead, grunting with effort, ears glowing pinker than ever as the sun shone through them. When all but one end of the board, which was inconvenient to reach, was covered with an uneven coat of paint, he descended the ladder proclaiming the job to be complete. Mother heard his words of accomplishment through the open window of Bloody Mary's room and came out to inspect the results.

"Why's that board sticking out like that," she said, squinting up at the sun splashed eave.

"Whadaya mean," Vince said.

"Why's that thing sticking out, instead of laying flat like these others," said Mother, swaying in dizziness, trying to focus her intoxicated eyes skyward for too long.

"Oh… that's the one I fixed," Vince said.

Mother shook her head, and I wasn't sure if she was making a silent comment or just trying to clear her own cobwebs. "Well, why is it so much brighter than the rest of the trim," she said.

"Well, it's brand new paint," Vince said, and I wasn't sure if Vince really believed that or not. "It will blend in once it gets some age and weather on it. If it doesn't, we'll go ahead and paint all of the trim that color."

"How about just painting all of that piece," Mother bitched, noticing the bare end of the cut wood.

"Aw, nobody's gonna notice that", said Vince. "It's hidden away from view. You wouldn't even have seen it if you weren't looking up at it."

"Mother was too impaired to contend with that lack of logic, and she turned to go back into the house muttering, "I hope nobody else looks at it, then."

Vince took one last look at his inadequate handiwork and began to pick up after himself. He brought out the garden hose to spray down the patio in a half hearted attempt to clean the paint left by the lid. After he finished soaking the slate tiles he bent to pick-up the live, bare wires of the extension cord where the saw severed it. “Yeow!” he screamed in the most feminine voice I ever heard emanate from the imposing man. His dark body hair stood straight out from his arms, and he jerked as if to throw the hot wires down, but he was standing in a big puddle of water, and the tenacious conduit held on like some kind of reptilian monster focused in on the kill. From somewhere deep in the recesses of my mind I recalled what to do and what not to do for a person in Vince’s predicament. I grabbed the other end of the cut board and landed it hard to his back. Vince, whose eyes had rolled into the back of his head, expelled an acrid breath of burnt air as he catapulted forward, landing in the soft ivy that bordered the patio. The exposed wire landed in the puddle of water I had been careful to avoid. It short circuited and blew a fuse in the house.

“Land sakes!” cried Bloody Mary. I dropped the heavy board and looked over at Vince. He was reclined, but mostly awake, leaning up on one elbow, shaking his head once again. Wisps of smoke hung over his arm like the remnants of a light morning fog over a dewy lawn, and his normally coiffed hair was mussed and singed.

“Are you okay?” I said, pinching my own arms to keep from bursting into convulsions of laughter and rolling around in the ivy next to Vince’s smoking hide.

“Yeah, I’m fine,” croaked Vince, trying to downplay an event there was no hope of downplaying. His eyes repositioned themselves in their sockets, and he tried to get up, but instead he said, “I think I’ll just rest here a minute.”

Mother didn’t bother to come outside, but she *did* poke her head out the window. “Vince, please don’t lie in that ivy. You’re going to smash it all down. It just started coming back after the fire. Come inside and rest on the couch if you’re tired.”

“No that’s alright,” Vince said, his voice coming back. “I think I’ll be getting back.” He made a Herculean attempt and finally struggled stiffly to his feet. "It looks pretty good, up there," he said, looking at the eave, noticeably bent over as he creaked toward the truck, giving wide berth to the sliced power cord, which lay impotent from the blown fuse. Mother didn't respond; her head disappeared behind the window sill. When Vince got to the driver side door of his truck, he turned and said, "Hey son, thanks for your help there." I just nodded, aware that I had saved somebody's life. No one else would know it – and Vince would acknowledge it only once again in the far future, when he and I were alone together – but I knew it. Vince drove away, while I finally gave into hysterics. Vince was a scary man, but his escapade that afternoon made him seem a little more vulnerable. I knew Vincent Palomino only from afar, and though I didn't know just what a criminal he actually was, I regarded him as a dangerous person. I didn't know it then, but my lot would be cast with his, and my childhood deed would stand me in good stead with the man whose favor everyone else in my world endeavored to curry.

V. Gracie Goes

Once the Rock was repaired to the best of Vince's ability, and Gracie's heart mended to tolerable resilience, summer settled back into a routine. It was a different routine though. Instead of Gracie and I sharing exclusive time with each other, Bobby and Eddie intruded into our lives. Vincent would drop by in the late morning with my new male companions just about the time Gracie was emerging from her house to start the day. I would be awake for hours, frustrated that Gracie wouldn't get up sooner so we could spend some time alone together. At first I wasn't sure how the three of them would get along, but Gracie, armed with natural confidence, took to Bobby and Eddie in seamless fashion. It was as if she had been part of our group ever since the two had been visiting the Rock.

Not that we all always got along. My friends were two curious boys on the early cusp of puberty, so sex dominated our conversations. Bobby often mentioned Gracie in suggestive ways when she wasn't around. Mother had slapped the sexual desire right out of me, but I was still mightily possessive of Gracie. In a moment of weakness – motivated both by ego and a jealous desire to stake my claim – I divulged to my friends the secret trysts Gracie and I shared in the garage. It was a mistake that would forever temper any future impulse to betray a confidence placed with me. Shortly after my indiscretion Bobby was making some provocative remarks to Gracie. When she snapped back, putting him down as only Gracie could do, he spilled the beans. "C'mon, Gracie," Bobby coaxed, undaunted by her rejection, "I know you let Charlie here have a peek. "Let's just go spend a little naked time in the woods, just you and me."

"Fuck you, Bobby," Gracie said coolly. "And fuck you too, Charlie. That was between us!"

My face burned in horror, and I felt more exposed than the

day Mother caught the two of us in the Cadillac. Bobby was in control by then, and he turned the table. “Oh, so it’s true,” he scoffed. “Charlie didn’t tell me anything. I was just guessing, and I got you.”

For the first time since that garage incident Gracie was nonplussed, looking hurt and apologetic toward me at the same time. “Well I’m sorry, Charlie, and fuck you anyway, Bobby,” she said as she stormed away in the direction of her own back yard.

“I know you want to,” Bobby taunted as I watched my dearest friend disappear in defeat. I was unable to muster the fortitude to take a stand. I should have gone to be by her side. Mrs. Willingham’s admonishment to stand by Gracie came back to me as I stood, overcome by inertia and feeling like the Apostle Peter I studied in religion class, who denied Jesus after the last supper. I was ashamed for not defending her; probably more damning was the fact that not only did I betray her confidence, but I let Bobby convince her I hadn’t.

The next day I awoke, happy that Bobby and Eddie were not scheduled to visit. I wanted to spend time with Gracie all alone to apologize for myself and for Bobby. In spite of my good intentions the encounter with Gracie was nothing like I expected. “Sorry about Bobby,” I said when she showed up in my yard. I was about to confess my indiscretion, and beg her forgiveness, but my timing was off. She spoke before I could continue.

“That’s okay,” she said. “It didn’t really bother me. I left for the dramatic effect. I wanted to come back, but Aunt Shelly wanted to take me shopping for school stuff.” As I began to launch into a confession her next comment shifted the dynamic of our conversation. “Do you think Bobby likes me?” she said, in a coy manner she never before revealed.

“What do you mean,” I said, stunned and hurt.

“Do you think he likes me, say romantically?” she said, being as inarticulate as she had ever been.

“I don’t know,” I stammered. “I mean no, I don’t think so.” I was processing her words and her mannerisms, and jealousy welled from my insides to the surface of my skin. As the color in my face intensified my spirit ebbed, and Gracie read my reaction.

"Oh, I'm sorry Charlie," she said. "I didn't mean to slight you at all. You're special to me. You're my best friend and nobody will ever replace you. But Bobby... he's just... well, you know, he's just so good looking. He's so... Clark Kent. I don't know how to say it."

Gracie was gushing, and she was unintentionally crushing me. I was suddenly as flat as a neglected basketball on a cold winter day. Any thought of confessing and apologizing was dashed along with my spirit. As she stood there practically tongue-tied she assumed the manner of the young schoolgirl that she actually was – the schoolgirl that must have always been there, but I could never see it until that moment. I was jealous, and wanted nothing more to do with her or Bobby for the moment.

"I'll say it for you," I said. It was my turn to be condescending, but instead I came off bitter and sarcastic. "You have a crush on a guy who doesn't care too much about anything, even you." I didn't mean to say it. It just came out, and I was instantly sorry.

"I guess so," Gracie said dreamily, clearly unaware of my comments or the bitterness imbedded in them.

"I'm going home," I said flatly, disgusted with Gracie and myself. "I'll see you later."

"See ya," she said, apparently unmoved by my comments.

So Gracie was gaga over the superhero Bobby, I had cooled on Gracie, and Eddie was oblivious to the subtle, adolescent currents running through our freshly formed foursome. For the rest of the summer we spent enough time with each other to form a tight bond. Bobby constantly flirted with Gracie, teasing her about her sexual allure, but he never offered his affection. This drove Gracie mad and intensified her lust for him. She temptingly taunted Bobby, firing suggestive salvos in his superhero direction, hoping they would land on a susceptible spot. But Bobby deflected her advances, preferring to torture her rather than woo her. Whenever their banter heated up I clammed up, feeling inadequate to join the fray – and feeling jealous frustration for not being adequate to enter the fray.

That was the summer I weaned myself from what Gracie called my *Gracie Dependence*, but I grew closer to her in another way. I also grew close to Bobby and Eddie, and we all went back to school as members of a newly formed family. Our common bond was that none of us had any siblings. We became for each other the brothers and sisters none of us ever before had. Throughout the following years we would all mature in different ways. Gracie, being an adult already, would change the least. Eddie showed early signs of being trouble, and as he aged, he went from trouble to criminal. Bobby, who was smoothest among us, and thereby unpredictable, would surprise us all with the path he took. But my future was probably the least predictable – and the most eventful.

……..

Once school started in the fall Bobby's and Eddie's visits were less frequent, but the weekend gave us a chance to gather. On Saturdays Uncle Vince would pull up in his late model Cadillac, let my friends out, and head off to tend to whatever illegal business he had going.

It was Eddie who, during the sixth grade, introduced our group to his father's stash of pornography. Eddie would bring his choice picks stuffed under his shirt, and once Vince was gone and Mother was securely ensconced in the Rock we would all skulk our way to the garage where Eddie would produce his trove of porn. There were Playboys and Penthouses in his selections, but as Eddie became a porn aficionado he found his own source of more graphic magazines. They were mostly magazines in foreign languages, laced with low quality photos of even lower quality women involved in a diverse range of perverse sexual acts; most of them were disgusting, and some were unnatural.

"That's just gross," Gracie would say as Eddie revealed one

fetish photo after another.

"Whoa," Bobby would exclaim, eyes wide with wonder and lust. "Hey Gracie, how would you like to have this stud as your boyfriend," he taunted, holding up a black and white of a pasty, overweight, over-the-hill woman captured in a compromising position with a horse that evidently found the poor woman attractive.

"Eeww," Gracie complained at first, and then said, "I don't know, for a boyfriend it beats anything around here."

Gracie quickly grew bored with Eddie's home version of show and tell, and the dirty magazines held no interest for my sanitized sensibilities. Even Bobby lost enthusiasm for the pulp depravity after a few weeks. Eddie still brought it, but we paid little attention. Besides, by that time Bobby was providing other forms of fascination for all of us. It was hard tearing Eddie away from his pages of iniquity, but he finally came around one Saturday when Bobby pulled out a fifth of scotch and a pack of cigarettes he filched from his inattentive mother. Gracie was out of town with her father in New York for the weekend, so she missed our first experience with alcohol.

Having never tasted liquor himself, Bobby assured me it had to be good because his mother and her boyfriends drank it all the time. Knowing how much Bloody Mary and Mother liked it, I had no reason to doubt him, and I voluntarily took the first swig. That caustic concoction violently assaulted my mouth. The liquid fire took my breath as I casually gasped enough cool air to loosen its grip from my throat. Tears filled my eyes, but I was able to conceal my angst well enough that Bobby made the same mistake as I did, with the same general ability to disguise his discomfort. Eddie on the other hand, overcome by the liquor, emitted such guttural and thunderous gags and coughs that it resonated through the trees rousing Bloody Mary from her stupor.

"Land sakes," we heard between curse words from a faint distance.

"You kids okay?" Mother called indifferently from the bedroom window. We didn't even bother to answer and

Mother didn't bother to investigate.

While we waited for Eddie to quit retching, Bobby and I shared some more cautious sips, and Bobby offered me a cigarette. Soon we were all three tipping the bottle and taking long drags off menthol Kools. My first experience with alcohol got me good and drunk, and the combination of the straight whiskey and dizzying, mentholated smoke impeded my brain function making me so ill that I would be repelled by booze and cigarettes for years to come. Based on that experience I was sure I would never fall prey to the vices that claimed my mother.

There was no way for even the most oblivious parent to overlook our drunken escapade, and when Vince came to pick-up my pals there was hell to pay. He and Mother found us rolling in the ivy, sick from our overindulgence. Eddie's stag magazines were spread wide open and stained with regurgitation. Vincent grabbed Eddie and me up in his menacing, tattooed arms, dragging us along while he used his feet to kick Bobby all the way out of the woods and down the hill to the patio. He dropped us to pick Bobby up and carry him like a football to the car. He came back for Eddie, and they were off without another word. That was one time I was happy to be staying at the Rock. Mother gave me a disapproving shake of her head and carried me inside to treat my condition. I never heard another word about it from her, but I didn't need to be punished; I learned my lesson of the evils of the vices Bobby introduced that day. I hated the harsh bite of the whiskey and the disorienting nausea that followed.

Bobby's mother handled his delinquency in much the same manner as mine. Eddie was prohibited from coming to the Rock for a month. During that time I found relief in having the quieter, less bombastic Bobby to myself. The booze and the cigarettes were gone for the time being. Gracie was spending a lot of time out of town, so Bobby and I got to know each other better since we had no one to entertain us but ourselves. Eventually Eddie returned while Gracie began to imperceptibly drift away from our group.

After school she spent the afternoons studying, and almost every weekend she went to New York with her father. During the summers she spent most of her break in New York, and Eddie and Bobby gradually filled in the time I used to spend with her. I unconsciously allowed myself to ignore her increasing absence, taking her for granted. Life was rollicking along for me. While I still maintained my high academic performance, my extracurricular activities were veering away from those of a higher purpose to those more familiar to my mother's circle of friends. For some ill conceived reason, Mother guided me in this direction, and I was like a loose and willing pebble being drawn along a raging riverbed, moving ever closer to the edge of a waterfall. Eventually the lighter pebbles get carried over, crashing to the bottom of the falls, and I was no heavyweight when it came to moral fortitude.

....

Reality crashed down upon me one morning of the summer of 1969 when I climbed the fence between Gracie's and my yard to roust her out of the house. She came to the door in a long t-shirt wearing apparently nothing else but panties. "Hey Charlie," she said with sleepy eyes focusing on the outdoor light.

"What are you doing?" I said, expecting her to invite me in to begin a typical summer day of reading and banter.

"Agh, I'm tired," she said. "I was up really late helping Dad pack. I've got to get back to it, but I'm trying to rest before he gets back with more boxes."

"Why, where are you going?" I said before I said, "Boxes? Boxes for what? What are you talking about?"

"Charlie, I haven't known how to tell you, but we're moving to New York," she said, looking at me with that adult resolve in her eyes."

"New York?" I said. "When... I mean when did this happen? When are you going?"

The barrage of questions was assaulting Gracie before her

still waking brain could respond. “We’re going to leave tomorrow,” she said. “I’m sorry I didn’t tell you sooner, but you had to know it was coming. You know how much time we’ve been spending there. It makes no sense for Dad to keep commuting. Mom was always from here, and she wanted to stay here. Dad hasn’t wanted to leave for sentimentality reasons, but time has passed and he has so much going on there with publishers, it just makes sense.”

The last move that I was told made sense was when my mother and I moved into the Rock. I dreaded that move, but on balance it worked out well for me, what with Gracie becoming my neighbor and confidante. But I was suddenly dreading news of this move.

“Are you sure,” I said stupidly, even as the moving vans were rumbling toward her home. “You could stay here with me until you get out of school…”

“Yeah, Charlie,” Gracie interrupted, “like I would put up with Bloody Mary and the Mary Widow. You know my feelings about that. Besides, I like New York. Dad’s got me in a great school there. It will be good to finish high school there. It will help me get into a good college.”

“But what about…” I stammered.

“What?” said Gracie.

“You know, us,” I said awkwardly. “This…” I was coaxing my hands between Gracie and myself as if there were some gravitational force keeping us close.

“Charlie, I love you, and I always will,” she said with such soft sincerity it seemed to make everything alright. “We’re just kids. There is so much before us we can’t imagine. We need to get on with it.”

Not knowing how to take her words of wisdom, I just said, “Yeah, but when will I see you again. Are you going to come back and visit?”

“I’m sure I will,” she said, but then she added, “I’m not sure when, but we can keep in touch with letters. You better write me, Charlie Lofton.” She smiled, completely disarming me.

“You know I will,” I promised as her dad pulled up to the

house.

"I've got to get back to work," Gracie said, "but I'll see you before we leave, I promise." With that I greeted Mr. Willingham and glumly climbed the fence back into my yard.

Suddenly Gracie's subtly diminished presence became conspicuous to me, and I began to miss her before she was gone. I regretted all the time I hadn't spent with her, and I wanted to make it up, but it was too late. For reasons I never knew, Gracie waited until the moving vans were practically in her driveway to break the news. No matter her motive, there was barely enough time to wish her well as I helped her carry some of her personal possessions to her father's over-packed Buick the next morning. As the vans pulled away from her big house Gracie walked up to me, planted a big kiss on my lips right in front of her father, and turned to get in the car. As the Buick turned down the driveway, she rolled down the window and called out, "Bye Charlie. I'll write soon. Steer clear of the bad butterflies."

That was a kiss I wouldn't forget. It summoned a flood of memories, and I realized I wouldn't have her around to say those familiar words in the future. I stood in her driveway, emptier than the house she just abandoned. Gracie's parting words were ominously appropriate, but for me there would be no avoiding the chaos that my father introduced to me when I was too young to understand. I didn't leave the lonely driveway until Mother called to me that Eddie and Bobby were there.

When I got to my own patio Bobby said, "What happened to you? Have you been crying?"

"No," I lied, and I would have been unable to defend the lie if Bobby hadn't been so preoccupied with another matter.

"Come on, let me show ya'll something," he said urgently as he led the way into the woods. When we were safely out of sight he shoved his hand into the crotch of his jeans and produced a pistol. Eddie and I stared in fascination at what turned out to be a .22 caliber revolver. As far as guns go it was a pipsqueak, but it didn't belong in the hands of a trio of adolescents – particularly our trio. Bobby took it from his mother who got it from a "boyfriend" who felt that, in her line of work, she needed some form of protection.

Bobby unloaded some bullets from his pockets and put them in the revolver's chambers with such composure I was sure he had been practicing with the weapon for quite some time. He had never fired it, though, since he lived in an apartment complex. Even Bobby couldn't have gotten away with discharging the gun there. Once the magnificent piece was loaded he assumed a shooter's pose, holding the gun with both hands and aligning his aiming eye with the sight at the end of the barrel. He pulled off a couple of pretend rounds, simulating the noise of the gun as his hands made an accurate recoiling motion.

Eddie was beside himself with anticipation. "Lemme see it," he begged, reaching to take the gun from Bobby's sure hands.

Bobby was careful with the object he knew required the caution Eddie wouldn't exercise. "Hold on," he said, "you don't just pick up a gun without knowing something about it. You gotta be careful with this thing. Have you ever fired a gun?" he asked Eddie.

"Have you?" Eddie shot back, with sharpshooter instinct.

"No, but I'm about to, and I don't think you want to be my first target," said Bobby. Eddie's ardor ebbed into conformed silence as I stood there considering the odds that Bobby would actually shoot Eddie. Before I could come to a conclusion, my thoughts and my ears were shattered by two explosions as Bobby directed his propensity for killing things toward an unlucky squirrel that happened to prance across a tree limb into his sight. I looked in horrified amazement as the poor animal dropped from the tree, dead before it hit the ground.

"Goddamn," I said, realizing I had used the Lords name in vain for the first time in my life. I wasn't sure if the uncontrollable utterance erupted from a startled reaction to the unbearable noise or from sheer astonishment that Bobby actually hit his intended target.

"Shit," Eddie cried, his face showing the distress of the sudden disturbance Bobby brought upon us.

"Land sakes," I'm sure Bloody Mary cried, although we couldn't hear it over the ringing in our ears.

"Charlie, what are you boys doing?" Mother called out in mellow inebriation.

Bobby had a look of satisfaction on his face as he answered my mother's question. "It was just a couple of firecrackers I brought over, Miss Lofton," Bobby called back.

"Well, you be careful," said Mother. "You boys don't want to start another fire."

"Okay Miss Lofton – just a couple of more," Bobby dared to appeal.

Of course she said, "Well just be careful," to Bobby as she undoubtedly went back to concentrating on her bartending. With Gracie's house vacant, there wasn't another neighbor close enough to suffer the full volume of the bang of the gun. We were free to experiment.

Bobby turned his attention back to the pistol, which he placed into my trembling hands. I felt the icy smooth surface of the white, faux pearl handle. For such a small gun it nestled heavy in my grip. I couldn't tell if it was the weight of the gun or the weight of the moment. I lifted it to imitate the same approximate pose that Bobby struck. I knew I wanted to fire it, and I knew I didn't want to kill anything with it. I got a bead on a pinecone hanging from a branch and pulled the trigger. The bang was less deafening when it was expected. The gun jumped upward as it went off. Leaves and sticks fell victim to the bullet as it followed its errant path, well wide of the targeted pinecone, and disappeared forever.

"Land sakes," cried Bloody Mary; we heard her that time.

"Lemme try," Eddie said, willing to pry the gun away from me just to touch it.

"Hold on," Bobby repeated. "You gotta be careful with this thing."

"Yeah, yeah; you let Lofton try it," Eddie complained as he grabbed for the gun. My finger was still in the trigger loop, and he was tugging so hard it was twisting to the point of breaking.

"Yeow!" I screamed, but my yelp would never be heard over

the ring of the gunshot. The pistol fell from my hyper-extended index finger, and Eddie fell backward, blood splattering from the left side of his head.

"Land sakes," cried Bloody Mary as Bobby and I both let out a terrified gasp.

"I'm hit," yelled Eddie, holding the left side of his head. I didn't faint, but my legs buckled, and I hit the ivy.

"Where are you hit," Bobby said urgently, but he stayed composed. He bent over Eddie and forced his hand from his head. "Geez," he said in a tone I couldn't interpret.

"What, what," I cried in a panic, trying to stand up, praying I hadn't just killed my friend.

"It's your goddamned ear, you moron," said Bobby. "You just barely nicked it, you pussy."

I had to see for myself, and I moved toward the crying Eddie with the trepidation of a turtle crossing a busy highway. It took every ounce of courage I had to look when Bobby once again pried Eddie's arm from his head. His upper ear was intact, but his lobe looked like ground meat.

"See, it's just a nick," Bobby said, nodding in my direction, trying to coax a positive response from me. I was too shocked to respond with anything.

"It is?" said Eddie, his crying decreasing to occasional whimpers.

"Yeah, well it's bleeding and all," admitted Bobby. "We better put something on it to stop the blood. Let's go see what we can find in the garage." He pulled Eddie up by the arms and we walked out of the woods. Eddie was still whimpering, I was trying to feel the ground under my rubbery legs, and Bobby was formulating a story to explain why part of Eddie's earlobe was missing.

We found a partially clean rag that Bobby told Eddie to press on his ear. Eddie obeyed, and after the rag became blood soaked we considered our options. Once most of the bleeding stopped the wound was less terrifying, but there was no doubt it would draw Vincent's attention.

"Let's see," Bobby said, fully in control of the situation.

"Yeah, it looks okay."

"Lemme see," Eddie whined skeptically. We positioned his face in front of the side mirror of Mother's Cadillac where Eddie's eyes stretched far to his left and squinted to focus on their sensory counterpart on the side of his head. "It's all torn up," he sniffled, his eyes leaking tears at the rate his earlobe was oozing the last of the clotting blood.

"It's fine," Bobby insisted. "Let's go clean it up and put a bandage on it." Bobby was right to do this, even though his motivation may have been to hide the injury with the bandage. He climbed up on the hood of the Cadillac and stuffed the blood drenched rag in a corner of the garage between the exposed ceiling beam and the rock wall. If anyone saw the amount of blood that escaped from Eddie's ear there would be hell to pay, and Bobby knew it. Once the evidence was securely secreted, Eddie and I followed our leader into the house. Eddie winced and wailed in the bathroom as Bobby tried to scrub the raw flesh with a warm wash cloth. Bloody Mary complained loudly about the noise, but by the time Mother ambled to the bathroom to investigate, the cleaning was complete and a neat patch of gauze and medical tape concealed the extent of Eddie's injury.

"What happened to you?" Mother said, unconcerned with the innocuous appearance of Bobby's handiwork.

Before Eddie could stammer anything Bobby chimed up. "A squirrel bit him in the ear, Miss Lofton," he said with such amazement in his own voice it sparked wonder in Mother.

"A squirrel bit you?" she said, rhetorically.

"Yes ma'am," said a dumbfounded Eddie.

"Why'd he do that?" Mother said.

"He was just hanging upside down from a little limb," Bobby spoke first. "We didn't know what he was doing, but he looked like he was sick or something, so we walked up to check him out, and he just reached out and bit Eddie.

"Hmpf," Mother muttered as she walked back to Bloody Mary's room.

I was astounded. The possibility of such a preposterous

explanation was so remote that I couldn't even visualize the imaginary event Bobby described. The thought of an aggressive squirrel hanging in wait to attack a human being and bite his ear was beyond the pale, yet Mother didn't bat an eye. The fact that Mother bought into it was just as remarkable as the lie itself. I could only explain it by her alcohol consumption until the news came that Uncle Vince believed the refined story in the car on the way home.

"Son, what were you boys doing bothering wild animals in the woods," Vincent reportedly scolded. "I swear to God. What the hell were you thinking?"

For Eddie, the lie may have been as painful as the truth; since it could never be hoped that the offending squirrel would be identified in order to test it for rabies, the doctor felt it prudent to administer a complete series of excruciating injections. Eddie took the medicine like a good soldier; he didn't want to test the consequences of admitting the lie.

As for me, I was carried away by relief: relief I hadn't killed my friend with that gun. And there was the guilty pleasure of knowing we cheated our due justice. The lesson I gleaned from the experience was that sometimes a lie – sometimes the most outlandish lie – is the best approach for avoiding trouble or even getting ahead. Unfortunately, I didn't learn anything about the consequences of the improper use of a gun.

VI. My Origins Revealed

Hugh McDowell Jr. had arrived at his destined station as the golden boy of our class, indeed of the whole high school. Saint Mary's endured years of sports mediocrity, but as the school grew – and with the influence of parents like Hugh McDowell Sr. who wooed student athletes to the school like a college alumnus might – the prospects for a good football program turned brighter with each new season. In the ninth grade Hugh Jr. made the varsity football team and was getting playing time as the back-up quarterback. It would be easy to say his father's influence created pressure on the coaches to give Hugh Jr. special treatment, but in fact, he was a great athlete and earned his playing time. I didn't begrudge him this success, and I didn't wish to be part of his crowd. I just wanted him to leave me alone. That wasn't to be, though. Whenever I crossed Hugh's charmed and disapproving path I cringed, hoping he was too preoccupied to hassle me. Unfortunately, with Gracie the Protector gone he felt free reign to not only acknowledge me, but to take the time to inquire about my family life.

"Hey Lofton, how are things at the Bottoms Up Lounge?" he would say, a snide grin overtaking his golden boy features. The entourage would snicker like young school girls. I was beyond shrinking in the face of his insults. Bobby's smooth demeanor had an effect on me, and even though I didn't have the physical tools to handle Hugh, I wouldn't allow him to steamroll me.

"I don't know, Hugh," I would smile back coolly, "Why don't you ask your father."

"Whoa," the entourage would gasp, as if to sarcastically say, "Boy Lofton, that was a real zinger. You really got Hugh on that one."

Sometimes the lot of them would just turn away, chuckling, leaving a hallway or cafeteria with me standing alone, suffering the stares from anyone who happened to witness the encounter. Other times, when Hugh felt up to it, he would engage himself in the battle of wits. The problem was, he was no match for me, and he always resorted to uninspired insults.

"How does it feel to have a mother who takes her clothes off in front of people for money, Lofton?" he would say. "Hell, you're right about my father; he's probably seen more of your mother's tits than you have."

"That's probably true, Hugh," I said one day, "but then I don't make a habit of ogling my mother. I'm sure your mother appreciates your sexual advances, since she can't get any attention from her husband." That comment led to a small jostling episode that was quickly broken up by Coach Banks, the varsity football coach who happened to be walking through the gym.

"What the hell…" he shouted as his muscle bound arms separated Hugh and me as easily as if he were parting curtains. The coaches were the only ones who had license to swear at Saint Mary's, and even they confined their profanity to the gymnasium or the practice fields. "McDowell, what the hell d'ya think you're doing."

"Well coach…" Hugh stammered to say something clever, but he had nothing.

"You were being stupid," the coach said, nodding his head until Hugh nodded in cowed, respectful imitation of the grizzly coach. "You know what'll happen if you get into some kind of fight with this guy? I'll tell you. You get suspended. And that means no football game on Friday night." Hugh was just nodding, stupidly. "Well that's gonna cost you laps after practice," said Coach Banks. "All of you," he added loudly, looking around at Cal Greer and Scott Trucks, fellow football players who stood dumbfounded and speechless.

"Yes sir," Hugh said as Coach Banks's power grip fell away from both of our arms. Hugh, Scott, and Cal slipped away ruing the idea that their butts would be dragging by the time they straggled off the practice field that afternoon, the last of Saint Mary's Apostles to hit the showers. By that time, I would have finished my assigned homework and delved into some extracurricular reading, waiting for Mother to leave to go to the work for which Hugh ridiculed her. Then I would run upstairs to my room. Even though I had grown to adolescence, I still raced past Grandmother's decrepit room, no longer from childish fear, but out of sheer habit. It had become a ritual with no basis; it just made me feel comfortable. By that age I was sleeping slightly more than when I was younger, but I still rose with the sun – another habit. Habit was a stabilizing force for me.

As part of my morning routine I would make sure Mother got home safely. The way she drank and drove made me nervous, but she wouldn't change her own habits at my behest. One Friday morning my heart skipped when I found her bedroom door open, and she was nowhere to be found. I stayed home from school and called Vince to see if he knew where she might be. He promised to check into the situation and I tried to occupy my time with any activity that would take my mind off my missing mother. I tried to eat something, but my stomach was too nervous so I put breakfast aside. Eventually I pulled out Gracie's latest letter to reread it. I often read her lovely words more than once, and that day they would provide comfort and ensure my overdue response would be relevant. I felt calmer the minute I saw her perfect handwriting on the linen page:

Dear Charlie,

I hope this note finds you well. I haven't heard from you lately. I suspect you and the two stooges are occupied with some sort of funny business. I trust it is not too sordid. Of course, if it involves Clark Kent and Eddie, chances are you guys are up to no good. Tell Bobby I still want his body.

I take my PSAT's next Saturday. I think I'll do okay, but I'm studying hard because by the time I get to the real thing I need to ace them. I'm looking at some colleges up here, and the better my SAT's, the better my choice of schools. Right now I am favoring St. Bonaventure in New York. I would like to study literature or journalism, and St. Bonaventure has an excellent program for either.

It looks as though Dad got me a job being a gofer with Craft Publishing for the summer. I would like to work in publishing, so the summer job sounds like a good opportunity.

I hope your school work is going as well as I'm sure it is. Don't let the stooges be a bad influence on your academics. I look forward to hearing from you soon. In the meantime, steer clear of the bad butterflies.

Love always,
Gracie

I began my letter back to her:

Dear Gracie,

Sorry it's taken so long for me to get back, but I have been busy with school and some advanced projects. I hope your PSAT's went well. Let me know how well.

I really have been busy at school, but I see Bobby and Eddie on the weekends. Lately we've been…

My words were interrupted by the back door opening, and I could hear the elevated voices of Vince and Mother in competition. I padded downstairs undetected and listened long enough to Mother's hysterical utterances to confirm that Vince had picked her up from the city jail after posting bail for her DUI arrest. That was all I needed to hear. At least she was safe at home. I stole out the front door, undetected, and walked to school.

By the time I arrived the day was half over, and I went straight to the cafeteria to get my first morsel of the day. My nerves were already frayed, and the last thing I needed was Hugh engaging me in his banal banter. It had been awhile since our last encounter, but that streak was not to follow me into the cafeteria that day. After a few cheap shots in front of a large table of starched Catholic students, Hugh proclaimed that my mother was a cheap whore who danced practically nude in front of perverts for money and then turned tricks for customers after hours. Finally, he announced I was a bastard son and that my mother had gotten pregnant and dropped out of high school after her junior year. Some of what he said was accurate and some wasn't, but the last part was all news to me.

Hugh was looking for a challenge; he had been waiting too long for the thrill of the fight. I just stood and looked thoughtfully into his eyes – for how long I can't say, but long enough to gauge them. They weren't cruel eyes, but careless eyes. They were the eyes of someone who didn't think and didn't weigh consequences. Perhaps it was a good quality for a quarterback who had to react with split second decisions and even sometimes take a hit for the team in spite of the personal risk, but it would not serve him well when it came to dealing with me. I realized that in an instant of clairvoyant clarity, staring into the careless eyes of my nemesis.

Hugh broke the stare, scoffed, and then turned and dismissed me for lack of a better response to my non-response. My musing turned to curiosity, but not about Hugh. I wanted to know the true nature of my beginnings. As I walked from the lunchroom, a new light shone on my family. I kept walking right out of the school in the direction of the Rock. Within fifteen minutes I passed through the kitchen door. I could hear the murmured inertia of meaningless babble from Bloody Mary's room.

"Mother!" I called loudly. Ice and glass rattled in startled response as Mother scrambled to answer my call.

"What is it, son…" she was saying as she rushed into the kitchen, and her tear stained face met mine with surprise.

"Mother," I demanded, "am I a bastard child?" Her body snapped stiff as if it were hit by a bolt of lightening.

"What?" she said. "Charlie, what are you talking about? Who told you that?"

"I'll tell you," I said, as intense as a laser poised to excise the truth. "Hugh McDowell, that's who."

"That bastard!" Mother cried reflexively, and she was referring to Hugh McDowell Sr. "He has no business telling his son something like that."

"Is it true?" I asked, but I already knew the answer from her reaction.

"Of course not," Mother said weakly, while her sad, drunken eyes exposed her lie.

"Mother, why did you tell me…" I said, but I didn't care to finish the question. "It was all a lie," I said before I went to my room to finish my letter to Gracie, which took on a different tone from its beginning:

…Well, you're not going to believe this. It seems I am a bastard – and it seems I am the last one to know. Hugh McDowell announced it in the cafeteria today. It kind of shocked me. I think I could deal with it if Mother had just told me, but when you're standing there among a whole cafeteria full of people you've grown up with, and the formal announcement is delivered by the big man on campus, it doesn't leave you with a lot of options. I asked Mother about it, and there was nothing she could say, so there you are. Your old buddy down here in Atlanta is the bastard child of a bastard child father and strip tease dancing mother. Sorry for ranting, but finding out that kind of thing doesn't do a whole lot to brighten your day.

Anyway, I do hope your tests went well, and I hope you are able to steer clear of the bad butterflies better than I am.

Gracie wrote me a chastening rebuke:

...You are my friend, so this is why I remind you that I endure my own bad butterflies, as does everybody. There will always be bad butterflies and much of your sense of purpose depends on how you react to them. There is not the sense of accomplishment when you succeed at something easy. School comes easy to you, Charlie, and you should be proud of your success, but perhaps it has been too easy. The real trick is to succeed when the chips are down. That's when you will know you've grown.

You're not a bastard. Hugh McDowell is the bastard. Quit worrying about what he or anybody else at that stuck-up school thinks and concentrate on your own independence and ability to thrive.

Sorry for the lecture, but you needed it. Everything previously stated notwithstanding, steer clear of the bad butterflies...

I should have pasted that letter to my mirror and looked at it every day when I woke up in the morning, but I didn't understand her admonition at the time.

VII. The Queen Succumbs

As Eddie, Bobby, and I grew older the boundaries of the property at the Rock became too confining for three miscreants ever anxious to expand our wayward world. We were not yet old enough to drive, but we could tromp through the large wooded yards in my neighborhood to foray out to the public areas of Buckhead, sparking nervousness among the shoppers and shopkeepers in the quaint, expensive part of the city. The wary adults we encountered might have been more distressed than they already looked had they known Bobby concealed his gun inside the waist of his pants wherever he went. We mostly just cruised the variety of shops that lined the grid of backstreets that made up the retail district.

At the record store Eddie would often pilfer a forty-five and sometimes nonchalantly smuggle an entire album under his jacket. Eddie just seemed to feel the need to take things, no matter whether or not he needed them – or however easy they might be for him to legitimately obtain.

One day in the shoe store a pricey pair of casual loafers caught his attention. The store was crowded that day and the understaffed crew was busy trying to cater to the paying public. It seemed the opportune time for Eddie to try on the pair. After the salesman handed him a box with his size then turned to answer a lady's question about some open toed pumps, he slipped on the shoes and began walking around to get the feel of the shoes. The salesman had a chance to ask him once how he liked them before someone else grabbed him. Bobby picked up Eddie's old sneakers as he and I walked out of the store. Eddie walked right to the exit with the new shoes connected to his feet. They were too polished and stiff to be coordinated with Eddie's sloppy ensemble, but their fine craftsmanship carried him brazenly out of the store. It seemed a clean getaway until I noticed the chubby manager pass through the storefront heading our way. At first we stayed calm and kept walking, but when he began calling after us we took off. He kept up with us until we reached Peachtree Street. Once we hit the intersection the poor, portly manager folded. Through his huffing we could hear him swearing as we put some distance on him. Suddenly, to our incredible misfortune, a cop on a motorcycle rode right up to the manager as if he was waiting down the street for this event to unfold. We didn't look twice, but kept running toward the Sears and Roebuck where Grandfather purchased the killer Craftsman Model 29DS grill. Bobby was leading the way, looking for a convenient place to get off the sidewalk and away from the street. I was close behind, but Eddie was lagging in the stiff, untrained shoes. We ducked into the woods behind the Sears, out of sight from Eddie and the policeman. By the time we reached Habersham Road, Bobby and I were home free, but we had no idea what became of our slow footed friend. As we slowed down, my breath relaxed to match our pace, and we laughed as we walked the rest of the way to the Rock.

As we climbed the driveway trying to guess how long it would take before Eddie showed up, I noticed the ambulance and the police car at the top of the hill. Suddenly, my body flashed hot and my lungs dropped into my belly. Bobby seemed scared and he hesitated, but continued silently up the drive with me. Everything that happened to that point was washed from our consciousness as I walked into the house. I could hear Mother's sobs from Bloody Mary's bedroom. I approached the half open door with the dread of a condemned man walking death row. Inside I could see Vincent's hand on my mother's shoulder as she sat on Grandmother's bed and wept over her ashen, lifeless carcass. I remember the precise feeling that it seemed outrageous that Mother should be so devastated by the death of the woman who had been the bane of her existence for so long. Even though Bloody Mary was of my own blood, I couldn't grieve. The old woman had been suffering and miserable for years, and she passed the misery on to Mother. Finally, she just passed on, and I felt only relief.

As they wheeled Bloody Mary out to the ambulance Eddie

was cresting the driveway trying to catch his breath. Bobby was staring in awe at the police officer who was trying to tend to mother and do whatever he was supposed to be doing in that situation. Everybody stood silently until the back of the ambulance closed. Vince began talking to Mother; that's when Eddie leaned over to me and whispered that the stolen shoes were in the mailbox. When Eddie saw the police car and his father's car at the top of the hill, he thought we were caught, so he ditched the shoes in the mailbox to be rid of the evidence. As the paramedics and police finished their tasks Vince hustled my friends to the car and followed the ambulance and squad car down the driveway.

I waited for Mother to disappear inside before I went to the mailbox to claim Eddie's special delivery. I didn't hear the car cruising slowly around the turn in my direction, so I didn't look up to see it was a police car with the manager of the shoe store inside. I pulled the shoes out of the mailbox and turned toward the driveway just as they spotted me. I couldn't believe the coincidence as the cruiser turned into the driveway. My hesitation was too obvious, but I tried to head up the hill as if I didn't notice them.

"Excuse me, son," said the officer from inside the car.

"That's him," I could hear the store manager cry. "That's the kid who took the shoes."

"Yes sir," I said. I was caught red handed and my face was flush with mortification as I turned to face the music.

The motorcycle cop saw us run into the woods behind the Sears and radioed a cop in a patrol car. He picked up the store manager and began slowly combing the neighborhoods in the area. The butterflies of bad luck couldn't have timed their arrival at my house more perfectly. Some people said Eddie and I favored each other, but I couldn't see the resemblance. I was sure the manager simply associated me with my friends and knew my face from the chase. Nevertheless, the manager claimed I was the thief from his shoe store, and I was holding the goods. It didn't matter, anyway; I was complicit in the crime.

The policeman put me in the backseat and we climbed the driveway to find my mother. I emerged from the car dreading the inevitable cataclysm that would surely result. Mother had just sent her dead mother to the morgue, and immediately her son was about to summon her so a policeman could tell her he was being arrested for stealing. I couldn't imagine anything more disastrous, and it was staring me right square in the eyes.

We got to the door, and the policeman told me to go inside and tell my parents what I did, and then bring them out to see him. I went inside trying to think of what I was going to say to soften the blow of the moment. I stood in the kitchen for a long time, at a loss for what to do or say. There is no telling how long I stood there completely confused, but it was long enough for the policeman to get antsy and ring the doorbell. I moved to answer it, hoping it was all a dream and I would open the door to a salesman or anyone other than the pair who was outside waiting for me. As I pulled open the door to face my nemeses Mother sidled up close behind me.

"Good evening ma'am, do you know why we're here?" said the policeman.

"Yes, I guess so" she responded weakly, her eyes swollen red, as she turned to face the authoritative voice. I noticed the policeman's shiny silver name tag.

"Well, this has obviously upset you," said Officer Crockett. He seemed a little surprised at my mother's extreme reaction, but he forged ahead. "This is Mr. Lacefield. He is the man in charge in this matter and he insists we need to go downtown."

Mother looked at Officer Crockett with tired eyes, and it was clear to me she did not have it in her to move from the house that evening. "Couldn't my son just go with you tonight," she said. "I'm just not up to it. I can go down in the morning."

Everyone standing on the front porch looked confused, except Mother. She was clearly the one who had once again misconstrued the situation. I learned the next day she thought Mr. Lacefield was from the coroner's office, and they needed her to endure some kind of red tape – to complete some forms or do something else bureaucratic. As I looked back, the dour

Mr. Lacefield, dressed neatly in his dark suit, could have easily been mistaken for a coroner.

"Well, I guess we can do that," Officer Crockett said, trying to gather his thoughts. He turned to Mr. Lacefield and stepped away, trying to put the matter to rest right there.

Things were suddenly happening so unexpectedly I had a feint hope the cloud of doom might, by some miracle, pass right over me. In fact, I am sure that, had it been Bobby in my spot instead of me, he would have dodged the storm entirely. But I didn't get that lucky. Mr. Lacefield had endured our smart asses loitering in his store for too long, and we weren't the only kids to breeze through and steal from him. He was sick of it, and he was eager to catch someone and make an example of him. When it was clear he was in no mood for charity, Officer Crockett said, "Well okay, Ma'am. We'll take your son with us. We will give you a call when you can pick him up."

Mother was a little perkier just knowing she didn't have to struggle out of the house. "Oh Charlie," she said casually, "Can you please call your Uncle Vincent when you're ready? I'm just too tired to deal with it, tonight."

"Yes ma'am," I said, eager to get away from her to avoid the big blow-up.

The policeman and Mr. Lacefield looked puzzled as they led me back to the patrol car and put me in the back seat. We drove silently downtown where I was booked at the juvenile detention center. Officer Crockett kept me out of the lock-up and let me call Uncle Vince for a ride home. I got Eddie when I called his house, and when he heard my story he refused to let me talk to Vincent.

"Hell no, you can't talk to him," said Eddie. "If he finds out you got arrested for shoplifting he's gonna know I was involved in it, and I'm not gonna let that happen."

"Listen Eddie," I said, "he's gonna find out anyway, and if he finds out later, and I have to spend the night here, he's damn sure gonna know you were involved. And I'm gonna let him know who walked out of that store with those shoes on his feet.

I know how far you had to run with those new shoes. When he sees the blisters I know you've got, he'll know who to believe. If you let me talk to him now, I'll tell him I did everything on my own, that you and Bobby had nothing to do with it. He might not be sure about that, but if I give him the real story he'll know the truth."

Eddie had no choice – and I had no choice but to confess to Uncle Vincent that I was arrested for shoplifting. I dreaded seeing him walk into the juvenile detention center that night, and I dreaded the ride home alone with him even more, but it didn't turn out as bad as I thought.

"Listen son," Vincent said, "I don't know what your mother thinks happened, but there's no need to bother her with all this after what happened with your grandmother today. We need to keep this between you and me. You're going to have to go to court and answer the complaint. I'll be sure to get you there. You just keep this whole mess to yourself."

Vince didn't need to stress the point. I would keep the truth of what happened to me from Mother. Eddie walked more than a mile in my damning shoes that day, and he would feel more pain in his blistered feet than I was feeling when Vincent dropped me off at the dark Rock that night.

....

Grandmother's funeral was pitifully scant. A few unfamiliar, older men showed up, but Grandmother didn't have anyone except Mother. Her acquaintances had been Grandfather's; in his crowd the women migrated in and out of their lives like disposable lighters, sticking around until the flame died out, only to then be tossed aside and replaced with someone fresher. There was always a little suspicion – never much mingling – among the women from my grandmother's day. Vince and Eddie came, but even Mrs. Palomino didn't make it. Candi and Bobby were there with Vince and Eddie.

After the funeral, depressing more for its lack of attendance than its reason for being held, Vince brought us all back to the

Rock. Mother, who was dealing with her grief the way she dealt with all her hardships, fixed herself a cocktail. I loitered in the suit Vince bought for me the day before, trying to cope with my friends' uncomfortable attempts to comfort me. There was no need for their attention; there was no grief. I was more concerned about what the outcome of my legal proceeding would be.

Just before Vince carried them away Bobby announced he was going to become a cop. I was astonished. Bobby was old enough to be serious about such an ambition, but he never struck me as good fit to wear a badge. Something happened when Bobby met the policeman at our house the day Bloody Mary died, and he was a new disciple of law enforcement. On the same day I was beginning to believe in my inescapable destiny as a Dutton descendant, Bobby was resolving to take responsibility for his future.

When the guests left and the alcohol delivered Mother into slumber I went to my room. Before I went to bed, I took time to write Gracie. It was only after receiving Gracie's reply that I realized how abnormally the events of the week affected me.

Dear Gracie,

Well, what can I say? This past week has been a humdinger. Bloody Mary passed away. You would think this is a sad thing for me, but I have to admit it's a relief. I mean, when you really think about it, all she did was terrorize me the whole time I knew her. I didn't really have anything against her, but I'm not terribly sorry she's gone. I guess I feel bad for Mother, but I'm not sure why she's so sorry she's gone. You know Bloody Mary was always on her case about every aspect of her life. Maybe she had a point, but she was relentless, and I'm just thinking; if Mother believes in herself, how did she allow herself to believe the abuse Bloody Mary heaped upon her? And if she believed what Bloody Mary was saying, why didn't she just conform and change her life.

Speaking of way of life, the same day Bloody Mary died, I got arrested for shoplifting. Mother doesn't know anything about it, so that made the whole evening a relief for me. Actually I technically wasn't shoplifting. Eddie was though, and when they accused me, I couldn't turn the tables on Eddie. So Uncle Vincent got me out of the juvenile detention center without Mother catching on to what happened. Of course, now I am going to court to answer the charges. I am hopeful the court will go easy on me, as I am generally okay, and I don't have a prior record.

But enough about me – how are things going with you? Steer clear of the bad butterflies.

Love,
Charlie

Dear Charlie,

Sorry to hear about Bloody Mary, but I understand where you're coming from on that subject.

Even sorrier to hear about the shoplifting affair. I am concerned about what you guys are doing with yourselves down there. You asked how things are going with me; well, I'm kicking ass in school and guaranteeing I will get into the college of my choice. I'm doing some volunteer work with a cancer center up here. At first it was to help my college resume, but it really means a lot to me to do this, especially with Mom's ordeal. Then I'm working with the publisher part time as a gofer. Since Dad got me the job, I pledged to myself to make him proud. So while I'm up here taking care of business, you guys are down there jerking each other off.

I hate to seem preachy, Charlie, but I know how much potential you have, and I want you to make sure you don't disappoint yourself. Good luck in court, and steer clear of the bad butterflies – and don't become your own bad butterfly.

Love,
Gracie

VIII. Hugh Jr.'s Comeuppance

Three weeks after Bloody Mary's funeral I was convicted of the crime of theft by shoplifting in a state juvenile court. I received a slap on the wrist – no incarceration, no probation, just a stern lecture by a judge who could strike the fear of God into God. I was told I was free to go, and if I stayed out of trouble until I turned eighteen, my record would be expunged. I was also told if I found myself back in the courtroom I would be in real trouble. I had no doubt the judge meant exactly what he said, and I was determined to do everything possible to avoid another meeting with the Honorable Fredrick J. Casper.

Bobby was making himself scarce after announcing he would become a cop. Meanwhile, Eddie and I were spending more time together. Since Hugh McDowell anointed me the pariah of my class at school Eddie became my main companion. I constantly found myself bored with Eddie who was possessed of stunted intellect and banal conduct, but when it came to companionship Eddie was available. Gracie was the best, most stimulating companion I ever had, and I longed for those days that were no more. Gracie was far away, both geographically and developmentally.

We were all becoming older, and by the time I was a senior, Eddie – the only one who could afford a car – became my de facto chauffeur. Eddie loved his new role, and by that time we were together more than I wanted to be. Bobby would occasionally join us, and whenever he did I was relieved to have a buffer from Eddie. Bobby was maturing faster than Eddie, and he was more interesting to be with than in earlier times. Those middle teens were the times that cemented a close relationship between Bobby and me. He knew I respected him for his rededication to school and his renewed sense of direction; he admired me for my academic prowess, but he was clearly concerned about my relationship with Eddie.

"When are you going to give up on Eddie and decide what you're going to do with yourself," he would ask me when Eddie was absent.

"I'll be fine," I would say, unwilling to acknowledge he had a point. Perhaps Eddie had become a bad habit; maybe he was my vice. I didn't have the common vices that influenced my relatives, so perhaps he was my vicarious vice. I was as fiercely loyal to him as Bobby was to me. Bobby understood that, so we didn't often discuss it. Besides, I kept privately believing things would be different once I was out of high school, away from my rumor riddled community, and in a college where my past didn't follow me. If I had to be burdened with a vice, I thought, Eddie was relatively harmless. I underestimated the destructive nature of my friend, my personal bad butterfly.

....

Bobby was an avid baseball fan. He would watch any game, from the big leagues down, and as the spring of Bobby's and my senior year rolled around we found ourselves hanging around the ball fields where the local high schools competed. Hugh McDowell played football, but the football coach required all his players to support the other sports programs at Saint Mary's. Hugh was always at the baseball games, and I scrupulously avoided him. The day St. Mary's played Eddie's school, Sandy Springs High, it was impossible to camouflage myself among the rest of the crowd. Eddie, who consumed a pint of his father's whiskey and smoked a joint before the game, was obnoxious in his support of a team to which he normally paid no attention. He began getting out of control, stoned and drunk and loud in otherwise passive bleachers. Fans from both schools were becoming fed up with us, and Bobby and I looked at each other trying to decide the best way to extricate ourselves from the scene. Finally, Bobby just picked Eddie up without a word and dragged him out of the bleachers toward the parking lot.

By the time we got back to the car Hugh and his buddies

were standing nearby talking to some girls. "Hey Lofton, who's this guy and what's his fucking problem?" Hugh said, walking in our direction.

"Nothing, we're getting him out of here," I said, trying to physically support our sloshed friend while Bobby dug into Eddie's pocket for the keys.

"What's your spic buddy doing, trying to give him a hand job?" Hugh said, looking toward his two companions who seemed to immediately turn their attention from Hugh and his comment. He knew, at once, he made a mistake.

Bobby paused and looked up from one knee. "What'd you say?" he asked, looking straight into Hugh's eyes.

"I asked what you were doing," said Hugh, suddenly less enthusiastic in the crosshairs of my well built friend's glare.

"Come on Hugh," said Cal Greer, "Let's leave 'em alone. They've got enough trouble with this drunk." It was already too late, though.

"No, exactly what did you say," Bobby demanded, standing to meet Hugh's troubled gaze.

Hugh looked back toward Susan Howard and Leslie Ames who were relishing the scene, waiting to see if he would stand up or shrink. He then looked at Cal and Scott Trucks to see what kind of support they might provide. Meanwhile Eddie broke from my grasp, stumbling forward as he slurred at Cal, "Drunk! Who you callin' a drunk?" I tried to grab him but he fell on his face in front of Cal.

Meanwhile Bobby wasn't giving Hugh a chance to save face, demanding again to have his question answered. Hugh spoke quietly. "I asked if you were giving your friend a hand job. It was a joke, you know," he said, trying to infuse reason into the confrontation.

"No, you called me a spic, didn't you?" Bobby said.

"Well..." Hugh stammered.

"Well? Well, you better get ready 'cause this spic's gonna beat your ass," said Bobby, allowing Hugh enough time to crouch in defense before he lit into him. In two shots to the head Hugh reeled backward in quick defeat, but Bobby was mad and he caught him and began unmercifully pummeling his beaten body. Cal pulled Eddie up by the shirt and took a swing, that missed wildly when Eddie collapsed back to the ground by his own dumb luck. Scott and I looked at each other, and without saying a word we knew what we had to do. Both of us seized Bobby's two arms trying to keep him from killing Hugh. It took us too long to react and longer to get him under control. Hugh's face looked like a bloody bowl of oatmeal, and he was whelping like a whipped dog. We looked around in time to see Cal pull Eddie back up, but before he could take a swing, Eddie leaned forward and threw up all over him.

"Oh God!" Cal cried like a little boy, arms extended in horror as he back away. "Did you see that? He puked on me."

The girls were tittering as they walked away. Eddie recovered from retching and was instantly less intoxicated. I got the keys from him and Bobby threw him in the car as I got behind the wheel and took off. We looked back to see Scott helping Hugh to his feet while Cal pulled his vomit soaked polo shirt over his head. Bobby was shaking with adrenaline and was still cursing as Eddie whooped and pulled a full flask from under the driver's seat. "You really took it to that boy!" he exclaimed.

"Shut up, Eddie," said Bobby in disgust. "None of this would'a happened if you weren't so goddamn obnoxious."

"Hey excuse me, but I'm not the one who tried to kill the asshole, asshole," slurred Eddie as he took another swig.

"If you don't shut up I'm gonna kill *you*," Bobby said, trying to calm himself. "Just get me home," he said to me. "I've had it with this guy."

I drove silently to Decatur to drop Bobby off before taking Eddie to Sandy Springs. "Don't you think you've had enough of that stuff," I finally said to Eddie when we were alone and he was tipping the flask.

"Who are you, my father?" he said.

"No, your friend," I replied, and left it at that. I dropped Eddie and his car off at his house and walked down the street to catch a bus home.

The next day at school Hugh looked better than I would have thought. Upon closer observation it became clear that he was sporting some pancake make-up, but he seemed generally okay. I wasn't sure how he was going to react to me, but I hoped he would appreciate the fact that I helped pull Bobby away before more damage was done. By the end of the day I had my answer. As I walked home from school down Andrews Drive toward the Rock, the unmistakably deep rumble of Hugh's convertible GTO approached slowly from behind. Cal was in the passenger seat as they pulled along side me. I felt the hot flash of fear through my body as the two got out of the car. Taking on Hugh was conceivable considering his condition; one punch landed anywhere on his cauliflowered face would instantly put him down. Cal, on the other hand, suffered only regurgitation to the shirt and was fully recovered. I knew I couldn't take on both of them.

The blow came from Cal, and it found my solar plexus, sending me to the ground. I gasped and waited for the next shot, which didn't come. The two attackers stood above me as I caught my breath while Hugh spoke. "Who's your spic friend and his drunk buddy?" he said. I still couldn't talk when Cal pulled me up by my button down, Catholic School collar.

"He asked you a question, Lofton," he said, spit spraying from his menacing sneer. I wouldn't have answered if I could. He struck another blow in the same vicinity as the first one, and I thought I would suffocate right in the middle of the street. I looked desperately around in the hope that someone would come along in the quiet neighborhood. Cal's foot struck my rib cage shooting waves of pain throughout my torso before the sound of salvation sent Hugh and Cal back to the Pontiac.

"You haven't heard the last of this," Hugh promised as they roared off just before the car came around the corner into sight. I picked myself up and tried to look normal to the passing motorist; I had no desire to deal with anyone at that moment. It was an isolated incident, I told myself. By next fall high school would be a bad memory, and I would be through with Hugh McDowell forever.

It would have been nice had that been the case, but the next day after school Hugh and Cal paid me another visit on the way home. They got in a few more slugs before another car came unwittingly to the rescue. No matter how bad it got, I wouldn't give up my friends. When I went to bed that night I considered my options. One thing was sure; I would have to change my route home.

Eddie was glad to skip his last period the next day and wait for me around the corner in the opposite direction of the Rock. That worked fine, and as the days went along I found other inventive ways to avoid the ominous hum of the GTO on after school walks.

One day during P.E. we were out playing softball when Hugh and Cal appeared from the cafeteria. Coach Harper made it a habit to retreat to the offices once our class was ensconced in an organized activity. As the period wound down, he would emerge from the school building in enough time to wrap up the games and send us to our next period classes. My nemeses, frustrated that I had been unavailable for after school beatings, decided to bring the interrogations to the softball field while Coach Harper was taking his intra-period break.

"Hello, Lofton," said Hugh as he snuck up behind me. "Haven't seen you for a while." Cal was standing next to him with one of the softball bats in his hand. I looked in panic for help from somebody. Even if anyone did have a notion to come to the rescue, no one had the inclination to cross Hugh McDowell in the process. Cal had the good sense to drop the bat, but I didn't have a chance against the two of them. They shoved me around and roughed me up until they got me into the woods out of sight. There they beat me until I made up two fictitious names to replace Bobby and Eddie and pointed them toward Riverside High. I was too bloodied to attend my next class, so I just left without checking out and found my way back home.

My fictional characters bought me one day until the names didn't check out. The next day I encountered Hugh and Cal on the softball field. The ritual began again. This time when they dragged me out of the woods I was beaten worse. Coach Harper was still on the field picking up the bases for the weekend when I was dragged back toward school by Hugh and Cal. I was happy that someone of authority was there to see what they had done to me. I had avoided telling anyone, reasoning that if I did it would only lead to trouble for Bobby. But it was beginning to be more than I could physically stand. So I thought the sight of Coach Harper offered a chance to put the ordeal to an end. The coach spotted us, undoubtedly aware of what had happened.

"McDowell, Greer, leave Lofton alone and get back inside," he shouted at us. He was less concerned about their football standing than coach Banks. Hugh and Cal dropped me without a word and hustled past the coach back to the cafeteria. I picked myself up slowly and walked toward the coach, my fat lip leading the way.

"Coach, I sure am glad you came along," I said in my manliest voice. Those guys were trying to kill me."

"Lofton, what'd you do to piss 'em off so bad, anyway?" he asked.

"Oh some guy went after McDowell at the ball fields awhile back, and they think I know something about it. They've been giving me a bad time ever since," I said.

The coach chuckled and said, "Lofton, if I were you, and I knew anything about it, I'd tell them boys whatever it is they want to know. They're some pretty tough cookies and they don't cotton to wormy kids like you."

"Can't you do anything to stop 'em?" I asked in dismay, seeing my last hope for deliverance dwindling before my sullen, swollen eyes.

"Nope son, I'm afraid I can't do that," he said, apparently unconcerned about my dire circumstances. "You see, if I go around fighting your battles for you, how're you ever gonna learn to take care of yourself?"

"So you're not gonna do anything to those guys?" I said in disbelief.

"Son, those boys are okay," he said. "They're just high

spirited. That's what makes 'em so damn good on the football field..."

I just walked away, the coach calling after me to get back to school. His admonishments carried no weight with me. I walked beaten and bleary eyed out of the schoolyard and straight to the Rock. Mother's car was gone when I reached the top of the driveway and the phone was ringing as I crawled inside. I recognized the voice of Father Baxter, the principal, asking for Mother. When I said she wasn't home, he asked me why I disobeyed Coach Harper's instructions and why I left the school grounds and where I had been when I was supposed to have been in Biology the past few days. I just hung up the phone; I didn't bother to tell him I had to skip my final hour in order to avoid Hugh and his GTO.

The deep end was at hand and I was ripe for taking the dive. Eddie called and we made plans to get together with Bobby on Saturday, then I went to bed for the day. I slept hard until five-thirty in the morning, when the squeaky sound of my mother opening the door after a night of dancing and drinking jarred me awake.

It had been almost fourteen hours since sleep carried me from physical suffering, and I woke up agitated, unable to relax. It took an eternity for Eddie to arrive thirty minutes past the time he promised, and I was more than ready when we left the Rock together, taking care not to wake my mother. I had never stolen anything in my life, but that weekend I covertly copped something from a friend. It was a crime I would pay for far into the future.

....

It took until third period Trig on Monday morning to get the summons to Father Baxter's office. This didn't surprise me, but finding Mother waiting there was a surprise. It might have been the first time she had ever been inside my school as a parent. Throughout my career at Saint Mary's I had been an excellent student and hadn't, until then, presented any problems. Mother signed all the papers and report cards throughout the years, but beyond that she was absent from my scholastic life. Now, at the homestretch of my high school career she sat in the principal's office to discuss my recent behavior, looking old for thirty-four. After a litany of charges was recited to us, we were both reminded of my excellent record and the scholarship opportunities awaiting me. The message of the meeting was, "Don't blow it now."

I was never asked why my behavior had taken such a sudden turn, but I wouldn't have responded anyway. The priest was smiling as if his simple lecture put the world right and he stood to indicate he was through with us. I never said a word about Hugh McDowell or Cal Greer. There was no reason to trust Father Baxter or even Mother any more than I could count on Coach Harper out on the softball fields. Mother smiled back at the principal and then at me, saying essentially that she was confident that the great Catholic School could guide me to salvation in spite of myself. "If anyone can get him through, you people can," she concluded blindly.

I went back to class, Father Baxter's talk having had the opposite effect on me than was intended. I had my mind on a little prank I intended to play during P.E. When the coach went inside I prayed for Hugh McDowell to show his face on that field, and unfortunately my prayers were answered. He and Cal took their usual cocky stroll along the windows of the cafeteria on the way to home plate where I stood counting their every step. The others watched the two in awe as they got within spitting distance of me.

"Well, Lofton..." was all Hugh could say before I whipped out the gun I took from Bobby's dresser drawer without his permission.

"Shut up, Hugh!" I screamed as he and Cal stopped dead still, eyes wide with terror. "You just **SHUT UP!**" I said for effect. By then everyone was gaping at me and Bobby's gun while I drew a bead directly on Hugh's head. He and Cal were speechless, as I alternated targets between the two. I could see that no one was moving a tick, and I was relishing the scene.

"You're so goddamned tough, you tell me what you're gonna do now, shithead," I said. "What are you gonna do when I put a bullet in that pea-sized brain of yours?" Hugh started to speak, but he couldn't find the courage. I fired the gun well above his head and his gray pants grew dark with pee where he wet himself. "You piss ant," I cried. "You wet your goddamned pants, you pussy. You're gonna look silly buried like that."

It was more than Hugh could take. He collapsed to his knees, sobbing, begging me not to kill him. Cal relaxed slightly, as amazed at Hugh as he was at the gun pointed in his direction. I howled with laughter, threw the gun into the woods as far as I could, and tore into Hugh like a Doberman. By the time Coach Harper pulled me off, I had turned the McDowell good looks into a worse mess than Bobby had. I was hauled back for my second visit in one day to the principal's office. The staff in the office eyed me in terror and shock as the coach escorted me in, my arms locked in an iron clad wrestling hold behind my back. He sat me down in front of Father Baxter who instructed him not to leave us alone. I was defiant, but calm; still the principal wasn't taking any chances with me.

The police arrived soon after an eager student retrieved the gun and delivered it to the office. They had a few questions, none that I was willing to answer. Before they arrived I never considered that I created a legal plight for myself. My stunt of self defense seemed rational until it was over. I knew I was never going to shoot anyone, so it didn't seem that serious an offense. I was *way* off on that calculation. When I saw the numb students and shaken faculty as I was wrested away from the scene, my focus on what happened began to sharpen. Then, with the police on the scene, I was aware enough to know that what I had done was beyond the pale of schoolyard antics. I knew not to say a word until I could get some advice.

Soon parents began arriving in a mild hysteria. I could hear them outside the cracked door of my office prison begging to find their children so they could see for themselves that they were okay. One minute I was incredulous that this personal vendetta between Hugh and me – and my indiscretion with a pistol – had ballooned into a school wide calamity. The next minute I was asking myself what I could possibly have been thinking. Still, a small part of me relished the vivid image of Hugh's embarrassing bladder failure and incoherent blubbering in front of so many of his admirers.

……..

I was charged with assault with a weapon and suspended from school. Vincent posted my bond, and Mother picked me up from the jail. My suspension from school was a foregone conclusion, but I believed I would be readmitted after a proper period. The next day Mother went to see Father Baxter and appeal for leniency. With my record of scholastic excellence I wasn't so concerned about school as my legal problems. That was another miscalculation.

In his humiliation Hugh pressed his father into indignant protest before Mother could make my case. Learning of Hugh McDowell Sr.'s outrage, Mother suggested a meeting among all the parties to try to reach a solution. Hugh Sr. wouldn't hear of it. He was a prominent member of the community, a big contributor to Saint Mary's school, and he wasn't about to consort with the likes of a stripper. Knowing what I knew of Alderman McDowell's penchant for adult entertainment, I could only laugh at the hypocrisy when Father Baxter showed us his letter of protest.

As for the school, they held some sympathy for me, but the McDowell's were important people. Besides, the incident shook the confidence of the other parents, and school officials weren't inclined to risk the support of the masses for my sake; I wasn't even supporting the school with tuition payments. By the end of the battle, Mother's less polished plea was no match for the influence of the smooth politician, and I was expelled for eternity. I was blindsided by the decision. It was inconceivable that, after all that time and effort, I was no longer a part of Saint Mary's School. I wouldn't graduate from there; my perfect grades would become meaningless. The scholarship opportunities would evaporate, and I didn't think I would be admitted to college even if I could have paid for it.

As for my trial in Juvenile Court, Vince provided a lawyer he kept on retainer, David Israel. I knew nothing about the business of being a criminal lawyer, but I could tell this lawyer deserved his obviously generous retainer. No matter how the McDowells cajoled the system to try to destroy my life for threatening and humiliating their bully son, David Israel, Esq. transformed me before the court as the model for youth in my day – a kid with stellar grades and a promising future who was unjustly charged in a matter that was best settled away from the court between the families involved. He was impressive, and by the end of my one day trial, I'm not sure it was clear to the judge how the gun appeared at school that day, or just what its involvement in the episode was.

I was feeling pretty good about the outcome until the Judge looked sternly over his reading glasses and dredged up the stolen shoes incident. I cringed, waiting for the other shoe to drop. When it did I had a momentary bout with dread.

Instead of finishing my last year of high school, I spent ten weeks in a juvenile detention facility in downtown Atlanta. It wasn't bad – mostly just boring. We performed busy work around the building, and the center provided classes in a futile attempt to continue our education. Most of my fellow delinquents had no interest in learning anything, and I already knew all that was being taught. We received counseling and went through tests intended to psychoanalyze us. From what I could gather, my counselor found me to be a relatively normal member of the human race. He explained my behavior in flowery and technical language, but he essentially attributed it to a lack of parenting, a conclusion I could have given him the day I reported to the detention center.

The juvenile justice system provided placement assistance for jobs and further education, but I wasn't interested in what was offered. I had no interest in going to a trade school, and I knew where my earning potential was going to be. I felt defeated and accepted what I thought was my inescapable lot in life as the descendant of neer-do-wells.

Meanwhile, my friend Bobby was joining the Atlanta Police force, and he would start school at Georgia State University in the fall. My friend Gracie was finishing her sophomore year at St. Bonaventure and was already anticipating going to graduate school at Harvard. She was taking her undergraduate Journalism major by storm – an odds on favorite to finish first in her class. She knew she wanted a graduate degree in Literature, and it looked as though she and Harvard would choose each other. Eddie had one more year of high school, and no one expected him to pursue higher education. He would scrape by Sandy Springs High by the gauge of a rolling paper.

Hugh McDowell and his father succeeded in altering the course of my education, thereby altering my vocation, so I would just have to adapt. I didn't have any ideas of avenging their assault on my future, but our futures would intersect once more, creating a chaotic impact upon their lives.

IX. HUGH SR.'S COMEUPPANCE

Mother's lifestyle ravaged her natural good looks making it increasingly harder for her to earn a living dancing topless among younger, fresher faces and figures. Finally, Vince mercifully told her he needed someone to manage the dancers, so he created the position of "house mother" at the club to give her a steady, although significantly diminished income. I had to do some work to supplement the household budget. Given my age, skills, and abbreviated education, my opportunities seemed limited, but Vince offered me the chance to make good money as a bouncer at the Bottoms Up Lounge. Like father, like son I thought as I accepted the position.

I wasn't old enough to be working there so Vince sent me to Lawrenceville to see Lance. *Lawrenceville Lance* was a former sheriff's deputy in the mostly rural community just north of Atlanta, but at some point he figured out that his hobby of forging local, county and state documents paid much better than the sheriff's department. I had no idea how he and Vince hooked up, but he gave me the impression Vince was an important client. The next day I received a driver's license certifying me as an eighteen year old. My evolving vision of the future was exposed to the possibilities that existed for those who were willing to exist outside the confines of the law.

The money was good at Bottoms Up, Vince made sure of that, but the work was unfulfilling. Still, in appreciation for Vince helping with a lawyer, I stuck with it. By the time Eddie graduated he joined me and his family business to work at the club. No one at the club liked him, but they had to abide the son of the boss. His fellow bouncers snickered behind his back, the bartenders shook their heads when he demanded drinks on duty, and the dancers rolled their eyes at his lecherous leers and uninvited gropes. Even Candi Wells was not immune from his attitude and sleazy innuendo. I tried to bring him along and teach him the things any simpleton with some muscle could do. While Eddie *was* a simpleton, the skills for the simple job seemed to escape him, mostly due to alcohol.

Eddie's drinking got increasingly out of control, and I was forced to cover for him. Once, after he unjustifiably hassled a regular, causing the man and his money to walk out in a huff, I concocted a lie to Vince to cover for Eddie. When it turned out the customer was a close personal friend of Vince's, not to mention a partner in some of his other affairs, I was summoned to Vince's office. His office wasn't in the Bottoms Up Lounge, but a couple of doors down Peachtree on the second floor of an old brick building that housed an adult bookstore.

"Come in son," said Vince, as he leaned back in a squeaky rolling chair, elbows relaxed on the tattered armrests. He pushed back from his desk. "What happened the other day with Gerald Towns?" Vince was one to get right to the point.

"Well, you know, he got a little fresh with the girls, Brandi in particular, and we just politely asked him to leave. No big deal," I said.

"You see, son, it is a big deal to Gerald, and to me," said Vince. "Gerald's a good friend; he has some mutual business with me. I've known Gerald a long time. He wouldn't lie to me. He tells me a different story."

"Well, you know how it is," I said, trying to keep Eddie out of the matter, "he had a few drinks. He probably doesn't remember just how it happened."

"No, he remembers," said Vince with what I hoped was a smile, "and Brandi remembers, too. Charlie, you're a good friend to Eddie." He paused for a moment. "But don't ever lie to me again." I interpreted whatever his next expression was as sinister.

"Yes sir," was all I could manage, not sure if he scolded me or threatened me. There was something in Vince's manner, especially since his electrical disfigurement at the Rock, which made everything he said seem like a threat. I started to get up, but Vince motioned that there was something else.

"Come with me," he said. "I've got something I need you to do." Vince got up and I followed him out to his car. I settled uneasily into the passenger seat, replaying the conversation we just had in my mind. We rode silently until we turned into a warehouse property just north of town. We pulled next to a rollup door marked D44 where Vince slammed the shifter into park before the car came to a full stop. Vince jumped out as the car quit bouncing. Fearing what he was capable of, I hesitated before I got out, but he waved at me enthusiastically.

"This is a little place very few people know about," he said as he clicked apart a padlock and hoisted a roll-up door, creating a hollow, metal screech. "This is where I keep private records for a business I share with Gerald Towns. You've proven yourself to be competent and loyal. You're here for a reason, so I trust you not to talk about this place – *to anyone*."

Vince's words were reassuring, quelling any concerns I had about his intentions. My tension fell away as I followed him through a warehouse into a small, undecorated office furnished with an old desk, threadbare leather executive chair patched with duct tape, and two plastic chairs to accommodate visitors such as myself. I plopped down on one of the uncomfortable chairs while Vince leaned forward and pulled a file from a drawer. It wasn't labeled, and inside was a plain business card and a hand drawn map of an area of Atlanta that I recognized. "Call this girl when we get back," he said. "She'll tell you when to meet her and what I want you to do. I'll make sure your shift is covered at the club. This is something I've never done to a client before, but I think this is necessary." Vince then did some work while I sat and stewed.

My apprehension returned like a boomerang as I held the file, trying not to imagine what Vince had in mind for me and a strange girl and whoever his "client" was. I resisted the urge to ask any questions; if Vince wanted me to know more he would have told me. Once I got back to the club I took the card out of the file and inspected it before I went to the pay phone. The bold type at the top of the plain looking card announced "Party Time!" with the name of Natasha and a phone number listed below. I picked up the receiver and unsteadily dialed the number.

"Party Time," said the sexy, smoky voice on the other end.

"Hi, Natasha please," I said, swallowing hard.

"You've got her, sweetheart," the voice said. "What can I do for you?"

"This is Charlie Lofton," I said. "Vince..."

"Oh yeah," interrupted Natasha. "When are you gonna come see me, darling?" she asked suggestively.

"Vince said..."

"Meet me at six," she said. "Come up Roswell Road 'til you turn on Copeland on the left, just before the perimeter. Go right at the first apartment complex past the shopping center. Follow the drive around to the right 'till it dead ends. Take a left. It's the second building on the right: number 2212, upstairs." Her voice implied rote boredom, and it was clear she had spoken those instructions a thousand times. She hung up before I could respond. The call produced no insight about my mission so I remained on edge until it was time to go, praying I wouldn't be expected to do something terrible, and planning my strategy if my prayers weren't answered.

At the appointed time I rang the bell at apartment 2212. The door swung open revealing a scantily clad blonde woman with a cigarette burning between her red lips. She was older than she sounded on the phone, possessed of a classic, but sad beauty. A closer look at her face, heavily caked with make-up, revealed the faintest brunette hairline contrasting with the wig she was wearing.

"You Charlie?" Natasha asked, uninterested in my response as she waved me inside.

"Yes," I said timidly as I walked into the sparsely furnished apartment. The living room smelled of weak incense and strong perfume blended with the redolence of stale smoke from the chain of cigarettes I could tell she burned all day.

"It's in here," said Natasha, walking into the hallway and motioning for me to follow. At the first door she turned the knob and we waked into a room where I found a video camera on a tripod wired to a reel-to-reel video tape recorder on the floor beside it. A metal chair rounded out the room's decor. The camera lens was pointed directly through the transparent side of a two way mirror into the bedroom on the other side of the wall. The set-up was obvious, but I still had to ask what I was there to do.

"Didn't Vinnie tell you?" said Natasha. "When the john comes in you're supposed to tape the action. You gotta keep this room totally dark so he can't see you from the other side; and be real quiet. I don't know what Vinnie's up to, but he must have a real hard on for this guy."

I was dumbfounded. The idea of sitting in that room, spying on a couple as they copulated sent my head into orbit. "I have to sit here and watch you two through the camera?" I protested.

"Yeah," she said, sounding human for the first time. "Sounded weird to me, too. But who am I to question why. Besides, Vinnie says there's an extra hundred in it for me."

My palms began to sweat, and I sat down in the metal chair, assessing *my* mettle in this situation, trying to convince myself that I could go through with it. "I don't know," I said. "It's just..."

"Relax, sweetheart," said Natasha. "It won't take long. They never take long with me." she said with a touch of pride.

I had to be sure I wouldn't be detected so I turned out the light and walked into the other room. There was a mirror affixed by clear plastic clips screwed neatly into the adjoining wall. I gazed deeply into the glass and satisfied myself that there was no reason to suspect it was anything other than a mirror. That only slightly allayed my anxiety. As I returned to the camera room I wondered if I could tape the affair with my eyes shut. I checked out the equipment, and Natasha gave me a quick lesson on how it operated. My throat was dry as I sat on the chair surrendering to the inevitability of the situation. I tried to remind myself it wasn't the worst thing Vincent could have had in store for me. Before I could change my mind the doorbell rang and Natasha isolated me in my dark, voyeuristic cell. I could barely hear the crack of the front door separating from its frame.

"Hey sweetheart," said the prostitute. "I'm Natasha."

"Where's Morgan?" asked the abrupt, familiar male voice. "I always meet Morgan here on Tuesday night."

"She had an emergency, dear," Natasha said with exaggerated warmth. "She asked me to take care of you tonight. I hope you don't mind."

"How about Rochelle?" said the john. "She couldn't make it either?"

"No, Rochelle doesn't work today, honey," said Natasha. "What's the matter? You don't like me? I'm real good; you'll see."

"It's not that. I just like to be careful. I've never seen you," said the john. They conducted a credit card transaction.

"Don't worry, honey," she assured him. "We're all part of the same crew. Come on, relax and let me take you on back."

I could hear the floor creak as they passed by my room. The light came on, and I could see Natasha tugging a hand behind her. I focused the camera on the next face to appear and almost gasped out loud.

"That was two hundred," said Natasha as she handed the credit card receipt to Hugh McDowell Sr. My adrenaline kicked in, and I was so intrigued with Vince's purpose for taping Hugh McDowell with a prostitute I forgot my reluctance to watch the two engaged in sex. "Make yourself comfortable," she said. "I'll be right back." She left Hugh Sr. alone to undress and lay on the bed naked. I focused directly on his face to make sure Vince could identify him and then pulled the zoom back to a wider angle.

When Natasha returned they got down to business. Mr. McDowell's sexual tastes were hilarious to me and embarrassing for him. I kept the camera steady on the action, despite my silent hysterics. The camera captured a further negotiation between the john and the whore whereby Hugh Sr. got premium services and Natasha was paid an extra two hundred dollars. Natasha left the room, and when she returned she was dressed in black leather. She assumed a nasty, authoritative tone as she ordered Hugh Sr. to lick the bottom of her knee high boots. Mr. McDowell obeyed and continued to obey until she had him on his hands and knees, paddling him, telling him what a bad boy he was. As he was being paddled, he began playing with himself. It didn't take long for his fetish to be satisfied. When he was done all four cheeks were red as beets – his ass cheeks from being beaten and his face from shame. The entire episode took about thirty-five minutes including the S&M scene. Hugh Sr. soon disappeared from the apartment of ill repute having no idea the degree to which he had just been screwed.

After Natasha shut the door behind him, she came into my room. "Did you get all that?" she asked, with a spiteful relish that I hadn't seen in her before Hugh Sr. arrived.

"Yeah," I said, wondering if she had any idea why this double cross was taking place.

"Good," she said as she rewound the tape and took it off the spindle. "Now, Vince told me to take care of you honey, so what's your pleasure?"

I was stunned by her proposition and had no idea what to say. I really just wanted to leave. "That's okay, but thank you anyway," I said, afraid I was offending the intimidating figure before me. I wanted nothing more than to get away from there.

Fortunately, for Natasha time was money; she wasn't concerned about my rejection.

"Fine with me honey," she said. "Now, you take that tape to Vinnie right away. I'll call him to tell him you're on the way." She patted me on the butt, rushing me out of the apartment.

"Fine," I said, and I was out the door and out of Natasha's life forever. As I drove downtown I reflected on the scene that I captured with the telltale video camera. I was privy to a secret no one else in the city knew about, and that realization made me laugh so hard I could barely keep my eyes on the road. What would Hugh Jr. think if he could see his father on all fours, spanking the monkey while a prostitute in black leather spanked him? I almost pitied Hugh at the thought.

Vince was waiting for me in his office. He took the tape

from me and watched it with a growing smile. "Excellent job," he said with a gleam in his eye. "What do you think we should do with this?"

"I dunno," I said, suspecting Vince already had plans for it.

"Whatever I do, I'll have to do it anonymously; Natasha's johns have no idea who's behind her business, and that's not something I want Hugh McDowell or anyone else to know," Vince said. Then he paused.

I had no idea what his plan was, but when I looked at Vince that night I realized how ruthless he could be.

"Okay, this tape's heading for a recording studio where some friends of mine are going to dub about fifty video cassettes of it. Then, some of the copies are going to all the radio and T.V. stations and newspapers in the city. Other copies are going to powerful people. This is going to become this city's underground tape of the year. Hugh McDowell is gonna pay dearly for crossing you. He'll never be sure it was you, but he'll always suspect. Besides, not knowing who screwed him will eat away at him. You just got your revenge, son."

The power Vince had, and his willingness to use it to destroy a man's life was frightening, but he was doing it for me and treating me as a confidant at the same time. It occurred to me that I was glad to be on Vince's good side; nobody would want to be at odds with the brutal hood.

Within two days reports were being circulated about some kind of embarrassing tape involving a prominent member of the community. By the weekend full blown accounts, delicately reported, dominated the local press. Businessmen who could count themselves among Atlanta's inner circle were soon passing copies of copies of the tape around amongst themselves. In less than two weeks Hugh McDowell Sr. resigned from what had become Atlanta's City Council, not to mention from the board of a local company and a charity he chaired. He was spending all his time trying to hold his family together, but there wasn't enough time in eternity. Andrea McDowell left him, taking Hugh Jr.'s younger sisters with her.

By that time, Hugh Jr. was at the University of Georgia

playing football. The dissolution of his family had to be a distraction. His promising freshman and sophomore years were followed by a lackluster spring performance. Eventually he lost his apparent inheritance of the starting quarterback position to his third string rival. He never regained his star athlete status, and he eventually became discouraged and quit football. Perhaps his decline in the sport would have happened, anyway. Perhaps he just didn't have the talent to be the starting quarterback in a major college program. I kept reminding myself of that possibility; I didn't want to be the cause of his dream going unrealized. I didn't have the same blind sense of purpose as Vincent.

X. CONTINUING EDUCATION

The downfall of the Hugh McDowells coincided with an upswing in my life. My growing rapport with Vincent was stronger than ever since our secret caper. The people at the club noticed my status, and most of them warmed to me, trying to get in good with the guy who was in good with the boss. It didn't take long to notice that Eddie, unlike my other colleagues, took umbrage with the mutual respect his father and I were enjoying. I tried to avoid Vince and his approving air when Eddie was at the club, but it didn't matter. Eddie's drinking was spiraling out of control along with his moods. When he was sober he was no problem. But once he had a few belts his demons bubbled to the surface and he became worse than any of the drunken customers in the club.

Not that I was the only one who bore the brunt of his tirades. One night, in an alcohol induced rage, he crossed a sacred line. The dancers' dressing room was sacrosanct – off limits to anyone except the dancers and my mother, the House Mother. Eddie was ranting unintelligibly when I noticed him stumbling to the back of the stage, and then, incredibly, he crashed through the door marked "OFF LIMITS". His timing was impeccably horrible. Candi Wells was completely naked and she let out a scream heard above the bump and grind music out on the dance floor. Eddie muscled her against the vanity counter and was berating her, leveling incoherently angry insults against her "snotty son." It was malice concocted in his mind thanks to the concoctions he was slugging down at the bar. Before the other bouncers and I could get to them he slapped her. We paused in horrified disbelief just long enough for Candi to clutch a metal nail file from the vanity and swing blindly in his direction. Eddie ducked late and the point of the file ripped a chunk from Eddie's good earlobe – the one that hadn't been shot off when we were kids at the Rock. By the time we got to them Candi crouched, sobbing, trying to cover herself with her own bare arms. Eddie stood above her holding his bloody ear and cursing at her. We caught his arm just as he cocked to land another blow. Everyone went down in a heap of sweaty humanity.

We wrestled Eddie into the manager's office trying to stop his bleeding. I sent a bouncer, Ralph Borden, to take Candi home and make sure she was okay while I looked for Eddie's only good lobe. I never found it. Eddie was livid. He was swearing at me and belittling the others who helped drag him out of the dressing room. I just ignored him and tried to get him to his car. He passed out as I drove him to my house.

Late the next morning I awoke to the persistent ringing of our doorbell. By the time I got dressed and got downstairs, Eddie was just stumbling off the couch, hung over and disoriented. I opened the door to see Bobby. He was furious, looking around me screaming, "Is the little bastard here!" Bobby caught sight of Eddie rubbing his eyes still in his rumpled, bloody clothes from the night before, and he pushed me aside. Eddie was stunned when he was grabbed by the shirt collar and lifted off his feet. "You son of a bitch," said Bobby in a cold, steel voice. "If you ever even speak to my mother again – I mean speak, like 'Hello' - I'll kill you. You got that?"

"Yes," came the reply and that was all. The pain in Eddie's eyes was replaced by astonished fear. It was obvious he didn't remember what he had done to incur the wrath of Bobby, but he wasn't about to inquire at that moment.

Bobby just stared into Eddie's bloodshot face still holding him in the air as if to hang him up on a meat hook. "Fine," he finally said, and threw him like a piece of dirty laundry onto the couch.

"Give him a break, Bobby," I said without conviction. "He was drunk..."

Bobby looked at me squarely and waved for me to stop. "That's no excuse; that's the problem. I've had it with him. He'd better heed my words. If he so much as even sneezes in my mother's direction he's a dead man. I don't care if I'm a cop; I don't care about anything. I'm never having anything else to do with him, but you can assure him for me, if he does, that's it. No questions, no warnings, he's dead. You tell him."

"But Bobby, it was the booze..." I began, but Bobby interrupted.

"No, Charlie," he said, palms in the air, facing my face. "His compulsions can't excuse his actions. He's responsible, and I hate him for it. If I didn't have to answer for my crimes he'd be dead right now. Take a good look at yourself, Charlie. What are you gonna do? Hang around this lowlife, forever? You're a smart guy. You can do better than what you're doing. Don't let this guy and his father take you down to their level."

I didn't want to argue. "Okay, Bobby," I said, knowing an era had come to an end. Bobby said things about Eddie he couldn't take back – not that he wanted to – and that relationship would never be the same. He walked out the door and off the Rock to be a cop, leaving me the responsibility of our friend Eddie with all his flaws.

Eddie was lying on the couch in a daze, trying to piece together the reasons he was on my couch with his ear bandaged. I turned to see him kneading his temples, and it was only then I remembered how pissed off *I* was at him.

"What was that all about?" he said.

"You don't even remember, do you?" I said in disgust.

"Well, why don't you fill me in, then," he groused as he pulled a joint from his cigarette pack trying to find some relief from another morning after.

"Eddie, what's your problem?" I asked. "First you get smashed when you're supposed to be working. Then you walk in on Candi Wells while she's naked and, completely unprovoked, in a drunken rage, attack her for I don't know what!"

"Well, what's the difference," he said. "She's just a ragged out whore, anyway."

"Don't talk like that," I said, angrily. "She's Bobby's mother, and she hasn't done a goddamn thing to you. And don't smoke that stuff in the house. Mother's still upstairs."

"Yeah, like it bothers her," Eddie said, his voice trailing, realizing he didn't want to venture into the subject of anyone else's mother.

"Don't even start with that," I threatened, "Bobby's right, you know..."

"Don't talk to me about him," Eddie interrupted. "He's gotten so self-righteous since he 'changed his ways'," Eddie said, his hands forming irritating quotation marks in the air. "Well, he's no better than me or you. He's the bastard son of a whore and becoming a cop doesn't change a thing about that."

Eddie's skewed slant was beyond repair and I sent him away to smoke his pot on his way home, but I couldn't get the ugly scene from the night before or that morning off my mind. Bobby's words to me before he left inspired me to put together a plan. The idea wasn't to improve myself morally; in fact it was a pragmatic determination to improve my economic status, moral considerations not withstanding. Hugh McDowell and his father ruined my chances for a stellar academic career, but that didn't mean I couldn't continue to study and learn. I would continue to work for Vince and the club, but I would educate myself outside the sphere of Vince's influence so I could one day leave the Bottoms Up Lounge.

....

My eleven plus years of private education prepared me better than some of the graduates of high school who were attending their freshmen years in college. I rejoined academia at the Emory University bookstore the week classes began. I couldn't get accepted there, but I bought the books that were on posted lists for specific classes. Literature and history were my favorite subjects, but I forced myself to concentrate on chemistry and biology. By studying on my own, and crashing some of the larger classes, I progressed more than adequately through a general science curriculum. Each semester I followed the same modus operandi for three years, including summers. By then I was sure I consumed enough of what Emory had to offer to place me near the top of the graduating class, and I was ready for more.

While I was matriculating in my own style, old run down tenant clubs such as the Bottom's Up Lounge were being replaced by glitzy, totally nude, upscale clubs spreading away from the strip, away from downtown, and toward the suburbs where the most desirable clientele resided. Our city's famous architect renovated the central business district and was encroaching on our strip. Our rundown area was becoming a political pariah, and soon legislation was passed that made it impossible to keep the adult bookstores open. The handwriting on the wall soon recorded the Bottom's Up Lounge's demise. Vince took a long term lease on a property just north of downtown and built a free standing monument to what would become the big business of nude dancing. *The Satin Club*, or *Satin* as it came to be known, would grow in salacious stature around the city at first, then around the country, and even in other parts of the world. Locals would mix with businessmen from out of town in the common areas of the club while celebrities from sports and entertainment were escorted to VIP suites and given special treatment by everyone from the dapper, darkly dressed bouncers to the entirely undressed dancers. Vince, himself, would chat up the luminous personalities who darkened the door of the dark club, and he became a celebrity among the celebrities who held an appetite for the fare he offered.

There was no role for Mother at the new club, so Vince allowed her to do some secretarial duties for him over at the warehouse I was once privileged to visit. I was skeptical of any contribution she could make, but Vince was surprisingly diligent in providing her work – and crucial income. Even as she started her new career at Vince's warehouse office, she continued to tumble down the same precipice of alcohol and drug abuse that was also claiming Eddie.

This transformation of the strip club genre provided me an opportunity to get out of the business. With all my knowledge, I didn't have a degree to vouch for it. I could have found other work, but I liked the hours and freedom I had working for Vince. Still, he didn't have anything for me other than working at Satin. I didn't want to do that, so Vince introduced me to a friend of his. Frank Machelli set me up as a bookie's assistant, distributing and collecting betting cards for people who wagered on sports. The job mostly entailed visiting various bars, creating a network of bartenders and barflies who did my work for me. There was never a shortage of eager gamblers no matter how little they knew about their hobby, and the money rolled in to my boss. Frank was all business when it came to the odds on any kind of game. He had extensive resources, experts and insiders from whom to gather information, and his love of all sports made him perfectly suited for the business. I was Frank's favorite runner, and he took particular pains to make sure I was well paid. He was a generous man and a free spender; when he had particularly good weeks he always slipped me a bonus for what he said was good luck. It wouldn't surprise me if Vince persuaded him to give me special consideration, but I also new I was one of his more productive runners. I brought in more bets than anyone else, and the money and bets were always in order. There was never a penny shortage, and my credit customers always covered their debts.

I had made myself a favorite of Vince, and soon enough I endeared myself to Frank for the same reasons. Still, I was privately committed to making more of myself than becoming a common thug. I was devouring every book I could get my hands on, both fiction and non-fiction. I picked up my grandfather's textbooks from dental school and began digesting the art and science of dentistry. It looked like it was something I could do.

At the same time I was reading a little known book at the time by Frank Abagnale and Stan Redding called *Catch Me if You Can.* It was the true story of a fellow who used fake documents to impersonate an airline pilot, a teacher, an attorney, and even a physician. It gave me the impetus to pursue a new career, albeit another illegitimate one. I decided to become a dentist, whether or not I could become certified to practice.

It didn't take long to learn the basics, but it was obvious that the material in Grandfather's library was outdated. Once I absorbed everything possible from the old texts, I began to purchase current texts and trade magazines. I couldn't get away with attending the cozy classes of dental school, but it was easy to pay the money and attend the continuing education seminars that dentists frequent to keep up with the most contemporary methods and developments in the field. My unstructured occupation allowed me to travel whenever and wherever I needed to be for seminars important to my training. There were some plush settings for these programs in beautiful resort areas, and many attendees chose the ones that offered the best golf or prettiest beaches. My choices were based strictly on content – whatever subjects were most important.

When I was home my favorite place to learn was in the backyard among the woods – old habits from childhood clung fast as the ivy on the trees back there. My income was sufficient for me to help support Mother, and she spent the time she wasn't in Vince's office inside the Rock with the television and her liquor. By then Vince visited only to pick her up and drop her off for work. Mother no longer drove, since a rash of traffic convictions found her without a license. She was eligible to re-apply, but she didn't have the drive to do it. Besides, she probably would have found herself in more trouble, so I preferred that she stay out of the driver's seat.

Forty years of hard living added at least twenty more to Mother's appearance, and any promise for a real life had eluded her. She was lonely, I knew, but loneliness was no stranger to the women who inhabited the Rock; it was a way of life. I furnished her with the things she needed, which were mostly cigarettes and vodka. She satisfied her other vices through other acquaintances.

I did try to offer Mother some books that I found particularly inspiring during my odyssey of self-education, but she was more of a T.V. person. The daytime talk shows found a home at our home. Mother learned of every dysfunction a human could have. In one way or another she could equate the miserable experiences of all the misfits that were paraded across the airwaves to her pathetic life. When she tried to tell me of these boring tales, I feigned interest until I could find an excuse to escape.

Mother's incessant anecdotes of absurdity served to drive me deeper into my work, whether it was studying or visiting my betting customers. Frank Machelli became increasingly pleased with my performance, and he eventually created another level of responsibility for me. I began to manage the other runners, leaving little time for me to take care of my own territory. That was okay with Frank; things were running so smoothly with me in charge, he just hired another runner to take my place.

As much as I hated to give up my territory the new assignment offered new challenges, not to mention more perks. One day Frank asked me to pick him up at the Mercedes dealership where he was getting some work done on his car. On the drive back to the office we got in a traffic jam.

“Whew, those fumes out there are killing me,” he said as he started to close the windows of my family Cadillac, which was approaching twenty-five years in service. I had to stop him.

“Don’t do that,” I said. “If you do, you’ll really get a snoot full. It’s coming from this thing, Frank.”

"Jesus Christ," said Frank. "Now that you mention it, I can tell it is. What the hell are you doing with this old bomb, anyway?"

"I don't know," I said. "I never thought about it. I don't drive it much. It gets me around."

"Yeah, but hell," he said, "how long do you think this thing'll keep running? Besides, what kinda image do you think you portray in this thing, anyway?"

"A low profile," I said.

"Yeah, but what about the ..." Frank stopped himself before he said "girls." "Oh yeah; I'm talkin' to Charlie ‘The Chaste’. I forgot." Frank constantly complained I never dated any girls, but I had better things to do at that point in my career.

"Forget it," I grousec, and we changed the subject.

The next day we were putting in long hours, tallying the betting cards before the weekend. Frank was antsy to finish and get to the dealership so he could have his car for the evening.

"Calm down," I said when Frank kept checking his watch and standing up to pace. "We'll get there in time. If it gets too late, I'll take you on home and we can get your car in the morning."

"No way," said Frank. "I'm not going one more mile in that piece of shit than I have to. I got a headache for hours after breathing that exhaust. Besides, I need my car. I've got big plans for tonight with a new woman, not that that means anything to you."

"Well we'll never get there if we don't get this stuff taken care of," I said. "Let's just finish it up and we'll be on the way."

Frank couldn't wait. "No, no, come on now," he insisted. "We can come back and do this later."

That was an irritating quality about Frank. If he had something on his mind, it didn't matter what needed to be done, it wouldn't be done until he was gratified. I had study plans for the evening and didn't want to have to come back downtown when we were so close to finishing work, anyway. But Frank was the boss, and it was a minor inconvenience of the job that generally provided so well for me.

"Let's hurry, then," I said. "I need to get done and outta here. I've got things to do."

"Oh yeah, what, you got a date or something?" said Frank.

I gave Frank an annoyed glance, but said nothing. I never discussed my continuing education with anyone. I even delayed mentioning it to Eddie until the day I would have to in order to advance my scheme.

On the way to AutoSport Imports Frank was antsy, telling me the best route to avoid traffic, urging me to go around cars and run yellow lights. "Frank there's plenty of time," I said.

He ignored me. "Take a left on Pharr Road," he said.

We pulled into the suburban dealership and Frank directed me toward the showroom. "Pull over here for a minute," he said. "I need to speak to a friend of mine in here. I'll be right back out."

I waited in the car for almost ten minutes until Frank and a natty salesman emerged talking exuberantly. Just then a Mercedes 280C, gleaming black pearl essence, pulled up behind my old Cadillac blocking me in. A young man in a golf shirt, baggy pants and Nikes jumped out of the car and approached my window. I rolled down the window and he shoved the keys in my face. "Here you go," he said.

"How do you like it?" asked Frank as he and the salesman walked toward me. I was puzzled, and it must have shown. "Go ahead, take 'em. They're yours," he said.

I hesitated, and then reached for the keys, in a fog. "You're kidding."

"No, it's all yours," Frank repeated, dancing around the new car, sounding like a little kid at Christmas. "Do you like it?"

"Yeah, of course," I said. "Thanks."

Frank had suffered the wait all day just so he could be the magnanimous person he really was. "Ah, it's nothing. You deserve it. Hell you need it more than you deserve it. I spoke to Vince about it, and he agreed. He helped me spring for it, so thank him. What are you gonna do with this old clunker," he said, patting the Cadillac's fender, with disdain.

"I'll probably keep it," I said, not knowing what a mistake that would be.

Frank laughed at my unaffected response. "I'm sure you will," he said. He slapped me on the shoulder and left to get his car from the service department. "See you back downtown." That brought me back to earth. I wasn't looking forward to finding myself at the office on Friday night, but the drive back home would be a nice one.

Back at the office I called Vince to thank him for his generosity. He said Frank thanked him for introducing us, and I had made him proud, so on that basis he felt I deserved it. Then he made a curious remark.

"Don't tell Eddie where you got it from, buddy," he said, seriously. "You tell him you spent some of that money you have hoarded up over there, okay?"

I agreed; I was thinking of asking Vince to keep his part in my new car quiet. I was glad when he said it to me first.

XI. THE CURSE OF THE CADILLAC

Dear Gracie,

Congratulations on your graduation. I am sorry I couldn't make it to New York, but I have been really busy. I know you do not approve of the occupation that keeps me busy, but there is something about that I want to tell you. I began attending a program at Clayton Junior College to become a dental hygienist, and it won't be too long before I can escape this lifestyle which you disapprove of so vehemently. I have to say, it's not all bad. I just got a bonus in the form of a new Mercedes. I know, it's not really me, but I didn't choose the car, and from a practical standpoint the old Cadillac is on its last legs. This is an inexpensive solution to that problem – inexpensive for me, that is.

Really, I am so proud of you and all you have accomplished for yourself. I hope my news will make you feel better about my future. Steer clear of the bad butterflies.

Love,
Charlie

It was my first big lie to Gracie. I wasn't enrolled at Clayton Junior College, but I justified the lie as the means to protect her from complicity in my carefully planned fraud.

The next morning Eddie was too hung over to help me retrieve the Cadillac from AutoSport, so I asked Bobby to give me a hand. I hadn't seen him for awhile, and I was glad to have the chance to talk to him. He was a cop for the Atlanta Police Department and was serious about the job. He was also a senior at Georgia State University studying Criminal Justice with the goal of going to Law School. On top of that was the news of a girl he met in a class. He was dating a girl named Eileen, and when he talked about her I could tell she had what was left of his time and attention.

When he got in my new car, he gave me a look of disapproving envy. He didn't make a lot of money in his job, and the Mercedes was a token of the corruption he forsook to embark on a legitimate career. I didn't ask for the car in the first place, but Bobby's look made me feel guilty as I sank into the provocative leather driver's seat.

Bobby laughed as we pulled cautiously out of the driveway. From the time I got my license I hadn't put in much time behind a steering wheel, and I couldn't get comfortable in the new car. "Boy, this thing just doesn't fit you, you know," he said. "This car doesn't deserve a driver like you."

I didn't take offense; I more or less agreed. But it was new, reliable transportation, and I was happy for that reason. "So where'd you get it?" said Bobby in an unusual moment of curiosity.

"My boss gave it to me," I replied.

"Whoa, must be nice," he said. "What'd you have to do to get it?"

"Take him to the dealership in the Cadillac," I said. Then I explained about the exhaust leak, and how Frank almost choked on the fumes, and how he had plenty of money, anyway, so what difference did it make.

"Just make sure you don't get too obligated," he said.

I didn't mind Bobby's advice. "Don't worry," I said. I felt like spilling the beans about my future plans. "I'm gonna be done with that soon enough."

"Is that right?" Bobby brightened at that news.

"Uh huh," I said cryptically. "I have plans." Then I told the lie to Bobby I told Gracie in my letter. "I haven't told anyone, but I have been going to Clayton Junior College to get an Associates Degree in Dental Hygiene – you know, kind of follow in the family tradition."

"That's right," he said with a smile, "Your grandfather was a dentist, right?"

"Yeah, and so I picked up some of his books and got interested," I told him. "Nobody knows yet, but they will soon, because I'm going out of town to do an internship with a dentist office."

That was all Bobby wanted to hear. "At least you'll be rid of those guys," was all he said and we moved on. How's that son-of-a-bitch friend of yours?" he said, unable to contain himself.

"You don't want to know how he is," I said. "You just wanted to call him a son-of-a-bitch."

"You're right," admitted Bobby. "He is a son-of-a-bitch. Worse than that, he's a criminal."

"So am I," I couldn't help saying.

"Yeah, but you're not a spineless, drunk, loudmouth, son-of-a-bitch criminal," he said.

"Eddie's got his problems," I said. "He drinks too much. He does everything too much."

"That's not his problem," cried Bobby. "That's his fault. He could do something about it if he wanted."

"I'm not so sure," I said. "It may be too late for him. He's in pretty deep. He needs help."

"Ha!" snapped Bobby. "He doesn't need help. He needs to change, which he never will – just like he'll never apologize to me or my mother. If I ever get the chance to pop him I hope you're nowhere near at the time, because I'll take him down. I'd like to see him do some hard time being some convict's bitch."

Neither Bobby nor I had any idea as we pulled alongside the run down Cadillac in my new car that Eddie would someday spend a short time in jail – at least someone pegged as Eddie. I handed the wheel over to Bobby and got in the old car to drive it for the last time back to the garage at the Rock where it would lie in wait, with one last gasp in store for us.

"Thanks for the help," I said to Bobby back at the Rock as I shook his hand. "You want to come in?"

"No," he said, "I'm going to Eileen's. We're gonna go work out."

"Well, tell her 'hi' for me. I'll meet her sometime, soon," I promised. Then I couldn't help but try to inject some closure in our previous conversation. "And hey, don't worry about Eddie. He'll probably create his own demise, so you won't have to do it for him."

"Forget it," he replied as he started down the driveway. His mind was already on more pleasant prospects for the afternoon.

Later that evening, I went to dinner with Bobby and Eileen Harmon. All the things he told me about her were true. She stood maybe an inch shorter than Bobby's five feet, ten inches. The warm light of the Italian restaurant echoed the deep shades of the silky brunette hair that fell freely to her slender waist. The sharp features in her dark complexion were softened by brown eyes that reflected the depth of her intellect. Not only was she smart, she was interesting, and interested. I wasn't sure what Bobby told her about my circumstances, so I tried to keep the subject on her. She didn't say it, but it was clear she came from a well-to-do family. She also grew up in Buckhead, but she went to the Westminster School, arguably the best private school in the city. Her father was an attorney at one of the old firms in downtown. I didn't bother to bring up the attorneys I met through Vince. They practiced in circles miles apart from Eileen's father. I silently thought if I needed a complex business deal put together I would want Mr. Harmon. If I were in serious legal trouble I'd take David Israel.

....

Eddie had been moved out of the club by his father who knew he was a liability. He became involved with Lawrenceville Lance in producing fake I.D.'s and certifications. They controlled a printing operation in the industrial west side of the city. During the evenings, when the employees finished their legitimate work for the day, a small staff of printing experts would arrive to produce false documents – mostly passports and green cards that brought in a tidy sum.

After I studied everything I could get my hands on and attended all the dental conferences that seemed important, it finally became time for me to get some hands on experience with real human teeth. I purchased the requisite mouth models from the supply companies and I explored every text required of dental students. The next step was at hand, and Eddie helped me move forward.

First I needed an alias, which was no problem. I wanted a name nowhere close to my own; there shouldn't be any reason to associate my temporary, fictional role as a dental hygienist with me when I became a full blown dentist. Eddie secured the moniker of Harold Peabody, an innocent, nerdy name that gave Eddie and me a laugh. The next step was to falsify a certificate from a vocational school declaring Harold a graduate, prepared for work as a hygienist.

I wanted to get far away from Atlanta while I trained. I looked in the want ads of several papers at the library until I found Dr. Lamb's blurb requesting help in Oak Ridge, Tennessee. That seemed remote enough, and I never encountered him at any of the numerous conferences I attended. I was confident I wouldn't be recognized. By the time we met in his office I knew more about Dr. Lamb than he would ever know about me. He was well into his sixties, as were most of his patients. His equipment hadn't been updated for at least twenty years, and I began to wonder how instructive it would be to work there. The advantages were: he never left the town, he knew only a few other people in the business, and he would provide actual mouths on which I could cut my own teeth. My credentials looked fine to the trusting old gentleman, and he never even called the number I provided to verify my education. The number was manned by Eddie, and if Dr. Lamb had called he would have reached a pleasant voice claiming to be the registrar's office at Clayton Junior College. Eddie had his script, and I prayed he wouldn't blow it, but I had no choice; he was the only one who knew of my scheme.

I told everyone I knew I was doing an out of town training stint to further my education as a dental hygienist. That shocked more than a couple of people. No one wanted me to move away, but I knew it was necessary to remain covert. Mother reluctantly recognized my inevitable departure after I explained how near I would be if I needed to return. We spent a nice last night together. She actually stayed relatively sober for awhile as she recalled some of the memorable times of our past. They say you recall only the good times – at least those are the ones you mention. There wasn't much to discuss.

As the evening wound down Mother was getting more consumed by liquor and drugs, and it became time to call it a night. Before she would let me go to sleep she insisted on dragging me out to the old garage. There she took on a serious tone, one she hadn't used with me since I was a child.

"Here," she said, "see up there in the corner – up there, that brick?" I had to squint in the dim garage to see the object she was so interested in showing me. It rested between the wood roof frame and the top of the stone wall. I could make out only one edge of it, since it was dark and the area she indicated was where the rafters of the roof angled down. "I could be a rich woman with what's up in that brick if I wanted to do it," she said, looking confused by something. She certainly had me confused.

"Yes," I said, wondering how that old concrete block could possibly hold any interest for her.

"There's a name and a phone number up there that you may need some day. I have it in case we need it. It is for both of us, so we will have something to live on. Oh, please don't go, Charlie…" Her voice was trailing through her tears as she began to fade into her nightly blackout. I had to hold her up as she continued to implore me. She was slurring as she said, "If anything should happen to me, you climb up there and get your hands on that. That holds the key to our future."

I had no idea what she was talking about. She was drunk and I was anxious to get to bed. I nodded and carried what was by then her fully limp body back to the house. She was so emaciated from her lifestyle it was no problem to carry her with my outstretched arms. I had a notion to go back to the garage to see what she was agitated about, but my mind was on my own future, and it had nothing to do with any name or phone number stuffed in the corner of the garage. I went to bed and forgot about the garage and the concrete block and the rafters.

The next morning I picked-up a three year old Chevrolet from a used car dealer so I could look more like an innocent dental hygienist fresh from school. Vince promised to look in on Mother regularly, and with that I was off to Oak Ridge for my first extended stay out of Atlanta. By the time I returned Bobby would be graduated and entering his first semester of Law School. Eddie and his vices would have developed an even closer relationship with each other.

....

After three months of work in Dr. Lamb's practice, I proved to myself I was qualified; in fact, I could have taught Dr. Lamb a thing or two about modern dentistry, but I dared not offend him or let him know my true expertise. I performed well enough to be an exemplary hygienist. He was pleased with my work, and his patients seemed to take to my quiet, deliberate manner. Mrs. Lamb ran the office. I had taken the place of the only other employee, Mrs. Greenfield, who had retired after twenty-three years with the Lambs.

The elderly folks we saw were more than patients; they were friends and neighbors of the old practitioner, and they accepted me as quickly and warmly as Dr. Lamb did. If I didn't hate my new name – and if the pay were better – I might have stayed right there. But my plans were firm and I was sure to be back in Atlanta in about a year. My stint in Oak Ridge would be abbreviated by bad news. Early in my seventh month with Dr. Lamb I had just completed a satisfying day at the office when I arrived home to the telephone ringing. It was Vince, and he sounded nervous.

"Charlie," he said in a rushed whisper, "son, I've got some bad news for you. There's been an accident."

The "accident" Vince was calling about was not an accident at all. At some point in the preceding thirty-six hours Mother ingested an acute amount of vodka, scribbled an addled message – something about her life being a sham – and then suffocated in the carbon monoxide pouring from the exhaust of the old Cadillac, which was shut up in the garage. Her body was discovered by the mailman who came up the driveway to deliver the care package I sent to lift her spirits. When no one answered the door the diligent, perhaps nosy, letter carrier looked in the garage to see if any cars were there. The Cadillac was still running when he came upon the gruesome scene.

I was not completely surprised as I packed my things and left a note to the Lambs to explain why I had to leave so suddenly. The note was understandably panicked, so they wouldn't wonder why I didn't leave a forwarding address. I didn't want them to be able to find me, so I told them I was going to Dallas where my mother died. That was my hometown from my resume, but the only address they had was the apartment I supposedly left when I finished school in Atlanta to move to Oak Ridge. My bases were covered during my six months with the Lambs when I let it be known that my widowed mother was remarried. I knew that once I left they wouldn't have a name to look for if they tried to track me down. I hadn't yet decided how I would go without leaving them my next address, but Mother's demise took care of that detail.

When I arrived at the Rock there was a composed stillness in the old stone castle as detectives milled around, speaking in respectfully low tones, finishing their routine investigation. The porch door was open, and the curtains along the back hallway into the kitchen were flapping nonchalantly in the uneven breeze. I couldn't help visualizing my mother in her last hours of life. Even without the autopsy report I knew she would have been in her bedroom – like Bloody Mary, she did her drinking in her nightgown close to bed. The television would have been turned on and tuned in to any show that offered a gray glow to the otherwise incandescent pall that saturated the room. I wondered whether it was something as simple as an inane daytime talk show that set her off, or if she had been contemplating suicide for some time. Her note was with the police, but it would leave no hint to answer that question or any others. It only indicated the level of her intoxication.

I found myself standing in the chilly kitchen, with no desire to pass through the hall that led to her bedroom. There was no reason to visit the bedroom before then, and there wasn't any reason at that moment. After standing for a long time, inert on the yellowed linoleum floor, leaning on the old gas stove, trying to gauge my emotions, I finally walked back outside to find the lead investigator with some uniformed police.

Detective Redmond introduced me to the two uniformed men. The preoccupied cops shook my hand and went about their business. I'm sorry about your mom, son," said the detective, looking directly into my eyes.

"Yeah," was all I managed before I walked away without tipping my hand. I didn't want to tell anyone, but I just wasn't grieving. I wasn't reveling in Mother's death like I privately did when Bloody Mary kicked the bucket, but I guess I felt like she wasn't suffering anymore. She was slowly committing suicide with her lifestyle; I saw that coming. The whole process was just accelerated by the Cadillac.

I retreated to the backyard and the comfort and solitude of my woods. At some point Vince and Eddie came by, patted my shoulder, and walked away to the front yard while I tried to look serious. Soon afterward I heard car doors close and engines start, and I knew everyone was gone. That's when I went in to write Gracie to give her the news and confess my lack of emotion. Gracie's response arrived in the mail after she breezed in and out of town for the funeral.

Dear Charlie,

Sorry to hear about your mother. I understand your thoughts, and I understand your mother was not the typical parent, but I do wonder sometimes about what seems to be a lack of emotion on your part. I am not making any judgments, and I know absolutely nothing about psychology, but as trite as this sounds, maybe you should see someone about getting in touch with your feelings. You invested so much grief when you lost your father, and I know how badly you hurt. Maybe you suppress your emotions. I'm not sure that's mentally healthy. You find too much humor in everything.

On another note, I've told you about my friend Austin. Well, I hope this is not a shock, but he's really more than a friend. We've been dating, and it looks like we're going to take it a step further. Bottom line is, we're engaged. I didn't tell you too much about our relationship, because I didn't know how far it would go, and I wasn't sure how you would take the news, but now we are committed. I hope this isn't too much of a shock for you, but I wanted you to know. I hope you will be happy for me.

I will catch a flight for the funeral and see you there. Meanwhile, steer clear of the bad butterflies.

Love,

Gracie

If I had received the letter before she came for the funeral, I would have disputed her ideas about my lack of emotion. I said I didn't feel sad about my mother, but I was suddenly grieving at the bombshell Gracie delivered. I tried to tell myself to be happy for her, but I couldn't be happy for her when I was so disappointed for myself. Somewhere in the back of my mind I believed Gracie and I would end up together, and I think she did too. That's why she was so reticent to tell me the truth about what was going on with her love life up there.

I scolded myself; I was usually so impulsive, but with Gracie, I let our lack of involvement go too long without doing something about it. I blamed it on my lack of experience with women. Well, her lack of full disclosure made me feel less guilty about my outright lie about my vocation.

……..

The funeral was arranged entirely by Vince, and it was another sorely unattended affair. He and Mrs. Palomino came, but Eddie was conspicuously absent. Bobby came with Eileen, and they brought Candi. I was a little surprised that Frank

Machelli didn't show up, but he wasn't one for funerals. Gracie flew in, and I was happy to be with her for the few hours she had available. She couldn't even stay overnight, though; she had to defend her thesis the next day in front of a committee of Harvard professors. It was the final step in getting her graduate degree, and I was gratified she made the trip at such a crucial time for her. The ever confident Gracie didn't seem too concerned. She didn't mention anything about the news her letter carried.

The ceremony was simple and quick, everything performed at graveside before the Mary Widow was perfunctorily buried next to Bloody Mary. Afterward, everyone was as antsy to get away as I was. I stayed long enough to see them off and thank them for coming. As I gave Candi Wells a polite hug, I noticed her unique necklace. It was a single strand of very thin, perhaps two inch long, triangular shaped silver links connected by small, smooth, shellacked pebbles. I noticed that all the glossy pebbles but one were roundish. One was noticeably flat. I almost gasped out loud when I realized what it was.

I looked at Candi and said, "Is that what I think it is," pointing at the tiny trinket.

She smiled back and nodded, "Yep, that's it."

I gave her another hug and wished her well as she took Bobby's hand to walk away. No wonder I couldn't find Eddie's earlobe that night at the club. Candi grabbed it during the fight and kept it. I never told Eddie that his missing earlobe was pierced and shellacked, and was being worn as a trophy by the one who relieved him of it. At least his earlobes were evened up by Candi's drawn nail file. I mused that she may have performed the first cosmetic lobe job.

I arrived back at the Rock, glancing once more at the killer Cadillac sitting satisfied as I rolled its sleeker counterpart beside it into the shelter of the garage. For the first time since being back I grabbed my suitcase and left the couch, which had been my bed for the previous two nights. I walked upstairs to my bedroom. As I passed Mother's room, I glanced inside for only a moment before I closed the door for the last time.

XII. Bad Business Practice

I spent the next few weeks visiting acquaintances, going to parties for Bobby and Eileen, and planning for my future. After their wedding, it was time to make the plunge and find a place to ply my trade as a full blown, fraudulent dentist. I began my search to find the ideal practice to join. It would be nice to be in Atlanta, but I knew too many people who knew too much about me. There was a risk of people running across me and catching onto my scheme. Perhaps just a little out past the suburbs I would find what I needed. There was no need to rush. I never spent any money, so I had plenty saved. A systematic and patient survey was required to assure the successful engagement.

In the meantime, Eddie and Lance forged the proper documentation for me to instantly become a legitimate dentist ready for an apprenticeship with a mentor. It was important to not be from a nearby regional school of dentistry; professional contacts made the risk of exposure too great, so my credentials came from an international school. The forged transcripts showed my grades to be only slightly better than average. I was afraid to go lower for such an obscure school, but transcripts reflecting high performance might trigger a more thorough investigation into my past. I ranked myself eighteenth in a class of thirty-eight.

After ten steady weeks of intense research, I found myself in the office of Dr. Eugene Powers in Acworth, Georgia. Acworth was just under an hour drive northwest of the Rock, remote enough in those days to protect my identity.

The image I had of Dr. Powers's office mirroring Dr. Lamb's set-up was quickly dashed upon meeting the crotchety sixty-two year old.

"Hmpf," Dr. Powers scowled as he looked over his reading glasses past my resume across his desk at me. "What kind of school is this – University of the West Indies? Is it even accredited?"

"Yes it is," I said. "It is recognized here in the state of Georgia. See my license signed by the Secretary of State?"

"Yes, I see it," he said. "Where the hell is it, anyway?"

"In Trinidad," I said.

"Trinidad?" he said as he put my resume down and leaned forward on his elbows. "Where the hell is that?"

"It's an island off the coast of Venezuela," I said impatiently. "You haven't heard of it?"

"I've heard of it," he snapped. "I just didn't know exactly where it was. How's the fishing there?"

"I don't know," I said. "I don't fish."

"You don't fish?" he said with a sneer. "What the hell do you do with yourself?"

"Well, mostly study," I said coolly.

"Well I fish," he said, "and I'm looking to do more of it. I'm sixty-two years old and I'm getting damned tired of this damned office. I get no respect from the staff, I can't get suppliers to deliver because we're too far from the city, and most of the patients around here are idiots. My wife died three years ago, and I don't have any relatives living anymore. You come along all young and eager; you think you can step in here and handle this crap?"

"I know I *can*," I said. "I just don't know if I *want* to. I don't have any relatives left, either. I just don't complain about it."

"Well suit yourself, son," he said flatly. "It's here if you want to take a stab at it."

I could tell something about Dr. Powers; he just wanted a certain type of person, and I fit the bill. As cranky as he was, it was easy to see where he was coming from, and I liked that about him. I was just as direct with him. The ironic thing was, even though my presence there was an utter ruse, I knew he appreciated my honesty.

Over a three week period, Gene Powers and I hammered out the finer points of our agreement. I would gradually take over, then after several years Dr. Powers would retire. The revenues from the new patients I brought in were shared until the old dentist hung up his drill for good, but he got no credit for them after that. He would receive a monthly payout for his patient base and the small building that he owned for a specified period and eventually the practice would belong entirely to me. Since Gene was at the end of his family tree, it was agreed that, if he died, I would inherit the business free and clear.

"You're getting away with murder; don't think I don't know it," he complained as we inked the deal. I smiled. Gene Powers had no idea what I was getting away with, but then I doubt he would have cared.

....

Dr. Powers came with a fifty-two year old receptionist and bookkeeper and a twenty-seven year old hygienist. Mrs. Lynette Jefferson, the receptionist/bookkeeper, had been with Gene Powers for sixteen years, and though she had a contentious relationship with the curmudgeon, I was certain she would retire when the old man did. When those two got together it was a contest to see who could out-cuss the other. She was married to a county building inspector about her age, and she needed to keep her job until his benefits kicked in to allow them a comfortable retirement

Ginger Arnold came to Dr. Powers a year and a half before I did, after her first child was born. She had to apply her training as a hygienist to subsidize her warehouse-worker-husband's income so they could afford to raise their baby girl. She was a native of Acworth with a country girl's natural beauty and striking red hair. Ginger had an upbeat demeanor, but she was intimidated by Dr. Powers's crankiness.

It didn't take long for Mrs. Jefferson – as I called her to show proper respect – to drop her suspicions about me. Ginger was warm from the start. Gene was giving me all the room I needed, pushing me onto some of his patients faster than some would have liked. Once they got to know me though, even the most skeptical took to my style. Eventually most people generally seemed happier with me than Gene. This was probably because I didn't moan the entire time I was assaulting my subjects' mouths.

I was also bringing in a new patient base of my own. As the word spread from existing patients, new people began to arrive to have the new young dentist poke and prod on their mouths. And, of course, I agreed to treat Eddie for all the favors he did for me getting my documentation arranged. I was worried about his mercurial behavior destabilizing my credibility with my new workmates, but I was obligated. My fear was initially put to rest. In fact, Eddie made quite an impression on Mrs. Jefferson. After his first visit, he began bringing flowers in to her. This softened the salty gal for a little while until Eddie began showing his true nature.

As he continued to spill deeper into drinking and drugs, his personality warped beyond his own ability to camouflage it. He eventually became oblivious to his own defects, so he made no attempt to cover for what was becoming untenable behavior.

Mrs. Jefferson had to endure Eddie because he was my patient, but she became grouchy on the days he had an appointment. There was no end to her profanity on those occasions. Even Ginger had a problem with Eddie, and she liked everybody.

"Oh, no!" Ginger would exclaim in her southern country accent upon seeing the appointment book. "Eddie Palomino's comin' in today. That so-and-so," she would mutter; then she would blush as if she had just called him a motherfucker.

Eddie actually had a thing for Ginger. Of course, Eddie had a thing for anything with breasts. It was impossible for him to keep his demeaning thoughts to himself whenever we encountered anyone of the opposite sex. It was no different when it came to Ginger, even though I constantly tried to remind him that she was married and I had to maintain a professional relationship with her.

"She loves it, ha ha," Eddie would erroneously state with an annoyingly self conscious laugh that had developed in step with his evolving psychosis. It was becoming useless to try to change him, so I just tried to always be there to run interference at each encounter. Once we were alone in the examination room, Eddie would start in, "That Ginger is a babe. Too bad I met her after she got married. I can tell we would have been good together. Hey do you have any cash I can borrow?" I would race to shove the nitrous oxide mask into his face before I had to endure anymore of his drunken narcissism.

The problem was exacerbated when Eddie began showing up on days that he didn't have an appointment. He would come on the premise that he wanted to go to lunch with me, but I knew what he wanted. He wanted to see Ginger, and he wanted to borrow money from me, which he never repaid.

....

The older Dr. Eugene Powers got, the more petulant he became. As we agreed, his hours at worked ebbed as he spent more time on the lake with the bass and the bream. But when he was in the office, he was becoming intolerable. He cursed and ranted at the slightest provocation, and even his patients weren't spared his unreasonable wrath. Posey Jackson complained that her son Mark learned the F word from Dr. Powers.

He was also getting forgetful. More than once he tried to send patients out the door before he had completed work on them. When he tried to send Luther Adams home, Luther still had the cotton strips in his mouth while he was halfway through a filling job. His overstuffed mouth wouldn't allow the words of protest as Gene ordered him out of the chair. It wouldn't have mattered, anyway. Even when Luther managed to pull cotton out of his mouth, Gene was insisting that his mouth was fine and he just needed to return in six months for another check-up. After I calmed Luther down and finished his filling, Gene became livid, accusing me of showing him up and taking over his patients.

"I'm not washed up yet, smart fella!" he screamed. "If you want your own fuckin' practice, go start one." Some sort of dementia doubtlessly was overtaking my partner. He needed professional attention, but he wasn't inclined to cooperate with any medical assessment, and there was no family left to force the issue.

I tried to conceal my concern, but the patients of Acworth knew the story and they felt sorry for Mrs. Jefferson and Ginger and me. I think Mrs. Jefferson would have just quit, but she was staying to support me. We got some of Gene's good friends and tried to convince him to get help, but he wasn't having any of it. Finally, there was no alternative. He was disrupting the daily course of business. It was agreed among our closest confidants that we would have to resort to the courts to get him help. There would be no immediate outcome.

The first thing to do was file documents with the court to request a hearing to convince a judge that there was probable cause to force Gene to undergo a competency examination. Then it was just a matter of getting the examining doctor to proclaim him incompetent. Based on my portrayal to my local attorney, Carl Meyers, there wasn't much doubt; if we could get him to the doctor, he'd be certified nuts. If that happened, a trustee would be appointed to tend to Gene's affairs and act in his best interest.

In the middle of the consuming battle, I had to leave early one Friday to go to Gracie's wedding in New York. It was refreshing to get away from the grind of the conflict, but I was still conflicted about the nuptials. I met Austin, and I couldn't say anything bad about him, but I just couldn't see what Gracie saw in him. Of course, my view was skewed by my jealousy. I met Gracie's best friend Toni Strunz, and I could see that she and Gracie were as close as sisters. I felt a little jealous of Toni, too. I told myself to get over it, and I *did* enjoy the weekend and the respite.

When I got back I had to endure two exhausting weeks of Gene's orgy of gripes and accusations before our court date. Carl did his job, I did my job and the witnesses did their jobs. It was open and shut; Gene was ordered to see a psychiatrist. Gene Powers would never make his appointment with the shrink. On Sunday morning, after the court decision, I got a call from George Madison, our mutual business attorney.

"Charlie, this is George. Some fisherman found Gene's boat out on the lake, but there was nobody in it. We can't find Gene anywhere."

"What?" I stammered. "What are we saying here? Do they think it's bad?" I couldn't speak my specific fear.

"They don't know," George replied. "He hasn't been seen since Friday, but that doesn't necessarily mean anything. Either way, they're gonna put divers in the lake to look for him."

It wouldn't be unusual for the lonely old loon to go unseen for a couple of days. But his boat being abandoned in the middle of the lake was not a good sign. "God," I sighed. "I'm really sorry, George," and I was in a way, but I knew if Gene did go overboard it would immediately right the good ship Charlie Lofton.

By Sunday evening the worst outcome was confirmed by the county's fire department dive team. I couldn't help but think some divine intervention played a role in relieving Gene from a future of diminishing mental capacity, and me from bearing the brunt of his illness. I had to smile at my luck – and Gene's deliverance.

After Gene was put to rest at a service attended by what seemed to be the entire town of Acworth, things settled back into a routine. For once the practice was unencumbered to flourish under my sole tutelage. As the weeks wore on, the shock of losing our scion wore away from the staff, and an upbeat air surfaced, not only among Mrs. Jefferson and Ginger, but also with our patients. It became easy for everyone to rationalize that Gene was now out of his mental misery. The business we lost in the dementia days was coming back to us while new patients were on the increase. I was a good dentist who had gained the confidence of my adopted town. The only thing that remained a problem was Eddie.

XIII. EDDIE'S COMEUPPANCE

Our practice became so busy I had to hire some part-time help just to keep up with the mundane tasks around the office. Lisa Lutz was the wife of a fellow who worked with Ginger's husband at the warehouse. Lisa was a plump woman in her mid twenties who lacked the work ethic of the rest of us in the office. As good a dentist as I was, I was inept at hiring, and we had to live with my choice of the first person to answer our call for more help.

Eddie Palomino found plenty of time to visit our office, usually coming in late in the afternoon, hoping to wait out the staff so he could convince me to give him a loan and a shot of the gas. He wooed Lisa, establishing another relationship to use to get what he wanted from me. He didn't have any designs on Lisa; he reserved his ill-placed affections for the lovelier Ginger who patiently ignored him. Lisa gave him an ear, even flirted with him, and this created a bond between them. She got the attention she craved and Eddie got the access he wanted. The rest of us got annoyed.

The practice was going strong and I was achieving something I had strived for since elementary school. Even if it were all based on a fraud, it was a fraud that had me anchored. But my career was built along a fault line of lies and misrepresentations, and any tremor might cause its collapse. In a corner of my mind, Eddie was a cauldron of seismic activity waiting to erupt.

From what Vince's minions told me, Eddie was so ill suited to the various enterprises in which Vince placed him, he was essentially idle – getting paid to stay out of the way. It was doubtful that Vince knew much about Eddie's extra-occupational activities. Besides dealing in drugs, Eddie was involved in pornography. He always had his eyes open for a girl who was marginally attractive enough and morally challenged enough to do nude photo spreads, which he sold to fringe adult publications.

"What do you think about Lisa?" he asked me one evening when we were alone in the office.

"What do you mean?" I said trying to concentrate on the filing Lisa couldn't complete before she went home early with – as she whispered annoyingly to me, fingers forming quotation marks – “female problems."

"There's a jack-rag out of L.A. filled with naked fat chicks. Lisa's not bad for a fat chick. I think she'd do it, don't you?"

"I don't know, Eddie," I said, "but please forget about that idea. This is supposed to be a professional office, you know."

"Oh yeah, I forgot, *Doctor* Lofton," he sneered, forming the same quotation marks as Lisa. "Now that you're a professional, you can't get your hands dirty working with scum like me or the old man." Eddie was intoxicated, as usual. As usual, this made him irrationally resentful. "Well just remember where you came from, buddy, and how you got where you are. I sure won't forget," he said.

"Come on Eddie," I said. "That isn't what I meant. I'm just asking you to help me by keeping everything on the level around here."

"Haven't I always been there for you?" he said.

Not knowing what he meant, I agreed and caved in to his pressure to give him a hit of the gas. I prayed the uncertain mixture of drugs wouldn't kill him.

The breaking point arrived like an arrow released at full draw, piercing the heart of my practice. It was the day of a scheduled wisdom teeth extraction for Hailey Baily, a seventeen year old beauty who had just graduated from Acworth High. I noticed Eddie, who always monitored my appointment book, made it a point to be around when my more attractive female patients were coming in, so it was no surprise when he barged in shortly before Hailey's appointment. As usual we tried to keep him at bay in my office, but Lisa was out because of one excuse or another, so as busy as we all were, we couldn't keep him pinned down.

The extraction would be simple – a lot of Novocain, an IV drip of thiopental sodium, and just pull the last two of Hailey's wisdom teeth. I had done it eight weeks before on her first two. This time I had Eddie in my hair. I just got Hailey to sleep when Eddie, who broke free when Mrs. Jefferson had to answer the phone, interrupted my work. Mrs. Jefferson frowned when she came back to find Eddie loitering in the exam room with me and my anesthetized patient.

The phone call was for me. Normally, Mrs. Jefferson wouldn't interrupt when I was in the midst of a procedure, but it was an urgent request for information from an oral surgeon. I reluctantly left Eddie with Mrs. Jefferson and Hailey for what I expected to be a short call. The surgeon kept me longer than I thought he would. A couple of lines were calling in, and Mrs. Jefferson made the mistake of leaving the exam room to quell the persistent ringing.

I was finally able to pry myself off the call with the doctor, and I hurried back to Hailey. Whatever emergency the wordy oral surgeon had could never have matched the crisis that was taking place during the time I was out of the room. If Hailey had been convulsing from a reaction to the drugs it would have been better than that instant the door swung open to reveal Eddie taking pictures of an anesthetized Hailey with her shorts pulled down to her ankles. I slammed the door shut and locked it in horror. Mrs. Jefferson reacted to the noise and came to knock on the door. “Is everything alright in there,” she said. I was too mortified to speak.

Eddie was caught and he knew it, but he had the presence to answer. "It's fine!" he said angrily, which didn't convince my militant, motherly assistant.

"Charlie, is everything alright," she insisted.

"Yes, it's fine," I managed to weakly respond as I glared at Edie in disbelief.

"Alright," said Mrs. Jefferson, sounding unconvinced.

When I could hear footsteps carry her out of earshot, I lunged for Hailey, lifting the small of her back as I pulled up her shorts in one unconscious motion. Only then was there time to deal with Eddie. "What in God's name were you doing," I started, and then said, "I don't know..., just get out for now."

Eddie started to say something, but he couldn't summon the courage, so he left. I had no choice but to go directly to work on my violated patient. Ginger finished a cleaning and came in to assist me. It was apparent there was something wrong, but I was thankful Ginger resisted the urge to pry.

Other than the Eddie disaster, the extraction went fine. When Hailey came to, Mrs. Jefferson gave her some juice and kept her in the waiting room for almost an hour until her mother came for her. While she was in the waiting room I reluctantly paid her a visit to see how she was feeling. She seemed happy with her treatment and oblivious to the abuse she unconsciously suffered. I was only slightly relieved as I retreated to my office to try to gather my wits.

Fortunately, the day came to a close on its own; if not, I would have ended it, anyway. Predictably, Mrs. Jefferson stopped by to ask what the problem was.

"I caught Eddie sniffing the gas," I said, trying to measure my outrage to the correct proportion.

"Hmff," she snorted as she walked out of the office. Mrs. Jefferson needed to say no more. Her disapproval was evident.

Once everyone was out of the office, the phone rang. It was Eddie. He had ratcheted his impairment by freebasing some cocaine and was waiting outside my office until he knew I was alone.

“It’s not nice to treat old friends that way, old buddy, old professional pal,” he said with a sneer that intensified as he spoke.

“Fuck you, Eddie,” I said. “You are sick, you know that? You really need help. That’s just advice from a friend. Now this is a demand; you are not ever to come to this office again. It is off limits, you got that? No more… You could ruin my practice, not to mention the crime you committed against that young girl.”

“Oh, I wouldn’t worry too much about her,” he said, his thoughts manipulated by drugs. “She’s legal, and she’s old enough to take care of herself."

"Not when she's unconscious," I said, but Eddie interrupted.

"On the other hand, you're wise to worry about that precious practice of yours. Speaking of crimes, I'm sure the authorities would frown upon the nature of your qualifications. Oh, and by the way, I happen to have a picture of a knocked out teenage girl, naked in a dentist's office that has your forged diploma plainly displayed on the wall. Anyone with a magnifying glass can identify the dentist who is doing such depraved things to his patients."

I hung up on him and put in a call to Bobby. I wanted to talk to a friendly voice – to calm down and reassure myself. I left a message and started home. What was Eddie doing, I wondered. Was he going to just hold this over my head to get his way with me; or was he going to go to the police, strictly out of impaired spite?

Bobby returned my call and invited me to dinner at his new house. That night in particular was one of mixed emotion. It was heartening to see how well he and Eileen were doing, but in light of the episode with Eddie and Hailey, Bobby's grounded development reminded me of just how tenuous my scam was.

Their family was happy and busy; it included a little girl, Courtney, who was going on three. She was curious, talkative and determined to keep her parents occupied. We discussed our lives between Courtney's interruptions.

Eileen was staying at home during the cold, early months of the year before gearing up for a spring rush of activities. Raising Courtney was her main vocation for the moment, and it suited her. She didn't need to work; her father's considerable wealth and connections helped pave the road of respectability for Bobby and his young family.

After graduating from law school, Bobby attended the FBI Academy in Quantico and went to work for the Bureau as a Special Agent. He was excelling at the Bureau, and thanks to his academic and occupational achievement, not to mention the influence of his father-in-law, he was on a path to join the U.S.

Attorney's Office in Atlanta. Even though he had a law degree, he never litigated in a courtroom, but he testified extensively in cases he worked. That and his experience in criminal justice made him eligible for the U.S Attorney's position, and with Mr. Harmon's support, it looked as though it might happen. His enthusiasm for his work was contagious. I was happy for him, but I was silently brooding over my own lot in life.

After feasting and catching up, Eileen took Courtney upstairs to read to her before putting her to bed. Bobby and I went to the den where he immediately asked me what the problem was. He was a great cop, and he had a profound intuition about things not yet revealed. He began his interrogation. "What's going on?" he said. "You sounded pretty stressed on your message.

"I don't know," I said. "I've got a problem with Eddie, and I'm not sure how to handle it."

"Oh," said Bobby, "I don't doubt that. What'd he do now?"

"Oh, he's just bothering the hell out of me," I said. There was no way to tell Bobby how Eddie was threatening my fraudulent career. It wasn't fair to him to let him know of my criminal activity and have him pit his loyalty to me against his oath to uphold the law – nor was it safe for my career.

"You want me to do anything about it," Bobby offered, a little puzzled.

I didn't know of anything he could do. "No, I can handle it," I said, skeptical of my own assurance.

"You need to get him out of your life, Charlie," Bobby said.

"He's my friend; I can't just shut the door in his face," I protested, but I realized Bobby had no idea how impossible it was for me to act on his suggestion.

"That's exactly what you've got to do," said Bobby. "My god, buddy, why do you think I don't ever see him, anymore. I can't afford to have someone like that in my life."

The room went silent for a minute. What Bobby said was instantly eye opening. My life consisted of my work. That had become my identity. That was what I had. I had no family. I had a couple of casual friends outside of my practice. Bobby was a good friend, but he was living his own agenda, and perhaps he couldn't afford to let me too deeply into his life any more than he could befriend Eddie. Without knowing the truth, Bobby drove home the truth – my life and career hung on the thread of fraud – and there was a substance abusing friend threatening to unravel the thread. I suddenly had visions of some sheriff barging in one day, rifling through the files, and then bolting the door to the gutted office. What would Ginger and Mrs. Jefferson think? These were the ones I had come to depend on every day. Whether or not ours was a friendship, we shared a bond that came from the steady little enterprise we all helped maintain. How could I face these comrades while a drug addict and a bunch of lawmen in uniforms were tearing down our practice file by file? Not only would I go to prison for a long time, but I would be open to lawsuits from former patients. My house of cards was a shaky one. It was getting increasingly shaky, if it hadn't already fallen. Bobby was right; Eddie had to go.

"Hey, you okay," Bobby finally said.

"Yeah, fine," I said. "You're right." I was too distracted to stick around. "I've gotta go. Thanks for the advice. Tell Eileen thanks for dinner."

"Sure thing," he said. "I hope it works out. If you need anything, let me know. "I'll help any way I can."

....

The morning brought a modicum of comfort when everything at the office was normal. Lisa was droning on about some bother in her life. I thought how nice it would be to have her trivial concerns. Mrs. Jefferson and Ginger seemed to have forgotten any unusual activity from the previous day, and the patients were routinely arriving.

Never one to break the routine, Eddie appeared late in the afternoon after everyone else was gone. I was in my office completing some charts, and just the sight of him brought back the queasy feeling that ebbed during the familiar ritual of the day. Still, I resolved to do what had to be done.

"Hey pal," I began, resolutely, but before I could utter another word he came at me, eyes drunk and angry.

"Don't hey pal me, *pal*," he said. "Your cop friend paid me a visit today. It's not real cool talking to the cops about me." He was standing over my desk, spitting venom, and I recoiled from the muffled volume of his hostile words. The tables immediately turned, and my planned lecture was out the window.

"I wasn't talking to the cops about you, Eddie," I said. "It was our friend, Bobby. I was just concerned because..."

"Your friend, not mine," Eddie said, his voice rising. "He reminded me again that he doesn't give a shit about me. He told me he was keeping an eye on me, and if I didn't watch my step, he'd see me behind bars. What the hell have you done to me?"

"I didn't want him to do that," I said defensively. "I was just concerned, you know. I've got a lot at stake here. This is my livelihood – it's my life. What you did threatened that."

"Well 'doctor'," he said, his unsteady fingers forming his quotation marks, "You'd better keep in mind just how much I can threaten your little bailiwick. Remember how much I know about the little scam you've got going. Oh, it's a sweet thing, alright. Just don't think you're any different than me. What you're doing is just as illegal as my thing. It's just wrapped a little prettier. You just put on a cleaner front. At least I'm honest about what I do."

"Eddie, come on, at least there are no victims with me," I tried to explain. "Let's be reasonable…" Eddie interrupted.

"Reasonable? You want to be reasonable? We are gonna be anything but reasonable. I know too much. I can rat you out to the good guys, and I can get the bad guys on your ass. Reasonable is the last thing we're gonna be. It's a new ball game, from here on, and I set the rules."

"What are you talking about," I said.

"What I'm talking about is you're gonna do what I say from now on. The day is over that you have this high handed attitude just because you've got some fake doctors' degree."

"Eddie, I don't have a high handed..."

"Shut-up, I'm doing the talking. From now on, you're gonna share some of that profit you make from your scam with me. That will be the price of staying in business. Also, if I want to take pictures of some of your more eligible patients, you're gonna arrange it. There's a big market for these shots. I got some good ones yesterday. You might be particularly interested in this one."

He pulled the snapshot out of his pants pocket and flung it down in front of my eyes. I was aghast. There was Hailey, asleep on her back with her shorts wrapped around her ankles. The framed certificate hung on the wall behind her with my name embossed on it. I didn't need any magnification to see it.

"That ought to interest the authorities," he said.

"You wouldn't do that," I said. "You'd be in just as much trouble as I would."

"Oh I'd be long gone if these were to turn up some place you don't want them," he sneered.

I knew what he meant by that. I thought about the false ID and all the cash he kept in his safe deposit box. I could find myself ruined and busted while Eddie would be sunning in another part of the world.

"We'll start with a thousand a month," said Eddie. "I'll see how that works for me. If I need more I'll let you know. Meanwhile, I hope I can count on you to let me know when it might be appropriate to plan for some shoots over here."

"Eddie, you can't be serious," I said. "It's me. I'm your friend."

"I've got no friends, and I know it," he said. "I *am* serious."

With that he turned and walked out. The drugs were deeply imbedded in his psyche. He was in a paranoid rage, and I was hoping he would be more reasonable when he was sober. It was a hope that would be dashed in the coming days.

……..

The busy activities of the following weeks would assuage the otherwise nagging reality of the Eddie problem. The Thursday Hailey Baily came in for her follow-up was a red letter day of relief. Hailey showed no sign of apprehension or unhappiness. She was as friendly and outgoing as always, and I hoped my awkward manner didn't betray the guilt and embarrassment I felt when she was there. Once she left, there was a discernable decompression from weeks of overwhelming pressure.

There was a letter from Gracie when I got back to the Rock, and it put my own problems in perspective.

Dear Charlie,

Well here's the bad news first. It seems my mom's genes are getting the better of me. I got the big C. I wanted to wait and see the outcome before I told you. It's breast cancer, but they already operated and we think they got it before it spread. Given my family history and the aggressive nature of the cancer, they did a prophylactic mastectomy. I don't give a damn; I told them to go right ahead and whack away if they thought it was best. The plastic surgeons gave me some new boobs, and they're a little too perfect. I'd rather have my own.

I don't know how Austin's taking this whole thing though. He's been freaked out. I know him, and I know he won't find my body sexy, anymore. He's been an asshole, anyway. He rarely even came by the hospital during my recovery, so I can see where this relationship is going.

So sorry for the bad news, but I feel good about my prospects. I'm just doing what I have to do to get back to my regular schedule. I will be doing more chemo for the next few months, so there goes the hair, another thing that will thrill Austin. Oh well, that's life.

I hope you're doing alright. How's the job? Are you keeping all the teeth of Acworth clean? I hope I can pay you a visit once I get done with the chemo. I wouldn't mind getting away from certain people around here. Do you remember my friend

Toni from the wedding? She's been really helpful, and maybe we'll get out of town together when I have a chance.

Steer clear of the bad butterflies.

Love,

Gracie

Even though Gracie managed to put my own problems in perspective, I still had to deal with them. I kept getting ideas – some rather gruesome ideas – and they were congealing into a vague but organized plan. The more I tried to push them aside, the more deeply they permeated moments of my daily thoughts. Eddie had already shaken me down for a couple of thousand dollars in hush money. To avoid the conflict, I paid him again, and then I made the phone call to Vince in an effort to divert my latent purposes. I decided to meet Vince and get a sense of where he might come down on the situation.

"Charlie Lofton," Vince said when he greeted me sitting behind his desk, looking tired. "What brings you down to the big city? I thought you were a staunch suburbanite these days." His tone was not inviting, so I deliberately felt my way along, dropping allusions to Eddie to see where he stood on his son.

"I was downtown to see Bobby for lunch; just thought I'd drop by," I said.

"Hmmf," Vince grumbled, "How's the Federal Agent?" There was no problem with me hanging around a law enforcement official per se; Vince had many of those kinds of friends. The difference was that his were tolerant of, if not involved with Vince, and Bobby was somewhere between unsympathetic to, and aggressively after, the likes of Vincent Palomino.

"He's fine, I guess. He's okay Vince," I said.

"Oh yeah?" said Vince. "You know he's a federal agent. He's become the real enemy. I know you're not concerned about such things, since you've taken your place in the world of cleaning teeth. But the heat is really on, and your buddy's just another ambitious bureaucrat in an organization out to destroy me and the rest of your old friends around here."

Vince's insinuation was too close to Eddie's language, and I catalogued that for future consideration.

"He's just a friend, Vince," I said. "We don't talk about such things, I can assure you."

"Is that why he paid Eddie a visit after you saw him awhile back?" Vince asked.

I was shocked. It was more likely that Hailey Baily would have sat up in that dentist chair and performed a strip tease for us than Eddie would tell Vince what had happened that day in my office. That told me where Eddie stood on matters of trust.

"What," I managed to eke in a pitiful voice.

"Well I was sure you knew," said Vince slyly, "since Eddie told you the very same day."

"Vince, I don't think you understand," I began to explain. History made it clear to me that Vince was one character I never wanted to cross, and I made it a strict policy to observe that rule throughout my adult life. Now, purely for self preservation, I had to come out with the truth about Eddie. "You don't know what's been going on..."

Vince cut me off. "I don't give a shit what's been going on," he glowered. "You keep your goddamn mouth shut when it comes to me, Eddie or the business. Better yet, you just keep the fuck away from that Federal friend of yours."

"Vince, I protested, "do you know what Eddie's into?"

"What Eddie is into is not the issue, son," Vince said in the calm formidable voice, which turns the blood ice cold for anyone who hears it. I heard it before, but it had never been directed at me. He had never even sworn at me. "I don't give a shit about Eddie's problems when it comes to people I trust saying anything to law enforcement about me or Eddie. We don't need you laying the groundwork for people whose purpose it is to destroy us. Now, you may feel like you're some kind of legitimate jack-off, but you've forgotten your roots. I set you up in life, and I can take it all away from you, just like that." Vince menacingly snapped his fingers.

"What the hell does that mean," I said. Predictably, Vince left the question ominously hanging.

"Get lost, Charlie," he said coolly.

"No Vince," I beseeched in futility. "What do you mean?"

"Hey Tomcat," Vince ignored me. "Charlie's ready to go. See that he does."

Vince's gigantic right hand goon gave me a subtle sigh and ambled in as if to say, "don't make this hard for me." I let him off the hook. I paused for an imperceptible instant to read Vince's face. Uncertainty washed over me once again as I walked out wondering what was in store.

On the way home, I wondered where I stood with Vince. He was obviously pissed off, but was that just one of his snits, or might he be considering my future – or my lack of a future. I hadn't felt like a target since Hugh McDowell had me in his sights in high school. That ended with the gun in school and my expulsion and Vince getting revenge for me. It seemed unimaginable that Vince would turn on me, but I was sure others had incorrectly gauged their relationships with Vince.

There wasn't even a gun at the house. I could get one from Bobby, just as I had in high school. Given the results of that episode, it seemed a bad idea. Besides, seeing Bobby was what created this rift with Vince, and there was no telling who was looking in on my activities.

I was getting angrier by the day. Eddie was emboldened. He was coming around more often with an attitude that he wouldn't have been able to sustain if not for the protection afforded him by the reputation of his father. There were constant demands for "loans" that I had to extend under the duress of threats of ruin. The situation was coming to a head, and the alternatives were boiling down to the inescapably destructive idea Bobby planted in my head the night I last visited him. I had to get Eddie out of my life.

My fate was sealed on a Wednesday when my source of consternation paid a visit. He was coked, stoked and looking for any enemy he could conjure for a confrontation. I tried to be reasonable. He demanded gas, so I administered it – too judiciously for Eddie's voracious appetite.

"Eddie, come on," I smiled, "what do you want. You want me to kill you? What kind of drugs do you have in your system? You know it can be dangerous to mix these things."

"You don't have to patronize me, Doctor," said Eddie. "Just pump up the volume, wouldja."

I carefully increased the potency of the gaseous solution. Eddie continued, more whacked than ever, "I was checking out the appointment book when you were in the head," he said, breathing in the elixir I hoped would mellow him. "I saw where Monica Keenan is scheduled tomorrow morning."

"Yeah," I replied trying immediately to move past Monica, "that's really enough gas for a little while, at least." Until then, I had been successful in staving off Eddie's demands to defile my unconscious patients with his pornographic photography.

Eddie just clutched the mask and took a deep breath. "Yeah, well you know what we need to do about that."

"What are you talking about, Eddie," I said.

"We need to work it out so that I get a little time alone with her and my camera," he panted lecherously.

"She's ten years old!" I exclaimed. "You can't be serious. What do you want to do with a ten year old?"

"Ten, that's perfect," he slurred. "I've got an underground magazine lined up that caters to people with a penchant for the nubile. I've promised 'em some photos and it looks like Monica's the lucky one."

"That's not happening," I resolved to myself and to Eddie. "It's folly. It's impossible. It's perverted!"

"Hey, one man's perversion is another man's pleasure," Eddie said icily. The chill of his statement gripped my soul.

"Well, forget it, 'cause there's no way it's gonna happen," I said, knowing I was right, but not sure what the consequences would be when it didn't."

Eddie ripped the mask from his blotched, swollen face and lunged unsteadily from the chair. The lines from the mask outlined his sneer as he tried to enunciate. "Oh, it's gonna happen. It's gonna happen because you want to keep your job here. You want to stay out of my father's sights, and you want to stay out of prison. So you just make the plans for tomorrow. I'll be here about ten thirty so we can get prepared. Now, I'll take my money before I take my leave," he mumbled, stumbling toward my office. "I believe we've agreed on two thousand."

We didn't agree on any amount, but the money was the least of my worries. "Okay," I agreed, "but I don't have the cash, now. I'll give it to you tomorrow."

"No good, bro," he said, looking stressed. "Gotta have it today." I was sure he had to have it to avoid the withdrawals he would experience when he couldn't pay for the drugs his deteriorating body craved, but I was wrong.

"I don't have the cash, seriously," I insisted. "If you want, I can write you a check out of my business account."

Eddie was clearly desperate. "Yeah, yeah, okay. But make it out to cash. I can turn that into money at the pawn shop. They know me there, but they charge me a premium, so add a couple of hundred."

I pulled out my checkbook to square with the extortionist. Eddie smiled sleepily as he staggered to his car. A fleeting hope that he'd crash and kill himself crossed my mind, then I realized the gas found in his system would be traced back to me.

Later, at the Rock my mind swam in the dangerous waters stirred by Eddie. As a stop gap measure, my only alternative was to call Mrs. Jefferson and tell her I was ill. She would cancel my appointments for the day. It would infuriate Eddie, but it would give me some time to try to save myself.

The call came from Eddie's car phone at ten thirty-four in the morning. "Real cute, pal," he cried, Van Halen blaring through the phone from his car speakers. "Don't fuck with me. You know better. You screwed my plans for today, but you're gonna straighten this out, or that's it. You got me?"

There was nothing to say. I just hung up. The die was cast. I could wait for Eddie to ruin me – or maybe for Vince to have me killed – or I could spoil it for both of them and take myself out of the picture.

When Tomcat came to the Rock that afternoon, I wondered if Vincent might beat me to the punch. Tommy "Tomcat"

Maroni was a Geechee fellow from somewhere in the islands off the Carolina coast. He and I always got along, but I knew he was Vince's henchman and his closest confidant so I was suspicious of his intentions.

"Hello Tomcat," I said, my stomach sinking to the pit of my soul.

"Hey Cholly," Tomcat called, in his unique accent, as he stepped through the doorway looming over me like a skyscraper.

"So what brings you," I said.

"Vince send me," said Tomcat. He was a man of few words. "Ah'm heya own behalf o' Vincent." It sounded like a rehearsed monologue. "He likes you, Cholly. He has been mo than patient, but you pushin' da envelope. You leaving him few options."

"What am I doing, now," I said. "What's he pissed about?"

"Eddie come to 'im," said Tomcat dryly. "They talk, now Ah'm talkin' to you."

"You mean that's all you're doing, just talking?" I asked in relief. "Vince didn't send you to, you know, beat me up – or worse?"

"Ah know," said Tomcat, "He been bitchin' 'bout you, and usually he don't bitch dat long 'bout somebody 'fo he do sometin' 'bout it. Ah'm glad dough, Cholly, 'cause Ah like you. Ah'd hate ta have ta hoit you, so please don't piss 'im off no mo."

"Tomcat, do you know what Eddie is doing," I said. "Do you know..."

"Hey, Ah don' wanna know nuttin'," interrupted Tomcat. "Ah'z jes doin' what Ah'z tole. Please, jes do what you tole, and we jes see each udder fo da good ol' times, kay?"

He rolled off the Rock in his Lincoln Navigator, and I was both relieved and intimidated. A phone call from Eddie that evening dashed any relief I felt. He sounded lucid, but it was hard to tell. I assumed he cashed his graft payment the night before, and he surely would have scored some good coke. And if he had the coke, there was a good chance he was putting it in his veins.

"I've been thinking about this, buddy," he began. "I paid a little visit to your office this afternoon. Since it was deserted, I was able to get a few things done. I checked the book for tomorrow. Jason Kolb has a two o'clock. We're gonna take some pictures or Monday the cops'll be on your doorstep with warrants in hand."

I was sure Eddie was finally all the way around the bend. "Eddie, are you okay," I asked. “Have you been shooting-up?"

"All night and all day, Doctor," came the reply. "Been in the booze, too. Does that go against your recommendation, or are you just trying to see if I'll have a change of heart in the morning?"

"I'm just worried about you," I said.

"I'll bet you are," he snapped. "Don't flatter me. I may be fucked up, but I'm not so fucked up I don't know your concern for me depends on your concern for yourself. Since you have such an interest in our mutual well being, I suggest you do what you have to do to take care of both of us. The first step would be to arrange things for young Jason Kolb tomorrow."

"Eddie, he's a boy, for god's sake," I exclaimed, just realizing that fact, myself. "I mean, little girls, that's bad enough. Since when do you take pictures of little boys?"

"Hey, they sell just the same," he said. "Matter of fact, I'll probably get a premium for the boy. That's one deeper level of perversion."

For one insane minute, I thought I could bring some reason into the conversation. "What the hell has happened between us? We used to be best friends."

"Times and circumstances change, pal," he said, bitterly.

"Don't you see," I begged, "you're pissed off because your father rejected you and kept his respect for me. Now you're just taking it out on me."

"Please spare me the amateur psychology, Doctor," laughed Eddie. "You're a dentist, remember? Oh that's right; you're not even a dentist. Don't forget that minor detail. Now I've got some other business to attend to. Just be ready for me around one thirty. This is your last chance. You can work with me tomorrow, or you can entertain the police on Monday."

With that he hung up. At that point, I considered two options. I could go to the authorities, give myself up and turn the blackmail tables on Eddie. That would mean tremendous legal problems, losing my career and incurring the ultimate wrath of Vince. It may inconvenience Eddie with an arrest, but he was prepared to disappear out of the country. That option didn't work for me.

The other option was to put an end to all of it. I could be rid of the problem with one swift, painless cardinal sin.

....

When a person is contemplating suicide, it is not uncommon for him to tie up the loose ends – to get his life in order. Going to the dentist for a cleaning would seem irrational for someone who wasn't going to be around past the weekend, but that was part of getting things in order. Once the sick call to Mrs. Jefferson was made on Friday, Dr. Glass agreed to see me that same afternoon as a professional courtesy. I also made an appointment to see Emmett Brandice, an attorney I used to write my will.

There were other things to do to prepare for the end. The big event would take place on Saturday. I wrote the note well in advance, fairly amused at the depressing words, which didn't describe my disposition:

To whom it may concern,

The wheels have come off. The people I care about may learn some things about me that may be shocking and disappointing, and they never would have imagined. To them I ask that they remember me as a person who tried to be the best at his job, even if it was a sham, and that they judge the veracity of any scandal against what they know about my past actions. I wish my life could go on, but it is out of my hands. I leave your world content to move to the next.

It wasn't profound, poetic, or particularly enlightening, but I guess you get only one shot at a suicide note.

The plan for the mechanics of the actual act gelled like concrete. There was need for only one rehearsal and good weather. The prolific foliage in the yard that canopied the Rock and washed the property in a rich, dark green hue most of the year had thinned during the brief winter months, and brilliant beams of light refracted through the sparkling glass panes of the French doors in the breakfast room forming ribbons of color on the outdated speckled counter.

A magnifying glass sat in a kitchen drawer, and I remembered how Bobby and Eddie used to toast bugs and slugs to death with the lens of the old telescope in the garage. A box of Blue Diamond wooden matches rested coincidently beside the magnifying glass. They would both play a part in the final act.

The one untidy part of putting things in order was to knock a pane out of the French door. I hesitated for a moment before tapping the glass into shards with a broom handle. It just didn't feel right, that single act of destruction to the only house where I'd ever lived, but it was a minor precursor to the devastation of life and property that would take place the following morning.

The thin plastic rim encasing the lens of the magnifying glass fit into the void that held the previously intact window pane with enough room to stretch tape across it and allow for an adjustment of its angle toward the kitchen counter. When the sun settled in for the morning, an intense beam of light concentrated into a burning dot on the counter top. As the sun arched its way across the late morning sky, the radiant dot moved along the counter in a predictable direction. A few matches placed in its path kindled successfully, once the dot converged on them. That was all that had to happen. I marked an X on the spot where the matches ignited and taped some cellophane on the outside of the door to cover the space left by the broken pane. I headed out, glad that Eddie didn't call before I could get away.

There was business at the bank: accounts to close, personal

items to get from a lockbox. Jan Dunlap took care of things for me, without a clue of what was in the offing. After leaving the bank, I had time pick up my dry cleaning before stopping at my office, which was closed early due to illness. It would be a brief and final visit – drop the suicide note on my desk, leave generous farewell cash gifts to Ginger and Mrs. Jefferson, change the name on some x-rays, take them, a tank of nitrous oxide, and some surgical gloves, and get out. Everything was left in its place and it was with calm resignation that I walked out of there for the last time. I wish I had checked my desk drawers to discover what Eddie already planted on his visit earlier that day.

Dr. Glass's hygienist, Martha, welcomed me and took me to an exam room. I watched as she placed my chart on the counter next to the chair. "Just have a seat and I'll clean your teeth," she said curtly, without looking at me. I couldn't help comparing her to Ginger. She didn't have the pleasant demeanor of Ginger, and there was a pang of sorrow that our little work group would never be together again. It hit me that over the past years Mrs. Jefferson and Ginger had become my close friends, and I hated leaving them in the situation they would soon find themselves.

Martha went about her work efficiently, and soon enough Dr. Glass came in to inspect my mouth. After some poking and mumbling, the good doctor pronounced everything to be in good oral order. We had some small talk and I walked out with him. As I got to the reception room I felt my pockets.

"Oh, my keys must have fallen out of my pockets," I complained. "These things are too shallow. That's always happening with these pants."

"Let me go check for you," said Dr. Glass.

"No, no," I protested, "I crashed in on this busy day. You get your next victim and I'll just run back and get them."

I politely pushed him aside before he could say another word, and found my way back to the exam room. I had to work fast without being able to shut the door. My file sat on the counter and I quickly pulled the x-rays from the folder and replaced them with the films I brought from my office under my shirt. No one walked by to witness the switch.

On the way out I leaned into the doctor's office and said, "Got 'em. Thanks. See you soon." There was no chance of ever seeing Dr. Glass again.

Emmett Brandice was patiently waiting when I arrived late for our appointment. We set to work, changing my will and reorganizing my finances. Emmett had no idea of my purpose for making the changes. Upon my death, he was to liquidate my entire estate and put the money into a trust to be invested only in US Government bonds. It was not to be touched for eighty years, after which time the surviving trustee was free to donate it to any qualified charity of his choice. That was the only smart thing I did that weekend.

There were two messages on the machine back at the Rock. One was Eddie – more ranting and threats. He said it was the last straw. According to him, I'd be either dead or in prison before the end of next week. How little he knew. The other call was Ray Smith, my broker. He was curious about my sudden liquidation of stock. There would be no call back for him.

I did call Eddie back, though. It was imperative to stall him for one more day, and to document the facts.

"Eddie, it's me," I began. "I'm sorry it didn't work out, today. I had to handle some things. I just can’t allow you to take pictures of my patients. It’s just perverted, especially because of the age of the ones you want. Are you into that child porn stuff, or is it just business for you."

"None of *you’re* business, you piece of shit! You do what I say or I’m going to the cops." he cried as he hung up the phone. He gave me what I wanted in that twenty second phone call.

I called him right back, but didn’t record that conversation. “Okay, Eddie, I give up. We’ll do what you want. I can’t fight it anymore.” The sheer lack of leverage he held over me made it tough to sound serious. "Please Eddie," I humored him, "Just give me one more chance. We'll do the deal. We have to be careful, but it's whatever you want. You're the boss."

"You should 'a come to your senses awhile back. You made

your bed," he scolded.

"Come on Eddie," I begged, trying not to overdo it. "Please, can we just talk about it? Come over tomorrow morning. I brought some gas from the office. I'll hook you up and we can talk." I knew the gas would break him.

"I'll see you in the morning," he said, before he hung up.

I made the last of the arrangements before going to bed. Sleep that night was surprisingly peaceful.

Saturday morning, Eddie looked like Keith Richards on a bad day. I was sure he had been up for the better part of the time since he hit me up for the two grand. There were fresh tracks on his arms. He was agitated, and I could smell stale liquor on his breath.

Maybe it was because this would be the last time I would see this person who used to be my oldest friend, or maybe I was trying to talk myself out of the whole thing, but I just had to try a reconciliation.

"Eddie, where did we go wrong?" I asked.

"What the fuck are you talking about," he said, looking around for the gas. "What happened over here?" He pointed to the cellophane window pane.

"I hit it with a broom handle," I told him. "You know, between you and me, what happened? We used to be tight."

"Fuck that," he cried. “You weren't worried about that when you were flying high. You hung me out, man. You don't give a shit about me or us. You're just trying to save your ass now that I've got it in a sling."

That was the most perceptive thing Eddie uttered in years. He was dead on. Anyway, he made the rest of our last meeting easy.

"Whatever," I sighed.

"Yeah, whatever," he sneered. "Where's that gas you were talking about?" His eyes were wired and tired. He was staggering.

"I've got it," I said. "Are you sure you need it? You've got to be careful, you know." I knew that would land on deaf ears.

"Like you care," Eddie growled, as if he knew what was up

and wanted me to go through with it.

I snatched the apparatus from under the kitchen counter. Eddie settled into the couch in the den. He pressed the mask over his mouth and nose. I released the gas and watched the drug ravaged face relax in lassitude.

"Remember, you've gotta treat this with respect," I warned as I had always done in the past. This time though, I didn't dilute the gas. I kept it going pure and mesmerizing until Eddie was comatose. I could have killed him right there, but there was another fatal fate awaiting my former friend.

Confident that Eddie would not be stirring for quite awhile, I moved to the kitchen to get the magnifying glass and matches. Outside, I cut an opening in the cellophane so the lens of the magnifying glass would get a clean shot from the sun and then taped the lens into place. I focused the light toward the counter where the matches were positioned, poised to release their destructive power. A check of Eddie and another shot of gas kept him asleep and afforded the time it took to lug the couch and the victim near enough to the breakfast area to guarantee the desired result. I took the cassette tape from my answering machine; then it was into the kitchen to extinguish the pilot light to the oven and disconnect the line that fed it natural gas. Some duct tape sealed the air vents and the cracks in the door jambs. As the gas spewed from the open fitting I administered one more dose to Eddie and stripped the clothes from his unconscious body. I retrieved his car keys and wallet from his pockets and walked outside to take one last jaunt among the grounds at the Rock.

February in Atlanta is a fickle, self-contained season which usually offers little to enjoy. Occasionally, though, it allows a day so beautiful as to deliver one from whatever weighs upon his soul, enveloping him in blissful ambience. That Saturday was such a day. The crisp air caressed my skin as the radiant sunlight toasted me from the inside out. No matter how heavy my burdens, the day breathed euphoria through me as I strolled among the flora and fauna of the land that had been mine since childhood. I found myself tramping in the woods, the unrelenting ivy refusing to give under my bulk.

Conventional wisdom puts one's life passing before his eyes when death is upon him, and it held for me. The horrible day we moved into the Rock immediately after my father's death returned in peaceful perception. Bloody Mary's rantings were so long ago, but were welcomed as I came out of the woods reminiscing the past. The image of Gracie and me playing together here allowed a hint of guilt for how she would receive the bad news about me, but the memories were so sweet the guilt vanished. I could remember only the comedy of the mischief Bobby and Eddie and I found ourselves in as we hid among those very trees. It's hard to say that the concept of time disappeared for me, but nearly a half hour passed before the task at hand delivered me back to the present.

When I passed by the house, I could see through the French doors, past the breakfast area, where Eddied lay serenely on the couch. The strong stench of gas was evident, even outside, where the torn cellophane allowed it to escape. I could see through to the counter where the matches were arranged. The intense point of energy from the lens focused itself about five minutes from the ignition that would set my soul free.

I grabbed the suitcase I packed earlier and stowed in my car the night before. As I settled into Eddie's car and drove out of the driveway I was careful to notice if anyone was around to see the car leave the scene of what promised to be a significant bang erupting from the direction of what would remain the Rock for only a few more minutes. It was shocking when the thunderous report from the explosion rocked the car before I could even turn the corner. Apparently, there had been a minor miscalculation in the time remaining until t-minus zero. Nevertheless, the instant the thunder jolted my bones it also shook me free – free from Eddie and his corruption and his extortion: free from the deceitful career that hovered over me all those years: free from one fraudulent life. I was to enter another brief one as Eddie Palomino. I was sure I could bestow more honor to his name than he did.

I could not resist turning the car around to make a quick pass by what had been the Rock. I drove by before the neighbors could recover from the bedlam to see what happened. The flames were majestic as they danced above the rubble, licking the grim, debris saturated swath of smoke that stained an otherwise lucent sky. My Mercedes, which sat outside of the garage, was engulfed and shot twenty feet skyward when the gas tank blew, strewing its metal skin in all directions. The windshield disappeared into thousands of tiny prisms showering refracted firelight throughout the shattered suburban surroundings. That was too bad I thought; I had just gotten used to driving the car Frank bought me.

The Rock was reduced to bits of little rocks that covered the yard, some still bouncing among the fallen trees and burning bushes. Glass and pebbles crackled under the car tires as I cruised slowly past the devastation. The neighbors' yards were littered in all directions on both sides of the street. I imagined the event would be huge, but I wasn't prepared for the scene before me. Only the stalwart stone garage remained standing, far enough from ground zero to survive.

There wasn't much time to absorb it before I had to drive to Eddie's to prepare\ for a long trip out of the country. On the way to Sandy Springs, I heard the radio station’s helicopter reporting on the tremendous house fire in Buckhead. Witnesses described two large explosions, but no one was speculating on any cause. It was too early to tell if anyone had been injured or killed, and no names were mentioned.

……..

Staying at Eddie's house was out of the question. I spent just enough time there to find the incriminating picture of Hailey Baily, which lay openly on his dresser, and to locate a forged driver's license and passport with a picture of Eddie that could pass for me. The name was Joseph Edward Paulsen, which was too close to the real thing for comfort, but what else could be expcected of Eddie's sloppiness. At least the address was in Cincinnati. There were also American Express and Visa cards in Mr. Paulsen's name.

I wore gloves the entire time I was at Eddie's. The key to his branch bank lockbox was right where he always kept it. There was a disappointing couple of thousand dollars in the open safe I had helped Eddie install in the floor of the closet a couple of years earlier. I noticed a new file cabinet in his bedroom since I had last been there. I thought about going through the files, but it was important to get out of that house pronto. Someone who knew me might come to tell Eddie about the explosion at the Rock. Before I left, I took some of Eddie's clothes and placed a call.

A cab took me to the rental cars at Hartsfield International airport. I was able to use my new identity to rent a car at the airport. If there was any reason for anybody to be looking for Eddie's car, either in connection to me or for anything else, I couldn't be found in it, hence the rental car.

Any hotel in the city would do, and there were plenty around the airport, but it would be safer to spend more time out on the city roads on Sunday than on Monday when more facts might come out about the events surrounding the Rock and me. I would have to be at the bank in Sandy Springs on Monday, so it was best to be ensconced in that neighborhood for the evening. I checked into a Sandy Springs motel under my new name and stayed in my room until I fell asleep.

By the time the Sunday morning paper was out, the burned out Buckhead house was identified as belonging to "Charles Lofton Jr., an Atlanta dentist who practiced in Acworth." The press speculated that the ravaged body parts found on the property belonged to one person, and that person was me, but the police would have to wait for a coroner's report. The cause of the disaster was still under investigation.

I was out of my motel room on Sunday just long enough to get food. The rest of the time I spent inside reading the paper, practicing Eddie's handwriting, tinting a right handed surgical glove to match my skin tone and brushing clear nail polish just beside the cuticle area. The time passed slowly, but it was bearable. It was interesting to read about myself in the paper.

At that point there was no hint of anything being awry in my life. There was no doubt the police visited my office and found the suicide note, but that had not made it in the media. I watched the local news reports during the day, and it wasn't until the eleven o'clock news that there was even a hint of a possible suicide.

My reputation deteriorated stupendously by Monday morning. Not only did the news of the suicide note become public, but that's when I discovered Eddie planted child pornography photos in my office before I could get to him. The police discovered the repugnant pictures, and an ambitious reporter ferreted out the information. There was enthusiastic speculation that the deviant dentist privately couldn't live with himself and his perversions, or was about to be discovered and did himself in, or was being blackmailed, or was being sued and faced financial ruin – it depended on what member of the media was doing the theorizing.

I was distraught. I was sure that eventually the news would come out that I falsified my credentials as a dentist, but I was hoping the child porn issue died with Eddie. The realization of the shock Bobby and Vince and Mrs. Jefferson and Ginger would be experiencing, and – oh God, Gracie – made me glad I left a self-exonerating nugget behind in Eddie's car. I wondered if it would be discovered. I hoped so, and I hoped it would be soon. I wondered if Bobby could ever believe Eddie drove me to suicide. Part of me wanted to call him to let him in on the real story, but that was impossible.

Late that morning was time to ignore the news, stow my emotions and get back to business. I put on Eddie's long sleeve coat and baseball cap and headed to the bank. I parked as close to the doors as possible, pretending to be on a cell phone, just peeking out from under the bill to see who was leaving. I had gone to the bank numerous times with Eddie so I was able to recognize when the girl whom Eddie made it a point to do business with left to go to lunch. I stepped into the bank carrying an empty briefcase, head down, cap side to the surveillance cameras I could spot. I showed Eddie's I.D. to the fill-in customer service person, Mr. Russell according to his nametag, a man of feminine qualities who was trusting and unconcerned about what I was doing.

The sleeves of the jacket covered the cuffs of the surgical glove on my hand as I deftly signed a highly respectable facsimile of Eddie's signature, leaving no direct finger prints. The pleasant man led me into the vault and I dropped my matching key into his palm with my ungloved hand. He unlocked the sterile steel drawer and walked away, leaving me to do my business in private. I began to clean out the drawer.

There was no time to inspect anything, but there was less cash than I expected. The records of offshore accounts were there along with forged documents, airline tickets, keys, letters and other unidentified papers. I cleaned everything out in minutes. Mr. Russell locked up the drawer, gave me back my key and led me out of the lockbox vault.

The room at the motel provided a secure refuge to make final preparations for my flight from the world of the dead Charlie Lofton. The contents of the briefcase spilled onto the flowery, faux-Laura Ashley bedspread. Among the clutter was a meager twenty-eight one hundred dollar bills. The blood drained from my head as I scratched it in disappointment. It had been a stretch since I was at the lockbox with Eddie, but the last time there were tens of thousands if not more than a hundred thousand dollars. Where had all the cash gone; where was the cash I counted on to fund the beginning of this new life? I tried to gather my wits and concentrate on the other documents strewn across the bed.

There were standby airline passes with open dates for passenger Nils Montgomery. A bank account ledger indicated twenty-three hundred dollars left in an account in Bermuda belonging to a Nils Montgomery. That was down from a high of almost two hundred thousand five years earlier. Since then, there were no deposits while withdrawals were steadily depleting the balance. I decided to abandon the paltry six hundred dollars left in his Atlanta account, rather than risk another trip to the bank.

There was a full set of documents for a resident of Bermuda named Nils Montgomery graced with Eddie's picture. I had no way of evaluating their quality, but Lawrenceville Lance, the forger, had a reputation for impeccable work. My fate lay in his hands.

There were also credit cards for Nils. I had no idea if they were activated or in good standing. The twenty thousand I took out of my own accounts helped, but it would have been ideal to have the ninety thousand in stocks and other investments I had to leave behind. I had Emmett Brandice put them in the trust, in case, through some unforeseen circumstances, I could ever get my hands back on them. Suddenly I couldn't imagine I would ever need it as desperately as I did right then. I just couldn't justify taking the money before my staged suicide; that would have raised too many questions. I thought Eddie's stash would get me by, but he managed to posthumously put the squeeze on me. I was scrupulous with money, but there was no doubt I would have to find a way to earn a living in a hurry.

These were considerations for another time in another place. Nils Montgomery picked up the phone and called to get on standby. Before the end of the night, I would be checking into the King's Square Hotel in Georgetown in Bermuda.

XIV. Eddie Disappears

Charles Lofton's chaos theory had not blown away in the havoc that was wreaked upon Eddie and the Rock. Old adages don't arise from the ether; there's no such thing as a perfect crime because there are too many factors to comprehend. And if one can't know all the elements surrounding a murder there's no controlling them. My crime was fraught with factors I couldn't know about, and two of them had me in a pickle:

- The staggering discovery that Eddie had no money when before there had been plenty. I couldn't know that drugs and pornography had consumed all but the crumbs of cash left for me. At least that's what I assumed happened to it when I made my count. That was not the only thing that happened to the money, and had I known the full story, I might never have blown up my friend turned foe in the first place.

- The planted, perverse pornography wasn't on my radar screen. Eddie threatened to use it against me, but it was serendipity that made him put that filth in my desk that Friday – the Friday that, unbeknownst to him, would be his last on earth.

Then there was Bobby. My idea was that he couldn't get his hands too dirty by his association with me or Eddie, particularly with his aspirations of becoming a U.S. Attorney, so he would let the results of my demise take their course without his involvement. I should have given that a second thought. The newspaper on my last Sunday morning in Atlanta brought the news of the explosion at the Rock to Bobby as he lay on the couch. Most of the emotions that took hold of him were predictable: shock, disbelief, grief. What I didn't count on was his irresistible detective's curiosity.

On the one hand, he knew from that night at dinner with me that something Eddie was doing was eating at me, but would I kill myself over it? This was a question he mulled over; would I actually commit suicide for any reason? He couldn't believe I would. If it wasn't suicide, could it have been murder? Might Eddie, in a whacked out state, have finally lost it and leveled his rage upon me to the point of whacking me? Or maybe my problems with Eddie had become an issue for Vince that had to be neatly checked off his list of errands. Those were the three possibilities. Of course, Bobby couldn't know all the factors in the crime any more than the perpetrator. First he learned that, instead of being a dental hygienist, I was impersonating a dentist. Then as the news continued to uncover new tidbits in what the press correctly called a bizarre case, Bobby learned of the pornography. Perhaps, he thought, he really didn't know me that well. But his training etched skepticism into him, and he never took new evidence at face value.

Where would he start? There was the practice; the women in my office probably wouldn't be much help, but they would be worth an interview. Then there were Eddie and Vince. They might be able to offer something, but if either of them were involved there could be a lot of disinformation. Just the same they were on his mental list of people to contact. That was where he would start – if he were involved in the investigation, but he wasn't.

After careful consideration Bobby placed his next call. When Eddie's voice mail came on he hung up. He called Gracie in New York to give her the bad news. After three more calls to Eddie, all unanswered, Bobby finally left a terse message for him to call back. Sarah Palomino answered his next call and summoned Vince to the phone. Bobby resolved to keep it civil, and most importantly to make it seem to be on a personal level.

Vince sounded shaken. "Oh, hey son," he said when he realized who was calling.

Bobby cringed at the "son" comment, but he let it go. "I guess you've heard," he began, in that always awkward first offering when broaching the subject of a friend's demise.

"Yes," was all Vince said.

"Well, I'm really shocked." Bobby broke the brief lull.

"I remember you boys as you grew up together," said Vince sadly. "You kids were really close, I know that, son. Charlie was a great kid. You know, Bobby, he just never could get the breaks. But he kept at it. He did well for himself. I don't know what went wrong."

Vince sounded bad. If he had anything to do with his friend's death, Bobby thought, he deserved an Oscar. But he couldn't stave off the thought of the other potential suspect.

"You know the child pornography thing is bullshit, don't you?" he said, convinced he knew me well enough to say it.

"I didn't know what to think of that, but I can't imagine Charlie and that shit," Vince said.

"Yeah, no way," Bobby said, hoping he could keep the faith, in spite of the evidence against me.

“You think it was a set-up?” said Vince, completely unaware it was his own son responsible for exactly that. Vince did privately worry about the role Eddie played in my death. He certainly had cause to worry about that.

"I'm thinking about it," said Bobby, wanting to leave it there. Then he said, "How's Eddie taking it?"

"Don't know, Bobby," said Vince. "I haven't been able to reach him." Vince's voice trailed into silence.

Bobby had a sense of Vince's thoughts, so he just did the right thing for the situation. "Eddie'll be just fine Vince," he said. “Do you know where he is?”

"I got no idea," came the melancholy response. "When I talk to him, you want me to tell him to call you?"

"Yeah, and I'll do the same, if I get him first," Bobby said, realizing the double meaning of his own words.

"Listen," Vince said, "I'm gonna make sure there's a service for Charlie. It'll be in the obits. Will you come?"

"Of course," replied Bobby. "I'll look for it."

"You're okay, Bobby," conceded Vince.

"Yeah Vince," was the only response, "I'll see you at the

service." There was a click and a dial tone, and Bobby tried again to reach Eddie.

As he tried to get to sleep Bobby thought about his conversation with Vince. His instinct told him Vince's emotion was real. Vince spoke more fondly of Charlie than he spoke of Eddie, he thought. Of course Charlie was the dead one. Not that anyone could blame him, anyway. Eddie was a bad seed even among Vince's crowd. Still, Eddie was his son. Bobby planned to see that son in the morning and get his take on the Charlie Lofton tragedy.

....

The next morning, Agent Albert Milton of the Bureau of Alcohol, Tobacco and Firearms, who was assigned to the Lofton case, received a page from Special Agent Bobby Wells. It was the child pornography and the explosion that had the ATF involved. Al Milton was anxious to meet with the FBI agent once he knew the deceased was his friend. He hoped Agent Wells could provide useful insight in the case. After all, the pervert was dead. There was no family to interview. The neighbors in this sprawled community with multi-acre grounds knew little of the person who lived in the old stone house on the hill. The FBI man would be one of the few who knew anything relevant.

It would likely be confirmed the explosion was caused by a spark that set off the gas from the oven the pervert was using to kill himself. Identification would be all but certain by the end of the week. Bank records might turn up something of consequence, but there was no guarantee. Perhaps he could gather additional facts to help pick up a sinister pornography trail. He welcomed anything Agent Wells could offer.

When Bobby arrived at the rubble known to him as the Rock, Al and his crew were sifting through the destruction. Some agents were looking for whatever might remain of pornographic material that had been in the house. They would find none. There was a team of explosive experts taking samples for lab tests.

The slender, tall guy wearing a navy blue, nylon baseball jacket with big white letters reading ATF on the back stooped past the crime tape and extended a firm handshake that enveloped Bobby's own hand.

"You Robert Wells?" Al asked. A direct manner was Agent Milton's way in all his investigations.

"Bobby," Bobby answered. "Albert Milton, I presume."

"So, Mr. Lofton was a friend of yours?" Milton nodded. "Sorry for your loss."

"Yeah, he was," said Bobby. "As you know, I'm not involved in the case. I'm just an interested party. Anything jump out at you so far?"

"Well, it's early, you know," said Al Milton, feigning an objectivity he didn't possess in this case. "It doesn't look good, I have to say. So far, we haven't found anything in the house that compares to the stuff in his office, but most everything was incinerated in the blast. I gotta tell you, though, the stuff at the office was bad – graphic kiddie porn."

"You figure it was his?" Bobby asked.

"Well, like I said, it's early, but do you know anything that would lead me in another direction?" said Milton. Both seasoned detectives were playing their hands close to the vest.

"Not really," Bobby said, "but I knew Mr. Lofton pretty well, and there was never anything about him that would make me think he would be into anything like that."

"Look, I know this guy was a friend, but let's face it; who's gonna find out these things until something like this happens? It's not the kind of thing anybody who's doing it goes around talking about," Milton said. "Do you know any specific reason he might have wanted to kill himself?

"No, not at all. Have you come across anything other than the fraud?" asked Bobby.

"We're looking into it," said Milton. "It could've been depression or guilt or something else related to the porn. It might have been completely unrelated. Was he depressed or anything?"

"Something was bothering him," Bobby responded, carefully. "It's hard to say what."

"Well, we're looking into all possibilities," said Al Milton. “We'll have financial records in a day or two. If he was being blackmailed, or something like that, we should get some indications when those come in. Can you think of anything else that might help this process along?"

"I'll be thinking about it," Bobby said. "I'll let you know."

"I'll let you know if anything new comes up," Milton said. "Do you know of anyone else we might talk to?"

"Charlie and I didn't see each other as much as we did when we were younger, so I can't tell you for sure." said Bobby. "We did have a mutual friend that he saw: Eddie Palomino. Eddie and I had a falling out, but I can locate him for you."

"We'll talk to him," said Agent Milton. "You know his address?"

"It's on Angora Trail in Sandy Springs. I don't know the number. I'll get it for you."

"Thanks," replied Milton, "we'll keep in touch."

Once Bobby was on his way from the crime scene he tried to reach Eddie without success. He thought by that time he would have been able to get in touch with him, but there was no telling what Eddie's routine was. Bobby wondered if Eddie was even aware of their friend's death.

He drove to the Sandy Springs house. Eddie's car was in the driveway, but the lights in the house were out. The temptation was too great. Bobby walked into the junk filled garage and tried thc door to the back hall. The door was predictably unlocked. He felt his way along the dark walls, bumping into the washing machine before he reached the light switch. The kitchen was almost neat. There were only a few pans and plates in need of a dish sponge. A quick look through the cabinets and drawers yielded only a corner of a baggie of marijuana. The rest of the house was routine, except for the bedroom.

There Bobby found the two drawer file cabinet. With his standard issue surgical gloves on he slid open the top drawer to find a clutter of papers, some in files that had been started but not maintained. Most were just lying on the bottom of the drawer. The files were labeled with names. Many sounded foreign, of the eastern European variety. Most of the files were empty, but in a couple were carbon copies of generic order slips embellished with Eddie's patented scribble. Names and phone numbers headed each slip in carbon blue. Below that were sexual categories and appalling descriptions with dollar amounts assigned to them. The scattered mess, which had never found a file, was abundant with such slips. They covered the spectrum of sexual deviance.

When Bobby opened the bottom drawer he was greeted with a disorganized stack of raunchy porn magazines. They were published in different languages including English, Russian, French and at least one variety of Asian. Most of them contained photos of children, both boys and girls. Bobby was repulsed, but the investigator in him compelled him to plow through the material.

Under the raunchy pulp were some still photos of more illegal filth. Behind this stack of smut were rolls of nasty negatives indicating Eddie was involved in taking the pictures. On one of the rolls, Bobby saw the image of a naked girl in the dentist chair. He could see the forged credentials of Dr Lofton’s on the wall even on the negative. Next to the negatives were video cassettes. When he popped one of the tapes into the VCR he wasn't surprised to find the same kind of smut come to life on the television for only a few seconds. He didn't want to take too long, so he rewound it to the spot it had started and popped out the tape, careful to replace it right back in its spot. Everything had to be just as it was when he found it. He quickly made his way out of the house. If Eddie came home it would be a manageable scene, but he didn't want Agent Milton to find him there. He glanced inside Eddie’s car as he was passing it. He saw something on the seat that looked like a small cassette tape. He opened the car door to inspect it more closely. He knew it was out of an answering machine, but he had no idea if it had any relevance to his friend’s death. He had to leave it there for Al and his crew to find.

On the drive back to the office Bobby breathed a tenuous sigh that the porn found in the office had to be related to Eddie. It was clear Eddie was the one with the porn. Eddie had the film from the camera that had taken the pornographic stills, including one from his friend's office. If he were blackmailing Charlie it could have been about his illegal dental practice. The pornography in the dentist's office could have been a frame job to infuse his extortion scheme with added leverage. That is what Bobby wanted to believe, and it was amazingly accurate. He hoped the incriminating photo of the girl in the dentist chair was taken without his friend's knowledge. He was almost right about that.

He cringed at the sudden realization of what he saw in the file cabinet. He was instantly filled with anger. Eddie was involved in crimes way beyond the pale, even for the scumbag he used to consider a friend. No matter how it played out, Eddie had to bear responsibility for the death of Charlie Lofton, whether directly or not. Where was the sonofabitch, anyway? It was time for a confrontation.

Bobby had to let Al Milton discover what he already knew on his own, after obtaining the proper warrants. He had his own work to do at the bureau. It was a case he was working in a support role with the US Secret Service involving counterfeit hundreds that had shown up in Georgia. It had been fairly simple to solve. The group involved was sloppy and painted a trail in neon. A few of the minor players were already secretly arrested. For them the shit had hit Agent Steve Langtree's proverbial fan, and they were ready to deal. The petty players sang like Wayne Newton at the Stardust. In order to save their own asses they changed teams and were working undercover for the good guys.

After seven months of careful execution the chain of counterfeit command was mapped. The problem was, the principals were two American master printers from Georgia working in Belgium. They were being observed by Treasury agents in cooperation with Belgian officials, but there would be some diplomatic red tape to get them back to the states when they were picked-up. Bobby had the tedious task of working with the state department through the U.S. Attorney's office to arrange extradition. Things were finally gelling, and before long, the two would be snared and on their way back to face the music.

That would be Bobby's last assignment at the bureau. He was slated to join the U.S. Attorney's Office in Atlanta by mid-year. After experiencing all the bureaucracy in dealing with the extradition he considered he might be happier right where he was. But then he couldn't anticipate the situation that would greet him soon after taking his new position.

XV. Nils Montgomery Finds Bermuda

Nils Montgomery found Bermuda to be more expensive than could be imagined. I stayed the first couple of nights in St. George until I could get my bearings. Given the limited resources I arrived with, two important courses of action had to be taken; I had to find cheaper accommodations, and I had to find a source of income.

The Commonwealth Trust Bank, which held my Nil's account, had its main branch in Hamilton. Bringing twenty thousand dollars cash into the bank for deposit merited some attention. As I turned from the teller window I was greeted by a banker in Bermuda shorts, tie, and jacket.

"Hello mate; I'm Clive Gaston," he said. "I'm the Manager of Customer Accounts here."

To look at the bank manager's rosy, round, whiskerless baby-face one would have thought his five-nine frame might be supporting extra weight. In fact, his tie draped comfortably against the flat waist of what I would later learn was the compact body of an amateur cricket player.

"I'm Nils Montgomery," I said, offering my new alias for the first time. It rang genuine, and I knew I would get along fine with it. "I've just gotten back from the states. I would like to stay awhile so I thought I'd fatten up my bank account."

"Well, we never have a problem with that around here now, do we?" Clive said with a grin and a slap on my shoulder. "I thought you were a new face. I just wanted to introduce myself. If there is anything I can do for you, my office is right over there."

"Thank you, Clive," I said, making a point to drill his name into my memory. "I'm doing fine right now, but I'm sure I'll see you from time to time."

"Look forward to it," Clive said with a wave. "Cheers."

I was out the door repeating Clive Gaston's name to myself.

I checked out some nearby hotels and made the instant decision to move into Hamilton. There were no rental cars on the island, and public transportation and taxis were expensive. The ferry came right to the pier in Hamilton to take people to different parts of the island for a price I could afford. It was clear there would be more job opportunities in Hamilton anyway, so the move made sense.

I liked Hamilton. It rests beside an emerald harbor dotted with yachts and commercial craft busily navigating the water by day and bobbing, tethered in marinas at night. During the week, large ocean liners dock stem-to-stern along Front Street supplying an endless horde of tourists to the pricey stores and restaurants in the area. At night the liners provide a festive display of colored lights that decorate their towering hulls.

I became intrigued with the professional men and women clad in garb unique to the quaint island. They worked almost exclusively in banks, insurance companies, retail outlets, or the hospitality industry. They spoke in the most polite British terms, and they were eager to engage any stranger in idle conversation. I could see this new life in this paradise would be agreeable. I knew the pangs of homesickness that visited occasionally would wane once I got on a stronger financial footing,. The life of Charlie Lofton from Atlanta, Georgia was beginning to seem like history.

I made it a point to stop by the bank on a regular basis and pop into Clive Gaston's office. Clive invited the interruption to his routine, and the two of us became casual acquaintances. It wouldn't take long to learn the habits of Clive, and that's just what I did. My intuitions formed from the past life hinted that Clive would be of value.

Like many of the denizens of Hamilton, Clive stopped in for a pint after his workday. One day, on a cold afternoon in late February, I intentionally ran into Clive at the Hog Penny. Usually he was surrounded by his cricket buddies, but on that particular day he was drinking alone. I moved up to the bar apparently unnoticed by the banker. It didn't take long for the amiable Clive to realize his customer had become his bar neighbor.

“Cheers mate. How are you?" he said,

I turned around with a surprised expression. "Fine," I smiled, coolly. "Nice to see you..."

"Clive – from the bank," he said, extending his hand.

"Sure," I responded. "I know it. It just took me a second – different scenery, and all. I remember though, you told me you came here."

“It’s Nils, right?” said Clive.

“Very good,” I said. “Can I buy you a beer? Whatcha drinking?”

“Don’t mind if you do,” Clive said, shaking my hand. “A Smithies”

“Two Smithies,” I said to the pretty girl behind the bar, having no idea what I had just ordered.

She smiled and drew two large steins of a tawny, lively liquid and passed them to us. Clive raised his glass and I followed his lead, clanking the two Irish ales together.

“Here’s to the expatriate American, wise enough to come to our little island,” he said. “How long do you plan to stay?”

“It’s open ended,” I said. “I’ve got no reason to leave, nor any desire.”

“Will the immigration blokes let you stay here?” he said.

I knew this was going to be a question, and I was prepared. I took a long drink from the crisp, effervescent Smithwick’s Ale before I launched into my lie. “There’s no problem with them,” I said. “See, technically I’m married to one of your citizens.”

“That right?” said Clive, moving a little closer.

“Yes, that was a lifetime ago,” I said adopting my role with finesse. “She’s a good girl; we just couldn’t get along in the end.”

“Right, sorry,” Clive said. “So you split up?”

“We never got divorced,” I explained, “but I moved out. Eventually I moved back to the states for a job opportunity. I’ve been living and working there for awhile, but I’ve been wanting to return.”

The bartender brought us a couple more Smithies and Clive

said, "Are you going to ring her up?"

"Oh, I've talked to her," I said, "but we will never get back together. We still like each other, but she's got a boyfriend."

"If she decides to get married, then you'll have to make the break-up official," said Clive.

"She swears she never will," I said, crossing my fingers.

Clive hoisted his pint and said, "Well, here's to … what's her name?"

"Gracie," I said, always knowing my imaginary wife would be Gracie.

"As long as Gracie keeps her word I imagine you're welcome in our bailiwick for as long as you want to stay," said Clive, finishing his toast to Gracie.

"Yeah, as long as I can afford it," I said. "Your little island paradise isn't the exactly a discount travel destination."

"No, you're right about that," Clive said. "You have money concerns?"

"Absolutely," I said, "All the money I have is in your bank over here. I need to find a job before I blow through it."

Pretty soon a third round descended upon us as a tipsy confidence settled into my personality. Clive seemed unaffected by the strong beer. "This might be your lucky day, mate," he said as he polished off about a quarter of his new pint with one gulp. "My wife Maggie works in personnel for the bank. She just got back from maternity leave, and she's got to fill a unique position within the ranks. It might just interest you. I'll set something up. Are you free tomorrow?"

"Only all day," I said. "So you just had a baby?"

"Right – a boy," said Clive. "Three months on Saturday."

That launched Clive's biography, which lasted through a fourth round. He married his university sweetheart. They had a two year old boy and their new baby. He played cricket in college and continued to play in a recreational club as an amateur. Clive tried to explain the arcane rules of the unfamiliar sport, but I couldn't have understood them cold sober, much less in the condition his Smithies had me.

While trying to comprehend my friend's explanation, I

suddenly knew I had too much and could no longer maintain any semblance of sociability. I finally excused myself after the fourth beer. As I was leaving, Clive reminded me to stop at the bank in the morning.

"I'll be there," I promised as I stumbled from the Hog Penny. The night air coming off the harbour was cool and it felt good against my face as I struggled back to my hotel room. I raced to the bathroom in the nick of time to throw-up. I had never drunk four strong beers in a sitting. In fact, I had barely drunk four beers in my life.

The morning after greeted me with my first hangover. It was barely manageable, and I wished I hadn't agreed to an interview with Clive's wife. I thought how lucky it was that I vomited the night before. It took awhile to get the cobwebs out, and it was late morning before I found my way to the bank.

Clive was bounding around jauntily, offering courteous orders to his charges, greeting the regular customers as they sauntered in to take care of business. It was as if he had never seen the inside of the pub the previous night.

"Right mate," he exclaimed when he saw me wobble in, the freshly purchased shades soothing his customer's shuddering eyes. I winced at the hearty slap on the shoulder. "We had a bit of the bitter last night, eh? You left me a little pissed. It was all I could do to get another two down before the 9:40 ferry home. Maggie had to pour me into the bunk without dinner."

It was all *I* could do to believe that Clive polished off two more pints and was standing there apparently immune to the afflictions that were punishing me. I had to put up a strong image. "Yeah, I know what you mean. It was tough getting up." I failed to mention the puking episode. "Sorry if I'm late."

"No, not at all," Clive said, grabbing a file and tossing it on his desk with a thud that echoed through my painfully pickled brain. "Let me give Maggie a call before she gets away for lunch. It'll just be a minute."

I had to take a seat at a desk in the lobby. Hot flashes were coursing over my skin. I wanted water, but was afraid it might make me throw-up. Fortunately, Clive didn't take long.

"Well Nils, Maggie's tied up most of the afternoon," said Clive. "Do you think you can make it to her office around four-thirty?"

The question was music to my ears. Had she interviewed me right then, I wouldn't have made it through without taking a bathroom break. The delay provided five hours to regroup. Clive's directions put Maggie's office just a few blocks west of the hotel. There was time for at least three and a half more hours of sleep. On the trek back to the room, I beamed at how prescient the move into Hamilton had been.

When the alarm went off for the second time that day my condition was much improved. The nap was just what the doctor ordered. I took a second shower of the day, dressed, and headed for Mrs. Gaston's office. It was in a plain mid-rise office building on Par-la-Ville Road just off Church Street. Maggie worked on the eighth floor. Her secretary showed me in and introduced me. Maggie was taller than Clive, with big bones, but a fit physique. She smiled and said, "Come in, love. I'm Maggie Gaston."

"Hello Ms. Gaston," I said. "Nils Montgomery."

"Yes," I know who you are," she said. "And it's just Maggie. Clive has told me a little about you and how you find yourself back in Bermuda, but tell me what you did in the states."

I dreamed up my story long before I knew I would be sitting in the office of the Personnel Manager of the Commonwealth Trust Bank. My story couldn't have been more appropriate for the available position. "I moved back to work with a friend who was trying to start a home building business," I said. "He was a fine person, but a terrible businessman. He didn't make it, but I stayed in the states and worked for myself doing odd jobs for homeowners. I worked as a handyman and did yard work – anything anyone needed to get done around their house." That was the story I invented weeks earlier to explain the large cash deposit I made at the bank. I would maintain that most of my customers paid me in cash and I held onto it to bring back to Bermuda with me.

"Surely you're joking," Maggie said with a smile of

disbelief. “The position we’re interviewing for is a handyman.”

It was my turn to be incredulous; what would a bank need with a handyman? “Is that right?” I said. “You need someone to maintain the property at your branches?”

“No, not that,” said Maggie. “You see the bank has a compound just across the harbour on Salt Kettle Road in Pagett. We use it to put up bank executives or clients from out of town – anyone the bank considers important. It’s really quite nice. It has five individual cottages, a lodge with complete office facilities, a couple of large meeting rooms, and a full restaurant style kitchen. Outside we have a pool and a putting green.”

“Sounds great,” I said. “You need someone to maintain it?”

“Yes,” she said. “We have a fine gentleman who has worked with us for seventeen years, but he’s ready to retire. He has some health issues, and at this point he doesn’t need to work. I’ll be frank with you; it is a slow paced, low stress job. It involves keeping up the grounds and making minor repairs. For major repairs we have contractors you would call. You would also be responsible for driving guests and shopping for supplies. We have a small apartment for your living quarters. There is a lot of downtime. When no one is there you have access to the facilities, and you can use the van for personal trips as long as you are available to our guests when needed.”

“I think I would be perfectly qualified,” I said, and I truly believed it. Whenever anything at the Rock needed attention I was the one who took care of it. I had learned enough over the years to be able to handle what Maggie was describing. “Not only am I reliable and competent, I would be friendly and helpful to your guests.” It sounded boilerplate, but I had nothing else to endorse me.

“Fine,” said Maggie, “do you have any references?”

It was a question I knew would come, and I had no good response. “Well, as I said, I did odd jobs so I didn’t have an employer,” I stammered. “I suppose I could try to contact some old clients to see if they can write something…”

“No worry,” she interrupted, “Clive likes you, and that’s

good enough for me, at least for the time being. We can give you a try with it. Assuming all goes well, you will keep the job, Mr. Montgomery."

"May I ask the compensation?" I said, already elated that I had the job in my pocket.

"I have to say," said Maggie, "it is not the highest paying position, but you get free room and board and a company car. With most of your necessities paid, you should be able to get along quite nicely. You know, of course, you pay no income taxes here?"

"Yes, that should be helpful," I said. "I would like the job if you would like to give me a shot."

"It's a deal. I'll hand you over to Rita, and she will get you processed and explain the details. Can you start on Monday?"

"Yes ma'am," I declared, and with that I became an employee of the Commonwealth Trust Bank.

XVI. Two Investigations and a Funeral

Vince arranged for my funeral to be on a Tuesday. Bobby and Eileen met him and the meager gathering at the chapel of Saint Mary's. Al Milton was there, undoubtedly to scope out the mourners for possible sources of information. Bobby introduced Eileen to Al and took a seat in a pew in front of him. A few of Vince's friends from the club were there. Mrs. Jefferson was there alone, looking stern, as only she could look. Ginger didn't make the journey into the city 'with all that traffic,' as she would put it. There were a few nuns, perhaps former teachers at Saint Mary's. Bobby spotted the familiar face of Gracie across the chapel. Eddie was conspicuously absent.

After the service Bobby and Eileen assembled among the mingling crowd in the chapel vestibule for a few uncomfortable minutes, anxious to get home to grieve in private. There was some stilted small talk, and Vince gave Bobby an uncharacteristic hug. The familiar face from across the chapel smiled as she walked up to the Bobby and Eileen.

"Hi, Bobby, it's Gracie," she began. "It's been a few years."

Bobby was relieved to see her, the way she immediately dispelled the discomfort of the scene. "Hi Gracie," he said as he gave her a genuine hug. "This is my wife Eileen."

"Nice to meet you," Eileen said extending her hand.

"You, too," Gracie said with a naughty spark in her aqua eyes. "So, this is the girl who married Clark Kent. I've read a little about you in Charlie's letters. You might not know it, but I used to have a big crush on your husband," she said, unabashed.

"Usually I have a crush on him, too," said Eileen, "but there are times when you're welcome to him."

"Maybe I'll take you up on that," quipped Gracie. "It's been awhile if you know what I mean. But enough of this inappropriate talk; we're at a funeral," she said, as her voice softened. "This is too weird. I can't believe I'm here for Charlie's funeral. It hardly seems real."

Of course, it never occurred to anyone – not even the intuitive Special Agent Wells – that indeed it was not real.

"I know," said, Eileen, "I can't believe it either. It's all just so sad. I don't know what to think of the whole thing. Bobby tells me all this stuff we read in the paper is a crock. I could never see Charlie involved in that stuff, but I never thought he would commit suicide, either."

"Let me tell you," the authoritative Gracie declared, "the porn stuff – there's just no way. I know I've been gone a long time, and I know you guys know Charlie, but we've stayed in touch with letters, and… there's just no way. You're right, though, I can't believe Charlie would do himself in. That's not his M.O. It's all too much."

"Well, Bobby's keeping up with the investigation, so if he learns anything he can tell anybody, I'll let you know," Eileen volunteered. "How long are you in town?"

"I fly out around seven-thirty this evening," said Gracie. "I just got in a couple of hours ago; it's a quick trip, but I had to come to this."

"If you want, there's plenty of time to come by our place for some snacks and something to drink; even if it's just coffee or tea," Eileen offered.

"Thanks," said Gracie, "but it's got to be something stronger than coffee or tea."

"No problem," Eileen said as she tugged at Bobby's sleeve. "Honey, lets go. Gracie's coming over and she needs time to get drunk before she has to leave for the airport."

People don't hang around any funeral for very long after it's over, and at this one the chapel hall emptied as if under a fire drill. All but a handful of the handful of people who attended the service were gone. Bobby shook Al Milton's hand, and they all thanked Vince before they went out to the parking lot where Bobby pulled Al aside.

"Have you got an update on your investigation?" Bobby

said.

"Not much since we talked," Al responded. "As you know, the dental records confirm the victim's identity as your friend. We're still waiting on some DNA tests to come back, but we don't have much non-degraded material to work with. I doubt we will get a full profile, but a partial profile will work for I.D. purposes, given the dental records. Call me at the end of the week, I'll fill you in."

"I sure will," he promised. "I've got the address of Eddie Palomino, the guy we talked about."

"Oh yeah," replied Al. Bobby related the information, frustrated that it didn't seem more important to Al. He couldn't blame him, though. The agent was working without the benefit of his knowledge. Bobby had entered and searched Eddie's house without a warrant, and he couldn't tell Al what he knew without jeopardizing a potential court case. He would just have to try to give Al a reason to get a warrant for a legal search.

Bobby turned away from Al in time to see Gracie getting in the backseat of a town car. Eileen leaned in for a final word before the driver closed the door and strutted smartly to his seat behind the wheel.

"I told Gracie where the house was, so we need to get back there. I don't want her to have to wait on us," said Eileen.

On the drive home Bobby was silently brooding that he would have to wait to see what his counterpart at the ATF would discover. He was already onto some important facts and he didn't want Eddie to show up and thwart the probe before Al could see the evidence. He automatically picked up the phone to call Eddie's house. As usual, there was no answer. He was getting more suspicious with every unanswered phone call.

Back at the house Gracie emerged from the luxury ride wiping tears from her face.

"This is a great house," she said to her hosts as she followed them through the garage door. "It's great to be back in the old neighborhood again."

"Yeah," Bobby said with raised eyebrows, "you ought to go back to your old yard. It changed dramatically the other day."

"I know," said Gracie, "I went by there this morning. It's amazing – the power of the explosion must have been something. There's nothing left but a pile of rubble – and the old garage." Gracie remembered the times she and her friend spent in the garage and a pang of sorrowful nostalgia nudged her thoughts.

"Well, Charlie never liked the Rock, anyway," Bobby said. "He succeeded in destroying that along with everything else."

"Honey, I want a drink," Eileen jumped in. "I want a vodka martini; how about you Gracie?"

"Whoa, sounds stiff for three o'clock in the afternoon," said Gracie, snapping back to the present. "I'll have one."

"I'll get 'em," Bobby said as he led them into the bar.

"Nice place, Bobby Wells," Gracie remarked, looking around at the spacious, comfortable home. "You've come a long way since back in the day."

"Yeah, I married well," Bobby said modestly, ignoring his own accomplished climb from his humble beginnings. "You look like you're doing okay, yourself, limo driver and all."

"I can't complain. I guess I was born well," Gracie said without a highhanded hint in her voice. "One can't live in Manhattan the way I do on my salary, darling." She inflected a haughty Cape Cod dialect into her confession. "I get a little help from Daddy, you know." She cast a limp hand in the air as she tossed her rich, blond hair and fluttered her eyelids.

"Yes, I can see how that might be hard for *one*, without Daddy," Bobby chided, as he shook the ingredients for three chilled martinis and dispensed them evenly into three glasses. "Let's see, twist for me, olive for Eileen, and what is your preference Luvvy?"

"Olives," said Gracie. "And that's plural, you know. Sheathe that cocktail sword in a stack of those olives.

"Wow, that sounded…passionate," Eileen said, fanning her face with her hand. Gracie never learned to temper the innuendo, whether or not she realized what she was saying.

"How is Daddy, anyway?" Bobby said, his thoughts darting to Gracie's mother and father.

"Not so well, Bobby," Gracie said as her voice lowered and she took a sip from her martini glass. "He's been in and out of the hospital. He's got heart problems, and he's put up a good fight, but I don't think he is too long for this world."

"Oh, I'm sorry to hear that. How old is he?" Eileen said.

"Only 62, but he's had a tough time, and he's told me when the time comes, he'll be ready," said Gracie with resigned practicality in her response.

"Yeah, that's too bad," Bobby said. "Gracie's dad was one of the good men around when we were kids," he told Eileen.

"Well thanks," Gracie said, a little surprised Bobby remembered enough of her father to feel that way. But then, there weren't any other respectable male role models around for our gang back then. Either way, the precocious boy she fantasized about in her youth grew to become diplomatic in his own time, she thought. "That's what Daddy's going through, but what do you think happened with Charlie?"

"Yeah, what was the ATF guy saying to you at the church," Eileen asked.

"Nothing new since I talked to him the other day," Bobby said. "We knew they got a positive match on dental records and they are doing some DNA tests, but it looks like we had the funeral for the right person. It's clear Charlie disconnected the gas line, but no one knows if he intended to asphyxiate himself or he intentionally blew the place up. Knowing Charlie, there wouldn't have been an explosion if he hadn't planned one. You know how his father died in that explosion; maybe he had that on his mind. On the other hand, if the level of gas were high enough to cause that massive explosion, it's hard to imagine Charlie would have been conscious to ignite it. So if he didn't do it manually, the question is how the explosion occurred, whether or not it was intentional. That much gas is going to be highly volatile, so any spark could have set it off. We just don't know what caused the spark." Bobby didn't betray his suspicions about Eddie.

"Like you said, Charlie never liked the house, so he must have figured this would get rid of it," Eileen said.

"I never liked the house, either," said Gracie. "His invalid grandmother and his mother just sitting in there all the time was creepy. Whenever I went in there it seemed like I was stepping into a black and white movie, like an Alfred Hitchcock film. If I were Charlie I would've blasted it too."

"Yeah, but he lived in it for all his adult years, after his mother and grandmother were gone," said Eileen. "Why didn't he sell it before all this?"

"Charlie knew it was a valuable piece of property," Bobby said. "We never talked about money, but I'm sure he was holding onto it, just waiting for it to appreciate even more. The way Charlie lived, he could retire on the proceeds from the sale of the house alone."

"I know he never remodeled or redecorated once he had it to himself, did he?" Gracie asked.

"Are you kidding?" said Bobby. "Charlie never spent a dime in his life that he didn't have to. He kept it immaculately clean and kept everything in good repair, but he never changed a thing in there."

"That's for sure," Eileen added.

"It's been so long," Gracie said through welling eyes. "Even though we kept in touch through the mail, I can't believe I went that long without seeing him, and now I'll never see him again." Of course in our world of chaos, Gracie had no idea how little she knew of her future with Charlie Lofton.

"I wouldn't beat myself up over it," said Bobby, pouring everyone a second martini and considering Gracie's comment. "Nobody knows when something this bizarre is going to happen. Hell, at least you kept up with him. I was in the same city, and we didn't see each other as much as we should have. You just don't expect the luxury of time to disappear like that."

They polished off their drinks with reverent small talk before it was time for Gracie to go.

"Thanks for the hospitality," Gracie said, with a slight zigzag in her gait on her way to the town car. "I hope the next time we see each other will be a happier occasion."

The next time they would get together would be an

astonishing occasion.

....

The rest of the winter passed swiftly for Bobby. The counterfeit case was coming together in a barrage of activities. He finally got confidential approval from the powers that be in Treasury to pick-up the rogue printers. The crooks would have their day in court to fight extradition, but there would be no political resistance for keeping them in Belgium. If there were no unforeseen snags Bobby would have the actual printers of the bad cash at his disposal within a couple of months. Meanwhile, he made certain to insinuate himself into the investigation of his friend's death. He kept in touch with Al Milton, and he made an appointment to see him. He arrived in the ATF agent's office to find him poring over files. Milton greeted him enthusiastically, happy to have something new to report. He started with the old news.

"We still don't have DNA results in," he began. "Your buddies in FBI lab are a little slow. The explosives team determined what we thought they would. The natural gas he used to do himself in exploded. It looks like he disconnected the pipe from the stove, and it was just pouring out of there. We can't tell what set it off. It could have been an accidental spark, or he may have blown himself up on purpose. The coroner can't come up with an absolute cause of death. He thinks the gas itself did it, but without much of a body there's not much to work with.

"A second explosion came from the gas tank of the car that was in the driveway at the time. They also found what was left of a tank of that nitrous oxide used in dentistry. Could be he got himself high on that before he did the deed. He might have been hooked on it. That kind of thing is not unheard of among dentists."

Bobby was sure that wasn't possible in Charlie's case, but he let Al continue.

"We got your friend's bank records. He had several

accounts, all at First Union. In the past few months he's been making some unusually large cash withdrawals on a weekly basis. It's way out of the pattern of his banking. Someone could have found out about the fraudulent dentist thing or the kiddie sex, or both, and was shaking him down. That could have driven him to end it all. We're definitely interested in that angle. That will probably get you guys involved in the case."

Bobby cringed when he heard the well meaning investigator make the offhanded accusation about his friend's depravity, but he continued to hold his tongue.

Al proceeded, "In his business account there's a consistent pattern of normal vendors he paid on a regular basis, but the last three checks he wrote were different. The last two were to his assistants, and they appear to be a gift that he made to them before he died. We interviewed them, and neither one had anything to do with this. The other check is one we can't explain. It was written to cash for twenty-two hundred dollars. On the back it's endorsed by a Joseph E. Paulsen. That one's suspicious. We checked out this Paulsen, and came up empty. The driver's license number the teller wrote down on the check when she I.D.'d him doesn't check out. It matches a farmer in Vidalia. He's about sixty and has no clue about any of this, so whoever cashed that check was using an assumed ID. That's where we're keying our resources.

"Mr. Lofton saw his attorney the day before he died. He changed his will and had his entire estate put into a trust, making his attorney the trustee. Can't figure that one out – not yet anyway. Your friend put everything in apple pie order.

"We've tried contacting your pal Edward Palomino, and we haven't had any luck. He didn't go to the funeral, as you know. Have you heard from him?"

"No, I haven't," Bobby said, the wheels turning inside his head. There was no way Charlie was doing the gas, he thought; he didn't even drink. He could have gotten it for the suicide, perhaps to bolster his courage or at least make it so he didn't care. He knew Eddie was wheedling gas out of his friend, but the complaint had been that he was going in and disrupting the office to get it.

"Do you have a copy of the check for twenty-two hundred dollars?" he asked. Al reached into a file folder, dug through some documents, and produced two Xeroxed pages of the front and back of the check. Bobby could see it was Charlie's handwriting on the front. Then he looked at the endorsement of Mr. Paulsen on the back. He was instantly sure Eddie was the one who endorsed the check. He made a quick decision to tell Al, but first he said, "Do you mind if we get involved and work with you on this?"

Al Milton was a professional. He had been with the ATF for twenty eight years, and he was long ago over being territorial with his cases. "I guess if you guys want to get involved, I can't stop you. I figured it was going to happen eventually, anyway," he smiled.

"I can tell you who I think endorsed this check," Bobby stated. "It's our friend, Mr. Palomino."

Al's eyes opened wide. "You sure about that? I can tell you've had a hard on for him; are you sure your not blinded by whatever bugs you about Palomino?"

"I'm sure enough to have it checked out," Bobby said confidently. "Nobody's seen or heard from Palomino since the explosion. I have personal knowledge that this is his handwriting. We could persuade a judge to at least let us get to his signature cards at his bank and have a handwriting guy make a comparison. Meanwhile, we can assign a detail to stake out Palomino's house in case he comes home. Then we could at least talk to him. Call my boss, and I'll go in and talk to her. We can put this thing on a fast track."

Al agreed, and he placed the call to the office of the regional director of the FBI. He didn't know what Bobby knew, and he wasn't so sure what this would lead to, but it was better than any other leads they had developed.

Bobby left for downtown to try to catch his boss before she got away for the weekend. He wanted to make sure somebody would be watching Eddie's house around the clock. He contemplated Al's report. Charlie knew he was going to die or he wouldn't have written the gift checks to his staff and tidied up his affairs. That made it almost certain he did himself in, instead of Eddie doing it directly. Still, the check from Charlie to the alias Eddie used had him involved in some way. Even if he wasn't directly responsible he may have driven Charlie to do what he did. Besides, Bobby thought, he did have it in for Eddie, and if he could get him popped on the child porn offense he would be happy to do it.

Jennifer Brannon was trying to slip out the door a half hour early to get a start on the weekend when Bobby intercepted her outside her office. "Did you talk to Al Milton from the ATF?" he asked.

Jennifer motioned him back into her office. "Yeah, about your friend's case," she said. "He wants us to get involved. They're looking into extortion. But I can see you already know all this, so why am I telling you? What have you been doing with Milton?"

"I was just interested – thought I could help, so I shared some thoughts with him, that's all," Bobby replied, cautiously. "Did the name Edward Palomino come up?" he asked.

"Yes it did," Jennifer said warily. "They have some inkling that he's involved; why? By the way, you know we're investigating his father."

"I know Eddie Palomino," he said, choosing his words carefully. "I know there was some friction between the two. I recognized the fraudulent endorsement of one of Lofton's checks to be Palomino's handwriting."

"And...?" Jennifer coaxed skeptically.

"And I want to be in on the case," he said.

"I thought you were almost out of here," said Director Brannon. "When do you join the Attorney's office?"

"There's some time. The exact date hasn't been set," Bobby said, aware that Jennifer knew that.

"You've got this big one you're working on with Treasury. How's that coming?" asked the boss.

It was all in Bobby's report, but he summarized for her. "We will pick-up Epstein and DeLon within a week. There's gonna be a hearing in Brussels that will be a formality. Everything should go smoothly. They could be here by spring."

"You'll send Phillips to Brussels," she said, indicating she had read his latest report. "I was going to talk to you about that. Are you sure you don't need to go there yourself?"

"Phillips will do fine," said Bobby. "He's more directly involved with the facts over there than I am, and he'll give competent testimony."

"Bobby, I know you have a stake in this other case with your friend's death, but if you step back it's petty. We don't need to devote anyone at your level to this thing. Are you sure you don't have some personal score to settle with Palomino?"

Bobby purposely avoided the question. "Jenny, who knows where it will lead? You've got a dead person, and I'm not so sure who's responsible. Then there's extortion and there was child pornography. We could be talking racketeering. Who knows how big it could get. And maybe it will help us get to Vincent Palomino."

"And if it turns into something you'll leave in the middle to go be a prosecutor," she countered. Jennifer Brannon liked Bobby Wells and respected his talents. She was inclined to let him have what he wanted, if only as a going away gift. "Okay," she relented, "but you keep Ted Reardon close by you on this one. If this develops into something, and you take off on us, I want somebody who can take over and run the investigation without starting at square one."

"No problem," Bobby agreed, hoping he could put the thing to rest before his boss's concerns became a problem. "I'm going to put a detail on Palomino's house this weekend. We need the surveillance."

"That'll make somebody's day," Jenny said drolly. "Whose weekend do you plan to ruin?"

"I'll have to check and see. Then we need to get a court order to get to Palomino's banking records," Bobby said, eagerly.

"Whoa, there," Jenny put up her hand in the motion of a traffic cop. "I've got out of town guests whose kids are destroying my house and terrorizing my kids as we speak. I've got to get home before it's too late. Besides, you won't find a judge in chambers at this time on Friday afternoon."

Bobby knew she was right. He thanked her for her understanding and went to his office to arrange the surveillance detail. He would not be popular with at least three of his agents once he made the phone calls.

....

In the past, Vince rarely expected to hear from his son. Eddie went months without touching base with him. Still, it had been months since Charlie's funeral and Eddie hadn't come around. Not only that, Vince was making calls to him that were not being returned. It was as obvious to Vince as it was to Bobby there was some connection between Charlie's death and Eddie's disappearance. He finally put Tomcat on the case.

Tomcat spent the next week looking for Eddie in the city. He went to stake out his place for a few days, but got spooked away when he saw the government car up the street from the house. He learned of Eddie's usual haunts, and none of them yielded any progress. He finally decided Eddie had to have flown the coop.

If Eddie skipped town Tomcat knew where to go. Thursday he was in Lawrenceville Lance's office. When Tomcat made an appearance it was understood that he was an emissary for Vince. That was all that needed to be understood. Lance fell all over himself to help.

He gave Tomcat a list of four aliases he provided for Eddie. Three of them came with forged credit cards and a driver's license. Those had to be temporary. The fake credit cards were linked to real people's account numbers and they would only be good for a few charges before either the credit card issuer or the victim himself caught the improper charge. That made it risky to use too many times.

The fourth alias, in the name of Nils Montgomery, was simply a driver's license and passport. Eddie had owned this one for quite some time. With Nils' I.D. Eddie could open accounts and manage money. If he were traveling, it would be under this name.

Vince had people on the take at US South Airlines. Some were baggage handlers who helped move large sums of cash and other contraband across state lines without detection. Others worked in ticketing and supplied his men with improperly discounted tickets worth thousands of dollars. Chances were, if Eddie flew out of Atlanta, he went US South.

On Friday Tomcat called Pete Kirkland, a computer jock on the joint payroll of US South Airlines and Vincent Palomino. Pete agreed to meet him after work that evening to search for a passenger of interest to Vince. Pete had no idea as he searched for Nils Montgomery he was trying to help Tomcat find Eddie Palomino.

Tomcat assumed they could find the name in some master database of passengers, but this was before the tragedy of 9/11 and the airline's systems had not evolved to such a sophisticated degree. There was no frequent flier account attached to Nils Montgomery or any standard reservation in that name. Pete explained that there were other ways for Mr. Montgomery to have gotten on a flight, and they would just have to wade through the thousands of flights to find the name. They could do a search on the name for each individual flight; he would just need a date. It was simply a matter of going through each flight on that date until they hit the right one – a cumbersome task, Tomcat thought. It didn't seem to faze Pete, and it occurred to Tomcat that Pete was well suited for his job. He was glad he didn't have to do that kind of work all day. It also struck Tomcat that he was cut out for his own vocation, so everyone had a talent for something; it was just a matter of finding out what it was. Tomcat would soon learn that different levels of risks attended various career choices, and the adverse consequences of his particular vocation were on a scale he never allowed himself to consider.

He knew Eddie had been missing since Charlie's death, so he had Pete start with the day the Rock exploded, and work forward in time. After hours of the boring and repetitive task

Pete shouted out, “Aha. So that’s what it is. Your Mr. Montgomery was holding an open ticket for any date for quite awhile. He redeemed it for a flight to Bermuda on this date, here.” Tomcat checked his calendar and saw that Mr. Montgomery flew out the Monday following the explosion of Charlie’s house.

"Disco," exclaimed Tomcat. "Good woik, Pete," he said as he popped a hundred dollar bill in his shirt pocket.

"What'd this guy Montgomery do," Pete asked with gruesome curiosity. "Is he done for?"

"You don' wanna know," Tomcat said wearily, as he walked out into the wee hours of the morning. He got what he came for, and he'd call Vince with the news after he got some sleep. That call would never be made.

....

Tomcat’s job was to do the high level bidding of Vince Palomino. He didn't get involved in the daily activities that comprised Vince's vast, illegal business interests. He put in his time over the years, working as a shylock, shaking down clients and running the parlay cards. He had never even been involved in the drug side of Vince's empire. That wasn't to say he wasn't keenly aware that Vince was making huge profits from it.

Tomcat wanted some of the action for himself, so he kept his ears open and made contact with some of Vince's distributors. Over time he built up a pat clientele of cocaine, crystal meth, and heroin users. He had no qualms about it, but he knew he would incur Vince’s wrath if he got wise to it. He had one rule; Eddie Palomino would never buy the shit from him. Everyone else in the world, though, was fair game, and the quality of Tomcat's inventory commanded a healthy segment of the high end druggie market in Atlanta.

They mostly came from Satin. The club had become the premier spot in Atlanta for celebrities from around the world who liked that kind of thing. No matter what professional sports team was in town, there were always players reporting to

Satin for a night of decadent entertainment. Tomcat was the dealer of choice for these athletes, other celebrities, and their entourages.

He also provided drugs to some of the girls who danced at the club. He was discreet with them, choosing only the girls who had their act together to be clients. The problem was, the more they did drugs, the flakier they became. This was a problem Tomcat did not anticipate, but it was becoming apparent to him. No new client dancers, he had vowed to himself.

There were still existing ones to take care of, though, and one of them was Sheri something-or-other. Tomcat was never close enough to any of the girls to know much about them, but he probably knew Sheri better than the others. She was a tall, twenty-three year old specimen of beauty and fitness. Her ample breasts had been enhanced to a pert D-cup by a plastic surgeon to get her a maximum return on her medical dollar investment, mostly in the form of ones and fives stuffed into her garter belt. Sheri was a body builder and she allowed herself to believe that cocaine helped alleviate joint aches that came from lifting heavy weights. Tomcat met the steroid infused iron-pumper who put that idea into her head. He, like all the other men who tried to date her, couldn't compete with her narcissism and swiftly fell by the wayside. By then she was snorting enough coke to relieve the whole club of arthritis, if only it had that effect.

Sheri had long since slacked off her activities in the gym. The coke kept her appetite in check, so her toned body had smoothed into lithe feminine allure, which oozed sexuality and kept the dollars pouring her way. Tomcat was trying to cut her off, but she was getting the drugs from other sources, so his feeble effort at reforming her was useless. What he didn't know was that she had been busted trying to score some coke in a local watering hole well known for its rampant drug swaps.

Tomcat was relaxing with a Bloody Mary in the sunroom off his kitchen on Saturday morning when his beeper started vibrating against the counter. Sheri's cell number greeted his blurry eyes as he stooped to grab the intrusive buzzing. He hesitated. The past week of searching for Eddie, capped off by hours in front of Pete's infernal computer screen had been a strain. Against his better judgment he returned the call.

"Hey," Sheri said after one ring. "Whatcha doing?"

"Callin' you back, baby; whacha tink?" came the gravelly response.

"I need to see you," she said. "Is that possible?"

Tomcat thought for a minute and then said, "Sho, why not."

"I need maybe four eights," she said casually.

"Whoa", Tomcat cried, "Don't talk ta me own a cell. Call me back." He punched the off button on his cordless, angrily. This bitch is brainless, he thought. Within three minutes his beeper went off with a number he didn't recognize. "Wheya you?" he barked when she answered his return call.

"At a pay phone," Sheri shot back, defensively. "Geez, sorry. You're paranoid."

"It keeps ole Tomcat outta jail. Whacha wont wid all dat," he demanded.

"To have a party," she said. "Me and some friends are going to Destin 'til Wednesday. We want some party favors."

"I hope id's a whole lotta friends," he complained.

"It is," she whined. "We need to leave soon; can you help me?"

"'Kay," he acquiesced, "meet me at IHOP o'er dere offen Holcomb Bridge. Make it twelve tirty, and don' be late."

"Thanks," she said, hanging up the phone, nodding to the DEA Agent who was monitoring her call.

Tomcat knew that twelve thirty meant one o'clock at the earliest to Sheri, so he finished his drink and moseyed through a long shower. Once he weighed out the product, wrapped it tightly, and stuffed it under a towel in a gym bag, he got into his Navigator and left his house. On the way out the driveway, he picked up his newspaper. The sports section would help bide the time until Sheri straggled along. Vince would be up by the time he got back, so he would call him after this errand.

As he pulled into the parking lot he was surprised to see the red BMW waiting for him. This is a first, he thought. He parked on the other side of the crowded lot. Knowing Sheri wouldn't bother to get out of her car, he grabbed the gym bag and started in her direction. As he got close enough to make out her face, the fact that she was on time and the expression she carried told him there was something wrong. He looked away and altered his course. As he scanned nonchalantly, he noticed a nondescript citizen getting out of a van. He didn't see the plainly clothed agent who stepped out from a car behind him and stuck a gun in his kidneys.

His blood ran cold. When the man from the van edged his coat aside to display the magnum stuffed in his waist, Tomcat stopped in his tracks and surrendered.

The DEA agent escorted him behind the van where he held a gun on him while the other guy patted him down. Once Tomcat was relieved of a gun, a switchblade, and the gym bag, he was cuffed and shoved into the back of the van. Another agent sat in the passenger side of the front seat, gun already trained on the captive. The men then put a hood over his head.

"Whad dis," Tomcat cried, literally and figuratively in the dark.

"What do you think, Tommy?" the driver said as he climbed into the van, "It's a bust."

As the van left the parking lot Tomcat couldn't believe what was happening. "Whad kinda bust, he demanded. I don' see no badges. This ain't no police cah."

"We've got badges, I assure you. If the gun doesn't persuade you, we'll be glad to provide I.D. when we stop," said the driver. Judging from the turns it made, the van headed south toward downtown, but it stopped short of the city's center.

Once they parked in an empty garage Tomcat's hood came off and the van was surrounded by federal agents. Tomcat was hauled out and taken into an office building. Double oak doors opened into what could have been the office of any important businessman. He was stripped naked and forced to sit down before an extravagant oak desk that harbored an imposing figure ensconced in a posh, leather executive chair.

Tomcat was not one to be intimidated, and he spoke first. "What da fuck's goin' own, heah," he glowered at the hulk wearing khaki pants and a thermal top exposed by a loud, half buttoned flannel shirt. The giant hunting boots left a rubber trail along the desktop as FBI agent Steve Langtree straightened up in the chair to reveal a massive upper body. Tomcat had never seen a guy with gray hair that looked so capable of taking him in a fight. He looked around to see two agents standing at the door with guns drawn.

"I'll tell you what this is, Tommy," sneered Agent Langtree. "This is the worst day of your life. This is a day you would do anything you could to avoid. Don't blame the girl. This day was coming; it was just a matter of when I wanted to ruin your life." He flipped his FBI badge on the desk in Tomcat's view.

"Fuck you," yelled Tomcat. "Ah don' say nutin' til Ah seez mah lawya."

"No, fuck you Tommy!" the Agent shot back. "There are no lawyers. There's only you and me."

"Bullshit," Tomcat said in confusion. "Ah know mah rights..."

"You have no rights," Langtree interrupted. "Look at me. I am it. I represent the full force and authority of the United States Government – the same government who eliminates undesirable nuisances around the world. I can snap my fingers and have you dead before you can shit. No one would ever know what happened to you. You're in a different world now, son."

Tomcat was disoriented. He had been in jail, in court, and in prison, but he always felt secure in his rights, knowing that ultimately the law limited what could be done to him. Also, he had Vince's network, outside and in the joint, to provide him special treatment. This was different. He was sitting there naked before one of the biggest men he had ever seen, and the guy was threatening to kill him in the name of the United States Government.

"What da fuck you wont," he said, quieter, trying to steady himself.

"There now," Langtree chided, "now we might get somewhere. What I want Tommy, is very simple. I want Vincent Palomino."

"Hmmf," groaned Tomcat, "Good luck. Ah won' cross Vince. Ah'd take ma chances wid you." He was surprised that Vince was even on the FBI's radar screen. Vince had built an organization designed to insulate him from the suspicion of men like Agent Langtree. At least that's what Tomcat believed.

"No, Tommy, you'll take your chances with both of us. That's reality. Now, I won't get you a lawyer, but suppose I did." Langtree reached into the gym bag and pulled out the thirty-two grams of coke. "We take you downtown and put you up on distribution charges. Your man comes down and tells you not to talk. That's the best he can do for you until Monday, earliest. Meanwhile you're nowhere to be found by Vincent. Come Monday you go to your bond hearing, but we delay that to obtain a warrant for your house. You may have Johnny Cochran for a lawyer, but the judge is gonna want to know what's in that house before he sets bail. Now I know you don't want us to find what's there, but that's beside the point, because once the warrant's executed we have as much as seventy-two hours to act upon it. We're in no hurry, and as you sit in jail Vincent gets real interested in why you haven't turned up. When we finally do get around to the warrant, we'll take that house apart brick by brick and leave it in a pile for you to put back together; you know why?" Tomcat wasn't responding, but he was listening. "Because we have the authority to, that's why. The federal drug and racketeering laws give me the authority to ruin an innocent man's life, so imagine what I can do to yours. I know whatever's in that house is good for a ton of time to a guy like you with the priors you've got – lots of drugs and illegal weapons, right? Who knows what else?

"By that time Vincent knows what's up, and that creates two problems for you. First Vincent is gonna know you were dealing, and that won't sit well with your boss. Second, once he knows you're staring at all those years in prison he won't be able to trust you. By then your only option is to deal, because every year you spend rotting in the joint is a threat to him. Vincent will always find a way to eliminate anything that presents a threat to him. You're gonna have to deal, one way or the other. You can save a lot of hassle, and it's a whole hell of a lot safer to do it early on – to take Vincent out of the position to take you out.

"Dat's if you convict," Tomcat said, unsure of himself. "You don' got probble cause to go in da bag."

"Tommy, Tommy, Tommy," Langtree lamented, "please don't be as dumb as you look sitting there with your belly hanging over your dick. We'll convict no matter what it takes." Either way, your relationship with Vincent will never be the same."

"Just da same, I needs ta consult a lawya 'bout dis," Tomcat said shakily.

Langtree shook his head in amazement. "Have you not heard a word I've said you moron? This is the last thing I'm going to tell you; then you have five minutes, that's it. If we don't come to an understanding the ball starts rolling, and it will roll right over your dumb ass. When I come back in, tell me what I want to hear."

With that, Langtree arose to his full stature of six and a half feet, looked down and snickered at the naked thug, and walked out. The two gunmen remained at the door staring at Tomcat.

There comes a time in many an organized criminal's life when the ultimatum is put to him, and he has the decision to make. Over the years the criminals convince themselves of their resolute loyalty to one boss or another, but as Agent Steve Langtree was known to tell his underlings, "When it comes down to the nut-cuttin', no matter how much honor there is among criminals, when the shit hits the fan the spineless bastards always deal."

The five minutes seemed like only seconds as his head swam for nonexistent options. There was nothing to think about, really. He was screwed. For an instant he wanted to crush Sheri's skull, but he realized what Langtree said was true. They were out to get him, and it was going to happen with or without

Sheri. The shit had hit the fan for Tomcat, and he was ready to deal.

"You're not as dumb as I thought" Langtree said as he dropped Tomcat's crumpled clothes in his lap. "Here's your new reality. Vince is no longer your boss. You now have a new boss – me. Vince is now your prey. The sooner you accept that and start thinking of him that way, the easier it will be to do your job and please your new boss. And you want to please me. The happier I am with your work product, the easier your life beyond this day becomes. So get a new attitude starting now. Agent Morgan will take you back to your car and we will escort you home from there. You will hear from us when we have an assignment for you. Oh, and don't get any ideas about running. We've got a lot of eyes and ears on you. You can't run far enough."

Within an hour Tomcat was back in his own home, stunned at how the day had turned for him. He never thought this day would come, but he was not totally unprepared. Steve Langtree had misread him. He had time to reconsider his situation once he was back on his turf. He would never double cross Vince, and he figured Langtree was full of shit if he thought he could keep track of him twenty-four – seven. There was no time like now to launch a plan, when Langtree's men would be thinking it would take him a few days to clear his head. He grabbed a cell phone that he purchased from a convenience store along with plenty of minutes. The phone was not in his name and the feds could not know the number to tap the line. He walked deep into his backyard and began inviting people over for an impromptu party. He had enough phone numbers of drug users who would drop whatever they were doing to come to Tomcat's house, especially when he was providing the party favors at no charge. By mid-afternoon his driveway was filled with cars and his house was filled with people.

It was Agent Josh Morgan's day to stake out Tommy Maroni's house, and when the unexpected guests started arriving he didn't like what he saw. It wasn't that Maroni didn't occasionally have guests, but after what he had been through that morning it didn't seem likely he would be feeling up to a party. Perhaps it was already planned, but Morgan figured Maroni would have canceled. He considered this and decided to make an appearance at the party. He was dressed casually; he didn't look particularly out of place as he approached Maroni's front door.

An emaciated girl answered the door, and looked a little startled when she saw the clean cut agent on the other side. "Is Tomcat here," he asked. The obviously buzzed girl just backed up and pointed him inside.

As Morgan walked through the house he measured the ambiance of the thugs place. It may be right that crime doesn't pay in the end, he thought, but in the interim it can buy you some mighty nice things. This criminal's house was twice as big as his own family's, and it was in a better neighborhood. The furniture and appointments, while not necessarily tasteful, were obviously expensive. He stepped into a large sunken room with a terrazzo floor generously dotted with antique silk Persian rugs. The back wall was glass, and French doors led to the pool with a stone waterfall and Jacuzzi. Two walls were lined with leather couches and a variety of chairs facing a big screen TV. There was a bar that ran the length of the other wall facing a pool table where a couple of zoned out home boys were engrossed in a game of eight ball. Tommy Maroni was behind the bar presiding over the eight ball of coke, which several attendees were attacking with cut McDonalds straws and rolled dollar bills.

When Maroni saw him he looked surprisingly unsurprised, which concerned Morgan.

"Whad's happnin' capp'n," Maroni said to the man who had abducted him just hours earlier.

"Not much," said Morgan. "Just passing by the crib, saw the cars, thought I'd check it out."

C'mon in an' cheel," said Maroni, "lemme show you 'round."

None of the bystanders showed any concern for the stranger who Tomcat casually greeted and no one made an effort to meet him. Morgan pressed his left foot to the right ankle holster he wore under his blue jeans nervously seeking reassurance that he was not in over his head. Maroni stepped from behind the bar and led his guest up the two steps through an arched passage into a hallway.

"And they say crime doesn't pay," Agent Morgan said, recalling his earlier thoughts.

"Not t'day," said Maroni in relaxed resignation. A left through a heavy, semi-opaque glass door at the end of the hall took them into a dark nook, lit only by flickering gas lamps on opposing walls. To the left was a walk-in humidor; to the right was an oak shelved wine cellar. "Caya fo a smoke," Tommy said.

Maroni was too composed for the experience he endured that day, and Morgan suddenly realized he was not in control of the situation. He began to back out of the room as he stooped to reach for his weapon, but the die was cast.

"Aw c'mon, now," said Tomcat, pulling a strategically placed nine millimeter from behind one of the gas lamps and pressing its barrel against Morgan's forehead. "Wheya you goin' in such a hurry? You jes got heya, and ah really won' you to stay awhile."

Morgan considered his options as he straightened up, and he knew they were limited. His host was just too big and too seasoned to try to disarm and overtake.

"Now whad's dis," Tomcat said, tapping Morgan's ankle holster with the toe of his shoe. "Sorry Mr. G-man, but Ah got a little rule in ma house; Ah'z dee only one dat carries a piece 'round heah. So, if you jes reel slow reach down deah and take off dat bulky ankle bracelet – and Ah do mean slow… Ah don' won' to add no killin' a federal offissa to mah list a troubles, and Ah'z pretty shoah you don' won' dat on mah conscience, needer."

Morgan's gut relaxed to the twinge of relief he felt as he deliberately removed his holster. Tomcat kicked the weapon aside. "Okay, dat was jes right," he said as he motioned Morgan into the wine cellar. "You know, you really made tings easier fo ole Tomcat by stoppin' in. Ah was gon' have to sneak bah you out deah, in someone else's cah, but now dat you in heah, Ah feel lot bettah 'bout ma 'scape plans. Ah'z sorry ta have to tell you 'bout mah 'scape, an' Ah know Ah had agreement wid yo boss, whads-is-name, Langtree? Da problem ees, Ah jes can' keep mah end o' da bargain. You see, as big as mah troubles are wid yo boss, they don' compaya to da problems Ah'd have wid my boss, iffen Ah cooperate wid you."

Tomcat closed the door, wedged a chair into the handle, picked up Morgan's gun and hurried away. He returned in less than a minute with handcuffs he secured to Morgan's wrists, through the sturdy iron wine rack. He knew when Morgan didn't report in, the next shift would come, find Morgan's car, and search his house. Morgan would be alright. The problem was, he didn't know how much time he had before all that would happen, so he moved quickly.

Tomcat gathered all the money he could put together, grabbed some extra clothes and headed for Lawrenceville. This time he was the one who needed a driver's license and passport. He felt sure Eddie was in Bermuda under the alias of Nils Montgomery. He couldn't call Vince to let him know where he was going. Vince's line might be tapped; besides, it was just too risky for even Vince to know his whereabouts. He would go find Eddie just as Vince had asked him to do. He had no idea what he would do after that, but he also knew he would never be able to return. Tomcat was a survivor, and at that moment he was in full survival mode. He would have to worry about the future once he secured one. Within hours, Tommy Maroni, alias Stuart Malcomb, was on a plane to escape his lack of options in the United States.

XVII. NILS'S VISITORS

Nils Montgomery was finding the caretaker's job the perfect answer to the quest for supplemental income. My modest wage for the minimal requirements of the cushy job that fell into my lap would sustain me indefinitely. Room and board was provided, and without any income tax, my simple lifestyle would be supported without dipping into any savings.

I was beginning to believe that I finally arrived at the place I was meant to be. I did odd jobs around the compound – nothing too complex to handle. There were a couple of trips to the grocery and office supply store each week to keep the compound stocked with supplies. I picked up the bank's guests from the airport and delivered them to various spots around town. Almost everyone I drove was relaxed from just being on the island, so there was rarely a hassle, especially since I was prompt and competent.

It was becoming apparent that often there were no visitors at the compound, and Maggie Gaston made it clear that I was welcome to use the facilities in this case. It was as if I owned the place much of the time. I even took to borrowing an old putter that lay around the compound and practicing on the putting green. It seemed almost everyone, from rich tourists to the working class, played golf on the beautiful courses that blanket the island, and I was developing an interest in a sport for the first time in my life. Clive invited me to play with guests on occasion, and after a few disasters it was apparent lessons were the only way to continue without being embarrassed.

In my capacity as caretaker I had frequent contact with compound guests and became the unofficial compound concierge. Soon I was recommending restaurants, golf courses, shopping and other attractions of the quaint island. Besides golf, one of my favorite activities was to accompany guests on fishing excursions off the island. I tried several charter companies, and finally decided Red Stevenson over at Castle Harbor was the best guide available. Red knew every mile of the coastline of Bermuda, and his fishing acumen and his patient tolerance for novices always left his customers feeling they got their money's worth. After a day with Red on the good yacht Doreen, guests were in a particularly good mood.

Neil "Red" Stevenson was a strapping mariner whose ruddy countenance and oversized, calloused hands were evidence of his forty-odd years of life on the sea. His buoyant swagger and sure, deliberate maneuvers on the deck of his yacht belied his sixty-odd years on the earth. He had a boundless sense of humor. As he put it, he "hailed from Scotland." Whatever landed him in Bermuda, I didn't know. There was just enough mystery about the Scotsman to make me feel we shared a kindred spirit.

Red never divulged why his boat was named Doreen. Discretion kept me from asking the question, but the veteran salt wore a wedding ring even though I knew he lived alone. The two of us became friends, and Red edified his landlubber pal in matters of boating, fishing, and the waters around Bermuda. He had a 52 foot Hatteras he used for his fishing tours and an old, teak Chris Craft inboard he taught me to pilot when there were no tours scheduled. Soon I learned the way around the island, mastered the art of docking the elegant craft and was tying a variety of knots that my maritime mentor taught me.

The reincarnation of Charlie Lofton to Nils Montgomery was quickly becoming complete. The previous existence of the studious, non-athletic, pasty skinned Charlie seemed a different lifetime. I had already developed some sun kissed color, and the new physical endeavors were exhibited by the muscles that were becoming more pronounced.

I was even going through a special form of puberty. At the pub women were becoming attractive. I was becoming aware of my ever improving physique, and for the first time I was able to appreciate the tanned and curved figures of some of the female companions who bellied up to the bar beside me. It had been a long time since the days of seeing bored, vacuous, near naked women all day, every day.

I was content, but for one thing; I missed a few people from the old life. I missed Bobby. I sort of missed Vince and the victim at the Rock. I missed Gracie's letters and missed being able to write her. If there were just some way to communicate with Gracie or Bobby, just to tell someone that mattered of my newfound joy, this new existence would feel more complete. It was a temptation that would be impossible to act on without threatening the very life I was enjoying. That fact sometimes made it hard to get to sleep at night. To compensate I would turn in about ten each night after a pint at the Hog Penny, which had proved such a lucky meeting place. I rarely had more than one pint, but sometimes it still took too long to fall asleep.

On a night before a golf lesson that was to start at eight the next morning, I wanted to be well rested, so I took an extra beer from the main kitchen to the cottage to supplement the beer at the bar. An Atlanta Braves game was coming over the satellite dish from the states as I went to the refrigerator for the beer. Before I could reach for the bottle opener, the bottle exploded in my hand with a deafening bang. I stood in stunned silence, staring at my wet empty hand unable to hear the struggle going on outside the apartment. There's no telling how long it took until I realized the ringing in my ears could not possibly have been caused by an exploding beer bottle. Eventually, the banging against the outside wall penetrated my inert state of disbelief, and it was clear there was something terribly wrong.

Charlie Lofton had never been one to deal well with emergency situations and Nils was no better. I was frozen as heavy footsteps made their way around the building to the door. There was a moment of silence as my heart pounded and my eyes grew as big as the golf balls sitting on the beer soaked counter. Suddenly the door crashed open and I emitted a guttural, involuntary scream at the large figure who returned an equally horrified wail. The AK-47 dropped from Tomcat's grip as the astonished thugs face turned to ash. He was staring at a ghost. The ghost was gazing back at the first familiar face it had seen since its last look at Eddie before the big blast.

"Jesus, Gawd, Cholly!" exclaimed Tomcat. "What da fuck... what da fuck you doin' heah?"

My liquid legs were barely supporting their quaking frame. "Tomcat?" I said trying to shake the ringing out of my skull. I didn't know what to make of Tommy Maroni's arrival in my Shangri la. "What are you doing here?"

"Ah'z huntin' Eddie fo Vince. Ah tracked him dis fah. Ah jes got to dis place, jes now. Deah was some shithead outside dat window deah aimin' ta waste one of yoos. Ah ambushed 'im, looks like jes in da nick o' time. Ah nailed 'im jes as he shot or you'd be daid. I tauht you *was* daid. What da hell's gon' on, anyway?"

I shook my head again as I noticed for the first time the bullet shattered window pane Tomcat had indicated. I stared at the jagged top of my broken beer bottle. I was as perplexed as Tomcat. Who was going after me, if it wasn't Tomcat, himself? The ringing ears and confusion of the moment made it impossible to think clearly.

"No, I'm not dead Tomcat," was all I could muster.

"Wheah's Eddie," Tomcat asked.

"He's not here, tonight," I said, the panic returning, the breathing quickening.

"Well whatevah den," said Tomcat. "Dat daid muddafucka outside was gon' do one a ya, and I'm guessin' it was Eddie, knowin' him. We gotta do somethin' wid his remains, ya know."

Tomcat could so keenly gauge these kinds of situations. Of course! Whoever was outside was going after Eddie. It was a case of mistaken identity. "Who the hell is it," I asked.

"Don't know," said Tomcat. "Tell ya one tang dough. He was a muddafucka. Ah aint had trouble wid no muddafucka like dat in a coon's age. Ah talkin bout he was PRO-fesh-a-nal. Foreign muddafucka. Ah'm sayin' Russian. Least he was talkin like dat.

Dis piece heah," he said picking the weapon up off the floor, "Russian made: A-K-fo-seven. Nice gun. Could be Russian Mob."

"Russian Mob?" I pondered aloud. The thoughts raced back to Eddie, and the pornographic pictures, and his deals with people from overseas. Who would have guessed Eddie had dealings with the Russian mob? No doubt he pissed them off and the dispatched killer was the result. If I had known the extent of trouble Eddie was in, I would have let the Russians do my bidding for me and continued life as Charlie Lofton in Atlanta. By assuming Eddie's alter-identity I had exposed myself to the most dangerous sort of criminal. Compared to the Russian Mafia, Vince's operation was college boys gone bad.

"Wheah's Eddie, anyway," Tomcat said, reading my mind, breaking the runaway stream of hysterical notions flowing through my ringing head.

Tomcat's question evoked the more immediate threat that he would discover the truth about Eddie. I continued to panic. "I can't tell you right now, Tomcat," I said. True enough – if Tomcat found out, he would surely finish what he prevented the Russian from doing. Either way, Tomcat or Russian mob, my problems had followed me to Bermuda.

"Well, help me out wid dis muddafucka, will ya," said Tomcat. I followed the massive mobster out of the apartment and around the corner to find the lifeless hulk of the would-be assassin crumpled against the wall surrounding the compound. Seeing the size of the dead man, I was impressed that Vince's seemingly out of shape Geechee goon could still handle such a menace.

I was even more impressed when the two of us had to lift the corpse and shuffle it to the porch stairs. I dropped the feet twice before we could complete the twenty-five foot relocation. Once the body was properly propped on the top step, Tomcat impatiently hoisted it over his shoulders and carried it inside. He went straight for the bathtub. I took him to the main house kitchen and he picked out various implements of mutilation. I handed him an entire box of forty-five gallon trash bags.

Without any discussion I excused myself and caught the ferry into Hamilton. Tomcat understood I didn't have the stomach for the gruesome task ahead of him. He took no pleasure in it, but he knew it had to be done. By the time I returned from the Hog Penny I was drunk, and Tomcat was done with his unpleasant job right down to returning the bathroom to pristine condition.

"Tomorra we gotta get oursevs some new luggage," the human butcher said wearily. We need some chains, too. Den we rent us a boat an' put da ole bags out to da bottom uh da sea."

Tommy Maroni was the expert at such endeavors, and I could only agree and stagger to the couch not wanting to think about where the filled garbage bags were being stored for the evening. I knew Tomcat would take the bed, whether offered it or not. There would be no golf lesson in the morning.

I awoke at ten after seven to Tommy Maroni standing over the couch holding a passport. "Ah got a passport outta yo pants wid da name Nils Montgomery on it, got Eddie's picture on it. Wha choo doin wid it?"

Still groggy, I groped silently, but could not find a good answer to Tomcat's query. "I'm using it," was all I could muster laying in a hung over fog looking up at the monster mobster.

"Uh huh," said Tomcat, "Jes wheah's Eddie?"

"I don't know," I said.

"Uh huh," repeated Tomcat, "Who wad dat daid at da Rock, anyway?"

"Hell Tomcat, I don't know," I protested, but it was plain the seasoned lug staring down at me *did* know. "Tomcat, just make it fast," I pleaded. "Just a bullet in the head, please God."

Tomcat just chuckled his ominous chuckle. "Hell, Ah ain' gon' kill ya, Cholly.

"You're not," I said, embracing Tomcat's answer with relieved wonder. "Why not?"

"Well see, Ah ain' zactly heah fo Vince. Ah got popped by some muddafuckin federal. He's a bad muddafucka, Ah tell ya whad, Cholly, it was eider tun on Vince or do da time – and Ah mean *doo da time*, bruddah. Heez ready ta frame ole Tomcat up, but good. Ah got no choice, but ta lam it, Cholly. Ah went straight ta ole Lance an' got mahsef some papers. Ah'z sposed to be lookin for Eddie anyway, so Ah put da heat on ole Lance ta tell me 'bout Eddie, an' he tole me 'bout Nils Montgomery an' Bermuda. So Ah come ta Bermuda ta find him, sose if Ah getz popped an' taken back, least Vince'll tink Ah'z heah for Eddie. Iffin Ah don't get popped den Ah through wid ole Vince an da whole ting. So Ah got no beef wid choo, see. Ah dint like dat spineless lil muddafucka Eddie, anyway." Tomcat wailed with laughter. I laughed with relief. The pair of fugitives ate breakfast and headed out to run our morbid errand.

....

Vincent Palomino was stressed and depressed. Not only was his son missing, but his right hand man had gone missing. When Vince last saw him, he was striking out to find Eddie. Whether or not Tomcat had made any progress, he surely would have made contact with his boss, but Vince hadn't heard a word from him. On top of all that FBI agents had been paying him visits, ostensibly to ask about Eddie, but he could feel the claustrophobia of a federal investigation closing in around him. Vince began to realize how much he relied on Tomcat, not only to get things done, but also for moral support. Vince's undiagnosed depression was taking its toll on him and he was sure Tomcat's presence would not only help solve problems, but would also lend some comfort to ease his intensifying sense of dread.

Instead, Vince had to worry not only about his son and the implications of Tomcat's disappearance, but about federal investigations. He had his people check out all the jails in the area with no results. He checked his usual haunts, but no one had seen Tomcat. It was time for him to launch another investigation. Normally he would turn to Tomcat for this assignment, but since he was the focus of the search, Vince would need to rely on less reliable resources.

....

Bobby had made the move, and he was officially an Assistant U.S. Attorney. His first assignment would be to help prosecute the counterfeit case he finished his career with at the Bureau. His involvement in that, along with the job change and the passage of time, put some distance between him and the Charlie Lofton investigation.

One day, Special Agent Ted Reardon called to tell him the FBI and ATF were officially putting his friend's case to rest. If they ever found Eddie, they would question him about his involvement in the Charlie Lofton death – but they had other reasons to find Eddie.

Months before, the handwriting comparison on the endorsed blackmail check yielded a positive correlation with Eddie's handwriting, providing the evidence they needed move forward. Ted Reardon and Al Milton put together an application for a warrant to search Eddie's property. Once the warrant was in hand, the team performed an all out search at Palomino's home. During their search they found not only the illegal material in his house along with evidence he was peddling it, they discovered the phone conversation on the mini-cassette I left in Eddie's car. That short conversation exonerated me and further incriminated Eddie on the child pornography charges, not to mention the extortion. They assumed he took it from me before the Rock exploded.

Ted Reardon was assigned to write summary briefs to keep Bobby apprised of the facts of the investigation. Bobby was glad Ted was on the case because of his quick instincts and his ability to extrapolate the most relevant details and produce a concise and meaningful report. Since Bobby was immersed in a complex counterfeit case, he needed this kind of support to handle the Charlie Lofton investigation the way he wanted it handled. He had breathed an incontrovertible sigh of relief when he read of the evidence on the mini-cassette.

But that was in the past, and his job now was to prosecute the counterfeit case. His quarry was in Atlanta. Interrogating the counterfeiters was the beginning of the second part of his involvement in the case, this time as a U.S. Attorney.

....

"Damn, aint nuttin cheap on dis lil island, is deah?" complained Tomcat as he and I left the store in Hamilton with luggage sufficient to send the dead Russian packing on his final journey.

"Tell me about it," I lamented. "I think I've spent more since I've been here than all the years in Atlanta."

This was a topic that was just being broached since we were reunited. "How much ya got, anyway?" queried Tomcat, not at all subtly.

I was immediately on guard. The big thug was forced to flee the U.S. in a hurry. There couldn't have been much time to garner funds. I paid for the luggage in the spirit of Bermuda hospitality, not to mention the fact I wasn't dead because Tomcat made sure the guy about to be stuffed into the luggage was. But it suddenly struck me that I might be taking on a dependent – one I couldn't afford. I was vague.

"I'm not sure," I said. "I know I've spent a lot since I got here. We can get some chains over in St. George. We can get a boat there, too. I guess we'll take the suitcases back on the ferry. We'll bring the company van back across the island."

Once we lugged the luggage the short block from the ferry landing to the cottage Tomcat packed-up what remained of the dead assassin. We grabbed the van and headed up Salt Kettle, then east on Middle Road toward the Castle Harbor. After I picked up the tab for lunch we went to get the boat. Red was replacing some lines on the Hatteras when we found him at his regular slip on the dock. I introduced my companion, Stuart Malcomb, as someone I met in the states, which was technically true. I wondered if we might take the Chris Craft out to show my visitor around the island.

"Aye," came the reply without hesitation. "The keys are in her. She may need some petrol. Keep her as long as you like."

With that, we set off to deposit our luggage in Davy Jones locker. The engine of the immaculately kept craft sparked to life with a throaty roar, as the chrome pipes belched bay water from its polished stern. Every peripheral implement in the boat was in its proper place, and once the tether lines were freed from the cleats of the dock, I coiled them and pocketed them in the side compartments just as the meticulous Red Stevenson trained me to do. When the boat was returned from its tarnished trip, it would be as trim as when it left. I had learned seamanship from the best.

First, we trolled our way around Ordinance Island where the passenger liners docked so we could pick-up the chains from the Market Wharf. Once laden with the heavy links, the vessel gathered speed and porpoised its way through the chops of St. George Harbour. As the hull of the craft slapped the lively wake of the bay, the spray cooled my outstretched hand. I scanned the sun glinted sea surface and took a deep breath of the salt air. The rush of the water and loud bellow of the engine allowed my thoughts to drift. I loved the outdoors and the sea and the life I was living. Things were going so well until the events of the previous night put a pall on my mood. The day before, I was playing golf, cleaning pools, and exploring the sea. After the thwarted assassination attempt I was preparing to load suitcases filled with mutilated human remains onto Red's boat and dump them in the ocean.

XVIII. THE RISE AND DECLINE OF VINCE

As Bobby perused the evidence in his counterfeit case he realized that no matter what kind of masterminded malfeasance he was investigating the players were generally stupid. Such was the case for the counterfeiters brought back from Belgium. After all the years, he wasn't sure why he expected these guys, David Epstein and Philip Delon, to impress him with clever schemes and a thoughtful vision of their crime. As most of the others, these two were a disappointment. The interesting thing about both Epstein and Delon was they had no prior record. Delon didn't have so much as a speeding ticket prior to this arrest. It was as though these skilled craftsmen just one day came up with a grand idea to score big at the expense of the U.S. Treasury.

There was no master plan. There was no vision. There were hardly any measures taken to conceal their criminal activity. Mr. Delon and Mr. Epstein were just a couple of talented artists and skilled printers who set-up shop in a foreign country and began selling their illegitimate wares to other criminals who probably weren't much smarter than they were. Perhaps on some subconscious level it disturbed Bobby that it took him and his colleagues so much time and effort to track down people like this.

These thoughts ran through Bobby's mind as he studied the reports in the Epstein / Delon file, which was actually a set of files taking up a small room in the Atlanta offices of the Secret Service. These craftsmen were mercenaries who did not limit their efforts to the fine art of counterfeit cash. They would print anything for the right price, and the materials recovered from their production facility revealed an extensive product line.

Along with the U.S. currency there were British pounds and German marks, and even attempts at Euros, but they apparently were never refined enough to reach the market. There were passports and drivers' licenses for various countries. There was even pornography. It was pornography of the most extreme nature – stuff that was illegal in the U.S. and most other civilized nations. It was mostly child pornography. There were whole underground magazines, in a variety of languages, devoted to perversion, depicting and describing the most depraved activities. It reminded him of the pictures they found in Eddie's house in the ongoing investigation of his friend's murder.

Bobby had to move past the pictures and the magazines. As an investigator he had experienced revolting situations of all kinds, and he could endure this depravity, too. He just didn't feel like stomaching it at the moment. He went to a drawer labeled "Associates". Inside were reports that linked Mr. Epstein and Mr. Delon to other persons both in the United States and abroad. Many of these people were innocent of any crime, but had some relationship with the pair by happenstance. Others were known criminals who were not suspected of specific involvement with these crimes. Then there were individuals the FBI believed to be involved in the case at hand. Some associates represented a lower echelon of criminal, deemed less important than the two in custody. There were a few who were heavy hitters – outlaw prizes for whom the Justice Department would give a break to Epstein and Delon if they could help nail them.

Bobby thumbed through the files of the more notorious villains. There didn't seem to be much of a criminal link between any of them and the counterfeiters. He took special notice when he came to the name Andre Petrov. The agents working on the case identified Petrov as a possible associate of the two. There were numerous meetings between his associates and them, but never in a place that was bugged. Neither Petrov nor his men had ever been introduced to any Secret Service or FBI agents, and there were no documents that linked him. If he were involved, Mr. Petrov was clever enough to distance himself from the captured criminals.

The dossier on Andre Petrov was enough to make any

investigator's mouth water. International law enforcement agencies had him pegged as Russian Mafia – one of the big ones, and one to be feared. He was in the U.S. on a work permit as an official with the Zhilsotsbank of Russia even though he had no known banking experience. His office, with its small staff, was in New York, but isolated from any of the bank's other facilities. Investigators working with the World Bank were pursuing their suspicions that Petrov and his underlings had diverted hundreds of millions of dollars from loans made to Russia for their own profit. That was the white collar side of his questionable activities.

The FBI suspected that he was fixing NHL hockey games by making terroristic threats against the families of Russian players who were still in their homeland. A vague pattern of nasty fates for the relatives of some of the apparently uncooperative players was beginning to develop. In the U.S., several individuals who had ties to Mr. Petrov turned up missing. There were few law enforcement agencies who wouldn't relish pinning something on the international gangster.

Epstein and Delon were the targets in the case, but if there were enough out there to nail Petrov, Bobby knew that Justice would be willing to cut a deal with those two. He had to spend the next week in Washington for some bureaucratic process he had to endure as a new employee of the Attorney's Office. After that he would schedule a time to visit his captives to see where they were on the Petrov matter. Even though it irked him to have to set up appointments to meet with charged criminals, they had the right to have attorneys present, and the counselors' schedules had to be considered in the process.

……..

Vince Palomino was falling deeper into depression by the day. He had Bud Bramlett looking for Eddie and Tomcat. Bud was as loyal as they came, but he didn't have the savvy and instinct of Tomcat. He was moving slowly and inefficiently in his search. Tomcat would have been further along – he would know what to say, how to reassure Vince. He had an intuition. He was also nowhere to be found. Vince had an intuition, also. His instincts were telling him an ominous future awaited him. But in his private depression he was thinking about the past – how things had been.

For a kid who grew up an only child in a lower class Italian neighborhood watching his father beat his mother until he, himself, was old enough to share the bruises of his father's drunken wrath, he had done pretty well for himself. Since he was fourteen he lived by his wits and the strength of his own self-reliance. That's when he started running numbers for the local mobster, Carmine Marino. His tough, shrewd manner caught the eye of Carmine and Paul Ducatto, and soon he was moving up in their organization. Young Vincent took care of them and they responded in kind.

When Vince asked for a meeting at the age of sixteen he arrived with a gash above a puffed eye, a bloody mouth and bruised kidneys. His mother was in as bad a condition as he, and was staying with a friend of hers in order to recover. That was the day he asked his gangster friends to kill his father. They didn't do it, but they scared the old sot so badly that he never laid a hand on his wife or his son, again. After that, Vince never associated with his father, but he held the newfound power he had over his old man's head whenever he felt he or his mother were threatened.

Within two years, Vince was out of the house for good. He was earning more money than his father, so he no longer had any use for him. Times were good. In time he paid for a divorce for his mother, and bought her a house in a better neighborhood.

Chaos theory was in full motion the day Vince left New York. He was hanging out in one of the Carmines haunts, a pool hall on the edge of the Bronx. Vince didn't play pool; he just loitered, taking in the conversation, making sparse, measured remarks when it was appropriate. Carmine, who was due to pay a rare personal visit to an adult nightclub owner to scare the shit out of him about a series of overdue payments, was on a roll at the pool table. He held the table for six games and there were already four more challengers waiting for a chance at him. He was taking all the money, and he wasn't inclined to leave.

While the next challenger was racking the balls he made his way over to Vince. "Listen, I need you to do me a favor," he mumbled out of the side of his mouth. I got this guy over in Times Square, supposed to meet me at his place in thirty minutes. I can't leave now. You can take care of it for me."

"Sure," said the eager young thug, "what should I do?"

"Here's the name of the place and the address. Just walk straight back to the office and knock on his door. Tell him you're there on my behalf, and he's to give you eighteen hundred bucks. Don't take any shit from him. Hell, that scar your old man gave you ought to let him know you're fearless and you're serious. He's been sandbagging us, and I've been letting him get by so far, but he gets no more time. Vincent, I want you to come back with that money, you hear? If he doesn't come clean – if you can't handle it, you call me on this pay phone and I'll take care of him. Here's fifty bucks for a cab to get you downtown and back."

Vince left the pool hall determined that Carmine would not have to bother himself further to collect that money. Everything should go smoothly as Carmine said, but if it didn't, he could take care of it. That would be another gold star for him in Carmine's mind.

As young Vince walked into the near empty, dank place, a voice was booming over the speakers, admonishing the few pitiful drunks inside to cough up the cash in order to coax the unattractive dancer on the stage to show more of her abundant flesh. He walked directly to the back, ignoring the cocktail waitress who accosted him to buy her a drink when he realized he didn't even know the name of the man he was supposed intimidate. He wondered if Carmine wanted it that way as he burst through the door.

"Who are you," wheezed the obese man from behind a

cluttered desk.

"I'm here on behalf of Carmine Marino, and I'm supposed to collect eighteen hundred dollars," Vince said, admiring the way he sounded.

The fat man leaned up on his chubby elbows and squinted at Vincent to assess his intruder. Vince stared right back, his expression giving up nothing. Finally, the club owner opened his mouth. "I don't think so, kid."

The condescension infuriated Vince, but he remained collected. "Come again," he said, again impressed with the tough confidence in his words. He took a chair across the desk from the man and leaned over the clutter to look into his eyes.

"I said I don't think so," came the reply. "If Carmine wants his money, tell him he can come see me about it personally. I don't do business with errand boys."

Vince could smell the liquor coming from the fat man. He maintained his resolve. "Look mister, I don't want to cause you any trouble, but I'm here representing Carmine Marino, and I will leave with what I came for one way or another. Why don't you make it easy on yourself?"

"Now you hear me you skinny little shit," said the stubborn man, his quivering jowls flushed with anger. "You get bumpkus. Now you get out of here and tell Carmine I don't deal with punks like you."

That was it; Vince couldn't help himself. "Hey you fat fuck. If you don't..."

That was all Vince could get out before the fat man grabbed a beat-up three iron from beside his desk and swung at him. Vince had to endure this kind of abuse his entire life, and he was ready for it. He ducked out of the way and jabbed the lard ass right in his belly. The man doubled over grabbing Vince's arm and locking his teeth into his bicep. Vince yelped in pain grabbing the man by the hair and ripping his own flesh away as the teeth tore free. The stench of alcohol tainted breath whistled around the skin still clenched in his enemy's mouth. The second swing of the golf club was weaker than the first, but it did catch Vince on the jaw just enough to piss him off.

Vince ripped the club from the wheezing fighter and whacked him in the temple. The blubbery human reeled backward, his eyes disappearing into their sockets, his left hand shaking violently. He had been rendered harmless, but that was not enough. Vince was in a rage. He was living his past, seeing his father beat him in a drunken fury. The transferred anger drove him on top of the surrogate tormentor, where he bludgeoned the man into an unrecognizable form.

He couldn't remember what made him stop, but he stood up, covered in blood, and went to the desk. In a deep drawer, he found a cash box holding a till filled with coins and bills from twenties down to ones. Under the till, the bottom of the box was littered with hundreds and fifties. He stuffed the bills in his pockets and, on a lucky whim, grabbed a handful of quarters. He strode quickly out into the club.

The waitress who solicited him earlier screamed at the sight of his blood covered clothes, and a tray with two beers crashed to the floor. He raced outside realizing he couldn't be out there covered in blood, so he ducked next door into an adult book store with peep show stalls.

He managed to whisk by the uninterested proprietor in the anonymous darkness of the den of iniquity. Adult bookstore patrons tend to avoid the eyes of fellow smut hounds, so he passed through the bookstore unnoticed. He was in a dark hallway lined by doors to the peep booths, and lit only by red floor lights. There was a pay phone in the back of the hall Vince prayed was working. When he got the dial tone he called the pool hall.

"Carmine," he said in an excited whisper, "there's a problem."

"What," screamed Carmine, "You tell that fat fuck that he…"

"No Carmine, I got your money," Vince said, wondering how to say what he had to tell his boss. "The problem is the guy's kind of… well, dead."

"Dead?" said Carmine. "Whadayamean dead?"

"It was like this," Vince said. "He attacked me and then I…"

“Never mind,” said Carmine. “Just get your ass back here ASAP, and we’ll discuss it then.”

“That’s gonna be a problem,” Vince said. “I’ve got blood all over me…”

“Jesus Vince,” cried Carmine, “what the hell… Forget it. Where the hell are you? I’ll come to you.”

“I’m in the adult bookstore right next to his place,” said Vince, knowing he had screwed the pooch. “There’s an open booth in the back. It’s third from the back on the right. I’ll wait there for you.”

“Stay in there,” Carmine said. “Don’t move until I get there. I won’t be long.”

Vince could hear Carmine snapping orders to his driver, Denny, before he hung up the phone. He took his place in the booth where he told Carmine he would be.

Once he locked the door he sat in the dark wondering how long it would be before help arrived – and if it would be before the police came searching the neighborhood. In the muggy darkness of the cramped space, illuminated only by a tiny light around a coin slot, time slowed to a crawl. It was silent in his cubbyhole, but he could hear the moans and sounds of sex surrounding him from the other booths.

Suddenly there was a knock on his door and he froze. "If you're gonna be in there, you gotta pay for the movies, jerk-off. Pay or zip up and get on your way."

"Okay," Vince responded, and he put money into the machine. He thanked God he had taken the coins from the dead man's office. He would never have been able to get change from the clerk without exposing his bloody appearance. He dropped ten quarters in the slot and the booth lit up as the peep hole came to life with a scratchy sex show.

Within twenty minutes Carmine was knocking on the booth. Vince let him in and Carmine handed him a bag of clean clothes. They spoke in a whisper as Vince changed.

"What the hell happened?" exclaimed Carmine in a muted scream.

"The guy attacked me, Carmine. I swear to God. I was as

nice as I could be, but the guy was crazy."

"Jesus, you sure he's dead?" Carmine asked.

"Yeah, I'd say so," said Vince trying to think of any other way it could be.

A thud struck the door. They looked at each other in silence. "Only one to a booth. You faggots break it up in there or I'll call the cops."

Vince quickly finished changing clothes as he wiped the blood from his face with his old shirt and stuffed it in the bag. The two hurried through the store front to find the proprietor at the register with his nose in one of his own magazines. They walked out into the brightness where Carmine's car was waiting. Vince looked out the back window to see the police cars outside the strip bar. As they sped away, Carmine spoke. "Jesus Vince, I said get the guy's money, not waste him."

"I know Carmine," said Vince, "but I couldn't help it. He attacked me with a golf club. I had to defend myself. Here, I got your money."

Vince reached in the bag and began drawing money from all pockets of the bloody rags. By the time they finished counting, it came to sixty-three hundred dollars. This helped to pacify Carmine.

"The cops are going to be looking for you. You're going to have to get out of town for awhile."

"Carmine, I told you, the guy attacked me. I was just protecting my life."

"Look Vincent," Carmine elaborated, "you were there to extort money from the man. You were in his office. You don't even want to try to explain that to the police. And I sure as hell don't want you to."

Within two hours Vince was on a Greyhound headed south. Carmine had a refuge on Wilmington Island in Savannah. There were friends there to take care of him. Before that Vince had never left New York, and he wasn't sure what to expect. But Carmine bought his ticket, gave him twenty-five hundred dollars and personally put him on the bus. If that was what Carmine wanted, that would be what Vince would do, and he wasn't going to complain about it – not even to himself. He could take care of himself under any circumstances. He looked forward to being at the beach in a different state, and he would be back as soon as the heat died down. He was sure of that as he rode south on US 11 through the fir lined hills of Virginia. Vincent would never make it to Savannah, nor would he make it back to New York to stay.

……..

The evening of the day Tomcat and I deposited my would-be killer into the waters off the Bermuda coast I took Tomcat to the Hog Penny to buy him dinner and a beer. The Saturday night crowd was different from the after work regulars during the week, so there was little chance of running into Clive Gaston. I was a little worried about explaining Tomcat to anyone I knew around town.

We were on our second beer when Tomcat pulled me away from the crowd at the pub and discreetly pointed out a suspicious bar neighbor. I noticed the new face the night before, but never had reason to suspect anything. Of course, at that time no one had tried turn me into the target of a Russian assault weapon. Tomcat noticed as the stranger got more inebriated his accent nuanced from one of a Yankee to one of a Russian. The square faced, fair skinned Peter Morton claimed to be an insurance executive from Connecticut, but the vodka he was swilling was blowing his cover. Tomcat suspected he was a partner of the man we just fed to the fish. Once again, the pangs of danger visited, and I was grateful Tomcat was around. As sharp as Tomcat was, I didn’t know how he measured up to someone like this. We rejoined the group where Tomcat set about handling the situation.

It wasn't long before the vodka worked its way through the suspect’s kidneys and he went to relieve himself. Tomcat arose and told me to pay the bill. He was right behind the suspected hit man about the time he pushed open the door of the loo. Soon the drunk man emerged, looking pale, with Tomcat eight feet behind. They walked straight past the bar and Tomcat motioned for me to follow. Once outside, Tomcat spoke.

"Okay, dis what we gon' do. We gon' git on da ferry and we gon' go on back to da house and we gon' straighten dis whole ting out. 'Til den, nobody sez nuttin'."

It took the ferry almost ten minutes to pull up to the dock of the Front Street terminal. Tomcat stood between me and the bogus insurance man and pulled both of us close to each side. Not a word was spoken, then or on the chilly ride back to the compound. We got off the boat and began the walk up the unlit road. After a minute, Tomcat suddenly lurched to the right taking the would-be assassin down to the ground. He drove the silencer end of a Makarov PM pistol into the back of his head. I flinched and turned, not wanting to see the results of the muffled explosion. But there was no gunshot – only Tomcat's muffled voice going off in a rapid succession of Geechee syllables.

"Okay, diz how's gon' be. Ah could keel ya right off. But Ah don' tink dat gon' do me no good, and Ah'z sho it ain't gon' do *you* no good. So heah's wut we gon' do. We gon' hike on up to da house, and we gon' tell ya a story. Ya gon' believe it too. Den ya gon' report back dat story ta whoever send ya, and ya gon' tell dem in English so weez all can heah. Now ya 'member, Ah could'a keel ya, so you do right when Ah let ya be."

With that Tomcat pulled the pitiful specimen to his feet and dragged him the rest of the way to the cottage. I followed behind in tipsy consternation.

Once inside Tomcat sat the Russian down and trained the gun on his dirt scuffed forehead. The man was shaking, and I didn't know if it was fear of his captor or fear of what the people who had sent him would do to him after he placed the phone call.

"Now, Cholly, ya tell dis man yo real name," said Tomcat.

I hesitated for a moment, but then realized only the truth could possibly quell the menace that was looming. I never went into detail of what had happened between Eddie and me with

Tomcat, and now I was about to confess to a stranger from a foreign land whose purpose it was to kill me. That's just what I did. I told the whole story of my friendship with Eddie, and the way Eddie blackmailed and tormented me, and when I could take it no more, the way I lured Eddie to the Rock and gassed him and blew him up and assumed his identities, and what I had been doing since I made it to Bermuda. When I was done it felt as if a heavy load evaporated. This confession to a couple of men of the lowest moral standards was cathartic, and even in this dangerous circumstance I felt a sense of relief.

Next Tomcat took Nils' passport and presented it to the confused man. "Look heah at dis picture - reel close - dat ain't da same man, see?"

Peter Morton squinted at the picture and then at me and said, "Hmm, I don't know."

"Come own man - heah look at da eahs in da pitcher. See dat? Aint no eah lobes dare, is it? See dare?" The sobering thug squinted silently and shook his head. Tomcat continued, "Look heah." He grabbed my head by the temples and roughly spun it so the mercenary could see an ear. "See dare? Eah lobes. See, yo man dint have no eah lobes, but dis man got 'em, and dayz all in one piece." He tugged on my ear hard enough to make my head porpoise like a bobble head doll. "See, I know how yo man lost his eahs, and he din' evah get 'em back. Dis man din' lose no eah. I sweah, dis aint yo man, see?"

Mr. Morton just nodded in agreement; there was nothing else he could do. "Now da way Ah see it, yo people don't tink much 'bout ol' Eddie Palomino, cuz – no offense – but dey ain't sendin' da A-team afta him. If dey was, Ah doubt ma buddy heah – or me, fo dat madder – would steel be heah. No, dey probly tink he gon' be easy. It time you call 'em, tell 'em what ya found out. Tell 'em dare man Eddie daid. He been daid, and he ain't gon' screw nobody no mo. You call 'em an' tell 'em right now."

Peter Morton picked up the phone and did as Tomcat ordered. He was white with fear. "It's Kobpa. I've got some info. No, not exactly. What I mean is Palomino's already, uh, taken care of. It happened back in the States. This guy here, we've been trying to get to; he did the job. I've got good evidence to support that. What should I do?"

"Heah, lemme talk to 'um," said Tomcat as he pulled the phone from Pete Morton's death grip. "Lissen heah, we don' know who you is an' Ah jes well keep it dat way. You don' know fo sho who we is. All Ah kin say is dat you aint de only one Eddie Palomino pisst off. Madder o' fac, if we knew you was gon' git 'im, we wuda let you do da deed. We dun it fo ya, so its dun. Now we din' know yo fust man dat come see us, and Ah'z sorry; we jes did wut we hadda ta keep alive. Ids nuttin' pusonal, an' I hope ya unnerstan'. Now we cudda wasted yo man heah, but we try ta do right by ya, cause we know you desuv da respect. Now, Ah know Ah cain't tell ya what ta do, but Ah'll send yo man back an' he kin give ya da whole story, an' Ah hope ya leave us be, den. But we won' stay heah, alive, so we do all we kin ta keep it dat way. Ya kin see we ain't no pushova like ol' Eddie wudda been."

Tomcat listened for a moment, then said, "Unh huh, okay den, tank ya," and he handed the phone back to Peter Morton. Peter said a couple of words in Russian and hung up the phone. He was only slightly relieved. Tomcat grabbed a disposable camera from the kitchen counter and snapped a couple of head shots of me from different angles.

"Now, you gon' walk on outta heah, an' go own down dare an' ketch da ferry back. Git dis film developed an' sho yo man da diffrence 'tween dis man an' whatever pitchers ya got a' Eddie. Sho 'em da eah, too. Den he know fo sho."

Peter Morton took the camera, left his confiscated weapon, and walked away without a word. Once he was out the door, I had to ask. "What'd the guy say?"

"Not much," Tomcat said. "Said okay, he unnerstood, an' he wud take it unner consideration. Ah don' tink we got too mucha worry 'bout, least fo awhile. Tuns out Eddie owes dem lotta cash. Dat's probly why Eddie wad takin' ya fo so much. He wad desprit ta get dese bad ais mothas offen his ais."

Damn, I thought, Tomcat is right. The Russians were

squeezing Eddie, and Eddie was squeezing me. But all Eddie had to do was ask, and I would have done all I could to help him. That just showed how paranoid he had become. He thought of me as an enemy and a target instead of a friend who could help him out of a jam.

……..

The next evening I took Tomcat back to the Hog Penny to spend a less eventful evening. The cruise ships were in from the states, and Tomcat wanted to check out the women who toured the local bars after a day of shopping and sightseeing. The bar was crowded as it usually was on the first day for the new tourists. We had a couple of beers, and I was ready to leave my buddy and get some sleep before an early morning airport run. I scanned the room before getting up, in reaction to the close call from the night before. When my eyes hit the exit I couldn't believe the vision coming through the door.

It was Gracie, there was no doubt. I hadn't seen her in person for awhile, but there was no mistaking her. She walked in boldly, her fine blonde hair teased by the steady breeze coming off the bay. She was laughing as she turned to her companion and said something with a naughty twinkle in her dancing eyes. I recognized her friend Toni Strunz from the wedding. They went straight to the bar, and my heart went straight to my head. I grabbed Tomcat by the arm and whispered the situation to him.

"Cholly, deah ain' no way ya gon' do nuddin 'bout dat. Ya jes can't. *You know* dat. Now ya jes need ta sit deah invisible like 'til Ah give ya da woird, den git up discreet like, an' git da hell oudda heah. Don' look back. Den ya gotta stay oudda sight 'til dem boats goan, ya heah me?"

I knew Tomcat was right, and it broke my heart. I sat with my back to her, craving another peek while Tomcat kept his eye on her. I was discreet as Tomcat ordered. I discreetly grabbed a bar napkin, scribbled on it and put it in my pocket.

Finally, Tomcat said, "Okay, she's gon' ta da badroom, so ya git yosef oudda heah in a hurry."

I stood and headed to the bar to pay the tab. I walked up behind Gracie's friend Toni who was guarding both their drinks, and I leaned forward to drop money off with the bartender. At the same time I dropped the folded bar napkin into Gracie's purse, turned, and went out the door. Tomcat saw my stunt, but before he could get to the purse to do anything about it Gracie reappeared from the loo. She sat down, put the purse in her lap, and ordered another beer. Tomcat watched her down the beer and leave the bar with her friend. He got up and followed them down the street toward the ships, weighing his options. He was ready to start his sprint toward the pair of girls and reach out to snatch Gracie's purse when he spotted a policeman too close to them in the cruise ship crowd. They got lost in the line that shuffled up the gangplank to board the big ocean liner. Tomcat missed his opportunity, and he went to catch the ferry to confront me at the compound.

I couldn't sleep just thinking about seeing Gracie that night. I was lying on the couch in a euphoric stupor when Tomcat burst in the door. "Whad da hell ya doin', Cholly?" he said in exasperation. "Ah tole ya not ta do nuddin'. Ya gon' screw tings up fo yosef, and me too."

I was shocked. Tomcat didn't miss a thing, and I should have known he would catch my reverse pickpocket. "Relax, Tomcat," I said. "I swear I didn't do anything to give myself away. I just wrote an anonymous note. I didn't identify myself, at all. It was just kind of a secret admirer note." I was telling only half the truth. "I won't go out again until the ships are gone day after tomorrow, I swear. But you have to promise if you see her again you'll watch her and remember everything she does – and tell me in detail what she wears, and how she looks and what she does. I won't go back out if you promise me that."

Tomcat agreed, and I was true to my word. I felt sure he would run into her again.

....

Gracie dropped onto the bed in her berth, too tired to put away her acquisitions from the day of shopping. She barley had the energy to take off her clothes. The beers with Toni at the end of the night capped off a long day, and she would sleep well and wake up refreshed for her snorkeling trip.

When she awoke the next morning she got a shower and went to the lounge for breakfast. Toni wasn't up yet so she ate a light meal alone and went back to her berth to get ready for the day. Since she didn't want to drag a whole purse around for her day on the sea she emptied her bag on the bed to pick out only the essentials. A mountain of receipts littered the normal inhabitants of the bag. She began to sort through them when she ran across the bar napkin. She didn't remember sticking it in her purse, and she almost threw it away until she noticed the pen lines on the outside folds. As she unfolded it she fell back on the bed. Her lungs struggled to replace the air that had involuntarily left her body.

She stared at the napkin with its surreal message unable to fathom how it could be there. She had to look again and shake her head to make sure she was awake. Finally, she was convinced it was real. She had no idea how or why, but she was holding a napkin inscribed with the words, "Steer clear of the bad butterflies." She sat motionless for a long time trying to understand. She eventually got up to start her day on the sea, but she couldn't get her mind off the mysterious note.

....

Tomcat went to the Hog Penny that night as he promised. He had a couple of beers and made as little small talk with the other customers as possible. A little after eight he watched the object of his friend's fascination come through the door. She was not as refined as the night before. It was obvious she spent her day in the sun and salty sea air, and while she didn't have the clean, posh style from the previous night, she exuded a healthy, radiant beauty.

Gracie walked through the Hog Penny tentatively, her eyes darting from one side of the bar to the other. She was clearly looking for something, and that something was someone in the form of Charlie Lofton, Tomcat was sure. He didn't know what was on that napkin, but whatever it was got her attention. Gracie was with the same friend as the night before, and she sat at a table at the back of the bar with her back against the wall looking over the entire floor. She was talking and smiling with her friend, but she was distracted and never stopped glancing toward every table and booth. She met Tomcat's eyes several times, noticing him notice her, but she wasn't aware of the big man's connection to Charlie.

After a salad and a beer she and her companion paid the bill and left the table. Gracie took one long, disappointed look around the bar before she disappeared to board her ship for her last night in Bermuda.

……..

Bud Bramlett was getting nowhere except on Vince's frayed nerves. Finally, Vince felt he had to take the bull by the horns. He asked Bud if he had paid a visit to Lawrenceville Lance. When Bud responded that it might be a good idea, Vince winced and dispatched the inadequate assistant to pay the forger a visit.

Lance was again anxious to help. He informed Bud of Tomcat's visit and how he told him where Eddie might be and who he most likely had become. Eddie confided his Bermuda intentions to his forgery partner should the shit ever hit the fan, and Lance knew which alias he would use. He told Bud how he gave Tomcat fake papers under the name of Stuart Malcomb. Lance did not want any trouble with Vince, and he was very clear about his conversation during his last meeting with Tomcat.

Based on Bud Bramlett's report of Tomcat's questions to Lance, Vince assumed he went to Bermuda to find Eddie, but why did he go under an assumed name. So it was possible his son was living in Bermuda and would not contact him, but he didn't know why. Then it was likely his top soldier had gone to Bermuda, but he had not been heard from, either. Perhaps there was something to the Bermuda triangle thing. Perhaps they had just been sucked up, never to be heard from again. Vince tried to laugh, but nothing was even slightly amusing to him, anymore. He spent days in his house staring at nothing, unable to assimilate what it all meant. Nothing was the same, and it probably never would be. Vince felt much older than he actually was, and his mind wandered back to when he was young, and he first arrived in Atlanta.

He got off the Greyhound in the downtown terminal about nine at night and had about an hour and a half layover. Never having set foot in another major city, he left the terminal to see what he could in the time that he had. He got in a cab and told the driver to take him to where the action was. The cabbie drove Vince five minutes north to the triangle formed by Peachtree Street and West Peachtree Street. There was a two block strip monopolized by adult entertainment clubs, theaters, and book stores.

Vince obeyed the barker who beckoned him into the door marked Bottoms Up. There was a staircase, barely illuminated by dim neon lights, leading up to bump and grind music at the top. Once inside the club Vince found a small bar surrounded by middle aged men who were mostly drunk and stuffing dollar bills in the garter of a dancer wearing a g-string and tassels on her nipples.

Vince took a seat at the bar and got a beer from the chubby waitress clad in black panties and bra. He drank slowly, bored, waiting for the time to pass before he could leave this depressing place to return to the depressing bus terminal. The action of the stripper wasn't much to see, but the action around her got heated. There appeared to be a small bachelor party getting out of hand. The guys were copping stray feels as they stuck money in the homely dancer's garter. They were getting bolder, ignoring the protest of the poor lady who was looking around for help. As the scene continued the men began crawling on the stage. Soon the drunks were groping the frightened woman, and they began taking the money out of her garter. She was desperately looking around for help, but there was no bouncer around to handle the situation. Finally, another girl jumped onto the stage and tried to help, but she quickly fell victim to the groping mob.

Vince thought about it for only a few seconds, and then jumped up on the bar. He grabbed a couple of marauders by the nape of their shirts and threw them off the stage. They tried to climb back and attack Vince, but the girl who came to help hit them both with a chair. Meanwhile, Vince had the other two. He kneed one of them in the crotch and then punched the other one in the face. He seized their limp carcasses and dragged them to the top of the stairs where he dropped them tumbling to the door at the bottom. He then moved back to the stage to take care of the drunks staggering up from the floor. They attacked him, but he was more of a fighter than either of them. Just as he was getting the better of them, he felt a violent yank from behind. Suddenly he was on the floor with the baton of an Atlanta cop pinning his neck to the ground.

Soon the violence was over. He and the other combatants were hauled up to their feet and handcuffed. They were being led out when a man identifying himself as the owner stopped the police from carrying Vince out with the others. They pulled off his cuffs and led him to a back office. Vince was cursing himself for getting involved. For all he knew, there was some kind of nationwide lookout for him from the New York Police. He sat alone in the office for nearly an hour while the police did their paperwork and sent the bachelor party to the city jail. He was wondering how he could be so stupid when the owner finally opened the door.

"Jesus son, I almost forgot you were in here," he exclaimed. "Hey, I took care of things between you and the cops. My name's Joe Howard. Thanks for helping us out. I don't know where that worthless bouncer of mine got off to. You look like you can handle yourself pretty well, especially for such a small fella. If you ever want a job you let me know, and I'll put you on the payroll, no questions asked." Those were fateful words for both Vincent Palomino and Joe Howard – and the other owners of the Bottoms Up Club.

By that time the bus was on its way to Savannah without Vince, and he was considering Joe's offer. He asked Joe to get him to a motel room so he could get some rest. He would call Carmine from there and explain what happened so they wouldn't be expecting him in Savannah.

The next afternoon Vince was at the Bottoms Up Club to apply for a job. Joe wasn't there, and he was sent to the Nitery two doors down the strip. There he found Joe in one of his many offices. As Vince walked in Joe stood up to greet him. Vince was taken aback by the gesture. The boys in New York would never show him that kind of consideration, even though he knew they liked and respected him.

"Well, if it isn't the hero of last evening," Joe said with a grin as he shook his hand and motioned for him to sit down. "What brings you back here?"

"You said something about a job," Vince said in what was then a thick New York accent.

Joe backed up, cocked his head and squinted his eyes in Vince's direction. "Yeah, I s'pose I did, didn't I. Hmf, I didn't know you would want one. Like I said, I like the way you handle yourself. Tell you what...what's your name?"

"Vincent Palomino," came the response.

"Whoa, that's your real name? Sounds like something out of the movies. Tell you what, Vincent Palomino. I'll give you thirty bucks a night, cash, to start. You show up on time, stay sober while you're at work, and keep your hands off the ladies. Do that and pretty soon I'll make it more. There are three clubs and a bookstore that we own here on the strip. You might be at any one of the three clubs. I'm always somewhere along here around six. You find me and I'll tell you where I need you. You can walk out when you get the last customer out the door around four a.m. What do you think?"

"Deal," said Vince and again Joe shook his hand. Vince had

heard about people in the south being polite, but Joe's affability took him by surprise. He thought he might enjoy spending some time in Atlanta, but he was sure he would soon be back with the people who really knew the score.

Joe took him out to introduce him to the employees of the Nitery, then took him a few doors over to the Gaslight Follies and finally to Bottoms Up. The girls were just getting into work, and most didn't seem interested in meeting this miniature bouncer who had the physique of a stick of Juicy Fruit. Once Rachel, the fighting dancer from Bottoms Up, recognized who he was, she took his hand and introduced him to her fellow dancers telling them the story of the night before.

The other bouncers eyed Vince with suspicion. They were all bigger than he was, and it was obvious they thought Joe was crazy when he told them Vince would be a bouncer. The new guy's thick accent made them even more wary. Nevertheless, Vince started to work that day, and he did just as Joe told him.

Vince acquired a strong sense of loyalty while working with his mentors in New York. He carried this with him to Atlanta. For two months, he was on time every day, stayed sober and professional at work, and had no trouble keeping his hands off the dancers. While there were a few young, pretty girls, he considered the others over the hill. None of them was very bright, and he didn't know any of them who didn't have personal problems. Vince knew he was the best bouncer Joe had on the payroll. For those two months the money he was getting was good, and he still had most of the cash Carmine gave him when he left New York. But Joe promised him a raise and Vince had kept his part of the bargain.

Joe was as friendly as ever and listened politely to Vince's reasoned petition. He said he had to talk to his partners, and he would get back to him. This irked Vince. He had met the other owners around the club. They were all silent partners, mostly businessmen who didn't have a clue about running an enterprise on the edge of illegitimacy. Since they were silent partners Vince was sure Joe didn't have to go to them for permission to give a bouncer a raise, but he trusted him to get back to him.

After almost two weeks Vince approached Joe again. Joe smiled politely and said how busy he had been, but promised to get back, again. Another week was all Vince needed. When he got no response, he was ready to make a move. That polite sonofabitch didn't respect him enough to tell him yes or no on a raise. His associates in New York lacked the pleasantries of his employer in this emerging southern city, but at least when they told you something you could take it to the bank.

Compared to Carmine, these guys were chumps, and Vince was tired of working for them. He could have just left, probably gone back to New York, since according to Carmine the police didn't have a clue about who killed the strip club owner – and didn't seem anxious to solve the crime. But he had another idea. He placed a call to Carmine and worked out a plan to shake down the Atlanta partners and take over the business.

Carmine was interested. He was surprised to learn how thoroughly Vincent developed the plan. It would be good to have operations in Atlanta. Not only was it an opportunity to expand markets in the south, they could use the Atlanta company for other various purposes, such as laundering cash and fronting for illicit activities. Vince wanted to head up the operation, but Carmine wasn't going to hand that over to such a young kid who was in Atlanta because he flew off the handle in New York. Over Vince's protests Carmine sent Paul Ducatto and a couple of lieutenants down to execute the plan. Vince didn't like it, but he had to defer to Carmine's judgment.

From the time Paul arrived the two were at odds. Vince knew how much he impressed Carmine, and he wanted to put his mark on this operation. Carmine's praise of Vince and his insistence on doing things his way was a threat in Paul's mind. Vince was instrumental in the process, but he constantly angered Paul who complained to Carmine. Carmine managed to keep enough peace between the pair, and in short order Joe Howard and his partners were in the clutches of Carmine Marino and company.

It didn't take long to tear down most of what Joe and his partners had built up, through blackmail and intimidation – including the after hours bombing at an empty club of Joe's. Finally, Carmine himself came to Atlanta and met with all the partners. He offered to buy the business out for a song, and that marked a new beginning for the adult clubs. When the meeting broke up, an embittered Joe Howard looked at Vincent.

"I should've known not to trust you," he said quietly. "I wish I had never taken you in."

Joe could have trusted him right up to the point he screwed him. But Vince maintained his decorum to further impress Carmine. "Hey," he responded calmly, "all you had to do was respect me."

That was the end of Joe and all of his partners, except one. There was a dentist there who wanted to reinvest. He offered respectability in the community as well as some local connections with police, which was attractive. Carmine considered it, listened to Vince support the dentist's position, and let Dr. Herbert Dutton stay involved.

That was the moment Carmine Marino expanded into Atlanta and set-up the business Vincent Palomino eventually operated. Vince and Herb Dutton ran the strip clubs, provided fronts for prostitution, and provided illegal parlay card betting on college and pro sports. Through Herb's local contacts, Vince muscled his way into the sanitation and laundry businesses and invested in several restaurants. Through these legitimate businesses, they washed all the illegal cash Vince was making. Vince and Carmine cultivated their business partnership and friendship in short order, and under Vince's leadership the southern operations made a lot of money for the entire organization.

Vince was well respected for the way he handled things away from the home office, and Carmine eventually brought him officially into the organization. The day he returned from New York as a newly made man, Vince went to celebrate at Tara, one of his restaurants in downtown. A pretty girl, whom he hadn't seen before, waited on him. The next day he took her out, and in three months Sarah Harland became Mrs. Vincent Palomino.

There were bumps in the road, but Vince was enjoying his life. After trying for three years to have a child, Sarah discovered she was unable to conceive. At first she was devastated, but the opportunity arose to adopt a son and both she and Vince were fulfilled. In a sincere and politically savvy move, Vince named his son after his surrogate father, Edward Carmine. The world became Vince's oyster.

Then something happened that would tarnish the pearl of a life he was leading. Carmine Marino suffered a fatal heart attack. Paul Ducatto ascended to Carmine's throne. Paul had not forgotten the uneasy relationship he and Vince shared when he was in Atlanta, and there continued to be friction after he took over for Carmine. Vince was too good an earner to make wholesale changes in Atlanta, but Paul didn't make things easy for him. In fact, he squeezed him in ways Carmine never would have. It was clear Paul favored Herb Dutton, which chapped Vincent. Herb wasn't even a made man.

Despite Vince's protests, Paul kept the heat on him. For awhile Vince thought about doing something about it, staging a coup or something, but he was too far removed from the scene in New York. Besides, even with the problems he was doing well. He eventually got used to the environment, but he never missed a chance to demonstrate to Paul what they both knew. Vince was smarter and more capable than his boss, but Paul had been the one who was in line to inherit Carmine's position. Paul felt threatened by Vince, and he wasn't entirely unjustified.

If Vince couldn't do anything about his competition in New York, he could damn sure make himself the only game in town down south. When Herb died at the hands of the exploding Craftsman Model 29DS grill, it was not his own stupidity that mixed up the gasoline with the lighter fluid, but Vince's calculating idea. He had been to a couple of Herb's barbeques and taken note of the way he soaked the coals for so long in the covered grill as well as how he soaked himself with alcohol.

He knew what would happen when a flame hit the confined fumes inside the metal case of the new grill, which could be lit without removing the top. Herb's only offense was to be more liked by Paul than Vince was, but that was a capital crime in those cutthroat days.

Vince purposely came to the party late that day, both to deflect suspicion of his involvement in the explosion, and to avoid injury. Too bad about the death of Charles Lofton Sr. and Mary Dutton's crippling injuries, but he justified them as collateral damage. After that, Paul extended an olive branch, but Vince, confident in his position, rejected his gestures of goodwill.

Now, in his depression, Vince felt regrets. His son and his top lieutenant were missing. He didn't know why. Was Tomcat involved with the authorities, or was he in bed with Paul Ducatto? Or had Ducatto done something to Tomcat... or Eddie? He was in the dark, feeling insecure. He didn't know why, but his gut was warning him of impending doom. He regretted the way he handled Paul Ducatto over the years. He wasn't sure if he regretted not taking him on and taking him over, or after deciding not to act against Paul, he regretted not treating him with more respect. But the chain of events that would put an end to his world had nothing to do with his strained relationship with Paul Ducatto. No, the butterfly of chaos for Vince was flapping her wings in Bermuda. A storm was brewing in the Atlantic, and it would land in Georgia soon enough.

....

Assistant U.S. Attorney Robert Wells signed in at the Federal Building the day he would meet with Epstein and Delon and their lawyers. The case was complex, but Bobby's men had been thorough, and they felt confident they would convict. It was unusual that the prosecutor who would be working the case was so intimately familiar with it. The lead prosecutor, Linda Egan met him outside the meeting room.

Their strategy was planned, and it was simple. Lay out the well prepared facts and see what the busted criminals had to offer. If they were going to be reluctant, Bobby would start offering areas where they could help themselves.

As Bobby and Linda suspected, this pair was scared. There was a team of three lawyers who were jointly representing them. They had never been in trouble before, and their attorneys were anxious to deal. They started with how the phony money was getting into Georgia. That cooperation would earn them only a little leniency upon conviction.

The money was being shipped into Savannah by freighter in big rolls of paper. The printers rewound the printed bills with a thick layer of unprinted paper. The bills of lading identified the pallets of bad bills, simply as "Raw Material – Paper". If any inspector cut through the wrapping to see what was inside, he would see white paper. Once the rolls were off-loaded, an independent and innocent trucking company picked them up from an expediter's warehouse and moved them to a warehouse in Lawrenceville. There it was unwound and cut into individual bills. From there, a character by the name of Lance Dawson got them into the marketplace through a distribution network.

Bobby was taking notes. Soon a judge would issue a warrant to search the premises of an expediter in Savannah and the address of Lance Dawson in Lawrenceville. They would also take Mr. Dawson into custody. Linda asked the lawyers what else their clients could offer.

"What are you looking for, and what will it do for my clients," asked one of the lawyers.

"Depends on what they can do for us," Linda responded. She ticked off the names of a few criminals Bobby listed. Epstein and Delon made a couple of veiled comments and consulted with their lawyers. When the name of Andre Petrov came up, Delon and Epstein became silent and couldn't avoid looking at each other. There was a long, loud hush.

"Gentlemen," Linda cut into the silence, "if you want to discuss Mr. Petrov, that could be beneficial for both of us."

The defense huddled and whispered. "How beneficial would

it be to Mr. Delon and Mr. Epstein?" one lawyer finally asked.

"That depends," said Linda. "If we pin something on Petrov and damage him, it could substantially reduce prison time. If we put Petrov out of commission for good, well your boys here have no priors, they'd be helping to put away someone the entire international community wants to get...I would think their problems would be minor at worst.

There was another huddle. "You understand our clients would be putting their own lives in danger by implicating Petrov," said a lawyer.

"That can be handled," Linda said. "If we get what we want, we put them in the witness protection program. As long as they do what we say and keep their noses clean, they'll be safe."

"Let us think this over and we'll get back to you..." the counselor began, but Linda cut him off.

"This is not a routine business deal, gentlemen. Your client's future is on the line. It's now or never; make your decision."

Bobby tapped Linda on the shoulder. It was the prosecutor's turn to huddle. They moved outside the room. "I say we give them some time," he whispered.

"Tell me why," Linda asked. Her experience told her to put the pressure on the perpetrators to cough up the goods. She knew Bobby was new, but he had been through the process as an FBI agent and she was listening.

"These guys are scared. They're scared of us, but they're probably more afraid of a guy like Petrov. We can put them away for a few years, but he can put 'em away forever. The lawyers here are competent, but they aren't the tops. They might not even realize how strong our case is. If we force them to decide now, they could panic and make the wrong choice. It's obvious they have something on Petrov. We can let them have some time; meanwhile we demonstrate more clearly to counsel how strong our case is, and how serious we can get about people screwing with our monetary system. And, it'll give us more time to think about how we want to proceed. After all, we'll have another one in custody soon. We can see what he has to offer."

Linda agreed. She turned to the adversaries and said, "You've got a week to come up with your answer. Let’s set up a meeting, and we will expect your answer then." The parties went their separate ways to consider their options.

……..

Bobby and Linda were in the holding cell of Lance Dawson. They were told it would be over an hour before his tardy attorney would arrive. In the meantime, Lance was given his rights, but they were lost to his strong desire to stay out of prison. Even though he had been in law enforcement and should have known better, Linda and Bobby were suddenly his best friends, and he was spilling his guts. Bobby took notes on the various players who purchased the fake money. The next day there would be more warrants and more arrests. Lance was turning state’s evidence without even securing a deal for himself. It was almost pitiful, Bobby thought.

Finally, once they soaked the arrestee for everything they could on his clients, Bobby took a stab. "What do you know about Andre Petrov," he asked.

"Whoa, man," Lance exclaimed, "I've heard of him. I've never met him, but I know he's a bad dude. I had a client. He was shipping out some sensitive material to Petrov’s operation. Evidently, he was getting paid for this stuff and getting pretty far behind in his shipments. Finally, he skipped town with some of the Russian's money. One of Petrov's men came to me looking for him awhile back. I didn't know where he was, but I can guess he's somewhere six feet under by now."

"What was this guy providing to Petrov," Bobby asked, trying to see what the Russian was up to in Georgia.

"Porn stuff, man," said Lance. "Bad stuff – kiddie porn. I didn't have anything to do with it, I swear. I just know the guy who was doing it and gave him some credentials to skip town.”

Bobby's head spun in amazement and he asked the question too eagerly. "Who was this guy supplying the child pornography?"

Lance must have suddenly realized how much he was talking, and how much trouble he was creating for himself. Perhaps his remote, non-relationship with the Russian Petrov made him feel insulated from him. But Vincent Palomino was in his back yard, and Vince represented a real and immediate threat. Whatever the reason, it occurred to him to clam up. "Oh, it was some nobody. I can't even remember his name. I'll try to get it for you, if I can find it."

"Let me help you refresh your memory," Bobby said, less like a lawyer and more like a personally interested party. "Was this guy named Eddie Palomino?"

Lance couldn't have been more transparent. His wide eyes shot straight into Bobby's, then darted toward an empty space on the wall. "No," he declared, too abruptly.

Linda looked at Bobby, puzzled. That name was nowhere in the documents they studied for the case. She let Bobby proceed.

"It wasn't?" Bobby said skeptically. "How can you be so sure? You just said you couldn't remember who it was."

"Well I know it wasn't him," Lance retorted indignantly.

"Oh, it wasn't *him*," Bobby interrogated. "Just who is him, this Eddie Palomino?" That's what Linda silently wondered.

"I think you know as well as I do," Lance spat back in frustration.

"Yes, I do," Bobby said, "and I want to find Palomino. If you know what's good for you, you'll give him up."

"Look man," Lance cried in desperation, "I told you, you're too late. That guy Petrov's wasted Palomino by now."

"You seem mighty sure of that," Bobby probed. "You said you didn't have any information on Palomino to give the guy. I think you did. I think Petrov's man came into your place and scared the shit out of you, and you were willing to give Palomino up to save your own ass. It's just like you're scared of me and what I can do to you. And if you know what's good for you, you'll tell me what you told Petrov's man."

Lance was nailed and he knew it. He gave up the most likely alias for Eddie and the most likely place he would be, but he reiterated that he probably had not survived the Russian. Maybe so, Bobby thought, but he was going to make sure.

IXX. THE RESURRECTION OF CHARLIE LOFTON

Once our second would be assassin was dispatched and Gracie sailed out of my fantasy world, the routine returned to Bermuda. Tommy and I were still meeting at the pub in the afternoons several times a week, but Tommy was going to a girlfriend's he picked up at the bar one night. That left me to my own devices at the compound. I was happy my buddy was becoming less dependent on me, but slightly suspicious of his motivation. After all, it was possible Tomcat was not keen on dealing with any more Russians over at the compound. That left me to worry about another visit from a man on a mission.

One Friday evening, Tomcat put down more than his share of beer. I was feeling no pain either, and I invited Tomcat over to cook out some steaks thinking it might be nice to have my menacing friend seen around the premises. Back at the apartment more beer flowed, and we got into a rare, alcohol induced heart to heart. In that state, one can never say how the conversation wends along from one subject to another, but it turned to the subject of killing for hire.

"You mean to tell me you don't take it personally when somebody comes all the way to this island for the sole purpose of killing you?" I said.

"Nah," replied Tomcat, his eyelids drooping under the weight of a full meal and intense inebriation. "Is jes bidness, nuddin pusinal. Ids a job an' somebody gotta do it."

"I know why you look at it that way," I said, sober enough to avoid pissing off Tomcat. "You're in the business. You understand the other side of it. What's it like? What's it like to have to kill somebody?"

"Cholly, ya 'magine too much," Topcat said with a sly grin. "Tings don' always happen like ya 'magine or somebody say. Ah din' go round killin' bunch o folks."

"Yeah, but you have killed before," I pressed.

“I kilt da man dat’s gon’ kill yoo,” Tomcat said. “Ya got a problem wid dat?”

“No, but you have done Vince’s bidding for him, I’ve heard,” I said.

“Ya can’ always believe whacha heya, now can ya?” said Topcat. Then he said, I din’ do a bunch a killin’ fo Vince. Ah had mah limits, too. Fo one, Vincent know Ah won'd do in no women. Vincent know dat."

"Women?" I was intrigued. I thought Vince only ordered violence against thugs like himself. I didn't know of any female gangsters around town. "Vince actually killed women?”

"Not offin. Ah know he wan' me ta do Mary Lofton. Ah sed no way. I tink he did dat hissef."

At first I didn't absorb what Tomcat said. I did a complete double take and looked at the sleepy hood. Did he realize what he just said? At that moment Nils Montgomery ceased to exist and my senses sharpened.

"What, Tomcat," I asked in disbelief. "What was that?"

"Ah say Vince did Mary Lofton, hissef," Tomcat replied, obviously oblivious to the ramifications of his disclosure.

"My mother!" I screamed. “Or my grandmother? Vince killed my mother?" I realized my grandmother’s name was Dutton.

This rattled Tomcat awake, and he realized what was happening. "Oh jeez Cholly, Ah fergot. Idz bean so long, and Ah so drunk, Ah fergot all 'bout huh bein' yo mama. Ah sorry Cholly."

I was suddenly wide awake, but still drunk. "Are you crazy? Why would Vince want to kill Mother?"

"Don' ass me," Tomcat said, clearly shaken awake at his own impropriety. He had been out of the game for too long. "Dat wuz 'tween Vince an' Mary. Ah din't wont nuddin' ta do wid it."

I didn't know what to do. Without another word, I walked out of the apartment, got in the company van, and drove blindly around the island. I was bewildered. It must have been hours, but finally exhaustion set in, and I found myself back at the compound where I fell asleep in the van.

Sleep was fitful, coming and going as I thrashed in the reclined seat. When the sun eventually pelted me with its infernal island heat, and my back ached intolerably, I climbed from the van and staggered my way into the apartment. Tomcat was snoring on the couch.

An exhaustion infused hangover brought on a lack of judgment. I found my way to the bedroom and threw a random assortment of clothes into an overnight bag along with my passport. Next, I grabbed a boxful of cash, unaware of how much it was, but sure it would last for my purposes. Back in the great room, I checked to see that Tommy was soundly slumbering, then rifled through his sport coat to find a baggie full of white powder he had been peddling around the bars to earn money. Thinking it would come in handy, I pocketed the crystal speed. In my last moment of any modicum of rationality, I put ten fifties back in the coat to replace the baggie. Completely ignorant of the value of the speed, I paused and stuck in two more fifties. On my way out the door, I grabbed a full bottle of vodka from the main building.

Driving the van to the airport I considered how ironic it was that Vince killed my mother behind my back, and I killed his son in the same manner. I tried to determine which was the bigger crime or the most sinful, but I wanted to hear Vince's take on that puzzle.

The bottle of Stoli was rolling down my throat as the van careened along Middle Road. Halfway to the airport, I pulled off on Tribe road, which was small and empty of traffic at the early hour on Saturday. It was a good spot to lay out the powder on the console of the company vehicle. I wasn't worrying about consequences at the moment.

By the time I got to the airport, I was wired drunk. There was one flight to Atlanta, and it wasn't leaving for almost three hours. I was able to get a first class seat on the flight, using Nils' passports and credit cards. I felt like another different person, and I simply wanted to travel in comfort. I checked my bag and prayed the flight would take off before Tommy could wake up, realize what happened, and find his way to the small airport. The single purpose of the moment was to get to Atlanta and find Vince so we could both air our dirty laundry. I was so slaphappy from lack of sleep and alcohol and drugs, I didn't consider the danger of the mission.

At boarding time the bottle of Vodka was two thirds empty, and there was a dent in the baggie from several trips to the men's room stall. The bottle went into the restroom trashcan, and the baggie was stuffed into my back pocket.

Once the plane was off the ground, I got a drink and made a trip to the head for a booster snort. If it weren't for the speed, exhaustion would have overtaken me and provided the sleep I needed to think clearly.

The drugs cleared customs in Atlanta. The disinterested agent asked the standard questions and got the standard answers. I was visiting the states for pleasure. I would be staying a week. I really believed I would be back in Bermuda the next day. No, I wasn't bringing any fruit into the country. A smile and I was past the customs counter. Next I held my alcohol saturated breath as the luggage passed by on the conveyor belt, but no one was interested in my cash stuffed bag.

The young man at the car rental counter displayed the most suspicion as he looked at my weary eyes. There was no telling if he could smell the alcohol exuding from my body as I tried to speak to him without exhaling. He took a deep last look and hesitantly handed over the keys to a Ford Taurus parked in space eighty-eight.

Walking out of the airport into the garage was like walking into a blast furnace. The moist, hot air, infused with jet exhaust, buffeted its way through man-made wind tunnels. The deafening roar of the planes lumbering around nearby taxiways ricocheted off the concrete components of the structure. As unpleasant as it sounds, it felt good to be back in my hometown. There was a welcoming familiarity to all of it.

The Taurus provided insulation from the airport environment. Even though it was suffocating inside the car, I used the key to dig out some speed and shove it up my nose before I started it up and beckoned the air conditioner to combat the heat.

Driving out of the dark cover of the parking deck directly into the sunlight of a summer Saturday afternoon in Atlanta, I felt as if a horrible hangover was waking me from the dreamlike encounter with Tomcat the night before. The drugs were kicking in about the same time as the air conditioner, and both were having contrasting effects as my eyes were adjusting to the bleached glare of the industrial area around the airport. There was a liquor store on Cleveland Avenue where I was able to restock on vodka.

Outside the rent-a-car, the humidity accentuated the rancid stickiness coming from the pores of my skin. There were three black men wearing battered jeans and construction boots sitting on the curb sipping from brown paper bags. It seemed they looked at me with pity as I struggled into the store. Their comments about me faded as the door slowly closed them out. At first I picked-up a fifth, but then decided on a half gallon, then a second half gallon. What the hell, I thought, and carried the fifth to the counter along with the two half gallons. The thought of confronting Vince from the grave summoned the need for courage I didn't possess. It had to be found in the bottles the clerk was ringing up on his register.

Back outside, the three men clammed up as I passed by them and fell back in the car. Once inside the Taurus, I took a cue from them by peeling the top of the bag down below the neck of the fifth, and unscrewing the cap to slug back a shot.

The skyline of the city dawned on the horizon as the Taurus wove around the curve and over the crest of the downtown connector approaching University Avenue. Sun glinted off the gold dome of the state capitol building in the foreground through the familiar summer haze of downtown Atlanta, as the skyscrapers loomed in a silhouette background. Passing the city on the left I broke into incomprehensible laughter. Trying to drive in my state of mind was more difficult while doubled over in hysterics, but it felt great to be there.

Vince lived north of the city, just outside the perimeter, but something drove me to drive into Buckhead. The car was being drawn to the scene of the crime, the neighborhood where I became all the things I had become – a fatherless kid scared of his own raving grandmother, an excellent student, an expelled student, a hood, a fraud, a killer, a dead man, and Nils Montgomery. Nostalgia visited itself upon me as Habersham Road wound along a rise, and finally around the turn that led to the big, ivy covered hill.

The slope had changed shape, and there was no ivy – only barren dirt where heavy bulldozers and dump trucks tracked their way back and forth to clear the land and begin construction on what a sign announced would be a big Italian villa. I had to take the rent-a-car up the familiar hill. All the rubble was gone and the only structure remaining was the garage, I peeked in to see that the contractor was apparently keeping it as a storage facility for equipment. I wondered how much Emmett Brandice got for the valuable property to put into the trust. Whatever it was, I was sure I wouldn't be able to get my hands on it. Perhaps the new house would provide better karma for its occupants than the Rock afforded Eddie.

The next stop would be Vincent's. After a couple of more snorts of vodka and crank, I pulled the rent-a-car up to the curb at the end of Vince's expansive lawn. The house sat perched behind perfectly manicured hedges, seemingly waiting for a visit from the one who wanted to sashay right up and inform its dangerous proprietor of the true fate of his son. Sarah Palomino would be at their San Francisco home this time of the year.

I walked deliberately to the front door and banged loudly with the oversized knocker. After waiting, I banged with more intensity. No one came, so I staggered back to the car and drove to a motel to check in for the night.

I hit the bed in exhaustion, and sleep quickly overcame me. I slept hard as uncounted hours of dreams floated through me. There were images of being back in the paradise of Bermuda, of fishing with my pal Red Stevenson. Then I would be puttering around the compound, trying to mend some minor malfunction in order to keep things nice for the guests. There were the golf courses and the trips in the van, showing the guests around the island. But the ever present butterfly was never far off, constantly circling overhead, determined to find a way to interfere with the pleasant dreams.

....

It didn't take agent Ted Reardon long to pick-up the trail of Eddie Palomino, a.k.a. Nils Montgomery, once Bobby related Lance's story. On a tip from Bobby, he checked airline records for the dates surrounding the Habersham explosion, and was pleasantly surprised at how quickly Mr. Montgomery's name came up on a US South passenger list dated two days after the incident. He made arrangements to meet with officials in Bermuda on Saturday morning. Eddie chose a beautiful place to spend his alias life, but Bermuda wasn't such a good place to hide once someone knew you were on the island.

The cliche, follow the money, rings true with FBI investigations. With the help of a magistrate, Ted was given the services of Officer Jon Hill and the proper documentation to inspect bank records to look for a customer account under the name of Nils Montgomery. The Commonwealth Trust Bank was fourth on a list of banks sorted in no particular order.

It was shortly after lunch that Ted was introduced to Mr. Clive Gaston, Manager of Customer Accounts for the bank. After the pleasantries, Ted spoke.

"Well, Mr. Gaston," he began, "we are interested in a depositor by the name of Nils Montgomery. We were hoping you would be so kind as to check your records for us."

Clive displayed a rather puzzled look. "Yes sir, well there's really no need to check the computer, Officer Reardon, now is there. You see, Mr. Montgomery works for the bank."

Ted brightened at the news. "Is that right," he said, thrilled that he wouldn't have to work very hard to track down this yoyo. "Is this Mr. Montgomery?" Ted asked, handing a picture of Eddie to the bank manager.

Clive studied it carefully, squinting to focus on the face. "It looks a bit like him. Maybe so," he finally remarked.

"What does he do?"

"He's a caretaker at a complex we have across the harbour in Paget. I know him well. What's he done," Clive asked with genuine concern.

"Let’s just say you may not know him as well as you think, Mr. Gaston," Ted said. “Where exactly is this place?"

"It's over on Salt Kettle. The ferry stops right at the dock at the end of the road. It's a short walk up on the left; you can't miss it."

"Right, I know where it is," said Officer Hill. We can go around the harbour in the car."

"Does he have a vehicle," the experienced investigator knew to ask.

"He's got a company van,” said Clive. “It's white I think. I don't know the license plate, but I can get that for you. You'll probably find him there, but if you don't, call me and I'll have that plate number for you."

To Ted's dismay there was no van and nobody at the compound. They called to get the tag number from Clive Gaston, and Jon Hill put in a request that the police look out for the van. The two law officers settled in to wait for their suspect to arrive. As the day wound down and Montgomery had still not shown, Ted called back to Clive's office. When he found out that Nils frequented the Hog Penny, Hill agreed to continue to wait while Ted took the ferry across the harbor.

After he watched the pub from a bar stool for an hour, Ted was sure it was a dead end for the evening. He checked in with Jon Hill on the radio issued to him, and waited to be picked up on Front Street. He considered the situation while he waited. Was it possible Palomino knew the FBI was closing in, and went into hiding? How would that happen? As Hill pulled up, Ted suggested they go to the airport. On the way they alerted security there and had them check the parking lot for the van.

By the time Hill pulled onto airport property, they got a call advising them that the van was found in the parking lot. Jon Hill dispatched a team to search the premises for the man in a picture he circulated and ordered surveillance on the van. Ted called Clive Gaston to ask when he last saw Montgomery.

"He took some clients of the bank to the airport on Thursday two weeks ago; I'm sure of that," Clive said after checking his daytimer.

Hill had the airport police start reviewing tapes from security cameras for the two week period. Then he and Ted went to the airlines to see if their suspect had flown out under the name of Nils Montgomery or Eddie Palomino during that time. Ted knew that this could prove a more tedious quest than his relatively easy breakthrough with US South in Atlanta. U.S. South was the first carrier he approached in Atlanta since it was their home office hub city, and they handled the most traffic in and out of there. During his search in Atlanta Ted was almost certain he was looking for a flight to Bermuda, and he had a fairly tight initial time frame with which to look. From Bermuda Palomino could have taken any number of airlines to any number of destinations. Nevertheless, he started with US South since that was the airline of Palomino's choice for the trip into Bermuda. They started their search with the date Clive had given as Palomino's last known day in the island. The U.S. South reservation agent assigned to the task was helpful, but slow. It took two more reservation agents until four the next afternoon before the Montgomery name surfaced on a passenger list for a flight bound for Atlanta. Ted picked up a phone in exhausted elation to notify his team in Atlanta. He thanked his host, Officer Hill, and caught a six-fifteen back home.

....

I finally awoke to static and snow emanating from the small TV of the motel room. The sunlight slicing through the blinds indicated it was daytime. I groped for the remote hoping the television would provide a clue as to where I was and what day it was. Slowly I remembered I was in Atlanta, and judging from the religious programming on a local channel, it was

Sunday. I spotted the crystal meth strewn across the nightstand, and I remembered pulling it out of my pocket and tossing it there before I stretched out to sleep.

I leapt from the bed still wearing the clothes I had on when I left Bermuda, and I opened the door to the outside. The sign hanging from the doorknob was showing *Do Not Disturb.* Fortunately, the staff had taken that request to heart. I closed the door and cleaned the powder from the table. Then I took a long cleansing shower. The overnight bag I brought had one change of clothes, which I threw on before heading out the door.

Back in the car I reassessed the wisdom of coming back to the states. A bank sign flashed the time and temperature. It was just past seven in the morning and it was already eighty-two degrees. I had to pull over and gather my wits. Alcohol and amphetamines consumed my time from Friday night until that moment. A thirty-four hour bender does not provide the optimal mindset for important decision making. It occurred to me I made a big mistake.

I pulled back out on the road to take a long drive and decide what to do. I still had a strong desire to visit Vince and clear the air about what each of us had done to one another's family members. I was curious; there had to be a reason for Vince to do such a thing to Mother. I had to understand, and Vincent was the only one who could enlighten me. The trouble was, I wasn't sure Vince would understand my position on Eddie's demise, and I didn't know how I could keep the truth from him.

The rent-a-car came to rest on the curb back at Vince's house. I returned to the front door and knocked, but no one answered. There were no lights on in the front section of the house. I crawled under windows, around to the back where the garage door was open. There was no noise coming from inside. A few padded steps across the garage floor led to the back door of the house. The brass knob turned in silence. The well maintained hinges did not announce my covert entrance into the kitchen. There was still no evidence of life in the home. I stood motionless and strained to listen, but my own hyperventilation was interfering. It was a big place, so there could be a circus going on in another area of the house and it might not be heard in the kitchen.

I moved into the great room, which was adorned with expensive art lining the walls and resting on expensive pedestals. This room reminded me of a museum, and it always seemed uninviting. I couldn't have felt less welcome at that moment. My tracks across the tile floor created an echo off the high ceiling. I stopped at the opposite end of the great room and pressed my back against the wall. There was the cranny of a tiny hallway leading to the bar.

The skies had clouded and a gray light greeted me when I entered the bar. I was looking at the back of the couch, which emitted a rustle, and I stiffened, suddenly wondering what I could possibly have been thinking by going there. I moved sideways, keeping my eye on the rustling sofa.

The pivotal moment was upon me. It was surreal seeing Vince swallowed by the down cushioned couch, dead asleep. For an instant I believed I was back at the motel, still in drunken slumber, dreaming of this moment. Vince had dropped weight he couldn't afford to lose. He was unshaven and looked disheveled. There's no telling how long it took me to assimilate the scene. At that moment, Vince didn't seem dangerous, at all.

As if on cue, Vince calmly opened his sunken eyes, which were looking beyond me. He surely thought he was still dreaming. "Charlie," he said weakly, "is that you?"

I was disarmed and swallowed hard. "Yeah," I managed to mutter. "It's me, Vince."

Vince, still in a stupor, focused on me. "What are you doing standing there?" he asked indifferently.

Gaining composure I said, "I'm not sure Vince." It was hard to believe the meeting was starting out with such serenity.

The fog was lifting for Vince. "What are you doing here? You're supposed to be..."

"Dead, yeah I know," I said, collapsing into a downy chair, my energy sapped from the stress of my invasion. "Well I'm not. Here I am, in the flesh."

"Whoa, that's great," he said, his face lighting up in surprising delight. The idea of Vince as a threat was so etched in my psyche I couldn't imagine why he would be glad to see I was alive. I had no idea what Vince knew that I didn't, but soon the truth would unfold before both of us.

"Where've you been all this time, son," he asked sitting up. He suddenly looked more lucid.

"Bermuda," I blurted carelessly.

Vince beamed. "Bermuda...with Eddie? You've been with Eddie?" The smiled drained from his face as he read my face.

"No," Vince shook his head. "No, no, tell me you didn't – not the explosion," he pleaded, but I just fixed my eyes squarely into his.

"Tell me you didn't kill my mother," I shot back.

"What," he said before he gave it away. "Where'd you hear...Tomcat."

That clinched it! He might as well have spelled it out in the blood that was on his hands.

"I didn't say who told me; you did," I said. "And by the way, I did do it. It was Eddie in the explosion, and he deserved every bit of it."

Vince's head dropped between his knees and shook in disbelief. "Why did you do it," he cried.

"He was blackmailing me," I said. "He was soaking me for money, and even as much as I paid him, he was hell bent on destroying me. He's the one who planted that porn in my desk at work. He's the one who took the picture of the young girl in my dental chair." Vince didn't know anything about the picture of Hailey Baily. "You see, he was in big trouble with the Russian mob. He was into them for a lot of money, not delivering the goods he promised. Vince, he was in so much trouble, if I hadn't done the deed, the Russians would have gotten him. Hell, they sent two guys to Bermuda to kill me because they thought I was Eddie."

"How can that be?" Vince said.

"Never mind about that," I said, "but tell me why you did what you did to Mother."

Vince cupped his hands under his forehead, elbows on his knees. "Son, son, you just don't know what you've done," he moaned. I couldn't imagine what he was talking about, but he started at the beginning. "I didn't want to...," he began. "I didn't want to hurt her, but I had no choice, at the time."

"What are you talking about?" I said.

"Okay, I'll tell you the whole story," he said, looking up from the floor.

Vince began to tell me how depressed he had been ever since I died and Eddie turned up missing and Tomcat disappeared. He told me all about New York and the club owner he wasted, how he ended up in Atlanta, and how, with the help of Carmine Marino, he took over the Atlanta burlesque scene and moved in on the Atlanta rackets. He spoke of how he met Sarah and married her.

"Yeah, yeah I've heard this before, Vince," I said. I was becoming bored as his rambling stretched into the afternoon. Suddenly amazing details overwhelmed me.

"Things were so good, Charlie," Vince gushed. "Then your mother came along. Do you know how young she was at the time, Charlie?"

I didn't answer.

"And she was so shrewd," he continued, "shrewd beyond her years. One day I'm at your grandfather's house on business, and suddenly she appears. She follows me down the street, pursuing me like a bloodhound. She caught up with me at a bar over on Peachtree. She was only seventeen at the time, but she was a knockout. I did try to resist her, but she made it plain what she was after, and I gave in to temptation. We found a motel room, and one thing led to another, and... well, you know. She seemed infatuated with me. I felt like a shit when it was over, and I just wanted to get out of there.

"That's not the worst thing, just that we did it. Later on, she comes to me, and she's real scared. She tells me she's pregnant. I'm telling you, Charlie, I about shit myself. I ask her if she's sure it's mine. She looks so hurt, and tears well up, and she says of course its mine; that I'm the only man she's ever been with."

By then, thoughts were racing like locusts through my over-stimulated brain. It was getting tough to concentrate as Vince continued.

"Well, I say we've got to do something about it – we've gotta take care of it while there was plenty of time. Then she starts wailing and saying something about being Catholic and she could never do such a thing, and suddenly it occurs to me that this young woman I fooled around with is really just a young, stupid, scared little girl in a woman's body. So now I don't know what to do. I can't let your grandfather find out I screwed his teenage daughter and got her pregnant – not to mention, I didn't want Sarah to find out. If Herb Dutton didn't kill me himself, he would have gone to Carmine Marino, and he had standing with the old man. I would have lost it all, Charlie. No matter how I try to convince Mary to have an abortion, she refuses. She then talks me into setting up an account in her name and putting a good chunk of money in it to take care of the child. It didn't seem like extortion, so I went along with it. Hell, I could have wasted her then, but I really couldn't – not that young pretty girl – not Herb's daughter. So finally, before it's too late for explanations, she comes up with a plan. We're gonna find some chump at her high school and she's gonna have sex with him and blame him for the baby. That way, nobody knows it's mine except Mary and me. We figure to pin it on the guy."

By now my head was swimming. Was Vince saying he was my father? How could that possibly be? I wasn't anything like him – or was I? For so much of my childhood I looked forward to becoming my father, but the butterfly of circumstances intervened, or so I thought. Look at what had become of me. Perhaps I *had* become just like my father. I didn't want to hear any more, but it was like passing a car accident, being drawn by morbid curiosity to look. I just let him spill his guts.

"Charles Lofton is the chump who goes to the prom with Mary and gets his rocks off and ends up stuck with the tab at the end of the date. So far so good. Mary tells your grandfather about this guy and what happened, and the shit hits the fan. What we didn't know was how noble this guy would be. He was abandoned as an infant, raised an orphan and he would never do that to a child of his own. He insists on being a stand up, do the right thing, kind of guy. He comes to your grandfather and they have a man to man, and Charles agrees to go to work for him while he pursues college. I figure he was smart with the books, but kinda naive when it comes to the real world. So, the chump's gonna be in the picture, but everything's okay for a little while, until one day, not long after you were born, Mary comes to me and says the doctors told her she was having another baby, this time by Charles. She could barely stand the effort of raising you, and she has no desire for another. I tell you Charlie, your mother's body was so fertile, it was made for making babies, but she wasn't built for taking care of them.

"Meanwhile, me and Sarah have been trying to have a kid for years, but we're having no luck. It was Sarah's problem, and that was back before all this in vitro stuff. There was no chance she was gonna get pregnant, and she was looking to adopt. This time *I* get the idea for a plan.

"Your mother tells Charles and your grandparents she has an opportunity to study one year in England on some sort of exchange program. It was a lame story, but both her parents were so out of it when it came to raising their own daughter, and Charles is so naïve and busy, it was easy to pull off. Charles spent the entire first year of your life raising you on his own while he worked and went to school. I don't know how he did it, but he was better suited to raise children than your mother ever would be.

"Your mother goes off to Europe, and I finance all of her expenses when she's there. I tell Sarah we have the opportunity to adopt a healthy baby from Europe. Your mother has the baby, and I go to Europe to pick-up Eddie. Sarah has no idea what the deal is, but hell, she doesn't care; she just wants the kid. By the time Mary comes back for good, she's slimmed down, looking good, and no one's the wiser. It would have been nice to keep you, Charlie, but it didn't happen that way. But I made sure I was always around you, and I knew, as long as your father was around, you would be well taken care of."

By now I was far from bored. It couldn't be true. I was still grappling with the idea of Vince as my father. Suddenly, Vince tells me Eddie was my half brother and the son of the man I looked up to and called father. Had I killed my own flesh and blood? I struggled to the bar, soaked a bar towel and tried to cool my steaming head. Before it took effect, Vince was pummeling me with more information.

"Now everybody's happy, right? Sarah's got a baby, Charlie and Mary have only one baby to support and take care of. Charlie's actually doing a fine job working for us downtown, and he's going to college making the deans list. Then Carmine Marino dies up in New York. Well, that asshole, Paul Ducatto, doesn't like me and he tries to make life difficult. It's like he's trying to cut your grandfather into the action and cut me out. Your grandfather's cutting into my income, and I'm supporting my family and an extra kid on the side, because your mother keeps soaking me for money, claiming that money's tight and hinting at exposing the whole ruse to her father. I didn't need any extra grief with everything else going on.

"So Paul and I are practically at war over our situation. Meanwhile, your mother is squeezing me for more and more money to raise the kid... sorry, to raise you – and I'm trying to help her out, but she's insatiable. I know Charlie – your father – doesn't know about the deal, but it's amazing that someone who was so smart would think they could live like they did off the money he was bringing home. I guess he thought your grandfather was helping your mother on the side, but he wasn't doing nearly as much I was. When I finally put my foot down, Mary's pissed, and she throws a tantrum, threatening to spill the beans on me being the father and all. I believe she would have done it, too. That would have made Herb Dutton too much of a threat to me, not to mention ruined my marriage. Well, I have to do something, and I thought about ridding myself of my blackmailer, but I couldn't bring myself to do that to the mother of my own child.

"About that time, Charlie's getting great grades at Georgia Tech. Herb's bragging about that, telling me how he's gonna have his big Memorial Day cookout to celebrate. Meanwhile, things between your grandfather and me and Paul Ducatto haven't improved. Well, I have this problem, and I know how your grandfather handles himself at his grandiose cookouts. I know he'll be out of his mind drunk long before it's time to actually grill the meal, so I hatch this plan to take Herb out. My people go into Herb's garage and replace the lighter fluid with gasoline, which I know he won't detect, as drunk as he used to get. I know how he soaked the coals under the tops of his grills. The boys plug the vents in the grill, and those gas fumes are just collecting under that top. By the time he's ready to light the thing, it's a bomb waiting to go off. Well, Charlie happened to be with him, something I didn't count on, I swear. I had nothing against him, and I knew he was going to provide a good home for you. He was just unfortunate collateral damage."

As Vince revealed this terrible secret, I caught myself staring through him with my jaw hanging open. By then, nothing was surprising me. My brain was soaking up the information like those coals had soaked up the gasoline, and it was ready to explode in amazement. It was my own real father, Vincent Palomino, who perpetrated the crime that deprived me of the man I thought was my father. It was as if Vince wasn't affected, telling me what he did. That wasn't the end of the story, though. Vince couldn't restrain himself, and he continued to blab, unconsciously.

"After the accident your mother was all alone, and even though she didn't know the real story, she was scared of me. I was the only one who could keep her and the family financially afloat. She was a victim of that fact. Much of her leverage evaporated when Herb Dutton died in that explosion. Still, I had a son, and I continued to support her and you and your grandmother, but I made sure she did her part for it. I put her to work as a dancer, and she made good enough money to subsidize what I was paying her directly. With Herb out of the picture, Paul and I had a kind of ceasefire. My earnings recovered. It took some pressure off me, and as time passed your mother and I formed a relationship based on a sort of tacit truce. That's when I started bringing your brother over so you kids would get to know each other and grow up together.

"Well, you were around from then on until you went off to Oak Ridge. You know how your mother got. She was drinking way too much, and doing coke. It wasn't helping her in the looks department, and I finally took her off the stage. When we opened the new clubs, I gave her some work at my office, mostly bullshit stuff, just so she'd have something to do to keep her sober. Finally she got so whacked out on blow and booze, I just let her sit at home. I kept taking care of her, though, especially while you were around. I took care of my responsibility when it came to you – for all those years.

"Even after you left town and were on your own, I made sure your mother had the things she needed to get by. I figured she wouldn't have been in that spot if Charlie had lived to graduate and get a good job."

No shit! And I would have had a father to raise me right and give me some guidance, even if he didn't share my genes. That went unsaid, but Vince could read my thoughts as he continued.

"But I did take care of her, Charlie," he answered my silent protest, "and I did what was fair. Do you have any idea how much she was blowing on coke? It was amazing. I'd give her five hundred bucks on Friday to last her a week, and it'd practically be gone after the weekend. And she hardly had any cost of living. The house was paid for, the car, everything.

"Shit, I finally figure out that I was supporting her habit. So I try cutting back on what I give her, making it smaller amounts at a time and telling her it has to last for awhile. She isn't having any of that. She's so irrational, by then, thinking I'm trying to cut her out. I'm sure she's gone totally mad.

"Then one day her sober side's revealed. She proceeds to spell things out for me. It seems all the time she was puttering around uselessly in my office, she was snooping around, also. I had been careless, and she picked up on some things that would not be good for me if they got into the wrong hands. She recites some very specific and damning details. As crazy as she had gotten, her facts were incredibly clear and accurate. Your mother demands cash, tells me I'm about to make her a rich woman, or else. She's trying to squeeze me. She's drinking so much Charlie, she had gone totally paranoid. But the facts were clear in her mind, and they could be used against me. I try to reason with her. I try everything, including begging her, but it's like she's on a mission to destroy my life.

"By then, I'm considering my options, but I gotta tell you, I haven't made up my mind what to do. Then Mary gives me what I need to decide. In pure drunken spite she calls me a chump. So I say 'What's that mean?'

"She proceeds to tell me how she's been playing me for a fool ever since that night I screwed her in that motel room – how she'd been balling Charlie Lofton for months before she seduced me. She says she'd relied on the rhythm method to stay out of trouble, and it wasn't so reliable. She figured this chump, Charles, wouldn't stand by her so she pinned the problem on somebody who was already doing pretty well – somebody like me. She never saw anything in me but a checkbook. She knew the score all along; there was no way I would let it get out that I screwed her and got her pregnant. Once I agreed to support her and the baby, she had what she wanted, including the bonus boy, Charles Lofton, who did the right thing, after all. You've gotta admit, that's cold for a seventeen year old girl. Of course, she was your grandfather's daughter.

"So now it's clear what I'm gonna do. Hell Charlie, if I hadn't done it, she would have put herself in the grave soon enough. I called Tomcat, but he refused to get involved with my personal situation, so I decide it's not a tough task. She's groggy from a coke bender and enough booze to make her pass out. So I agree to give her the cash she wants. I get her real drunk and put a gun to her and tell her to write a suicide note. It was worthless; she was too drunk. I give her another drink and when she's out, I carry her to the garage, put her in the car and start it up. I close the door on the way out, and that's that. I swear that's the best way to go. She didn't feel a thing. Like I said, it was bound to happen to her the way she was going, and it could have been a lot worse.

"So that's it son. That's the whole story. I don't know how you feel about it, but that's the story. I tell you, I'm not the one who got your mother pregnant, and I'm not the one who spent a lifetime of deceit and extortion. Finally, I'm not the one who's so different than you."

Suddenly learning Charles Lofton was, in fact, my father changed my mood.

"No, Vince," I said, almost dizzy from the range of revelations, "and we both found ourselves in the same situation. And I guess we can acquit ourselves with the position that our victims were heading for their fates one way or the other. We just kind of hastened the outcome."

"Yes, but you killed your brother, Charlie," Vince said, not to accuse, but to express real regret it happened.

"Don't remind me, Vince," I said as I stood up without another word and left Vince to his obvious depression.

I unconsciously got to the car and began driving to the airport. Every word, every revelation was replaying itself in my head. Amazement overcame me as the essence of what was divulged gradually unfolded. So Vince wasn't my father, and he wasn't Eddie's, either. But Eddie was my brother and my father's son, and I killed him. It was astounding to me that Mother did to Vince exactly the kind of thing Eddie did to me with the same demented, drug induced malice. I could empathize exactly with what Vince had gone through. Still, he killed my father, and I would always blame him for that, even if I couldn't blame him for Mother.

As the Taurus carried me down the road, I mused that Eddie must have gotten more of Mother's genes – those maniacal, blackmailing genes. Vince and I were merely killers. My frazzled mind darted back to the matter of genes. Perhaps I inherited more of my father's genes. Was it the genes? What if the butterfly's wings had stirred the winds of fate a little differently and I had been the one handed over to Vince and Sarah Palomino? Would I then have been the Eddie, and would he have been me? Would we have chosen the exact same course? Would I have been the blackmailing drug addict if I grew up in Vince's household? Or would things have been a little bit different for both of us?

It was about six o'clock when I dropped off the rent-a-car and caught the shuttle to the airport. There were no available seats on the limited flights from Atlanta to Bermuda until twelve-thirty Monday afternoon. There was a seven-forty a.m. out of New York. I was eager to get out of Atlanta and the country, so I arranged for a 9 p.m. flight to Kennedy and the next morning's flight from there to Bermuda. I paid for the ticket and wandered around the terminal looking for something to occupy my time.

XX. A Case of Mistaken Identity

Special Agent Barry Irvin received the call from Ted Reardon on Sunday afternoon. He jotted some notes and called Agent Robin Reo.

"Ted called from Bermuda," he began briefing her. "He's picked up the trail on Edward Palomino."

The mention of Eddie took Reo back to an unpleasant memory and excited her at the same time. She had been on the manhunt with Irvin months before. It began with weeks of a stakeout of Palomino's house that produced nothing but monotony. At the time they were just looking to question him regarding the residential explosion that killed Charles Lofton. When Palomino never showed, and his family and acquaintances couldn't be of any help, they became more interested and stepped up the investigation. She wasn't sure how it evolved, but they received a warrant to search the home based on a forgery situation. She was part of the team that discovered the debauched photos and magazines along with forged documents, cryptic ledgers and drugs. After a search of the house Edward Palomino was wanted for a number of criminal violations, and the bureau stepped up their efforts to find him.

Since then Robin worked peripherally on the investigation, but as time went on, all the leads dead ended, and the case became stale. Her part had focused on the father, Vincent Palomino. The FBI already had an ongoing investigation into his activities and his ties to organized crime in New York. Robin's insights into Vincent during the search for the son finally landed her on that case with Steve Langtree, full time.

It was a difficult case, because the people involved were the very good at concealing their criminal activities. Their reach was extensive, and their intimidation tactics were effective. They didn't make many mistakes, and their ability to conceal money and records within ostensibly lawful businesses created a labyrinth for investigators to negotiate. It was tough for the FBI to get enough probable cause to convince a court to give them access to the ostensibly legitimate businesses that they were sure held a gold mine of incrimination. They mostly had to rely on wire taps and hope these very careful characters would make a mistake. The office in New York made inroads, but getting to Vincent Palomino would help the bureau work its way up the food chain. Because of the tangled trail, Robin was enmeshed in tedious details and mounds of paperwork. She found there was often more superfluous material than relevant information in the documents. Not only would it be satisfying to catch up to the son-of-a-bitch who traded in child pornography and drugs, but putting the squeeze on the son might help put the finger on the father.

"Where is he," Robin asked Barry.

"You'll never guess," he said. "We think Atlanta. Apparently he's been living in Bermuda, using the alias of Nils Montgomery. Someone by that name purchased a ticket back to Atlanta yesterday. Don't know if he's still in the city. We've got this Montgomery's credit card data. I'll get on the horn and see if he's made any charges around town. Why don't you pay a visit to your buddy Vince and see if he's had any contact with him."

Robin headed out the door, jumping into the chocolate brown Crown Victoria. There was an accident going north out of downtown. She was eager to get out to the suburbs before the opportunity to possibly snag Edward Palomino eluded her. It didn't take five minutes of sitting on a six lane interstate that was barely moving to make her place her blue light on the dash and begin cruising down the emergency lane. Still it was over a half hour to the Palomino house.

Vince looked startled when he opened the door to Agent Robin Reo's face. "What do you want," he scowled.

"Nice to see you, too, Vincent," Robin responded coolly, taking a patronizing tone with him right off the bat. "I may have some good news for you, if you'll let me come in."

"You got a warrant," Vince said, almost automatically.

"Hey, I just want to talk," she said. "You mind?"

"Come on," he said, turning his back to her as she followed.

"You don't look so good, Vincent," Robin said, honestly.

"Like you care," Vince shot back. "To what do I owe this honor, you coming out after hours and all? Shouldn't you be off somewhere doing whatever you cops do when you're off duty?"

"I'm working day and night to help you out, and you treat me like this," the agent chided, following Vince through the house. "I'm hurt."

"Yeah, I really appreciate your concern," he said, as he plopped back into the couch that had born his bulk for the bulk of the day. "Take a seat."

Robin sat in the same chair I vacated a couple of hours earlier and got right to the point. "We believe your son is in Atlanta. I thought you might be interested to hear that. I thought you might also know something about that."

Vince didn't betray his secret. I represented less potential problems for him on some foreign island than I did in custody in Atlanta. His reaction was steady. "That's good news. I've been worried about him. I haven't been able to find him for a long time."

"So you haven't talked to him?"

"Nope," he was able to honestly say.

"And you haven't communicated with him any other way?"

Vince sighed impatiently. "No, I haven't."

Robin persisted. "And you haven't seen him? You know nothing of his whereabouts?"

Vince shot her a frustrated expression. "Agent Reo, you know more about where he is than I do. You're not gonna get any closer to him sitting around here. If you can find him, I wish you would get to it. I'd be thrilled if you did. I would like to see him again. I'm sure whatever you think you have on him can be straightened out and I can have my son back for good."

"That's why I'm here, Vince," she responded sarcastically. "A servant of the people, you know. Anything I can do to put a little joy into your life."

"Well, if that's the case, I'm kinda tired, so if you could excuse me, I would be filled with joy."

"Okay, then," Robin relented. "If you do hear from him, I'm sure you'll contact me right away." She offered her card.

Vince put out his hand in a stop motion. "Don't bother. I have a few of those, remember? You give me one every time you come to see me."

"Fine, Vincent," she said. "It's been so nice seeing you again. Thanks for your hospitality."

Vince showed Agent Reo to the door and closed it behind her, snickering to himself. If only she knew, he thought. He wished there was a way to contact me to warn me how close they were getting, but he had no idea where I went after I left his house.

Once Robin was on her way she reached for the phone to check in with Irvin. Before she could dial the number, she got the call from him on his cell phone.

"Where are you?" Barry Irvin asked.

"Just left Vince Palomino's house," she said.

"Head for the airport," he commanded.

"What's up," she asked.

"The credit card company gave us a charge he made at Hertz down there, Saturday. We called down to Hertz and the guy turned the car in just a little while ago. I've got those bozo's down at security looking for him, but they're not to approach him if they see him. I'm getting in my car now. I want to get down there in a hurry before they fuck this thing up."

"Okay, see you there," Robin said as she turned the blue light on and mashed the accelerator. The traffic was light, and the trip through town was a high speed one. The Ford pulled up to the security office at the airport exactly seventeen minutes after the phone call. Irvin, who had only just arrived from downtown, was impressed.

Security had not yet spotted the man whose picture was faxed to them. The FBI agents went directly to US South who seemed to be the suspect's carrier of choice. There was no Montgomery on any outbound Bermuda flight passenger lists.

Irvin mentioned that Palomino might have just turned the rent-a-car back into Hertz, then left the airport by another means. Barry asked the US South Airlines staff to continue searching passenger lists and went to the Hertz counter to verify the man in the picture was the man who turned in the car.

Robin headed for the concourses hoping she might get lucky and spot Palomino. Assuming he was on a US South flight, the most likely place to look would be concourse A or B, since US South dominated those gates.

Barry Irvin arrived at the Hertz return and presented the picture to the woman behind the counter. It had been a slow day. The rental agent pulled the paperwork for the specified car, gazed at the photo and back to the paperwork. She remembered someone who resembled the man in the picture, but she couldn't be sure. That was good enough for Agent Irvin, and he took off for the terminal to catch up with Robin Reo.

....

The aircraft bound for Kennedy International pulled in from Miami late to gate A12. I watched anxiously as the Atlanta bound passengers deplaned and the crew set about readying the plane for its continuation to New York. My apprehension made it seem as though I was the only one interested in getting out on schedule. The ground crew looked like it was moving in slow motion. It was obvious the flight was only partially full and the gate agent was assigning seats to standby passengers until the last minute. Finally the call came for first class passengers to board. Once the man with the microphone saw that the few who were going first class weren't enough to form a line, he called for general boarding. I quickly stood and shuffled along with the crowd toward the ticket taker.

"Edward Palomino."

The sound of the name rang hollow for an instant, and then my stomach dropped as I turned to see a woman with a badge in one hand grab my wrist with the other hand. I was helpless as she pulled me out of the line holding my arm with inhuman pressure. She shouted excitedly into a radio, and I could see her chest heave for breath as sweat ran down her forehead. She dropped the radio, reached behind for handcuffs, and spun me around in a painful motion to manacle my wrists. I could feel the heat from all the faces in the area staring at the scene in which I was the central character.

"There must be a mistake," I declared weakly. "My name is Nils Mongomery."

"Perfect response," the FBI woman said as she sat me in a chair on my hands. "Nils Montgomery, Edward Palomino, Joseph Paulsen, and a few others if I recall from the documents we found in your house. We found some other interesting items, too."

People were gawking as I tried to hide my face. "It wasn't me," I said honestly, and then I went silent. Suddenly I wasn't sure what to say. My world collapsed in that stark terminal, no matter who I turned out to be. More law enforcement arrived, and I was suddenly surrounded by dark business suits and uniformed cops. I was grateful for that, since they were screening me from the curious crowd. A man in a suit pulled me up from the underarms and I was hustled off in a VIP cart provided by US South Airlines. I was a very important person at the moment, but for very wrong reasons.

An Atlanta police car transported me down to the city detention center. The officer driving the patrol cruiser had no interest in the prisoner behind the metal screen in the back seat. I had nothing to say to him either, and we rode in comfortable silence into downtown Atlanta.

The Atlanta City Jail is a massive brick structure just south of the heart of downtown. It's the most attractive building in a neighborhood teeming with bonding companies, a couple of package stores and an assortment of dilapidated storefronts. As we approached the processing entrance, I could see the brightly lit signs of companies like AAAA Bonding, ALL Time Bail Bonds, and A Speedy Bail Bonding. The idea of springing myself on bond was only fleeting. As naive as I was about the criminal justice business, even I knew that a judge would not allow bond to a flight risk such as myself, whether I was Eddie Palomino or Charlie Lofton. The realization made for an unpleasant enrollment into Atlanta's correctional facility.

Walking into the jail from the dark Atlanta night is a shock to the eyeballs. It has to be the most brilliantly lit place in the city. Endless rows of fluorescent lights clash with randomly placed incandescent yellow lamps creating a hostile glare off garish yellow walls. A greeting party of indifferent clerks in uniforms performs various tasks to get the new arrivals processed. A woman at a typewriter processed me as Edward Palomino. That's how they knew me already, so there was no harm in letting that ride until I could talk to a lawyer. After the typing they confiscated all my possessions, fingerprinted me and assigned me a prisoner number. Then they put me into a holding cell with other offenders of the law. If the offense was relatively minor a prisoner would stay there until he could make bail. People like me had a different fate awaiting them.

The overnighters were taken as a group and stripped of all our clothes – not to mention our dignity. We were then given a group shower and finally deloused before we were allowed to don some yellow, government issued jump suits with a "City of Atlanta Jail" monogrammed on the left chest and "PRISONER" printed on the back. Each of us was tagged with an I.D. bracelet as if we were being admitted to a hospital or a rock concert. They gave me some sort of moccasins which felt like Styrofoam on my feet. This was before we went to the General Population of the jail.

We were divided into groups, and my group was led to Pod A. There I was placed in a cell with Marvin Dixon. The amenities in my new cell consisted of a toilet with a sink next to it in the middle of the room. It didn't have the space of the Rock and it lacked the charm of the compound in Bermuda, and at that moment I wondered how I would adapt to this place or a place like it for as long as I would surely be put there.

Marvin Dixon was a black fellow who didn't talk much at first, which suited me. He told me he was in for disorderly conduct. I wasn't sure what that meant. He said disorderly conduct could cover a range of things. Since he didn't seem eager to discuss it, I didn't pursue it. Marvin did ask me about my transgression, and it was then I realized I didn't even know precisely what the charges against me were. I knew what they would be if the truth were ever discovered.

"I'm not sure," I said, seemingly satisfying the barely interested Marvin. Eventually, someone would discover the whole story, and the charges would change to murder. That possibility was impossible to consider and still remain composed, and it was important to maintain composure in jail.

Marvin the Disorderly appeared unaffected by the entire process we went through together, and it was obvious this wasn't a new experience for him. He was tired and wanted sleep, so I let him choose the bed that suited him and left him alone. I, on the other hand, could not possibly sleep. I was groping for ideas to get out of the grave trouble I was in, but none existed. I asked about a phone call that the guards promised to provide. Suddenly, it was late at night, there was no guard nearby, and the outlook looked bleak. To my surprise, within half an hour after Marvin began snoring in a disorderly manner, a jailer appeared and called into the cell.

"Palomino!"

"Yes," I responded, still trying to get used to the name.

"You wanna make a call?"

"What time is it," I asked, stripped of my confiscated watch."

"Two ten," came the reply. "You wanna make a call or not?"

"Yes," I said, unsure whom I could call. "What's my bond?"

"They didn't set one. You're our guest care of the feds. You have to go to a hearing in the morning to see what that'll be."

That sounded encouraging to a naïve and hopeless optimist. When one is in a dire situation such as prison, he will clutch onto any ray of hopeful information, no matter what the source. As the guard escorted me to a telephone, I thought to myself how it would have been good for the moment if Vince were my father. He would have to bail his own son out of jail. I looked through the phone book and got David Israel's home number. A groggy voice answered after a couple of rings.

"David," I said,"

"Yeah," he said automatically.

"David, this is Charlie," I said.

“Charlie?" he said, "Charlie who?"

"David, it’s me, Charlie Lofton," I said in a hushed voice.

"Charlie?" David shouted into the phone, obviously confused. "Charlie, is that you?"

"Yes," I said, trying to calm him. "It is me, David."

"But how can that be?" he asked. "Where have you been besides dead?"

"It’s a long story," I said. "I need your help."

"Where are you Charlie," said David, still trying to assimilate the world into which he awoke that early morning.

"At the Atlanta jail," I said, with nothing more to add.

"Oh God," David sighed. "What are the charges?"

"It’s a long story, David," I repeated. "I'll tell you when you get here."

"What's your bond," he asked.

"They haven't set one," I said, listening for his comment and tone of voice. It wasn't promising.

"Great. Okay, I've got early morning court," he said, by then fully awake. "I'll be out of there about ten-thirty. I can get to you around eleven. How's that?"

"That's okay," I responded despondently. That meant at least another nine hours in jail, rooming with Marvin. "Oh, by the way, David – when you come to see me, ask for Edward Palomino. They think I'm him."

"Whoa, this is a good story, isn't it," said David. "I'll get there earlier if I can."

Surprisingly, I was able to sleep for a few hours until our section was roused by the terrible, bright lights and a blaring, indecipherable P.A. system announcing something about waking up. Marvin groaned, sat up and nonchalantly moved to the commode where he proceeded to empty his bowels. I tried to look in any direction but his, vowing to never go to the bathroom again if I had to go like that.

To my relief, we were soon retrieved by a couple of fresh

guards who came on duty for the morning shift. They took us to a large dining room where we moved through a line while prisoners in white jump suits slopped food on metal trays we held in front of us. It was supposed to be bacon and eggs, but it was more like fat and a runny, powdery mix of some yellow, unearthly mess. One bite was all it took to know that I could at least wait until lunch to satisfy any hunger I might feel. Maybe before that, David could do something for me...maybe.

....

Bobby was on the way downtown to his office when his cell phone rang. The display revealed Ted Reardon's cell phone.

"Hello, counselor," said Ted, his voice full of excitement.

"Agent Reardon," Bobby smiled in the car. "What has you up so early in the morning? I thought you would have slept in. Don't you start your weekend about now?"

"Its Special Agent to you, counselor" he shot back, but nothing could hide the giddiness he felt. "I may just take the rest of the week off, after the coup we had last night. You wanna guess?"

"Why don't you just tell me, sweetheart," Bobby said. "I can tell you want to so bad."

"Edward Palomino."

Bobby almost drove off the road. He shouted into the phone, "Eddie Palomino? You got him? You know where he is, or what?"

"I thought that would impress you," came the smug reply. "We got him. He's here in Atlanta."

By then, Bobby was on the side of the road, unable to concentrate on driving. "You're kidding! Where is he?"

"Oh he's in the custody of Atlanta's finest, downtown," Ted said. "We're gonna snatch him outta there around nine and take him over to our office to have a little talk. Thought you might be interested in popping in to pay him a visit."

Bobby couldn't have quit smiling if his head had rolled right off his neck. "Yessir," he replied. I've got to stop at the office, but I'll be there before you get done with him, I promise. Did he lawyer up, yet?"

"Don't know, pal," said Ted. "I don't think so, so far. We'll read him his rights, again…see what we can get from him before he does. His old man will probably have somebody down there pretty fast."

"Okay, I'll see you there," Bobby said. "Good job, Special Agent Reardon."

"That's more like it," said Ted as he hung up.

Bobby hung up, happily surprised at how the Monday morning started. That wouldn't be his last surprise of the day.

……..

After breakfast we were shuffled back to our respective cells. Marvin went straight for his bed. I calculated that it would be another three hours before David would be there to try and rescue me. Time crawled. At what must have been eight-thirty, guards were coming around calling names and prisoners were being lined up outside the cells. Soon they marched off, led by the uniformed officers.

"What's going on with them," I asked Marvin who watched apathetically.

"You never been here, have you?" he said, smiling. "They going to their bond hearing. Don't worry, they be by to get us, directly."

Marvin was half right. The prison guard did come to our cell, and they did get Marvin and put him in the line with the other prisoners. But they had no use for me. As the others were marching off, I spoke in a hopeful tone. "What about me?"

A woman in uniform looked back and said, "Oh you're not up here. The feds will deal with you separately."

Marvin turned and looked at me, impressed. I was simply depressed.

I remained, sitting on my bed, marking time until I would see David Israel. The pod was quiet. Most of its residents were absent. They were in court, learning what it would take to be liberated from the place of bright lights, incessant noise, and bad food. I was alone in my cell, wondering if I would ever see a day of freedom again. I knew I would never live the life of Nils Montgomery in Bermuda. I would never see the Gastons. I wondered what they would think happened to me. I assumed they would discover me missing and finally call the police. I had no idea the police involved them in their search for Mr. Montgomery. I wished I had never come back to the states, but there was no use thinking about that. My stomach was knotted. I took advantage of the opportunity to go to the bathroom in privacy.

……..

"Edward Palomino," the call came from a guard.

"Yes," I said, leaping from my bed, relieved that I was not altogether abandoned. It was too early for David to arrive. Maybe they had some sort of court hearing for me. No matter what it was, anything was better than sitting alone fretting.

Back in the processing area, two U.S. Marshals handcuffed me and led me out of the artificial glare of the building into the natural brilliance of the summer day. My momentary elation at getting out of the oppressive jail was tempered at the idea of losing the freedom to enjoy such a simple pleasure as the morning air. They sat me in the back of an unmarked government car for a short ride with the two men. Not a word was spoken by any of us.

The car pulled into a parking lot behind a tall building, which was familiar, but I had never known its purpose. We went into a back entrance and got on a freight elevator which took us to the eighth floor. It could have been the eighth floor of any office building in Atlanta – carpeted, fluorescently lit hallway, doors on one wall marked with department names, a recess on the other wall with a water fountain and bathroom doors.

We took a right into a large open office divided by gray cubicles. There were a few men and women milling around, carrying files and papers. I walked by, slightly self conscious in the handcuffs. I was hardly noticed; it was a routine spectacle for these people. They led me by the arm into a conference room, took off my handcuffs and shackled my feet so I could sit at a long table.

"Stay here. Someone will be with you soon," said one of the marshals. It was professional and polite, as if I had come in for a job interview or to apply for a loan – except for the shackles. I sat alone imagining I was there for a job interview, just to stay upbeat. At least I was out of that jail, I thought to myself.

After what seemed an eternity, the woman who arrested me and a man who was there with her stepped into the room and closed the door. "Good morning Mr. Palomino. I'm Agent Reo and this is Special Agent Irvin. How'd you sleep last night?"

"I was in jail," I said, a little too insolently.

"Well, you might as well get used to it," Agent Reo said coldly, causing a chill to course through my gut.

"Now we read you your rights last night," she continued, "but I'm going to remind you. You have the right to remain silent and you have the right to have an attorney and have that attorney present when we speak to you. If you choose to speak without your attorney, anything you say can be used against you when we go to trial."

"I have an attorney," I said. "He's supposed to see me at the jail at eleven."

Agent Irvin spoke up. "You won't be back there by then. Who is your attorney? We'll have him sent over here."

"David Israel. I know his office number," I said in an effort to seem cooperative and helpful, as if it might earn me points with the agent whose purpose it was to incarcerate me.

"Oh yes, Mr. Israel, your father's attorney," said Reo. "Don't worry; we know how to contact him. Have you spoken to your father?"

It sounded strange to hear someone refer to my father, since I hadn't had a father since I was five. It was clear whom she was referring to, but I didn't know how to answer the question without getting into more trouble. "I would rather wait to talk to my attorney before I say anything."

"You don't even want to answer a simple question like that," said Reo. "Whew, I can see you're going to be real cooperative. I guess we won't feel the need to be cooperative when Mr. Israel approaches the prosecutor on your behalf."

I wanted to blurt out my true identity and spill the whole story. Agent Irvin was scrutinizing my face, and he spoke before I could. "Did you have some kind of plastic surgery?"

"No," I responded, uncomfortably.

"So you will talk about some things," Reo chided.

I felt outwitted already, and I decided to clam up completely. Just then there was a rap on the door and a head poked through, causing me to audibly gasp. As Bobby turned to face the sound, his face paled, he fell back and the door closed him out. The two FBI agents looked at each other, puzzled, until the door immediately reopened.

"What are you doing here," I asked, glad to see him, and embarrassed at the same time.

"What are you doing here is a better question," Bobby said, in a mixed state of emotion.

"What are you two talking about," Reo said in her own state of confusion.

"Uh, could you guys excuse us for just a minute," Bobby said to the two FBI officers. They both glanced at each other warily as they managed to stand and leave the room. Bobby walked around to my side of the table slowly, with trepidation in his eyes. After all, they were staring at the ghost of his dead friend.

"Are you kidding me," he said in a hushed tone. "You're okay? You didn't die in that explosion? You were positively identified - dental records, DNA."

"I can explain. I switched the dental records."

"Wait a minute," Bobby cried, his hand in the air.

"Bobby, can I talk to you?" I said, my mind racing. This was my best friend, and he worked for the very people who would be aiming to put me away, either as Eddie the child pornographer, extortionist, etc., or as Charlie the murdering, fraudulent dentist. For all I knew he might be the one to do it.

"No," he blurted. He went to the wall where he flipped some switches. "This room is miked. See that mirror? If anyone's back there, they can see you, and I'm sure Robin and Barry are back there, right now. I just turned off the microphone so they can't hear us. No, you can't tell me anything..."

He was too late. I had to give my friend the whole story. "It was Eddie, Bobby. It was him. I did it. I killed him." The dam broke and the confession was spilling from my mouth as the damning details flooded my friend's ears. "Eddie knew I was a fraud. He knew I didn't graduate from dental school. He was blackmailing me. He framed me with pictures of naked children. He took a picture of one of my patients naked in my office before I knew it, I swear. He was pushing me, Bobby. I couldn't take it, anymore; he was bleeding me dry and he was pissing me off. I had to do something, so that's what I did. Then I used his alias to get out of town. Please help me Bobby, please. I don't think prison is the life for me.

"Oh God, Charlie," Bobby interrupted, "You shouldn't have done that."

"I know, I know, but what can I do now," I said.

"No, you shouldn't have told me this. You just put me in a terrible spot. I'm a U.S. Attorney. You can't confide in me. You've been given your rights. What you've told me will be used against you. It has to be. I mean, I have to do it."

"Bobby, there's got to be something you can do, please," I said, then added, "Oh God, I wish I had never come back home."

"There's not, Charlie," he said definitively. It doesn't matter, anyway. We were onto you – or onto the person we thought was Eddie, nevertheless. We would have caught up with you in Bermuda."

"I came back because I found out Vincent killed Mother," I said. "I had to see him. I had to make sure it was true and figure out why he did it."

"You're joking," Bobby said, as his mouth dropped open. Bobby had been in law enforcement for so long he was unflappable, but this circus of circumstances captured his imagination. "Vince Palomino had your mother killed? Why?"

"She was doing to him what Eddie was doing to me. Eddie must take after Mother...oh you don't know. Eddie and I are brothers. Vince thought he was my father until the night he killed Mother."

"Come on!" Bobby leapt to his feet so fast the chair flew back against the wall upside-down. "That doesn't make any sense. How are you and Eddie brothers?" Then Bobby remembered the final report from ATF agent Al Milton. "Of course, that would explain the DNA match," he said, unable to keep the discussion on course. "How are you and Eddie brothers?" he repeated. "You killed your own brother?"

"I know, I know, Bobby, but I didn't know it at the time," I said. "Neither did Eddie. Vince just told me, yesterday."

By now Bobby was pacing the floor in disbelief. I knew Reo and Irvin were watching the whole thing, and I couldn't imagine what they were making of the scene in front of them.

"You saw Vince Palomino, yesterday?" he exclaimed. "This is too unreal. I've got to be dreaming." Bobby wanted to tell me of the FBI's investigation into Vince, but he couldn't. "You were over there yesterday?" he repeated, shaking his head.

"Yeah, we all knew he was a mobster", I said. That's why I tried to put some distance between us a long time ago by getting into something legitimate… well I know I wasn't exactly legit, but at least I was not with Vince. But Eddie, well you know..."

Suddenly Bobby interrupted, saying, "Hey Charlie, you've got one chance to help yourself out. If you know enough to help us get our claws around Vince, we can maybe strike some kind of deal." Bobby tipped his hand slightly trying to help me and help the Justice Department at the same time.

"What are all of your problems? You might as well tell me, now. You're already in too deep. You've got the murder rap, which is a state matter, but you'll be looking at arson and insurance fraud, too. Then there's the dentist thing. You've got a host of federal problems there, mail fraud just for starters.

Then you were traveling with false documents. Do you have anything else? I mean something completely different I don't know about?"

Bobby's litany of charges was doing nothing to encourage me. But there was the Vince factor I tried to remind myself. "I don't know, Bobby," I said honestly. "I didn't even know I had done all the things you just named."

"Well that's enough to put you away for a long time," he said, sternly. "You're gonna need to really have something that will move the government to bring a case against Vincent Palomino if you want to help yourself. If you don't, I can't help you. But if you do, I can get you to the right people."

"Well, I told you he killed my mother," I said naively. "Oh, and he also killed my father and my grandfather. He killed some nightclub owner in New York when he lived there. He told me all about it, I swear."

"What," said Bobby, "he killed your father and your grandfather? What are you talking about?" Bobby was beginning to think I was delusional; perhaps I had a personal persecution complex about Vince.

"He told me, Bobby, I swear," I said. "He didn't seem himself, you know."

"You're the one who doesn't seem himself, buddy," he said. "You're not going to get anywhere with those claims. That was years ago. It's hearsay, and it's coming from someone who's out to do anything to save his own skin."

"You don't believe me?" I said.

"Charlie, it makes no difference to anybody but you, me and God what *I* believe," Bobby cried. "What matters is what these officers believe, and more importantly, what they think you can testify to and make a jury believe. There's got to be evidence around to back up your story. Think of what you know of his business affairs. You said you knew he was tied to the mob."

"Well, it was pretty clear to those of us who were close to him," I said. "You should know the people he associates with..."

"Charlie, I'm sure we know the people he associates with,"

Bobby said in exasperation. "You can't put a guy away for who his friends are. You've got to have concrete evidence to convince a jury to convict someone of the kinds of things that are worse than what you did, Charlie. Is there anything you have first hand knowledge of – that you can prove? That's what you will need to parlay into some kind of deal."

"I don't know, Bobby," I said, trying to concentrate, but realizing I really didn't have any firsthand knowledge of his activities other than running the betting cards for Frank. Then I realized I couldn't even directly tie Vince to that activity. All I knew was Vince was an associate of Frank Machelli's, but not necessarily involved in the betting cards. Even I knew that was a far stretch to connect Vincent, when he had lawyers like David Israel to distort the testimony of a rookie like me. "I just know how he is, and I know what he told me yesterday. I'd be willing to testify, if you could get me a deal."

The shit had hit the fan for me, and I was ready to deal. I did have second thoughts, because I did stake my fiber to loyalty – on being true to the people I grew up with, and who had been there for me. But it didn't take long to justify screwing Vincent – he killed my father, and that was enough for me to defend turning states evidence on him. The problem was, I had no evidence.

"I don't think anything you've told me will get you anywhere, Charlie," Bobby said. "All I can do is put in a word for you, but I will not do anything unethical. I'm sorry Charlie, but I've worked hard to get where I am, and I have a Constitutional responsibility. Unless you can give us something significant against Vince, I'll do every ethical thing to help you, but chances are you're looking at some serious prison time, and there's not much anyone can do about that."

Just when I was thinking how good it was that Bobby arrived when he did, his words made me grasp the weight of my problem, and even he couldn't carry that load. In fact, since I confessed my crimes to Bobby, he was more of a threat than a help. Bobby could see me fretting and tried to offer some comfort.

"We'll see what we can do, buddy," he said in a more encouraging tone. "I just don't want to give you false hope."

That consolation was enough to dangle a thread of relief. "How have you been, anyway," I asked him as if we were meeting in a bar.

"Fine, Charlie," he said. "Everything's okay with me. Eileen and I were shocked when we learned of... thought you were... you know."

"I know," I replied, "dead."

"Yeah," Bobby chuckled, "I'll tell you, Charlie, if it were up to me, I'd pin a medal on you. If anybody deserved to be blown up at the Rock, that son-of-a-bitch Eddie did. I should share in whatever punishment you've got coming to you just for what I have in my heart. I've killed him a thousand times in my mind. I still go by the Rock and look at what they're doing to it. It'll be prettier than that depressing old house, but it won't have the memories. I'll rue the day they finally tear down the old garage. We had some times in there."

I was facing a future worse than anything the Rock had to offer, and I was wracking my brain to find some glimmer of hope when something Bobby said triggered a flicker of hope deep in my memory. He was talking about the garage – a dusty old place that held such vivid memories. I hadn't thought about it for a long time, but I caught an image of the inside of the dank and musty old structure. I remembered the aroma of dirt and concrete we used to smell when we lifted the tilting door and adjusted our eyes to the coolness of the shaded garage: the lair where fractions of sunbeams would filter their way through the dust on the glass panes of the windows. I remembered the wonderful times Gracie and I shared. Then when Bobby and Eddie came along it became a place where mischief brewed and usually spilled out beyond its confines. I remembered the fire from the matches and the lighter fluid we found in the old garage. It provided a shelter for the alcohol incident and the pornography Eddie provided. And when Eddie lost his first earlobe to the errant gunshot, we retreated to the garage where Bobby tried to stem the bleeding with the rags he stuffed up in the concrete blocks under the rafters. Out of the blue, I remembered Mother and her crazy claims of our fortunes being tied to something up in those concrete blocks under the rafters. Suddenly her voice came back to me – something about a brick or block of concrete up in the rafters with a name and phone number. At the time I thought her alcohol addled mind was deceiving her, but I didn't know then what I found out from Vince just a day earlier.

Mother was blackmailing Vince. Vince said it just the day before…“tells me I’m about to make her a rich woman...” A stroke of serendipity caused the statements to click in my mind. On top of digging into Vince’s illicit affairs, had she been smart enough to document what she knew? Vince spoke of how lucid she was when it came to reciting the damning details. If she did document her findings, why didn’t she tell him? It might have saved her life. Perhaps she committed a sort of passive suicide. Maybe Vince was nothing more than the assistant in an assisted suicide, as I had been for Eddie.

She failed to set things up so that if he did anything to her he would pay the price. She also failed to be clear enough with me about why the garage played such a role in her financial future. Or maybe my poor impaired mother, in some prescient moment of clarity, did everything exactly as she should to get me through this jam in which I found myself. Perhaps she sacrificed herself to save me at this very moment. Perhaps my mother had become my savior. There was a glimmer of hope that the butterfly of chaos might flap some favorable winds my way.

Bobby was still talking as my mind churned, and without realizing it, I broke into his nostalgic ramblings. "Bobby, I may have something," I shouted. "I just thought of it..."

"Well don't tell me about it," he interrupted. "You'll screw yourself if you talk to me, now. You need to see a lawyer before you say another word. Do you have one?"

"Yes, David Israel should be on his way," I said.

"David, Israel," Bobby asked. "Isn't he Vince's lawyer?" Bobby had read the reports from Reo when he was still at the

Bureau.

"Yeah," I replied, "that's how I got hooked up with him."

"Charlie, you can't use him if you're going to betray Vince," Bobby said. “He'd have a conflict of interest. Besides, if Vince is who we all know he is, you don't even want Israel to know what you're doing. Now that is the last bit of advice I can possibly give you. I'm already conflicted all over the place, but I couldn't let you do yourself in. Do not say another word except that you need a lawyer. I have a name for you: Harvey King. He’s the best. Now I'm obligated to tell these officers what I know about this situation. I pray you can tell them more about Vince than I can tell them about you."

Bobby left and brought the agents back into the room. He spoke forthrightly. "Agent Reo, Agent Irvin, this man is not Edward Palomino. This is Charles Lofton." He paused to let that sink in.

Irvin searched his memory bank. "You mean Charles Lofton from the explosion?" exclaimed Reo.

"That is correct," Bobby stated, choosing his words like an attorney. "Mr. Lofton has made certain facts known to me. It is his contention that Edward Palomino is deceased, that his was the body at the Habersham address, and that Mr. Lofton caused his death. He further contends that he may have certain information that might prove helpful to the government as it relates to an ongoing investigation. I have no knowledge of what the information is or how valuable it may be. As you may know, Mr. Lofton is a friend of mine. I have a conflict of interest in this case, and I am going to withdraw myself from it right now. I'll leave you to continue questioning Mr. Lofton." With that, Bobby turned and walked out the door. I was impressed with what my friend had become, and how professional he was, even if he did just give me up for murder to two FBI agents.

The two agents prodded me for information, trying to intimidate me, but I hung tough, demanding to speak to an attorney. Finally, David Israel arrived and demanded to speak to me in a secure room. We were led to a smaller conference room and the agents left us alone.

"Charlie," David said, "It's so good to see you and to know you're alive. I thought I was dreaming last night when you called. What's going on here?"

"Well, David," I said carefully, "it's a real long story. I don't really want to bother you with it. I know you've got bigger fish to fry. Can you just recommend a good lawyer for me?"

"Charlie," David's tone turned patronizing, "if you've got problems I'm your man. Now what's all this about them booking you as Eddie Palomino?"

I knew David would have spoken to Vince before coming to see me, and I knew he knew the answer to his own question. "Like I said David," I responded nervously, "it's a long story. You might guess, since they think I'm Eddie, it might be a conflict for you to represent me."

"Charlie," David said, looking concerned, "you're not thinking of doing anything stupid, are you?"

"David," I said, "I'm not going to do anything stupid. I've just got some legal troubles, and I need to get a lawyer who can best represent me."

David protested. "We can handle your problems, Charlie. We can take care of you and protect everyone involved, at the same time."

That was all I needed to hear to know I had to find someone to represent me who would be concerned for me, and me only. I also knew better than to trust David to recommend a lawyer.

"David," I protested, "I will be on trial for my life. I'm a small client for you. Besides, I couldn't possibly afford your services for a case like this."

"Don't talk about money, Charlie," he said. "If you need money, it will all be taken care of."

"No, thanks anyway," I said flatly, refusing to be railroaded. "Please, I'd rather do it my own way."

David's tone changed. "Okay, Charlie, but hear me good. *Do not* do anything stupid. No matter how much trouble you think you're in now, you don't even know what trouble can be until you cross the wrong people."

His threat struck deep against my spine, helping to cement my resolve. Sweat popped from my forehead as I steeled myself and stared directly into his arrogant face. "Do not threaten me, David," I said. I turned my back, and he stood to leave the room with a parting shot.

"Okay, suit yourself. It's your funeral."

There was no doubt that he had just issued a threat, but that was okay with me. I had already survived one funeral, and I was convincing myself I could avoid another one. David left. Agents Reo and Irvin returned to the room, looking gleeful.

"I want to call a lawyer named Harvey King," I said.

"Harvey King," Reo said. "Look at you. You *are* in trouble."

They got me the phone number and left me alone to make my call. Just talking to the attorney on the phone made me feel better about my future. He didn't say anything to give me false hope. He listened to the cliff notes of the complicated story and asked questions to get insight into my plight. I could tell this was the person I wanted to work with to try to extricate myself from the legal mess threatening to consume me. He promised to see me that afternoon. In the meantime I could only wait and wonder what was in store.

Both Agents left me alone, which suited me. Any time spent in the comfortable office building was time away from the harsh accommodations of the City Jail. I relaxed slightly, allowing myself to grasp the straw of hope that there was something in the old garage to help my new acquaintances at the FBI so they would, in turn, help me. As I sat in solitude, my thoughts wandered back to the jail. I wondered what court was like for Marvin Dixon. He was okay, as prison roommates went, and I hated to lose him just to have to try out another convict. I shamefully hoped the judge invited him to stay for awhile. It was getting past lunch time. The inedible breakfast left my stomach devoid of nourishment. I wondered what kind of gourmet lunch I missed while I dickered with my captors. The regular growl of my empty stomach marked the time as it inched through the afternoon. I had to pee, and there was no one around to tend to my call of nature. When it became unbearable, I called out. An unidentified staff member opened the door. I explained my plight, and the unsympathetic individual left to find someone who knew who I was. After an excruciating interval, Agent Reo finally came into the conference room, smiling.

"Got a little problem," she asked, cruelly.

"Yes, but if I don't hurry and get to the bathroom, someone else is going to have the problem," I replied desperately.

"I wouldn't be so sure about that," Reo said as she freed the leg irons from the table, but left them around my ankles. "We've had people clean up their own messes in shackles before." She led me, step by hampered step, to the men's room where she walked in with me. I would have complained if I hadn't been about to explode. The tears blurred my vision as I shuffled as fast as possible up to the urinal, unzipping just in time.

As I sighed in relief, I asked, "You always watch men while they pee?"

"I do when they're in as much trouble as you are," said Reo. "Don't worry about it. It's nothing I haven't seen."

As she guided me back to my forsaken room, I couldn't keep myself from asking if Harvey was on the way to see me.

"I guess we'll see," Reo said smugly.

I resisted the urge to ask how long I would be waiting to see. It would be at least another hour. I waited in nervous anticipation, anxious to get things moving. The most stressful thing was not knowing how many days of uncertainty lay ahead.

When he walked in, he looked more like a librarian than a lawyer. He was tall and thin. His slightly graying hair was pulled straight back and was collected by a colorful band to form a generous ponytail. He looked to be in his mid-forties until he placed the half lens reading glasses at the end of his sharp nose. They added a couple of more years to his appearance. His dress was informal but neat. Well worn jeans were topped by a sleeveless V-neck sweater over an open collar oxford cloth shirt. When he sat down and rested his feet on the long conference table I could see the argyle socks he wore under a pair of two toned Docksiders. We shared some small talk, but I was ready to talk about my problems.

"Just a minute," he said, putting a finger up to his lips. He left the room for a minute and when he returned he had Agent Reo in tow.

"We need to get these shackles off him," Harvey said. "He's had them on all day, and as I understand it, he hasn't even been arraigned."

"Counselor," Reo protested, "we've had him here all day for his own benefit. We can't unshackle him; he's under arrest. What's to say he won't take off? He's been out of the country on the lam while we were searching for him."

"As I understand it, you guys were looking for Eddie Palomino. You haven't been looking for my client, Mr. Lofton," Harvey said.

"That's because we thought he was dead," Reo said. "We were looking for the man who killed him."

"Not true, Agent Reo," Harvey replied in his lawyerly way. "You were searching for Eddie Palomino on charges completely unrelated to the death of my client, here." I sat next to him trying not to laugh at his ridiculous statement.

"Just the same, Counselor," Reo said in frustration, "we consider him a flight risk."

"Come on, Officer," Harvey said, "look at him. Does he look like the kind of guy who's going to make a break for it down here at FBI headquarters? He's just your average Joe who's gotten himself into a jam."

"This average Joe has committed murder and managed to fool law enforcement about his identity and whereabouts for a long time," Reo said.

"And shame on law enforcement for that," Harvey scolded. "Now come on, Agent Reo; as an officer of the court, I'll be responsible for keeping Mr. Lofton in his place right here in your offices. Its inhumane to keep someone shackled up like that for so long."

"You have a funny way of asking for favors, Mr. King," Reo

complained as she relented, unchaining me from my anchor.

We were escorted to a bare office containing only a desk and a few chairs. Harvey inspected the room to see if there were any obvious bugs. He didn't see anything, but just the same he kept his voice low and admonished me to do the same. Then he got right down to business, tossing a blue paged legal pad on the table and producing a *Mont Blanc* from under his sweater. He prepared to take notes as I began to relate what had been happening since the Rock incident. The more I spoke, the more he made me back up to fill him in on events leading up to all the incidents involved in the case.

At some point he stopped me, and said, "To be clear, you blew this Palomino up in your own house? But he was your own brother."

"Yes, I know," I said, already tired of answering that charge to everyone who leveled it. "But I didn't know it at the time."

"Okay," said Harvey, shaking his head at the quirky facts.

By the time we were finished I felt as if I had told him my life's story.

"Okay," he said, "you think you may have something the government may be willing to bargain for?"

"Well, like I said, I know my mother had something on Vincent Palomino," I said. "She was blackmailing him, and that's why he killed her. She told me about something she had hidden in our garage up at the old house. She said she put it up in the top of the wall where the rafters meet it. I don't know for sure what's there, but that's where you'll find whatever it is."

"We're going to need something good," Harvey said, snapping me from the false sense of comfort I was beginning to feel. "You blew up the house; is the garage even still there?"

"Yeah, it was detached from the house. They're building a new house on the property. They're using the garage to store equipment," I said.

"Don't hang your hopes on this," he warned. "You evidently know Palomino pretty well. You take the night to try to think of anything you may know that might prove beneficial to the case against him. We'll see what we find in the garage. If we don't turn up anything of value, I'll start probing, helping you to determine what may be important that they may want to know. The more we have, the better off we'll be. Even if we can't strike a bargain with these guys, we can work on a good defense for you."

"What about keeping me safe from Vince; can we do something about that?" I asked, hoping to avoid going back to jail.

"Not at the moment, Charlie," he said. "Lets see what we come up with, tonight. Then we'll see if we have anything to even worry about with regard to Palomino." With that, Harvey was gone, and an unidentified marshal shackled me to transport me back to the city jail.

When we arrived back at the jail, I was reprocessed. New mug shots and fingerprints were taken and attached to my proper name, and a new bracelet was strapped to my wrist. I had no idea if the charges against me were changed. My fate was in the hands of these bored city employees for the time being. It did no good to ask questions, since the guards seemed to delight in keeping prisoners uninformed about what was happening in the yellow place with harsh lights.

Marvin Dixon was waiting back in our cell. Waiting was an apt occupation for Marvin. He seemed perfectly suited to it, content to sit and stare and wait for the next thing to happen. His eyes barely moved to look up when the guard slammed the heavy metal door behind me.

"Here come the federal man," Marvin said flatly. "Where you been all day?"

"Talking to people, that's all," I said.

"You missed the recreational period. We'll be in lockdown for a few minutes before they take us to dinner," he told me, sensing my apprehension.

"What happened to you in court?" I asked.

"Five thousand muthafuckin' dollars is what they want to get me outta here," he said with only slightly more emotion.

"Five thousand," I exclaimed thinking more about what it meant for me than for him. "Why so much?"

"It's 'cause of my record, man," he replied, with a resigned calm. "They charged me with all kinds of things that sound bad, something about terroristic threats, assault, things that could land a fella in jail for a good while, when they look at priors. I told the judge I didn't have that kinda money, and she said I'd just have to sit here 'til trial."

"When will the trial be?" I asked, still trying to relate his situation to mine.

"It ain't set yet," he said. "Hell, could be months. First they gotta get me a public defender to take my case. They don't do you no good. They assume you guilty and try to get you to plead out, just so they can move on to their next case and do the same thing. You get you a lawyer?"

"Yes," I said, leery of the question.

"There's a good man, come around here every day, Jeff Curry, he's pretty good. He gets a lot of people off. There was a cat here last time; he was here on receiving stolen property. He was caught dead to rights – three or four stolen cars taken apart in his garage. Old Curry got him off on some technicality. I need somebody like that. If you can afford him, you ought to talk to him. Who'd you talk to?"

I figured Marvin, being familiar with the entire community of players in the criminal law system, might be a good sounding board to check my progress.

"You ever seen a guy around here named Harvey King," I asked.

Marvin sat up and looked wide eyed straight at me with more enthusiasm than he exhibited the entire short time I had known him. "Sheeeet," he exclaimed. "Hell no. I know who he is, but not from around here. He don't need to come around here looking for customers. Everybody know who he is. Harvey King? Is that who you got? You either got a lot of money or you in bad trouble. What'd you do to get the Feds all after you and get a big time lawyer and all?"

"It's a long story, Marvin," I said, thinking the lethargic cellmate would drop it. Suddenly Marvin was animated.

"No man, I gotta know. What's a goofy white guy like you

doing here in more trouble than the rest of us put together?"

So, once again I recounted my story as Marvin sat riveted, tossing in comments, here and there, like "you killed you own brother, and didn't even know he was you brother?" to which I replied, "I know Marvin. I wish people would quit reminding me," to which he replied "oh, sorry, but the same man that killed you father, killed you mother about twenty years later?" to which I replied, "Yes Marvin. Weird, isn't it?"

The story was interrupted by an abominable dinner of some kind of processed meat, watery mashed potato mix, and canned green beans, all swimming in a bland, yellow gravy. Marvin and I sat together, but neither of us said a word. Marvin looked around jealously as if to protect his personal gem of secret information. He was clearly eager to get back to lockdown, and it didn't disappoint me when the tinny, echoing, indiscernible PA system herded us back to our cells.

We had a roll call, then the doors were unlocked and we were free to move to the common area, which consisted of a single television and rows of uncomfortable chairs. There was a prison store that sold snacks and toiletries. I must have missed the day's shower, which didn't matter, since I hadn't made book. According to Marvin, that means nobody on the outside had come to put money on my prison account, which would allow me to charge things. Marvin was generous enough to offer to charge a toothbrush and some toothpaste, since his wife brought thirty dollars to put on his books. I thanked him, but declined, thinking the prison could at least provide a toothbrush. I went down to the store where the clerk informed me that nothing was free of charge. Even a toothbrush cost money.

"What's your number," he asked cocking his head to read my bracelet.

"It doesn't matter," I said. "I don't have anything on the books."

"Let me see," he said. "Sometimes people bring you money and you don't know about it."

"I doubt it," I said.

"Well, you'd be wrong," said the clerk. "Says here you've

got seventy-five bucks on the books."

That surprised me. I would find out later that Bobby was kind enough to deposit that in my name. I got a toothbrush, some soap, and a Snickers bar for me and one for Marvin. When I returned to the cell, he was waiting on the edge of his bunk for me to resume the account of my criminal activity. We ate our candy bars while I finished my story. I couldn't understand Marvin's fascination, but from his point of view he was rooming with an uncommon criminal. That broke the monotony of jail time for him. My first impression of my cellmate as an inert bump on a prison cot was changing. His enthusiasm grew with each new detail of my misadventure.

Finally the story was told, so I asked about him. Marvin was from New Jersey. He didn't know his father, but his mother was a public school teacher who died when he was eleven. He was sent to Los Angeles with one brother to live with an older sister while his other two brothers stayed with an aunt in Jersey. Adele, the Los Angeles sister, was strict and kept the two boys in school and made them go to church. Marvin got a good foundation until, when he was sixteen, Adele's company sent her to Germany for a two year stint. The two brothers rejoined their other siblings back in New Jersey. The situation at the aunt's was a disaster. The children were already in trouble with the law, and Marvin fell right into the life his oldest brother was leading. Soon they were standing before a judge charged with auto theft. Marvin got probation for that, but when he was convicted for armed robbery, he went to prison for the first time. Adele was transferred from Germany to Atlanta, and when Marvin was released he came down to start over. He got back on track for awhile, but then he got into a drug habit. That caused him to employ various illegal methods for acquiring the funds necessary to feed his activity. Pretty soon he was back in jail for selling drugs. When he got out, Adele took charge and made sure he went through the prescribed drug treatment program. She got him a job, and tried to keep him away from the bad influences that helped land him in prison.

Marvin started working for a Coca Cola bottling plant. He

got married and had four children. There was a minor incident of recidivism when he got a DUI coming home after meeting some coworkers at a bar. He lost his license for six months. The lack of license did not discourage Marvin from driving. One afternoon, while picking up his kids from school, the policeman presiding over the after school traffic pulled Marvin over for not having his kids in seat belts. When Marvin could not produce a driver's license he went back to jail. This caused him to lose his job. His wife, Janita, became severely ill with untreated diabetes, and had to quit her job as a waitress at *Waffle House* for awhile. Money got tight while they were both unemployed, and they were in so much debt they were still trying to get out from under it.

When Marvin got out of jail again, he found work with a small cabinetry company. He enjoyed the work and things were back on track. Then on Tuesday night he went out to a bar with his coworkers. He claimed he had only three beers. When he passed the convenience store who had sold him a twenty-five dollar *Plasti-Com Card* to buy long distance he went in. The card did not work and he asked to get his money back. The clerks at the store denied any responsibility for the cards and an argument ensued that lead to Marvin's arrest.

"I mean it just weren't right," he explained. "I paid them men twenty-five dollars of my hard earned money so I can talk to my oldest daughter who's in Statesboro at college, and I hadn't got to speak one word to her. They had my money and wouldn't give it back. I told 'em I was gonna stay there 'till they gave it back. Pretty soon the cops come and they didn't want to hear no part of what I had to say. One thing led to another and they brought me in."

"I suppose I'm just one of those people who's got the problem of finding myself in jail from time to time – lately for little things, though," Marvin concluded. It didn't seem to bother him too much; being an occasional inmate had become a way of life for Marvin. I fell asleep thinking about how different Marvin's experience was from my own. I wished I had his problems instead of mine.

XXI. Two More Investigations

Jason Jordan received a call from Harvey King Monday evening. The retired GBI agent with a PHD in *Criminal Justice* did investigative work for the attorney from time to time. Harvey paid well for his services, and Jason was good at what he did. Harvey requested he go to a construction site on Habersham Road and look for a document that was hidden in the rafters of an old garage on the property. Harvey didn't know what the document contained, but it was imperative that Jason find whatever was there as soon as possible. He wasn't busy, so he decided to leave right away and take a look at the property. Approaching the bulldozed lot he could see that whoever was building the house had money. Jason pulled up the driveway where he was greeted by someone who looked like a superintendent. There were some Hispanic men working with concrete on the foundation of the house.

"Can I help you," the man asked Jason.

"No, I'm just driving around the neighborhood looking at houses," Jason said. "This looks like its going to be a big one. Who's building it?"

"It's a couple," the man responded. "The guy's a dot com millionaire. He's about thirty years old. His wife's a doll. Too bad, huh?"

"Guess so," Jason responded. He could tell the man was a talker, willing to volunteer any facts he knew, and some he didn't. "They got you working late?"

"We're trying to get some of this foundation poured before the rain," the man said. "We'll work until we can't see anymore. That won't be too much longer."

"Thanks for letting me check it out," said Jason as he began turning his car around to leave.

He drove off to get dinner and feed his dog. He returned to the construction site when it was dark and the crew was gone.

His flashlight revealed a chain and padlock on the garage door. That presented no problem for Jason, who had the equipment and expertise to get past the lock. Just the same, he walked around to the side of the building and tried a window. It felt stuck at first, but it finally popped loudly and began to slowly open. The investigator climbed through the narrow opening, flashlight in his mouth, brushing cobwebs out of the way as he landed on the packed dirt floor. He trained the spot from the flashlight up along the edge of a concrete block wall. As the beam hit the corner, he thought he saw the edge of some paper. The construction company obligingly parked a Bobcat toward the back of the garage, providing an ideal stepping stool by which to get to the top of the wall.

He put the flashlight in his mouth and climbed up on the tractor's shovel where he was able to reach his target. He grabbed something, but it felt more like fabric than paper documents. He gave it a tug and an old rag peppered him with dust as it broke free from its perch. It was stiff, and when the beam of the flashlight hit it Jason could see it was stained with a dried brown substance. He suspected blood, but he thought it could be paint or a wood stain. He decided to hold onto it until he was able to thoroughly analyze it, even though it had nothing to do with a document. He directed the flashlight back toward the top of the walls. The spot of light didn't reveal any evidence of paper, but he wanted to be diligent for his client, and he was already covered in dust, so he climbed on top of the roll cage of the Bobcat and began searching from a higher vantage along the edge. In the far corner, he could see something that could be paper, but it wasn't above the Bobcat.

With flashlight in mouth, he pulled himself up onto a crossbeam and began stretching his steps from one beam to the next until he reached the other corner. When the light hit the top of the wall, he cold see a hole in one of the blocks stuffed with what appeared to be a piece of paper. He worked the crumpled ball from it's confined cubbyhole and smoothed it out to find what looked like a lockbox key and bold magic marker across the legal size page reading, "Charlie – Call

Attorney Grover Hewitt at this number. He has valuable information you might need." Jason had no idea if he held what Harvey was looking for, so he trained his light around the perimeter of the wall again. When he was satisfied the stained rag and the note with the key were the only treasures hidden in the garage he jumped to dirt floor and stole his way back to his car. On his way home he called Harvey, correctly guessing he would still be in the office.

"Harvey, Jason here," he said. "I may have what you're looking for."

"Good, JJ. Have you looked at it?" Harvey asked, knowing that the investigator wouldn't be able to resist. "What is it?"

"Looks like a piece of paper with an attorney's name and phone number on it," said Jason.

"Hmm, that's all you found?" Harvey said.

"That and an old rag that's stained with something that looks like it might be blood," Jason said.

"Hmm," repeated Harvey, "that's odd. What's the attorney's name?"

"Grover Hewitt," said Jason.

"Doesn't ring a bell," said Harvey after testing his memory for a moment. "I'm knee deep in another case right now. Can you be in my office first thing in the morning?"

"Not a problem, Counselor," Jason said, curious about what role this piece of paper or the rag would play in one of Harvey's cases.

....

The unintelligible, echoing P.A. system and the unfriendly lights woke me up at 6:45 in the morning. I stayed in bed long enough to let Marvin do his business in as much privacy as one can hope for in those very public environs. When the toilet flushed, I got up, relieved myself and got ready to leave the cell for breakfast. Marvin grumbled as the guards escorted us to the stark dining area. When we got our food, Marvin made sure to stick close, still protecting the treasure he possessed. We continued to talk, while I refused to eat the slop on my plate. Marvin was willing to clean my plate for me.

When the guards came around to collect people for their bond hearings, I was called to join the line. We got into the courtroom and waited while we watched what appeared to be complete disorganization in the front of the courtroom at the judge's bench. Once in a while a name would be called, and an inmate would be led away from our pack to join an attorney in front of the bench. It was impossible to hear what took place, but it took awhile to dispose of each case. The waiting was excruciating, since I didn't even know what I would be facing when it was my turn. I looked around and didn't see Harvey. I didn't know if he was even aware of this hearing.

Finally, my name was called and I was taken to see the judge. A woman in a business suit met me at the front. "Hi, I'm Sandy Miller," she said casually and quickly. "Harvey King sent me to represent you at this hearing. Let me do all the talking."

The charges read against me were numerous and complicated, but the ones that sank my spirits the most were arson and murder in the first degree. After that, I couldn't comprehend anything until Ms. Miller said, "Not guilty to all charges, your Honor."

"Okay, we'll go to trial on this one," said Judge Katherine Skiles. "What are the people asking Mr. McKenzie?"

"Your Honor, Mr. Lofton is accused of a capital crime," said the starched prosecutor. "He also faces numerous federal charges. He has proven himself to be a flight risk, as he has already fled the country under an assumed name. Therefore, the people ask that the defendant be held without bail."

"Ms. Miller?" said the judge to my representative.

"Your Honor," my attorney said, "at this time we will not contest the people's request."

"Okay counselor," Judge Skiles sighed, "we'll put this on the docket and notify the parties. Thank you Ms. Miller. Take Mr. Lofton into custody." A man with a sheriff's uniform gripped my upper arm.

I couldn't believe my ears. Was this person I'd never met forsaking me to spend an unknown amount of time in jail until my case came to trial without so much as a fight. I started to say something, but Ms. Miller just looked at me and put her finger to her lips. I was led away to wait in the back of the courtroom for someone to take me back to prison. Ms. Miller smiled at me, and without a word, left through doors behind the judge's bench. I sat in the back of the courtroom hoping Harvey had a better plan than the fiasco that occurred in front of the judge. I wasn't the only one in the courtroom wondering what just happened. David Israel had one of his assistants there to find out how things were developing in my case.

The remaining activity in the front of the courtroom passed before my eyes without meaning. Any time spent away from the jail was welcome time, but I was stewing about the prospects for getting out of the jail, at all. I tried to relax and listen in to get a feel for what was happening to the other defendants being paraded before the bench. It was all finished before lunch. We were herded back to yellow headquarters to have a yellow lunch.

Seeing Marvin Dixon back in the cell proved an odd sense of comfort. He was the one person I identified with, not to mention he was a mentor on useful tips for prison practices and procedures.

"How'd it go," Marvin asked lazily as he lay in the bunk staring at the cruel lack of sky above him.

"Wonderful," I said. "They're going to hold me with no bond. I'm stuck here until… who knows."

"Hmpf," replied Marvin, "that right? Whatcha charged with?"

I could hardly bring myself to say it. "Oh just about anything you can do. Everything from practicing dentistry without a license, to murder in the first degree."

"Murder, eh," Marvin perked up. "Well there you go. They don't usually grant bond in murder cases. Nothing even your hotshot lawyer can do about that."

It was a wonder how Marvin knew everything about the law.

"My hotshot lawyer?" I said sarcastically. "My hotshot lawyer didn't even show up for the hearing. He sent some woman I didn't know to stand up there with me. She didn't do anything. She didn't even try to get bond for me."

"That right?" asked Marvin curiously. "That don't seem right. What'd she say?"

"Nothing; she just smiled and put her finger to her lips."

"That means something, there," said Marvin. "That's a good thing. They cooking up something good for you, Charlie."

I wanted to grasp onto any straw available. "You think so?" I asked as I felt my heartbeat decelerate at the suggestion.

"Oh yeah, man," Marvin said. "You got *the* man, and he cooking up something me and you don't even know about, yet. You might get outta here before you know it. There's no telling."

Marvin's sudden enthusiasm helped a little, but I had no illusions of walking away from the jail anytime soon. As time passed and I considered the odds, my confidence that Mother actually had something on Vincent was eroding. I didn't believe her to be competent enough to document anything. Still, as Vince put it, she recited some very specific and damning detail. I had to nail my hopes to Vincent's words.

....

Jason Jordan got to Harvey King's office at seven o'clock sharp, about an hour and forty-five minutes before I was taken to court for my bond hearing. Harvey greeted his investigator with a cup of coffee Jason accepted and put down without a sip. Harvey was known for his bad coffee. Jason knew better than to have anything until the rest of the law office staff showed up and made something potable. Harvey briefed Jason on the case and gave him an office where he could call Counselor Hewitt.

Jason assumed it would be too early for most lawyers to be at work. He tried the number and got a recorded disconnection notice. A check of the phone book revealed a different number for Grover Hewitt. Jason tried it and got the anticipated voice mail. He left Harvey's office number and went to the kitchenette to dump Harvey's muddy concoction from his cup. He heard Harvey's secretary settling in for another intense day of lawyer administration, and he smelled a fresh pot brewing thanks to Tyler Cannon.

"Morning Tyler," Jason said as he held his empty cup out to her like a beggar.

Tyler took the cup with a sympathetic smile and said, "JJ. How are you doing? It's been awhile. What brings you here at this uncivilized hour?"

"Your boss," said Jason. "How have you been?"

"Busy, as usual," she said. "We've got a lot of cases going. I'm trying to do Harvey's work and keep the rest of the staff on track. How about you?"

"Doing fine," Jason said, aware of how competently she performed her duties. "How is Jessica?" he asked.

"She's fourteen. She's a pain in the ass," said Tyler with a smile. "But she's my pain in the ass, and I love her."

Jason knew Tyler's daughter because he had been to her home and met her. Tyler was a divorcee who was not a classic beauty, but something about her late thirties look attracted him. He had worked with her long enough to grasp the depth of her intellect, so several years earlier he took the plunge and asked her out. They had several dates, but they couldn't make the leap from the friend stage to the romantic stage. Before things got too awkward, they mutually agreed to leave things as they were. They remained friends and worked together whenever Harvey brought Jason into a case.

Tyler answered the phone and transferred the call. She pointed Jason to the phone and he went back to his space to answer it.

"Mr. Jordan," the voice said. "Grover Hewitt returning your call."

"Yes Mr. Hewitt," Jason said, "I'm calling to see if you have a client by the name of Mary Lofton."

There was a pause on the other end before Grover answered.

"I don't recognize the name," he said.

It didn't take the investigative intuition of Jason Jordan to know Mr. Hewitt was lying. He pressed the lawyer. "It would have been a few years ago," he said, calculating the time since Mary Lofton's death. Harvey was thorough in his briefings and Jason retained information almost photographically.

"I'd have to look back to see," Grover said. "Of course, if I find something it would be confidential between my client and me."

"I understand," Jason said, and he understood much more about his phone conversation than lawyer-client confidentiality. He read the situation perfectly. "I am calling on behalf of Harvey King. Do you know Mr. King?"

"I know of him," said Grover Hewitt. "What's his interest in this Mary Lofton?"

"That is also a matter of confidentiality for the moment," said Harvey. "I think you and Mr. King should have a meeting to discuss Ms. Lofton."

"Mr. Jordan," Grover protested, "I'm very busy with current clients, and I don't have time to spend on mysteries."

"If you can meet with Harvey, it won't be a mystery, Mr. Hewitt," said Jason. "I *will* say that it is most important. A man's future is at stake."

"Just the same, I don't see how I can help," said Grover. "I do not recall any Mary Lofton. If I did it would be…"

"privileged information." Jason finished his sentence for him. "I think you are apprehensive about who you're talking to and what my purposes are. Mr. King is so keen to talk to you, he will do it on any terms you dictate. But I have an idea. You should hire a security detail to accompany you to the meeting. I could suggest someone, but I don't think you trust me. You find a few men who are good with their fists and with weapons. Mr. King will pay the cost. You meet him at the city jail at the consultation area. What can go wrong there? Time is of the essence, though. Can you try to do it today, sometime after two?"

"Mr. Jordan, I really do not see…" Grover was interrupted.

"Please Mr. Hewitt," implored Jason. "A man's future is at stake. We will make it worth your while, I promise."

"Let me check my schedule," Hewitt said reluctantly. I will call you back to see what I can work out."

Jason hung up the phone and waited for Harvey to finish an unrelated call. When Tyler showed him into Harvey's office, he sat across the desk from him. "I think we have something, Harvey," he said with an urgency that captured the attorney's attention. "I talked to Grover Hewitt. I'm sure he knows something about Mary Lofton, but he is scared. So whatever he knows is big enough to have him covering it up. I had to push him hard to even get him to consider speaking to us. I offered to pay the cost of a security detail for him to meet you. Then I suggested the city jail as the place to meet. I figure he'll feel safe enough around a bunch of cops and prison officials. If you and he come to an arrangement, he would be right there at the jail to confer with your client."

"Thanks for spending my money," Harvey said dryly. "What time do we meet?"

"He's supposed to call back to let me know for sure, but I told him after two as you instructed," said Jason.

Harvey looked at Jason in amusement. Even after all this time away from the GBI, Jason had not completely shaken that starched collar, pecking order mentality. "Well, you take instruction well, JJ," he chided. "Let me know when he calls back, and I'll talk to him. Now, you may be excused."

"Fuck you, boss," Jason said.

....

Jason and Harvey watched a lawyer walk nervously into the spacious consultation area at the city jail. "Think that's our man?" said Harvey as Jason stood to greet the man in the dark, off-the-rack suit and button-down white shirt and red tie.

"Mr. Hewitt?" Jason said, extending his hand. Grover Hewitt's eyes darted in his direction and then to the legendary Harvey King sitting at a table. "I'm Jason Jordan, and this is…"

"Harvey King, I know," Mr. Hewitt said in a hushed tone.

Harvey stood and shook Hewitt's hand. "Let's step into a room," Harvey said as he led the way into a small conference room with a table and five chairs. Harvey spoke as they settled into the hard, wooden chairs adorned with pen etched graffiti. "Can I call you Grover? And I'm just Harvey. I can tell you are apprehensive about meeting us. Frankly, we feel the same way. I can only say that while I represent defendants in criminal cases, I conduct my business with absolute propriety. I do not do the illegal bidding of criminal clients. I have a client now who needs to know what you may know about Mary Lofton."

"I can appreciate what you are telling me, Harvey," said Grover, "but as I told Mr. Jordan, I would not be able to divulge any confidential information of any of my clients."

"I understand," Harvey said. "I am going to go out on a limb and reveal that my client is Charles Lofton, the son of Mary Lofton."

That comment shook Grover, and he began to perspire. "It doesn't matter because I don't know anything about Mary or Charles Lofton," he said.

Jason chimed in. "I think it might be helpful if you check the records here. You will see that Charles Lofton is alive and currently residing in this very building."

Grover could not help divulging a puzzled stare. "I really don't see the need, but I'll humor you," he said, trying to regain his facade of ignorance.

When he left the room, Jason said, "I think you can tell him the story, buddy. He's simply too scared to admit what he knows. If he had any ties to Palomino, he wouldn't be acting like that." The two waited in silence for a few minutes until Grover returned.

"I thought Charles Lofton died in a fire at his Buckhead home," Grover said. "Tell me the story, and I'll go out on a limb and try to help you."

Harvey gave Grover the same briefing he gave Jason earlier that morning and told him where Jason unearthed his name.

"So in order for my client to get consideration from the US Attorney, he needs to come up with some substantial and damning evidence against Vincent Palomino."

Grover sighed a relieved breath and said, "You came to the right place. And you gave me the password – Charles Lofton." Mary Lofton came to me a few years ago with documents she stole and copied from Palomino's office. She wanted to make affidavits about the contents of the documents and she wanted me to maintain them in case she needed them. I didn't think anything about it at first. I didn't know who this guy was. Then, when I saw some of the things she was bringing me, and recorded her testimony about them, I began to realize the gravity of the information. I didn't know what her purposes were; I was afraid she was blackmailing Palomino, but she told me she wasn't. Just having that material scared the hell out of me. I did my best to impress upon her how dangerous it would be, and I convinced her not to tell anyone what she had, including her son. It would be dangerous for me and anyone else who knew about the information we had. She promised she would keep it between the two of us, but she signed a Release of Information, allowing me to communicate the particulars to Charles Lofton should he ask about it.

I got a safe deposit box at the Marietta Community Bank and put all that damning information in it. I would bill Mary Lofton once a year for the cost of the box. Then, when I didn't hear back from her one year, I looked into it and found out she committed suicide. I wasn't so sure about that, though; I had seen and heard what this guy Palomino was capable of. Then, when I saw the news about Charles Lofton dying in the explosion at the home he and Mary lived in, I was sure there was some foul play. I wanted to destroy the information to wash my hands of the whole thing. Then I thought if Palomino caught wind of my involvement, it would be good to have the goods on him for self preservation. So it's all up in Marietta stuffed in that safe deposit box. It's not very organized; I didn't even want to get into all that stuff. But it's there, and if Charles Lofton is your client, you can have all of it. I will be glad to have more people in the know about all this."

"Alright, then," said Harvey, "Jason will go with you to Marietta and we'll see what we can put together."

....

Wednesday morning Jason brought the jumble of papers, computer disks, CD's and video cassettes into Harvey King's office. "Here it is," he said to Harvey, "such as it is."

"Have you looked at it, at all," Harvey asked.

"Haven't had time, yet," said Jason. "I'll get it into some kind of order, and then we'll go over it."

Jason took the papers into his assigned office and dumped them across a big meeting table. As Grover Hewitt had warned, it was a jumbled mess, but a few key glimpses indicated they contained information about an enterprise of some kind. Jason saw names of people and restaurants he recognized, with dollar amounts. There were checking account statements and handwritten notes. It was pretty clear the papers could be used to blackmail some people, but it would take some studying to understand what the files held.

"Files" was a loose term for what Jason had spread on the table in front of him. As he worked through the mess, there were two things he became certain about the woman who squirreled the documents away with her lawyer. First, she knew nothing of organizing paperwork into any kind of digestible arrangement. Second, she knew the right kind of information to get her hands on for the purpose she had in mind. In almost three hours of shuffling, calculating and diagramming, Jason knew he had something special. Each page he turned, and every figure he recorded heightened his exhilaration. Finally he stood and left the office, locking the door as he went to find his client. Harvey had a client in his office. It was all Jason could do to keep from bursting through the door and interrupting.

When Harvey finally emerged from his office, he found his investigator practically standing in the doorway. "Whatcha got, JJ," he said, shifting his focus back to the Lofton case.

Jason pulled the attorney back into his office and slammed the door. “It’s big, Harvey,” he said, “real big. If I knew last night what I know now, I probably wouldn’t have slept with that file in my house. I mean this is the kind of stuff that gets people killed. You can see it didn’t pan out too well for Mary Lofton.”

“Big, huh?” said Harvey. “That’s good news. This guy may have a chance, after all.”

“Oh yeah, he’s got a chance,” said Jason. “It’s the people mentioned in those papers that don’t have a chance. They’re nailed, dead to rights, Harvey. I’m not just talking about Vincent Palomino, either. There are things in there which implicate members of the New York mob. Not to mention, there are some local and national celebrities who probably wouldn’t be too thrilled to see that information go public.

“I mean, it’s prostitution, money laundering, phone card scams. It spells racketeering all the way. And it spells trouble for us if he finds out we’ve got this. We need to get copies of this stuff and secure them for our own protection.”

Harvey was shocked. Just forty-eight hours earlier, when he met with his new client, he had no idea it would lead to the kind of things involving the kind of people Jason was mentioning. He didn’t doubt his detective’s words. JJ was a seasoned professional, and the way he was reacting to what he saw made Harvey an instant believer.

“All right, then,” he said, “let’s immediately get someone to start making copies. We can’t give this to the copy service. You supervise the process, will you? I’ll contact Henry Lipscomb and arrange for him to deep six a copy for our protection. Then I’m going to put an associate on these things with you, probably Donald Travers. I’ll also get a CPA in here to work with you. We’re going to have to keep this down to as few hands as possible for everybody’s safety.”

“You’re right about that,” said Jason. “As a matter of fact, I’d feel more comfortable doing the copying, myself. I’ll get it done quickly enough. You just get me a secure room to do the work. I got my laptop, so I can make copies of the disks, too, but we may need to get some software in here to read what's on 'em. I think it would be wise to let me speak to Don Travers and your CPA to make sure they understand what's involved – to give them the option on the work. If there's any hint of a leak, or any kind of threat, I can work on providing security for the team. It's your man behind bars that we have to think about."

"Yeah," said Harvey. "So, I can assume you believe this is going to help save his ass?"

"Hell yes," boomed Jason. "I can't imagine why the Feds wouldn't want to *kiss* his ass when they realize what he can provide."

"Okay then," Harvey said, "Make three copies: the originals we'll secure with Lipscomb's firm and then you'll have three working copies for your team."

"Make it two for the team," interrupted Jason. "The fewer the better; and there's enough information there that three people can work efficiently with two copies – and it will save a little time at the copier."

"Okay, we'll make it two," agreed Harvey. "How long will it take?"

"I've got some work to do to get it organized," Jason said. "Give me today to finish organizing. Thursday to get copies made and files downloaded and software arranged. We should be good to go by the end of the week. I'll put in some extra hours."

"You're just milking me for overtime," Harvey said.

"I'll earn it, and we'll both be alive while we work the case," Jason said.

"The minute you get enough to get my client protection, let me know and I'll start the process with the Feds," said Harvey. "I don't know when to tell this Lofton guy he hit the jackpot. It might be better if he doesn't find out until we can negotiate a deal to get him out of there."

"Absolutely," Jason said, rising out of his chair. "This guy can't know. For his own protection, you keep him in the dark until we can get him isolated."

……..

Whenever Marvin and I and the rest of the inmates were taken to meals and other activities, Marvin continued to stick close to me. He was constantly scanning the area to make sure that his prized cellmate remained in his custody. Marvin was disappointed that I was beginning to be hungry enough to choke down whatever it was they were serving. I had no choice other than to starve. He did manage to get my stale roll every time, and he used that to sop up the last bits of yellow stuff from our plates.

At the jail, everything was always the same: yellow paint, yellow lights, yellow jump suits, yellow food. We got up at the same time every day. We ate meals at the same time every day. The meals were all the same every day. We got out on recreation and milled around and went back to our cells several times a day. Then the guards would finally deliver us from those infernal lights, which burned through the eyes, so we could try to sleep until we started the same routine the next morning. I did not relish the prospect of spending years – or the rest of my life – trapped in this routine.

Conversation with Marvin was one way of keeping my mind occupied and off the subject of my predicament. I began looking forward to the periods in the cell where he and I had privacy. I could listen to him talk about almost anything. Much of his ramblings were not so reliable, but I was glad to listen and let my mind wander. Harvey hadn't contacted me since my bond hearing, even though I placed as many calls to his office as the guards would allow. I was losing faith in my first impression of Harvey King.

I got up Friday morning feeling more exhausted than when I fell asleep. Finally, midway through the morning milling around routine, I was called out to the attorney-client area. There sat my lawyer, looking as though he had just come from weekend brunch in his causal attire and long pony tail. He was trying to smile, but gravity was etched in his face and saturated his words as he spoke in quick tempo.

"I couldn't get back to you sooner," he said without as much as a hello. "I was kind of busy."

"Kind of busy?" I complained. "You're my lawyer, aren't you? I'm paying you whatever this is going to cost, aren't I?"

"Well now that you mention it, Charlie," he said, as he peered at me over his reading glasses, "we haven't spoken about money."

Harvey explained he agreed to see me after my call from the regional office of the FBI. That was the kind of rare and bizarre call any attorney would respond to, no matter who the client turned out to be. Now that he had a general understanding of the case he would take me on, and he could afford to invest some under-billed time on it. But there were going to be costs, and he wanted to spell out the facts and know what I was prepared to spend.

"Something like this can run into some dollars," he continued.

Here we go, I thought. "Yeah, I'm sure you're concerned about that. Are you concerned about me, is the question. I'm on pins and needles over here, and I can't even get a phone call from you. You'll get your money, don't worry. How much are we talking, anyway?" I asked, suddenly unsure how that was going to happen.

"Well this is a serious matter, Charlie," Harvey said. "We will need to do research. That takes staff, and even outside consultants. There are security costs and we have to interview and depose people. I have some highly qualified people working on your behalf, and it will take a lot of my time, too. I bill out at five hundred dollars an hour. This whole thing will doubtlessly run into five figures, and I can't tell you it won't run into six. But we're fighting for your freedom."

The spiel was good, and Harvey was smooth. I couldn't read him – was he really that sincere, or was he just good at feigning sincerity.

"I can afford it if you will get me outta this thing," I said, knowing I could get money from the trust I set up with Emmett Brandice.

"Well, Charlie, I'm not going to tell you we're going to get you out of it at this stage," he responded, evenly. "There are simply too many factors. If I told you that I would not be honest with you, and I believe you deserve my honesty."

Harvey's answer contained another vague duality. Was he being honest with me, or was he reciting a disclaimer by which he could take my money and say, 'Hey I told you there were no guarantees,' as I was being carted off to the big house. Still, Bobby *did* recommend him.

"All I want to know is, can I trust you?" I asked, searching his eyes for an answer.

"Yes, you can trust me," he said.

"All right," I said, "I know I can cover five figures. I can probably get into six figures."

"Can I trust *you?*" he asked.

"Yes," I said.

"Fine, then I would like you to arrange for a deposit of five thousand dollars, as soon as you can," he said, sounding as if he were asking for five dollars.

"Hmmm, that might be a problem," I said, trying to think of the mechanics of getting to the trust Emmett established.

"Charlie, I can let you float on some time, but we will have cash outlays, and I don't want to be spending my own…"

"It's done," I interrupted. "It might take a couple of days, but I set up a trust with an attorney named Emmett Brandice before I left town." I didn't say, 'before I killed Eddie.' "I had around ninety thousand in the trust. Then he must have gotten money for the property on Habersham. If you help me arrange getting it, I think that should cover a whole lot of advocating."

"I'll contact Mr. Brandice, and we can start on your case right away," Harvey said.

"Now, what about the case?" I said. "Is there anything we can do to get me outta this mess?"

"It's hard to say so soon," Harvey answered too ambiguously for my taste. "There are several ways we can approach it depending on how things unfold. It's too early to talk about, right now."

I was almost afraid to ask the next question. "What about the garage? Did you find anything there that might help?"

"I'm not sure we will have anything there," he said, with that infuriating cloudiness in his response. "Along those lines, though, if we do get something, or if you come up with anything on Vincent, are you willing to deal with the prosecutors to reduce your criminal exposure? Keep in mind, that would mean you may be putting yourself in danger, and you might have to go into a witness protection program to stay safe."

The question gave pause. Bobby brought that up on Monday, but I hadn't thought of the implications until that very moment. It was the idea of having to change identity and start a new life, yet again. I had done it once, and it had worked out well. Besides, anything was better than the alternative of prison. "Yeah, I'll do it," I said, wanting to get back to the garage, but Harvey was pushing forward without hesitation.

"All right," he said. "Just one more thing, Charlie; you're dealing with a super sensitive subject for some people. It could be a dangerous subject. It would be wise for you to not mention this to any of your neighbors in there. This must be kept in the strictest of confidence for everyone concerned." I didn't know what he meant by *everyone concerned*, but his comment triggered thoughts about what I told Marvin, and what Marvin told others. Harvey stood up. "Well then, I probably won't talk to you over the weekend, and we'll see what the new week brings."

"But wait a minute," I said, desperately. "Can't we talk a little more?"

He looked at me sympathetically. "Any more conversation at this point would be feel good chit chat, Charlie, and that would be expensive therapy for you." He smiled and turned away.

Of course he was right. I just wanted him to reassure me that everything was going to work out for me. That wasn't going to happen. I left the conference room a little wiser, but no less concerned. My mind started racing and my heart picked up the pace. There was more I should have asked. What about getting bond? When would I hear from him again? By the time I was greeted by Marvin back in the cell, I was thinking I failed to maximize my brief time with the man who would be working on my behalf.

……..

It was eleven Friday morning at Harvey King's office and Jason was about to see the accountant from *Harris, Taylor and Oates, P.C.* He and Don Travers, a lawyer in Harvey's firm, met earlier to discuss possible candidates to do the auditing. Jason spelled out the task and the risks of being involved in such a mission. Don was a married father of two, and the detective's blunt description of the parties and the stakes involved brought the dangers home in a real and disturbing manner. It was with a degree of trepidation he agreed to work on the research. He was already ensconced in the locked conference room, beginning his initial perusal of the papers when Tyrone Jones, CPA was called into Jason's temporary office.

"Mr. Jones, come in," Jason greeted. "I'm Jason Jordan, a private investigator retained by the firm. I know you've worked with Harvey's group over here in the past, but give me a recap of your experience."

Tyrone hadn't been briefed on the case before he arrived and he thought interrogation by this private-eye to be odd, but he played along. "You want my experience with Harvey King, or my entire work history," he asked.

"I'm sorry, your work history, please," Jason replied.

"I've been with HTO since graduation, eight years ago," he began. "I've been in auditing the entire time. In recent years my role has been Audit Manager on engagements for my firm."

"What kind of clients?" Jason delved. "Have you been specializing in a specific industry?"

"It runs the gamut," Tyrone replied. "In a firm our size we don't compartmentalize like the major firms. If anything, I'd say I've worked a lot of health care organizations. Here at

Harvey King I've been involved in some embezzlement issues and some auditing for divorce cases. That's been awhile, though."

"That's okay," Jason interjected, "what about your personal life? What's your family situation?"

"Look, Mr. Jordan," Tyrone said as he shifted in his seat. "I'll be glad to answer any questions you have, if you can give me a reason. I've worked with this firm in the past, and I think you'll find my performance was more than satisfactory."

"Please," Jason implored, "just indulge me for another minute and it will be clear. I assure you I'm not questioning your competence."

"Okay then, I'm single," Tyrone said. "I've been seeing someone for almost two years – no children, obviously."

Jason chuckled, "This day and age, maybe that's not a given, anymore. What about your immediate family – parents, siblings – anyone in Atlanta?"

"My parents are in Maryland with my younger sister," Tyrone responded. "I've got a younger brother in Virginia. But what is this all about?"

"One more thing, please," said Jason. "If I told you that there was an element of danger involved in this engagement, how would you react to that?"

The comment piqued Tyrone's interest, and he thought for a moment. He was the working manager on three live audits, and he had a pile of administrative work back at the office. It had been a long time since he worked in the Harvey King law office, and he considered himself too experienced for that kind of work. The things he worked on there could be handled by someone with much less experience than his. That's why he was surprised when Roff Taylor asked him the previous evening to make the visit. He was put out about it the entire morning, and Jason's grilling didn't do anything to mollify him – until the last question.

"That's an interesting question," he said. "What kind of danger?"

"Let me first state, emphatically, that anything you hear from me this morning must be held in the strictest confidence," Jason said in a tone so grave, it had to be taken seriously. "If any information were to be leaked from this office, it would likely endanger peoples lives, mine being one of them. So I ask for your word on that."

"You can count on that," said Tyrone, now salivating to hear more.

"May I call you Tyrone? And you call me Jason, please," the detective said, getting down to the crux of the matter. "We have a room full of documents that we believe could be used to indict some important and ruthless people in this city and perhaps beyond. These people have ties to the mob in New York, and they would do whatever it took to prevent this information from getting to federal law enforcement – I mean anything, such as commit violent acts, even murder. At this moment we are confident they have no idea we have this evidence, or that it even exists, but you can't even imagine how quickly and easily circumstances in matters of this nature change. Right now, the only people who know about this are Harvey King, Don Travers – I think you know Don – you and me. Oh, and maybe your man Roff Taylor has an inkling of knowledge. Information of this kind takes on a life of its own; it can not be contained for long. I'll be happy if we can keep it quiet throughout the weekend. That's why we're going to have to work Saturday and Sunday to try to stay one step ahead of the detection process. What do you think? Are you up for it?"

If Jason were right about the tight security surrounding the secret, Tyrone couldn't imagine how it could be exposed that quickly. He felt sure he wouldn't be in danger. "Why are we doing it," he asked, pointedly.

"We're trying to get enough information so someone can turn states evidence and cut a deal with the Feds," Jason explained. "Poor sap – even he doesn't know what we have our hands on."

Tyrone was fascinated. He couldn't refuse the opportunity. He agreed and the two of them joined Don Travers in the locked conference room. Jason had done his usual proficient work to prepare for his team. The long table had three laptops spaced apart with plenty of room between them to accommodate the mounds of material they would be handling. Next to each computer was a calculator, legal pads, pencils, pens and erasers. At one end of the table was a television with a VCR plugged into it. At the other end rested portable file boxes filled with hanging files. The files were stuffed with yellow papers. Next to the file boxes was a floppy disk container holding perhaps twenty yellow disks. Beside them was a replica of the yellow files, except the pages and disks were blue. The color coding would allow the three researchers to use the materials and replace them without getting them confused. Against the far wall, looking out of place, was an imposing safe large enough to hold all the contents in the room. Beside it sat a large waste basket crowned with a shredder. Each laptop was loaded with the spreadsheet, word processing and accounting software necessary to use the PC files on the disks. Jason's also had a utilities package that would crack almost any file the other software couldn't open. Tyrone made a call back to his office and the three men immediately went to work.

……..

That afternoon after lunch I was milling about with Marvin by my side. Second thoughts about Harvey were creeping into my restless mind. At least with David Israel I would have gotten priority attention, and I would have had Vince and his crew on my side. Since I spurned David for Harvey, Vince would certainly not be an ally. I was a little insecure about Harvey's commitment to my cause. I wasn't sure whether I was doing the right thing or not. It was like speeding down a dark winding road, not knowing what to expect around the next curve, and not being able to put on the brakes. Still, some inexplicable inner compass kept me on the path I paved for myself. My next challenge was going to take all the gumption I could muster. A guard took me from my cell and let me into the private room where inmates use secure phones to communicate with their attorneys.

David was on the other end of the line sounding warm and cheerful. “How are you, Charlie? Did you come to your senses? Are you ready for me to pay you a visit and see what we need to do to move your case along?”

“Not really, David,” I said, trying to return the friendly tone. “I’ve got Harvey King on my case, and I think that’s the best thing for me.”

“Charlie, you hurt me,” said David. “You’re going to choose Mr. King over my service? He’s good, Charlie, but I can do better for you, trust me. Think about it, will you?”

“Yeah, I will,” I said, wishing the call would be over.

“Meanwhile Charlie, you keep me and Vince in mind,” David said, in a benign tone, but the implied threat was clear.

“I will,” I said. The die was cast and I was hoping I was making the right choice. I wanted to discuss it with someone. Marvin Dixon was my only adviser, and I suddenly had to be careful about what I said to him.

....

No matter how professional people are, they never cover one hundred percent of the bases. Just as there is no such thing as the perfect crime, there is also no perfect procedure for what Harvey was trying to accomplish. There were too many variables. David Israel was not on Harvey’s radar screen, and he had no reason to warn me not to speak to him. If I had not been so conflicted about my choice, and if I had known what Harvey knew about the documents, I probably would have had the sense to not mention Harvey King to David.

As it was, within five minutes of my conversation with David, Vince knew Harvey was my lawyer. Bud Bramlett was called in and given his marching orders. Vince had no idea whether I was going to rat on him, but he was going to monitor the situation. He rounded up some support in the form of Frank Machelli and Miguel “Mickey” Alverez.

Frank looked up Harvey King in the phone book and drove to the address on West Peachtree Street in midtown Atlanta where he found a modern, twenty-four story office building. In the lobby, he noted the suite number of sixteen hundred for the law practice. He was done with his part of their investigation for the moment.

At six o'clock that evening, Mickey Alverez gathered with the rest of the mostly foreign cleaning crew at the loading dock of the building where the security office was. The guard made each worker sign in, and then issued temporary badges to be worn while they cleaned. Mickey signed an alias, and received his badge.

When the crew supervisor began to give out assignments, he noticed he had one more head than he was supposed to have. He wasn't going to complain about the extra help, since his office usually left him shorthanded.

Mickey was given his assignment, which he promptly traded with a coworker for ten dollars; he wanted to get to the sixteenth floor. When he got off the elevator, he was greeted by two large frosted glass doors etched with a stately logo identifying the offices of *Harvey King, P.C.* In due time, the supervisor arrived to unlock the door and turn on the lights to the office, which occupied most of floor sixteen. Mickey entered and began emptying waste baskets until his boss left to unlock more doors on other floors. Once alone, he began checking out the offices. All of them were unlocked, including Harvey's. He couldn't find anything related to Charles Lofton or to Vince, but this firm had shredders on almost every trash receptacle it possessed. He placed bugs in strategic areas of the office, and in Harvey King's office phone. He couldn't determine whether they actually had a problem based on his observations, but he hoped they might get something from the bugs. Then he came upon the conference room, which was locked. It had double wood doors and he tried to jiggle the handles until he was startled by a man opening the door in his face.

"Can I help you," boomed the voice of Jason Jordan. The

large gentleman didn't have the look of a lawyer, as he stood blocking the doorway.

Mickey feigned his best lack of English as he said, "Trash, senor?"

"No, thank you," the man said gruffly as he closed the door.

Something was going on in there, Mickey was sure of that, but who knew if it had anything to do with Charlie Lofton. It was almost eight p.m. and there was activity in that room on a Friday night. He tried to discreetly look past the man who confronted him, but he couldn't see much. He caught a glimpse of colored papers strewn across a table. He didn't actually see another person, but there was motion behind the man, and noise from inside the room. He tried to pause for a moment after the door was abruptly shut to listen for conversation, but the room was practically soundproof.

Mickey proceeded to the back of the office where he located a door that led out to a deserted part of the outside hallway. There he deftly applied a patch of duct tape over the latch and closed the door. The worst part of this assignment was that he would have to actually complete cleaning at least that office, so as not to arouse suspicion. He got out the vacuum and set about the menial tasks. By nine o'clock, he noticed two white men and a black man emerge from the locked room. By then he was dusting, and he kept to his chores while he watched the man who confronted him wrap a heavy chain around the door handles and attach a high security lock before he joined the other two. All three men left together. There would be no getting in that room on Friday night.

When Mickey was alone, he assessed the job he did on the office and was satisfied to see it was spic and span. Soon the supervisor returned, complimented him on his work in Spanish, locked up the office, and accompanied him to Suite 1650, a small ad company with four offices. That was the only other suite on the sixteenth floor. The supervisor told him to just lock the door behind him when he was finished and proceed to the seventeenth floor. As soon as the supervisor was gone, Mickey found the coworker he traded with on the twenty-third floor, and paid another ten dollars to trade back with him. Once he had the man working in Suite 1650, he headed back down to the security office. The inept guard looked sideways at him as he turned in the badge and signed out for the night.

"Sick – sent home," he explained in his worst English. The guard shrugged and waved goodbye. Mickey was gone.

When Jason Jordan said good-bye to Don and Tyrone that Friday evening in front of Mickey the cleaning man, he was finishing thirty-two hours in two days. He covered a lot of bases in that time. Not only did he organize all the material his team was working on, he made all the copies in duplicate, all on color coded paper. He analyzed the computer disks and copied them and the VCR tapes before he arranged for the secure delivery of all originals into the custody of Henry Lipscomb. Before the office closed, he had a safe installed in the conference room where his team would be working. Next he purchased two laptops, software and other supplies critical to the project. It was all expensive, but Jason was determined to do everything he could to keep it under wraps. Finally, unbeknownst to his cohorts, he arranged for on-call security surveillance with some trusted colleagues. Jason worked with only ex-GBI, FBI or military personnel. He had grown to distrust the local police. In fact, his distrust was born out in the evidence of a couple of crooked cops in the documents he was studying for this case. Indeed, Jason worked hard to cover all the bases, but he, like Harvey, couldn't cover everything.

When he got to Harvey's office on Saturday morning, he signed in with the guard in the lobby of the building. He automatically inked a false name and the company name of an office on a different floor of the building. He recorded his destination as that company's suite. He failed to tell Don or Tyrone to do the same. As the three analysts worked through their Saturday, Frank Machelli entered the building and signed in, checking the few names above his and where they were going in the building. Two names were signed in to Harvey King's office. One was Don Travers who was with the firm. The other was Tyrone Jones who jotted down *HTO* as his company's name. On the ride in the elevator he jotted down the information. When the doors opened to the sixteenth floor, Frank proceeded down the hallway toward the back office exit Mickey prepared for him the prior evening. He was both disappointed and interested that there were people already in the office on Saturday. He hoped to compromise the security of the conference room Mickey hadn't been able to enter, but that wouldn't be possible with others around. He wondered if Messrs. Travers and Jones were there for the Lofton case or an entirely different matter.

The taped door opened slowly and silently as Frank peeked in to find an unlit office area, partitioned by cubicles. He stepped into the big room slowly to avoid detection, but there didn't seem to be anyone in the immediate vicinity. "Test, test," he said quickly and quietly to test the sound for the bugs as he moved to the front reception foyer. Just past the foyer, he spotted the double doors to the conference room, and he noticed that they swung to the outside, exposing their hinges to him. Light crept from under them indicating that was the most likely location of the two men. Mickey was right; he wasn't able to discern any conversation coming from the room.

Frank moved stealthily into Harvey King's office, where he picked up the phone, punched one number to eliminate the dial tone and spoke into the receiver. A quick glance around the office and in the desk drawers confirmed Mickey's report that there was no obvious evidence of anything related to the Lofton case. There was no point in hanging around any longer and risk getting caught, so he instead caught the elevator back to the lobby where he signed out and re-checked the names on the guard's sheet. Then it was out to the van where Bud was monitoring the wired office.

"There are two guys holed up in the same office Mickey was talking about," Frank said. "Who knows why they're there. Did you pick up my tests?"

"Sure did," Bud said, "but I don't think we're going to hear much from the bugs today."

"One of the guys is from the firm; one is from a company

called *HTO*," said Frank.

"What do you think?" Bud asked. "We have anything to worry about?"

"Hard to say," Frank opined. "They're hot on something in there. There's no getting in that room while they're around. They're augured in, and I don't think they're coming out until it's locked up. We can get in tonight when those two leave."

"Meanwhile, we'll check out this Jones guy and see what this *HTO* company is," Bud said. "Mickey said there were three guys in there last night. The third one must be taking the weekend off. Our man down at the city jail says Charlie's locked away not talking to anyone, but pretty soon we'll have to make a decision about what to do next. I'll be talking to Vincent in a little while and I'll give him the lowdown. Get on the Tyrone Jones thing." Frank left to research Mr. Jones, while Bud waited for Mickey to relieve him on wiretap duty.

It didn't take long to decipher HTO. Frank simply went to the yellow pages and began looking up law practices that began with H. None of the H firms had the initials HTO. The next logical move was to look for accounting firms, because firms with initials for names were usually professional firms like attorneys, accountants, and architects. Frank didn't imagine they were making blueprints in Harvey's office.

There it was, right after *Hardy, Gerald, CPA – Harris, Taylor, Oates, PC.* It was the only one that fit the HTO pattern. Frank put in a call to Vince who called his accountant. Richard Stockton was able to look in a professional directory of state CPA's to find the only Tyrone Jones certified to practice public accounting in Georgia. It listed his home address and phone number, and confirmed his employment with HTO.

Vince preferred to be as discreet as possible, but if they couldn't figure out what was being pursued with such urgency, his people would have to have a conversation with Mr. Jones or Mr. Travers. He was anxious to know whether Frank was going to get any information when he revisited Mr. King's office later in the evening.

....

The only reason Don, Tyrone and Jason left Friday night after the cleaning man arrived is they had to get some sleep. If they could have, they would have worked through the night, driven by fascination for what they had been auditing. There, before their eyes, was enough incriminating evidence to put several men behind bars for the better part of their useful lives, several local politicians and police officers out of work, and many married men out of their houses. They just needed to get enough sleep to recharge for another long day on Saturday. And after working another ten hours, the trio was no more eager to leave than the night before.

There were records describing a gambling operation that handled large transactions and debts among some of the most well-known people in Atlanta, not to mention some celebrities famous throughout the U.S. and beyond. There were spreadsheets containing schedules of sports events, with point spreads and records of monies paid and owed. There was an illegal lotto that did well among the less affluent and influential, until the state sponsored lottery came along and put a dent in that business.

Some of the same people were customers of the prostitution side of the business. Regular charges of constant amounts were billed to willing customers' credit cards in the names of the restaurants owned by Vincent Palomino. Not coincidentally, the same names were entered in a computerized day planner schedule, matching girls names with the customers on the same days the charges occurred in the restaurant. Much of the prostitution appeared to be billed through Satin, the most well known nude bar in Atlanta, and beyond. Tyrone was working on the details to connect individual charges at the club to specific acts of prostitution.

There were memos from New York, albeit with code names, describing various schemes to make and launder money. Don uncovered one such plot which involved using the help of airline employees to move boxes full of cash from Atlanta to

New York on commercial flights. Tyrone found extravagant expenditures on Satin's books to bogus shell corporations in New York for consulting services, which were probably never rendered, thereby completing the cash laundry cycle. Another memo, accompanied by working papers, detailed a nationwide scam, where the mob set up flimsy companies to purchase long distance time at the wholesale level and sell the time on cards through a pyramid scheme. By the time the cards got to market, the companies would fold, with massive liabilities to the long distance providers, who would simply inactivate the cards for which they hadn't been paid. This left poor bastards like Marvin Dixon holding worthless cards.

Just as frustration about the code names in the memos set in among the three men, Don turned up a word processing file that appeared to be a simple key, matching code names to their rightful owners. It was somewhat out of date, and many of the names were unfamiliar, but it was clear the feds would have a field day with it.

Even though the trio had been put together hastily, and somewhat randomly, they worked well together, and by seven o'clock Saturday night, they felt good about leaving. They knew much of what they were going to know about the materials. There were plenty of loose ends to tie up, but there would be time for that. Besides, in the long run, the feds could tie up many themselves. They all agreed that noon to five on Sunday would allow them sufficient time to finish and write a report for Harvey and his client on Monday morning. They went their separate ways for the evening.

....

Frank had no idea whether the people in Harvey King's office were gone or not, when he first arrived back at the building at six-thirty in the evening. He casually walked to the guard with the sign in sheet, took one look and exclaimed, "Damn, I just realized I left something I need. I'm going to have to go back. I'll see you in a little while."

The guard shrugged, uninterested, as Frank headed out the door, frustrated. He was frustrated that the two guys were still on the sixteenth floor. His mission would take some time, but first he had to be up there by himself to do it. He went to get a beer at *Complex*, a quiet midtown bar Vince owned. Frank ran plenty of football betting cards through the place, and he knew all the regulars. That night, betting was not on his mind. When Greg Shippe, a loser who spent most of his time and money in the bar spoke to him about placing a bet, it was the wrong time.

"Pay the money you owe for the last motherfucking bet, and we'll talk then," he barked, immediately sorry he said it. Even though Greg was a loser, he was actually one of the easier people to take, and he never owed too much money for very long. In short, Greg was a decent customer, and while he would be back when Frank was in a better mood, Frank felt bad.

At eight-thirty he went back to the office building and looked at the sign in sheet. Finally, the pair was signed out, after about ten straight hours of work. Frank noticed a Domino's Pizza driver signed in and out of that office at around two that afternoon. There was only one poor soul left working in the building up on the fourteenth floor. If he hadn't had three beers, he might have noticed how close the fourteenth floor guy's in-time was to the two in the King office. Frank signed in and got on the elevator. The briefcase in his hand contained no office supplies, whatsoever; it instead held the tools necessary to pick locks and remove doors from their hinges. He would be able to get into the conference room, no matter how well they had it secured. He got off the elevator, and walked toward the office's back exit. The taped door swung open slowly to reveal the big room, dimly lit only by the hallway behind him and some light coming through the windows in the offices whose doors were open. There he paused for a long time, listening for any sound, and trying to sense if any immediate risks lurked in the darkness. When he was satisfied, he crept toward the conference room. The doors were chained and padlocked with quality hardware. Frank turned on the hall light. When he could see that removing a door from its hinges was the best alternative, he set about the task. The job took almost twenty minutes, and even when he had the pins removed from the hinges, the chain on the handles was so tight it was tough to twist the doors away far enough to climb into the room.

When he got up from the floor on the other side of the doors, Frank found the light switch on the wall. The moment of truth was at hand when the switch flipped to reveal an empty room. There wasn't a scrap of paper, a pen, pencil, legal pad or laptop in sight. The only thing in sight was the furniture, including the large safe at the far end. If the material they were working on was anywhere, it was in there, and Frank was not qualified to crack safes. He did peruse the room carefully, and he could see the construction dust on the carpet around the safe, indicating it was recently installed. He strategically placed bugs where they wouldn't be detected, and when he was sure he wasn't going to get anything else from the room, he struggled out and proceeded to replace the doors. Before he left, he stopped by Harvey's office to make sure they hadn't put something on his desk. He was not surprised to find it empty, also.

Frank's report to Vincent told him no more than he knew when David Israel called to tell him Charlie had been arrested. Vince didn't want to do it, but he put the order out to Frank.

"Okay look, you gotta go to one of those guy's houses. Make it that Jones, the accountant. Travers has a big family. Jones lives alone; it'll be less complicated." Vince learned quite a bit about the two subjects earlier in the afternoon. "Now listen, play it real cool. Don't let him know what your interest is, and don't show him your weapon unless you have to. Just surprise the shit out of him, and then ask him what his business is at Harvey King. He'll probably be scared so shitless he'll start singing like fucking Ethel Merman. If he needs some coaxing, be subtle, but try everything you can to get the word from him. Only show him your piece as a last resort, and for God's sake, don't use it. The last thing we need right now is a dead guy associated with the people representing Charlie."

Frank wasn't keen on bothering the guy, but he had his

marching orders, and he knew the implications of the situation. It was almost ten-thirty when he turned east from Harvey King's office in the direction of the Morningside area of Atlanta. Within fifteen minutes the Cadillac pulled slowly past the address Vince gave him. The house, like so many others in the quaint neighborhood, was a twenties, craftsman style two story, with a front porch looking over a tiny front yard to the street. It was a fixer-upper in which Tyrone Jones invested a little money and a lot of sweat, and it was probably worth twice his original purchase price. Frank hated the neighborhood for one reason. All the driveways were so short most people had to park at least one car on the street. It was always a major coup to find a place to park anywhere near the intended destination within the neighborhood. Frank finally found a spot on the street around the corner from the Jones residence.

The air was heavy with steam coming off the sun scorched street. It was the kind of night Frank hated, and he was looking forward to the end of summer in Atlanta. He watched as the descending house numbers guided him until he stood in front of the home of Tyrone Jones. An Acura dominated the space of the tiny driveway. From the looks of it, there wasn't a light on in the whole place. He guessed the hours Mr. Jones was putting in were putting him in bed early.

The old houses in the neighborhood were a cinch to penetrate. The only consideration was the possibility of an alarm system. If he had to, Frank could compromise most of the rudimentary systems the residents usually installed, but it didn't appear Tyrone Jones felt the need for an alarm. After tonight, Frank thought, he would reconsider and make the investment. Frank made his way to the back of the house where none of the neighbors would notice him. The back door had a lock from the nineteen-fifties. It was a fifteen second job. He quietly swung the door toward the inside of the house. As he was ready to step in, the cold steel muzzle of what felt like a high caliber pistol pressed into his temple.

"Wrong house," came the voice behind him.

His knees went limp. Weapons had been pulled on him

before, but that feeling was one to be assiduously avoided. He tried to turn to face his interceptor.

"Don't think so, pal," came the indistinguishable voice as the power behind it pressed the gun harder into his skull. "You can walk or die, you decide."

Frank doubted he would be shot dead by his interceptor, but he knew when to cut his losses. He turned away from the voice and calmly walked away from the property without saying a word. It had been a shit day from beginning to end. He was just happy to leave without more of a hassle.

Tyrone Jones, CPA would never know how close he came to getting the shit scared out of him, Frank guessed as he retreated through the heat back to his car. Whatever this guy was involved in, it was big enough to keep him under protective surveillance. That was all Frank knew about the situation. He wouldn't know that he had been shadowed by Jason Jordan since he left Harvey King's headquarters.

Once the three men parted ways that evening, Jason hung back to check the security of the office. He didn't bother the night before, since the cleaning crew was in the way. In the morning, he swept the conference room for bugs, and it was clean, but he had seen the line light up on the conference room phone when Frank picked it up to test the bug. It took him only a moment to discover the tape on the back door. Clearly someone planned on entering after hours, and Jason knew whoever it was would be waiting for his team to clear out. He decided to wait for awhile to see if his hunch was on target. It took an hour and a half, but sure enough, as he sat invisibly silent in Grant Duncan's office, a growing swath of light appeared at the rigged back exit. He held his breath and fingered his pistol as he sat, statue still. The area outside Duncan's office remained dark, and Jason thought he could hear whoever came in moving away. Suddenly there was a touch of light coming from down the hall. Jason got up and peeked out of the office into the big area, now lit at one end. He crept toward the lighted hallway. He could see the man's reflection in the big glass doors of the main entrance. With the angle he had, he was at an advantage, and he sat in one of the clerical chairs just around the corner. Jason watched with some degree of amusement as the determined intruder worked up a sweat trying to break into the conference room. He knew the man would be disappointed once he saw the spotless room. He also knew he would have to sweep for bugs, again, before his team started back to work.

While the intruder plugged away at his futile mission, Jason moved away for a minute to call his surveillance men and put them on heightened alert. Then he went back to observe the keystone crook. Once all the hullabaloo was over, and the doors were put back into place, Jason retreated back into Grant Duncan's office until the intruder pulled the tape from the back exit door, and walked out, latching it behind him. Jason jumped up as fast as he could. He waited for just enough time for the man to be out of sight, left through the same door, and bolted down the stairs to the fourteenth floor. There he rushed down the hall to punch the elevator button. Sure enough, when the doors parted, there stood a tired looking sap, briefcase in hand. Jason stepped in with a smile.

As the doors closed the two men in, Jason spoke. "Gotta love these hours, don'tcha?"

The man looked surprised and suspicious that the elevator had stopped to pick-up the only other guy working in the building. "Yeah," he grunted, trying to maintain his cool.

The two rode the rest of the way down in silence. In the confines of the elevator Jason picked-up the smell of beer on the guy's breath. As they approached the guard's stand Jason veered off to the lobby water fountain. He wanted to leave the building last. Within five minutes he was tailing the man in the Cadillac out of midtown, and then followed him in the direction of the Morningside neighborhood. The closer they got to Tyrone Jones' home, the surer Jason was of the man's intentions. He phoned ahead to warn Alex Culpepper.

"Looks like our guy is heading to pay a visit to Mr. Jones," Jason told the surveillance man assigned to Tyrone. "If you *do* encounter him, just send him on his way. Make as little conversation as possible. No police; we don't need any of Palomino's people arrested. We need to keep as low a profile as possible."

"Gotcha," acknowledged Culpepper as he got out of his car and moved across the street to blend into the darkness in a corner of Tyrone's yard. Once he intercepted the goon and sent him on his way, he returned to the air conditioning of his car to spend the rest of a boring but lucrative night on stakeout.

XXII. SALVATION

Vincent spent the weekend gathering what little intelligence he could, trying to decide on a course of action. There was definitely something afoot at the lawyer King's office. He wondered what other cases Harvey King was working on, but he had no way to get that information. David Israel warned him that I represented a threat, given the dire legal battle before me. David suspected I was soft and would use any means available to improve my legal lot. He had my bond hearing monitored to understand my plight. Vince wasn't convinced I could hurt him and wanted to play his cards intelligently. If there were no need to arouse suspicion he wanted to leave me alone. David pointed out that I was surely working on something, or I would have retained him as my lawyer. Even if I didn't have anything of significant value, he felt Vince needed to fire a warning shot of intimidation across my bow. Besides, David cautioned, I killed his only son. Vince was surprised at his own ambivalence about the death of his adopted son. He was actually just as happy to see me alive as he would have been Eddie – the problem child. Now, suddenly I was the problem.

New York weighed in on the matter. It was their opinion that something should be done. They were giving Vince the call for the time being, but the pressure was on him to act. On Sunday morning he reluctantly made a decision about how to handle the Charlie Lofton situation. By Sunday afternoon he made the call.

....

While the skullduggery played itself out between Vince and Jason Jordan, Marvin and I had our own problems in prison. We had to contend with what Marvin termed the weewars, or weekend warriors – the short-time prisoners who were hauled in on Friday and Saturday nights on more mundane charges than the regulars. They were there too long to stay in the holding cells, but they would be gone before the weekend ended. There were a lot of habitual drunk drivers, and drunk fighters, and just plain drunks crammed in with the rest of us. The population of the jail swelled on the weekend, making life even worse than it was during the weekdays. It was tough enough to get any sleep in the yellow place anyway, but it became impossible when we were besieged by the noise of the weekend warriors. There was a poor man in our pod suffering from the D.T.'s who screamed hysterically from the time he was brought in early Friday evening until four Saturday morning. Other weewars just screamed and laughed back and forth all night for no apparent reason. The weewars came and left, and we were left to our own devices to cope with the resulting pandemonium. As in every other situation there, I looked to Marvin for guidance. He didn't much worry about the weewars or the noise they made.

"Don't bother with those boys," he said. "They'll be outta here before we know it, and everything will settle back to normal." He said it as if normal at the jail were a good thing. I was amazed at how much I was looking forward to the end of the weekend. Anything was better than the zoo we were caged in for those two days.

Sunday afternoon, Marvin was called to the visitors lounge to see his wife. I was left to exist in solitude. I spent so much time with Marvin, I didn't know what to do with myself when he wasn't around to keep the conversation running. I sat alone in the cell trying to maintain a positive attitude. At lunch I choked down a few bites. Lunch was the meal with the least offensive food – it was sandwiches made from something that resembled meat. At least it wasn't yellow. I was determined there would be no leftovers for Marvin at this lunch. I had to make an effort to eat. In the few days I had been incarcerated I lost a noticeable amount of weight. Suddenly, my internal thoughts were interrupted by a voice outside my cell.

"Hey Lofton," a guard I didn't recognize spoke to me.

For an instant I was excited. Whenever someone of authority addressed a prisoner by name it usually meant something was going to happen to break the monotony.

"Vincent Palomino sends his regards," he said. "He told me to look out for you and take care of you whenever necessary. I told him not to worry, I'd be glad to take care of you if circumstances called for it. We'll see each other again."

As he turned away he smiled a look that sent a shiver throughout my body. Great, I thought. Now Vince is using guards employed by the City of Atlanta to intimidate me and possibly do worse than that. As I thought about my plight I halfway wished the guard had come in and finished me off, right then and there, just to be done with the whole ordeal, but I put those thoughts out of my mind. One suicide per lifetime was all one gets, I decided. Before long Marvin returned to our cell, and I was never happier to see him. He laughed about his wife and how mad she was about his stupid behavior.

"She say to me," he scoffed, "'Marvin, what the hell got into you, you gotta be so stupid to get youself locked up over a lousy phone card?' But what she don't know is how hard I work for that lousy money that bought that card. We got kids and expenses, and I gotta hold onto every penny I can."

Marvin's desperation about money, and his sincere intention to meet his responsibilities, was as heart wrenching as it was palpable. I thought about the history of finances in my life. There were times when money was tight, but I couldn't remember having the problems that plagued Marvin. While I didn't consider myself rich, compared to him, I was unencumbered by poverty or responsibility for others. Marvin was having to squeeze every penny, and this setback wasn't going to help matters. His employer was trying to hold his job for him, but he couldn't protect it forever. Marvin needed to get out of jail, or be prepared to start looking for a new job. Still, he was nice enough to offer to share some of the measly thirty dollars his wife managed to leave for him. Even in jail I was financially comfortable, and I was going to be sure to share my prison funds with Marvin. With this in mind, I fancied myself an individual with at least some redeeming value. The idea was comforting enough to allow sleep to overtake me and close out the first of what I was afraid would be uncountable weekends in prison.

Monday morning broke the same way every day broke in the city jail, but with less commotion from the cells than on the weekend. Marvin, like clockwork, did his business while my dreams were replaced by the reality of my predicament. My uncertainty clocked in with the same regularity my cellmate possessed. My finicky nature was Marvin's gain at breakfast when I was able to choke down but a meager half glass of bitter juice.

After breakfast, back in the cell, I needed to tell Marvin what should have been said all weekend, but wasn't. The visit from Vince's prison guard underscored Harvey's admonishment to keep quiet, and I was freshly motivated to put a cap on further information about me. After Harvey's warning I had quit discussing myself with Marvin. The problem was that he knew too much already. I had to warn him to clam up, not only for my good, but also for his. Marvin was going to have to forget about me as an item of gossip. Before the guards opened our cages for the morning milling around session I spoke to him.

"You know what happened to me yesterday when you were talking to your wife," I said.

"No, tell me," said Marvin.

"A guard came by and threatened me – or at least let me know he was watching me for Vincent Palomino," I said, shuddering again at the thought.

"That right?" said Marvin, sounding happy to hear more of the intrigue that surrounded his fellow inmate. "What'd he say to you?"

I was annoyed at the way he relished the news. "Yeah, that's right," I shot back. "He said he'd be watching out for me, and he assured Vincent he would quote, 'take care of me,' if it became necessary."

"Whoa, is that right?" Marvin said sitting upright in his bed.

"Yes, that's right, Marvin," I repeated in frustration. "I guess they think what I know might be damaging to Vince. I wish I really did know what they think I know. But here's the point; if you start talking about the things I told you, you might get me into real trouble. And if word gets around that you know the things they think I know, you might have problems, too."

Marvin didn't seem fazed. "Oh, I don't know they worry too much 'bout me," he smiled. "I know what you saying 'bout you, though. Don't worry Charlie; I don't think nothing's going to get you in worse trouble than you already in."

Marvin's words were both comforting and unsettling. His words were sincere, but his opinion of the depth of my problems struck a sharp chord in my gut.

"Okay," I said, "Thanks, I think."

"And one more thing," Marvin added. "As long as you my roommate, I ain't going to let nothing happen to you. You can count on that, Fedman."

That was reassuring. Marvin was a rare character. We had known each other about a week, and it was as if we were the best of friends. We both knew the other's history, and we got along well in our confined cell. If only I could take Marvin with me to wherever I was going to end up, I thought, prison might be almost tolerable.

During the milling around session, and again at lunch, I noticed Marvin guarding me with the same zeal as ever, but it was for a different reason. Perhaps he was being a little dramatic, but it was clear he was ready to put up a fight if anything happened. How effective he would be was unknown, but he survived prison in the past, and I was happy to have him by my side.

During the afternoon recreation period, Marvin was right there as usual. Suddenly my name was called, and he spun around to get a view in all directions. He was jumpier than I was. The guard who called me came in my direction.

"You Lofton?" he asked, looking at my I.D. to verify my name and number. "You got a lawyer here to see you."

My mood instantly improved, but Marvin looked suspicious. I followed the guard toward the attorney-client conference area.

Marvin followed both of us as far as he could before he was turned around at the door. The guard put the shackles on my ankles and wrists as usual, and led me into the room, where my heart began to race. There was no Harvey – no lawyer at all – just me and my escort and two guards waiting in the isolated room. Dread took over as one guard looked at the other two and said, "Here he is. Take care of him."

I went limp. "No," I screamed, "please no. I haven't said a thing. I swear to God, I don't know anything!" I was kicking and writhing violently as the two guards picked me up by the underarms and dragged me out of the room, my feet resisting whenever they touched the floor. I was pleading and shaking and begging for my life when I realized I was in a carpeted hallway. There were other staff members around staring at me, taken aback at my hysterics. Harvey King appeared from an office doorway looking horrified.

"Charlie, what's wrong," he cried as the guards dropped me on the floor.

I looked up, possibly more mortified than I had been moments before when I thought I was being taken for a beating. An entire office staff was out in the hall to investigate the commotion as I lay shackled before them, beads of sweat drying on my forehead.

"Harvey?" I said, at a loss for any other intelligible utterance.

"Pick him up," Harvey commanded the two guards who shrugged and hoisted me onto my feet. "Come in here, Charlie."

I looked at the guards for permission, who again shrugged, and I waddled to Harvey, chains clinking along. He shut the door. "What was that all about?" he asked. I proceeded to report everything I told Marvin, and how David Israel acted when I told him about Harvey, and the threats from the guard on behalf of Vince. My composure was just beginning to return.

"So, that's what's happening," Harvey said. "That may explain some things that have been going on in the office."

"What's been going on?" I asked.

"Listen, Charlie," he said, "some big things are in the works that I've got to fill you in on." Harvey's poise returned after the trauma of my tantrum, and the normal sense of urgency was back in his voice. I became focused on his words as he continued. "It seems that, while your mother was a sloppy record keeper, she sure as hell knew which records to keep." I sat in amazement as Harvey related the story of the garage and the records Grover Hewitt kept for Mother. He gave me a concise synopsis of their content. When he got to the part of the long distance card scam, I had to interrupt.

"What kind of cards were they – what brand?" I said.

Harvey looked frustrated. Here he was telling me of the most explosive information that anyone from the Justice Department could ever hope to get his hands on, and I was concerned about a seemingly irrelevant detail. "I don't know," he replied, "something like Plastic Card or…"

"Plasti-com cards?" I asked.

"Yeah, I think that was it," he replied. "Why; you know about that, or something?"

"No, it's nothing," I responded. "Don't worry about it." I couldn't believe it. I had no idea Vince was involved in that business, but I knew of poor Marvin's plight. Vince's actions indirectly landed Marvin in jail. My father had been right. One event caused by Vince was rippling out, influencing many other events, one of them being the arrest of my new friend. Vince was proving to be quite the bad butterfly, creating ill winds throughout my world.

Harvey finished his explanation of the potentially huge bargaining chip we held, and as an aside he mentioned the rag that Jason had finally determined was stained with blood. "We just can't figure out the significance of that being up in the rafters of that garage," he said. "We wondered if your mother found it in Vince's office and it had something to do with violence against somebody; but you don't know anything about that, do you?

"Hey, that was from Eddie's ear," I said, suddenly

transported back to that simpler time. “You see, he shot off his earlobe, and Bobby…”

“Okay, that’s not relevant,” Harvey said, getting somber. He told of the bugs in his office, and the thug who broke in and was later intercepted trying to enter the house of someone working on the case for him. “I’m telling you, Charlie,” he warned, “this is a deadly serious game at this point. I don’t believe Vincent Palomino has any idea the extent of documented information we have about him and people even higher up than he is, but we need to strike a deal with the Attorney’s office and get you into protective custody. The sooner the better, but until that happens, be vigilant in here.”

Vigilance was fine, but even if I were aware of some imminent attack against me, what could I do. I always had Marvin, but he would be a minor impediment if Vince wanted to get to me. “What does all this mean?” I asked, getting back to my potential bargaining position.

“It’s good,” said Harvey. “I won’t say how good. The charges against you are serious; I’m not going to lie. If you didn’t have this information, and you were convicted, you would spend significant time in prison. Now, this is the kind of information the feds will have an incentive to get. Normally the problem is the negotiation process. We need to entice them to give our client the best deal possible without giving them so much information they don’t need him anymore. In your case it’s different. We have so much, and it’s all documented so well, we can tell them what kind of information we have for them without having to reveal the specifics. It should earn you consideration. I don’t want to predict, but I will get you as good a deal as possible. What’s your relationship to Bobby Wells?”

“We’ve been friends for a long time, since we were kids,” I said. “He’s really been my best friend – until I disappeared to Bermuda. Either he or Gracie…” I was rambling before Harvey interrupted again.

“That’s not relevant right now,” he said, not exasperated, but trying to stay on subject. “That’s good. It never hurts to have friends in the Justice Department. I’ll be meeting with them as soon as I leave here. We'll know something soon, and we'll try to get you somewhere safe. Meanwhile, watch your back."

Harvey stood and smiled as we shook hands, and we walked out of the office. Once they heard the door open, the guards walked toward us to escort me back to my yellow accommodations. They approached me warily, considering my unexplained behavior on the way in to see Harvey. It had been perhaps thirty minutes since the guard first came to get me. In that period, my outlook went from one of resignation to a life behind bars, to fear for my life, to nervous anticipation of what Harvey might be able to do for me. I volunteered to carry myself back to the jail without their help.

Once my shackles were removed I grabbed Marvin and took him aside to a remote corner of the milling around area. I wasn't specific with him, but I told him things were looking promising.

"That right?" said Marvin, evenly. "That's good news for you. When you talking to that hotshot Harvey King, get some advice for me, will you? I could use somebody like him to help me out with my problem."

I could see a distant look in his eyes. As steady as he seemed about being locked away, the time away from earning money – and the possibility that he might not have a job if he didn't get out soon – was eating at him. I wished I could pay Harvey to work his case, but first I would have to see what my problem was going to cost.

As we talked, a guard with the name tag *Dugan* called me aside, again. He walked me back to the cells, which sat empty until roll call. Suddenly, my carefree elation at Harvey's news evaporated and I recalled his admonition to watch my back. As I turned to grasp for public exposure, his elbow caught me under the chin. I went down, my head ringing from the blow. Pain shot through my legs when he struck the crotch of my knees with his night stick. I winced in agony when the second blow caught the small of my back. Out of the corner of my eye I could see the club rise to strike me on the right side of my head. I used my arm as a shield and it bore the crack of the unforgiving stick. My arm dropped away in limpness as the club went back up for another shot. I cringed, but the strike never came. Suddenly, there were groans as the guard struggled above me. I was able to turn around to see Marvin in hand to hand combat with my attacker. I tried to get up to help, but my beaten legs were slow to react. I pulled myself along the floor until I got to the recreational area, where the guards took one look at me and reacted to my pleas to help Marvin.

By the time they got to the two men they had both gotten in their licks. Marvin suffered the worst of it, since the guard had the weapon advantage. They untangled the combatants, giving Marvin a few extra jabs and kicks in the process.

“You okay?” one of them said, once order was restored.

The bloodied guard stood up, trying to catch his breath. “Yeah,” he panted. “Those two were going at it pretty good. I tried to separate them, but then this dude here jumped all over me.”

“That’s bullshit,” I cried, hobbling back to the scene, but to no avail. Marvin and I were carted away to the jail’s dispensary where I was treated and sent back to my cell. Marvin was in worse shape. He had a knot above his right eye, presumably from the club, and he was bleeding from his mouth and his right ear. His eyes were cloudy, and his speech slightly slurred. The doctor told him he probably suffered a concussion and sent him to Grady Hospital for tests and treatment.

I heard the guards speaking around the corner. They watched Marvin being carried away on a stretcher, assuring him that he earned another court appearance to answer for his attack on my attacker. I felt terrible that Marvin found himself deeper in trouble just for my sake. I couldn’t believe he kept his word to protect me; it was such an unselfish act.

Back in my cell I relaxed, as the pain subsided. I was leery of any prison official passing my way. I kept my eyes on the corridor. Thanks to our altercation, the whole prison population was in lockdown. Dinner would be delayed. The calls from inside our pod were of a threatening nature, and I imagined a fellow prisoner doing as much harm to me as a guard. There was no telling how long lockdown would last, but as far as I was concerned it could go on forever. As long as my fellow inmates were in their respective cells no one was going to get to me.

After a long, blaring, inaudible announcement over the PA system, which presumably admonished everyone to calm down and threatened to punish any misbehavior, dinner was served. It was an hour and a half late. The annoyingly loud buzz announced the opening of all the cells at once, something I dreaded. I walked out sheepishly, feeling a powder keg of stares as we walked toward the mess hall. A couple of under the breath threats accompanied a few unfriendly jostles as inmates maneuvered for position at the long awaited buffet of slop. I was able to find an empty table to try to choke down a morsel.

Before I took two bites, three tattooed and greasy characters moved over to my table. They were no agents of Vince, but they were dangerous. I tried to toss an indiscreet glance toward a guard, but not one of them was concerned about the inmate who was partly responsible for the assault on a fellow officer.

"Hey man," said the inmate with the most tattoos, "whatcha mean, fuckin' the whole day up for the rest of us. I'm so hungry, I'm gonna need that turkey you got there."

He reached across the table with a quick stab and snatched the meat off my plate while his eyes remained fixed on mine. I was surprised to learn that it was turkey I was eating. "Is that what that is?" I asked sincerely.

"Hey dude," the biggest of the three said, sneering, "don't be stealin' the dude's food. This is the man. This is the *federal man*. This is the dude that stupid nigger's been talkin' 'bouts gonna be a big man; gonna git hisself outta here, cut some deal with the EFF-BEE-EYE. Don't take the dude's meat, man. You piss him off, he might get his FBI agents after you.

"The last thing you could do to piss me off would be to take this food off my plate," I said, in a futile attempt at humor. It was lost on the dim trio. As repulsive the idea of another bite was, I scooped my fork toward some apple sauce and forced it down trying to seem unaffected.

"You pissed off, dude?" said the big guy as the other two crowded in tighter. "You gonna git your agents after us, or you gonna take up fer yourself?" They clearly didn't understand my comment.

Fear gripped my body into a catatonic state, except for my right arm, which kept shoveling slop into my mouth. I stared straight ahead, afraid to alter my pattern of movement.

"He don't seem intersted in talkin' ta us," said the previously silent one. "What's wrong, ya don't kier fer our kind? He'll talk to the niggers and the feds, but he won't speak to us."

Unable to provoke a change in me, the frustrated Mr. Tattoo grabbed my eating arm by the wrist squeezing my hand open. The forked clanged against the metal tray, which was surprisingly empty, drawing the attention of the entire room, including the guards. No one noticed the mini cavalry moving in from the free world. Just as the guards closed in, a man in a suit stepped into focus.

"Hold it right there," announced the well dressed man I would later find out was in charge of the jail. Six more suits surrounded our table, all holding FBI badges in the air. Before I realized what was happening, I was snatched up and removed from the room. They carried me through the maze of passageways, and out of the secured area of the jail. Once I was placed in an empty office the agents clamped handcuffs on my wrists in front of me. Reading my thoughts, the man I recognized as Special Agent Irvin explained concisely.

"Looks as though you might have hit the jackpot, Mr. Lofton," Irvin said dryly. "That is, if you can deliver what Harvey King claims. We're here to take you away from all this," he scoffed sarcastically and waved his hand in a sweeping motion, indicating the disgusting place.

FBI Special Agent Irvin was my savior. I was in the slammer only a week, but hope for getting out of there was fading until he swooped in to snatch me from the clutches of the tattoo trio. As suddenly as I found myself incarcerated, I was just as suddenly being driven away from the city jail on my way to a defunct hotel on Peachtree Street near Midtown Atlanta. My escorts were jabbering on their radios, sounding very official, coordinating plans. I was even given a nickname – *Cain.* It took a little while to figure out they were referring to me, and even longer to get the significance of it, but it finally hit me; Cain slew his brother Abel, and I blew up my brother Eddie. I wondered if there was a position in the FBI devoted to coming up with code names cleverly descriptive of their subjects. It would be a perfect position for Gracie, I thought.

The car pulled into the driveway along the starkly lit face of the empty hotel, then turned right around the corner into darkness. When we reached the back of the building there was an impressive congregation of government vehicles hidden from the rest of the city. Men stood chatting casually in the unseasonably mild summer night, vapor from their tightly held *Starbucks* cups disappearing against a gray background. Shotguns and pistols were in evidence as I took in the awe inspiring scene. There was a pang of paranoia causing me to wonder if I was being chauffeured back there to be summarily executed for my untenable crimes. Then there was complete amazement that all of this was for me – then the ominous realization all of this was necessary to ensure that I remained alive.

I could have been the President of the United States, except for the handcuffs, the way Irvin and his crew stepped out of the car and scanned the area, speaking to the awaiting team, finally deciding it was safe. I was taken from the car surrounded by my personal security staff. We strode, en masse, toward an occupied room facing the back parking lot. The people in the post rush hour traffic on Peachtree would have no idea that the faux Miami style building with the real estate sign in front was about to become temporary quarters for an endangered stool pigeon and a half dozen or so federal agents.

The quick turn of a key provided access to a warmly lit room. I walked in with my entourage and looked around at the comfortable surroundings. I didn't know it at the time, but every piece of furniture had been removed from the entire building months before my check-in. Everything that was there upon my arrival – the beds, couch, table and chairs, refrigerator, microwave, and television – were installed by the Justice Department, and they did it in a hurry. The room next door was also furnished to accommodate the contingent assigned to keep me among the living. It was all quite a production. The owners of the property had been trying to unload it for quite some time. It was finally sold to the U.S. Treasury Department who planned to build Federal Reserve offices on the site. The existing building was scheduled for demolition, but for the time being it would be my refuge.

Harvey was waiting for me inside and jumped up to greet me. "Charlie, how are you?" he said cheerfully as he shook my hand first, then Agent Irvin's. "Here you are, buddy. This is your home for awhile, until we finish up with the negotiations and interviews. You should be safe here. What do you think?"

"Nice," was all I could manage. I was surprised and slightly embarrassed by all the attention.

"Good then," Harvey said. "Special Agent Barry Irvin will introduce you to the men who will be in charge of your safety. Listen to him, do exactly what the officers tell you, and you'll be fine. We should be able to wrap this up in due time, and we'll know where we go from here."

I had no idea what Harvey meant. I didn't know what the process was, or what the ultimate outcome would be, but I was so glad to be out of the jail that nothing else mattered. The basic accommodations in the abandoned motel were five star compared to my former residence. Agent Irvin removed my handcuffs and spoke up.

"Okay Charlie, this is Agent Jonathan Mailer," he said. The tall, broad Agent Mailer nearly crushed my hand with his oversized handshake. Irvin continued. "He will be your roommate. Agents McDonald and Berman will be next door." They both shook my hand. "We'll leave two officers on duty outside at all times. We're going to leave off your handcuffs, but you're still under arrest, charged with serious crimes. You are to obey Agent Mailer and the others at all times. Do what they say, and you'll stay in our good graces – and remain alive."

"Yes sir," I said, respectfully. Their attitude toward me had swerved one hundred eighty degrees from the time we first met in the FBI offices the previous week. I responded in kind. "Good gentlemen," said Harvey as he made his way to the door. "We'll meet downtown in the morning, around nine." Harvey wasn't one to waste words, and that's what I liked about him as a lawyer. He got to the point. I hoped his brevity was minimizing his billable hours.

Harvey, Irvin, McDonald and Berman left together. Jonathan Mailer and I were left alone.

"I'm staying in here with you," Agent Mailer said, "to keep you here, *and* to keep you safe. I'm pretty easy to get along with, as long as you're not going to be a pain in the ass. You're not going to be a pain in the ass, are you?"

"No sir," I assured him.

"Fine," he said, "and don't worry about calling me sir. It's just Jon. We're going to be together for who knows how long, and I don't stand on ceremony. If you just cooperate, that's enough for me."

Very un-FBI-ish, I thought, rubbing my wrists, happy to be out from behind bars and unshackled. Mailer was shaping up to be another decent roommate.

"I like watching the TV while I go to sleep," he said. "Hope you don't have a problem with that."

I was so elated at the turn of events, I didn't have a problem if the guy wanted to parade a brass band through the room all night. "No problem," I agreed.

"They got some items in the bathroom there for you," he said. "I think they'll get your things from property down at the city, tomorrow. Meanwhile, there's a toothbrush and other stuff in there."

The TV came on and I went to the bathroom to take a real shower alone – for the first time in awhile. After a half an hour of refreshment in a room that was private enough to collect steam on the mirrors, I walked out to find Jon sprawled on the bed that most directly faced the television. It was clearly his call and he made it. I was happy to default to the other bed. Before whatever show he was watching returned from commercials, I was asleep. It would be the soundest seven hours of sleep I had since my nights in Bermuda.

……..

Vincent Palomino got the news I was taken by FBI from the jail about the time I arrived at the hideaway the FBI coined *Eden*. He was perplexed. He knew I had a general idea of what he was about, and I had worked with Frank Machelli on the betting cards, but it would be hard for me to make that link to him. None of that was enough to get me the kind of attention the feds were paying me.

Whatever was going on, it was disturbing, and too late to prevent. The guard Bud Bramlett ordered to work me over botched the job, and I subsequently became inaccessible. Vince could feel the insulation that came with his position deteriorating before his eyes. His panic and depression deepened. He summoned Frank Machelli and David Israel to counsel him on what his next move should be. It was clear that Frank was at a loss. There was no apparatus in place to penetrate the protective shell of the FBI, so there was no way of knowing what I was saying to the feds.

David tried to reassure himself and Vince that whatever I was telling them was embellished to try to save my own ass. In the end it wouldn't hold up in court – if it ever got to that point. The opinion was viable to Vince, but it didn't explain why his intuition was sending different signals. He was a man who could rely on his intuition. It served him well in the past, rarely steering him wrong, and the damn sense of impending doom that had been with him for a long time was intensifying with each day's developments. Options ran through his head, but the possible courses of action required more energy than he possessed. He was able to hide his panic and bark logical orders to his lieutenants, but inside he was unraveling.

....

When I woke up a little before seven, feeling rested for the first time since arriving back in the states, a local program was previewing that morning's *Today Show.* Jon Mailer was already showered and was crunching on a bowl of corn flakes with milk. He offered me some, but the involuntary stuffing my arm committed upon my belly the night before still weighed heavily. I washed up while he munched and Katie Curic interviewed the author of a diet book. As I was dressing, a local news segment came on. I wasn't paying much attention to the story about a water main break affecting the water supply of a neighborhood and creating a traffic nightmare in the area. But then, in the background the words from the newscaster began to filter into my thoughts:

"In other news, you may remember last week we reported the story of the man who police believed to be dead for more than a year resurfacing after being out of the country under an assumed name. As we reported, Charles Lofton is now being charged with the slaying of Edward Palomino, who police say perished in an explosion and fire which consumed Lofton's Buckhead home. Now, in a breaking story, we learn that last night Lofton was removed by the FBI from the Atlanta Jail where he was being held without bond. We have more from *Five Alive's* Ken Lacefield at the jail."

Ken Lacefield appeared looking serious, the facade of the jail looming in the background:

"That's right, Samantha. It was last night around eight o'clock that federal authorities entered the prison and took Lofton away, right in the middle, as we understand it, of dinner. It seems earlier there had been some type of altercation between Lofton and another inmate. That inmate required treatment at Grady Hospital, and authorities say he will be returned to the jail tomorrow. There is no indication that the altercation had anything to do with the actions of the FBI. You may recall the alleged victim of the Buckhead fire is the son of Vincent Palomino, the owner of Satin, the well known adult entertainment club here in Atlanta. If there is a connection between that fact and the FBI's action, we don't know what it is. There is some speculation that Charles Lofton was removed from the jail for his own protection, but that is only speculation at this time. It looks like we will just have to wait for more details to emerge in this sudden turn of events in this already bizarre case. Samantha."

There I was, right back in the news, like the day I left town. I got a sensation that the entire time since then was a dream, and I was waking up to the next day with the latest news update. The news was no more flattering than the day I left.

"Whoa," said Jon, "look at all that about you on the TV. How does it feel to be a celebrity, buddy?"

"How would you feel if that was being said about you?" I asked. It was hard to know how to take this Agent Jonathan Mailer. In the little time we spent together, he came off as a person who lived in the moment, upbeat, but with a personality that resided on the surface. I didn't know at the time that my protector was Jon Mailer, PHD, with a doctorate in psychology specializing in antisocial behavior. He wasn't assigned to me for the purpose of analyzing my psyche, but his orientation must have caused him to lead our conversation in that direction.

"I don't know," he responded. "Is it true?"

"Some of it," I said, and his silence begged elucidation. "If you want to know, did I kill Eddie Palomino and set fire to my house to cover it up, you'll have to wait for my lawyers to allow me to answer that."

"Ah, yeah," he said, "leave it to the lawyers. Pass the responsibility on to someone else. I guess that makes it easier, but it doesn't make you better."

"What do you mean?" I asked.

He gave me a stern but honest look as he spoke. "Just that your lawyers can use all sorts of tactics, facts and negotiating positions to help you beat the rap, but you're the only one who can ensure your own freedom."

"What do you mean," I repeated.

"I mean you may be free from a prison cell and all of the trappings that go with it, but you will remain a prisoner of your own demons until you confront them and at least learn to coexist with them to prevent them from destroying you from the inside out," he said.

"Okay," I said, "I want to feel completely free from demons, but if I get out of this, I've got a pretty good feeling I'm going to feel pretty damn good. But for argument's sake, let's say, hypothetically, someone did do the kinds of things they're saying I did. Let's say he killed a friend or even a brother. How can someone who did that ever redeem himself? How could anyone like that ever be free from his conscious again?"

"I'm sure I don't know," said Jon. "Perhaps he can't – not totally. As long as we're speaking hypothetically, let me ask you; is killing always wrong, in every circumstance?"

"I suppose there are times when it *is* justified," I said. "Maybe self defense, or to protect the life of someone else."

"Self defense," Jon posed, thoughtfully. "Is that the same as self preservation?"

I guess so," I said, wary not to fall into a trap, "if they both mean protecting your own life – you know, kill or be killed."

"So you're saying it's only justified to prevent your death," said Jon. "What if someone wanted to unjustly imprison you? What if the only way to win back your freedom was to kill the person who was holding you against your will?"

"I suppose that could be justified," I admitted. "But you said unjustly imprisoned. What if the prisoner deserved to be locked up, just not by the person holding him hostage?"

"Well that makes it more complicated, to be sure," said Jon. "That gets into the motivation of the one doing the detaining. Nothing is black and white. I think if his motivation is to keep the detainee from harming society or to punish him, it's not unjustified. However, if the motivation is purely selfish on his part, a case could be made the detention is unjust, and violence against him might be acceptable."

I had to get to the point. "So you're saying if my victim was trying to destroy my life, even though I might deserve to have it destroyed, if he was doing it for his own selfish reasons, I would be justified in killing him – hypothetically?"

"Not necessarily," Jon said. "I couldn't possibly know the answer to that, nor could anyone else with any certainty. All I'm saying is that there are many sides to an issue, and degrees of guilt. It's just something to think about. You indicated you weren't too proud of the television news report. You're the only one who knows what your circumstances and motivations were when you did whatever it was you did. That's why I asked if what they said about you is true. If not, I would think you would have a right to be upset. If it is true, ignoring the lawyers and judges, your reaction to the news story can only be influenced by how you feel about the motivations and justifications of your actions."

I couldn't believe this FBI agent was saying what I heard. I challenged him. "So you're saying, hypothetically, if someone blackmails you for something you did wrong, and he threatens your way of life, you're justified in killing him?"

"Not at all," said Jon. "I'm saying there are degrees of guilt and one must look to himself to answer that question to his own satisfaction. Let me ask you something else. Do you think the value of all lives is equal?"

"I guess so," I responded, "at least in the eyes of the almighty."

"No," he explained, "I mean here on earth, are all lives of equal value? Say you're trying to rescue two people who are about to drown in a flood. One is Charles Manson and the other is Mother Teresa. You've got only one lifeline left and they're both sinking fast. Are you going to toss it out there randomly for the first one who can get to it, or are you going to try and give the good mother the edge?"

"The nun, of course," I said, "but so what?"

Agent Mailer looked at his watch and said, "We have to leave in a few minutes, so get ready. But think about what you're about to do. You are going downtown to try to keep yourself out of prison by putting someone else there in place of you. You have to decide if his life outside of prison is more valuable than your own. If so, perhaps you shouldn't feed him to the wolves. However, if his crimes are more numerous and severe than yours, maybe his freedom should be sacrificed for yours. Again, that's something you have to decide... oh, I guess you and the US Attorney."

There was a brand new red jumpsuit laid out for me with *Federal Inmate* stamped across the back. It wasn't a label I relished wearing, but at least it wasn't yellow. All my other clothes were still at the Atlanta jail. Agent Mailer didn't handcuff me. I stepped into my new outfit, and he assembled a team to escort me to the federal building where I was taken the previous week. Harvey was there sporting a fashion contrast to the crisply suited Justice Department personnel. First, he and I met privately in a secure room.

"Charlie," he began, "this is where we begin to decide your fate. As I've told you, you have quite a bit of incriminating evidence against Vince Palomino and some of his cronies. I've given them a preview of the information they can expect from you. It's stuff you probably have no idea you have on Vince. They know nothing about the documents, but I have little doubt these guys are already salivating to get their hands around the evidence I have told them you can provide. The rub is, they want to get it without having to give in too much to you – or me, as your attorney. It's kind of ridiculous, because it is really of no consequence what happens to a minor player such as you. I think it is just the plain principal of it. These guys spend their time trying to put criminals behind bars, and they don't like seeing any lawbreaker get away scott free."

I took no offense at Harvey's minor player remark. The thought of a murderer being a minor player put Vince and his crowd in another echelon.

Harvey continued his explanation, "We, of course, are trying to get the best deal for you, and we don't mind giving up the entire enchilada if it gets you the best deal. What we have to decide is what we should reasonably expect to be the best deal for what you have to offer. I have mulled this over, and I believe, in the long run, they ought to settle on a short stint in prison, and some extended period of probation – say six years. That's just my opinion. They will probably have another view, but they also want what we can give them." Harvey was in his urgent oration mode, so I let him go on without interruption. "First we give them a taste of something fat. We'll let them chew on it for awhile and see what they offer. It won't be serious, so we'll hint at better things to come. It will be back and forth, like any other negotiation, but this is high stakes for us and them. We will work this out until we get to their real final offer. If it's acceptable to you, we agree, and that's the end of it. If not, the problem at that point is, if we want to string them out further, it means going back into the prison system and letting them stew for awhile until they finally give in. Meanwhile they're leaving work every night, going to their comfortable homes. I'll do the negotiations without you for now. Sometimes it's easier to keep the emotions of my client out of the process. Besides, I don't want them to see how clueless you are about Vince at this point. Got any questions?"

That was the most verbose I had seen Harvey, and I wondered how much that lecture cost per word. Still, his explanation worked for me. Harvey was going to do what he could, and I would wait to see how good the deal was.

"What do I do, in the meantime?" I asked.

"You sit around here," said Harvey. "I'll get you a newspaper and other reading material. This could take all day, or even several days. You'll be the guest of the Feds while we work through this. I'll have some lunch sent up for you around noon."

With that, Harvey was off to engage in some power negotiations. My role was defined, and it was something I could perform with aplomb; the Atlanta City Jail had prepared me well. Soon afterward, a gentleman brought me a Danish and coffee along with the local paper, a *Wall Street Journal* and a *Time* magazine. I couldn't believe how quickly my fortunes had changed. I was not out of the woods yet, but whatever happened, I was going to get some kind of break for the terrible crime I committed against my brother. Meanwhile I was relaxing in a quiet office building away from the yellow jail with its yellow apparel and yellow food.

After a delectable lunch from the corner sandwich shop, I decided to tackle the local newspaper. The *Journal* and *Time* lasted the morning, but it was time to face the hometown pages. That meant reading the reports of my reprehensible crimes. Jon Mailer's advice helped only slightly to assuage the embarrassment, but it's never good when your life is an open book to an entire city – especially when there are people there you know and the press brings up the old charges of child pornography. Everyone involved with the case knew I was innocent of those charges, even though they were still pending against me. The airing of the murder charges seemed almost bearable; after all, it was undeniable, but the perversion was mortifying.

Fortunately, there was only a sketchy article on page two of the Metro section. After I choked the article down with an afternoon latte from Starbucks, complements of Harvey – and ultimately myself when I paid his fee – I perused the rest of the paper. That's when the blurb about Tomcat caught my eye. The title read "Man Extradited to Face Cocaine Charges." The article began:

"Thomas Maroni was back in federal custody today after eluding authorities for months. Maroni was apprehended in Atlanta last year for possession of a controlled substance with intent to distribute, but he escaped and disappeared. Maroni fled to Bermuda where he lived and worked under an assumed name. Authorities gave no details of his capture, saying only that he was returned to Atlanta today, under heavy guard, where he will be arraigned."

As I read, I was sure my actions caused him to be found in Bermuda. At the time, I had no knowledge of Bobby's counterfeit investigation, and the arrest of Lawrenceville Lance. I was feeling guilty when Harvey broke into my thoughts. He looked slightly haggard from what was obviously a long day of haggling.

"Okay, we're done for the day," he said, seeming upbeat.

"How's it going," I asked anxiously.

"We're doing fine," he said. "It's just a complex case. There's a lot to discuss. I'm dealing with Robin Reo of the FBI and Jerome Calloway from the Attorney's Office. They're both reasonable, but stubborn. They huddle up a lot, too. That delays everything, so we'll be back at it tomorrow. I think Robin's pushing hard to give the concessions, but she's playing it cool. She's been working a long time to get to Vincent Palomino, and this would be a godsend for her and her team. Jerome wants Vincent too, but he's going to make things as difficult as he can for as long as he can. He doesn't feel the pressure to nail Palomino like Robin, but he knows what a successful prosecution of someone like that will do for his career."

I wanted to delve further into the chances of various outcomes, but there was no point in it. Harvey told me everything he knew and, beyond that, the result was anybody's guess. Soon my escorts gathered me up, and Jon Mailer and I found ourselves together again in our private motel. Pizza was brought in for dinner, and that was followed by a night in front of the television. When I couldn't take the absurdity of whatever sitcom was airing at the moment, I interrupted Jon's viewing.

"Hey Jon," I started, "have you ever heard of chaos theory?"

"Yeah, I've heard of it, but I don't know much about it," he said. "It's a lot of math, which I never studied."

I proceeded to explain what I knew of the subject, which had nothing to do with math. I told him about the butterfly and how so many factors affect so many outcomes that, in turn, affect an exponentially greater number of outcomes, and so on. I explained, according to the theory, complex events were hard to control, and outcomes were hard to predict because of the infinite number of influences at work at any given time.

"But, unless I'm wrong, the theory does contend that there is a mathematical approach to predicting events," said Jon. "But where are you going with this? What's it all mean?"

"I don't know," I complained. "Sometimes I wonder what factors have affected my life, and how I might have turned out if circumstances were different."

"Oh, I see now," said Jon skeptically. "Are you trying to pass the responsibility for your problems off to uncontrollable causes? I'd say that's a stretch. No matter what outside influences affect a person, assuming he is able and sane, he has to be responsible for what he does. That's the only way the law can work. People, nowadays, use that tactic to try to avoid punishment, and sometimes they get away with it. Every time they do, it erodes our judicial system a little bit, which erodes society."

"Whatever," I said, realizing the truth in his rebuttal. I couldn't argue, and I spent the rest of my waking hours processing his perspective and honing my attitude to conform to his wisdom.

When Jon finally woke me at eight fifteen there was little time to shower and dress before we had to go downtown. There would be no philosophical exchange that morning.

Back in the FBI offices, Harvey briefed me and gave me a pep talk, then left me alone with my newspapers and coffee and Danish. There were no further reports about me or my friend Tomcat. The coffee had a warming effect in my belly, providing a sense of comfort I hoped was warranted. For a moment I became frustrated with the slow process and lack of anything to do but wait for the lawyers to haggle over my fate. In the monotony, my mind wandered back to the jail. It would be about time for lockdown after the morning milling around session, before the laughable lunch. I quickly brightened at the fact I wasn't there with my former jail mates.

As I began thinking about what the accommodating Justice Department would be allowing me to have for lunch, Harvey walked into my adopted office. I checked his expression before he expressed himself.

"Charlie, I've got to tell you where we are," he said seriously. "Basically, they've given us the farm." Harvey's smile became as broad as I had seen it. "They must have had a powwow last night, and evidently they really want what we've got. We got as much as anyone can hope for. Four years to serve two in minimum security. Then five years probation, that's it. We hit the home run!"

I looked at my lawyer in disbelief. After everything I had done, and all that happened – the fraud, the arson, the murder, fleeing my crime, Nils Montgomery, Vince, the arrest, the threats – it was all washed away. Thanks to what? There was Harvey, and Bobby for steering me to Harvey. Of course, there was Mother who collected and saved the evidence. A big, oppressive cloud was suddenly blown away on the wings of these butterflies of the future. I hugged Harvey.

"Thank you, thank you," I cried. "I don't know what to say. I can't express my appreciation."

"Thank your mother, Charlie," Harvey said. "She gave you a straight flush. We just played the hand."

That was the perfect lead in for what I was about to ask of Harvey.

"How strong is the hand, Harvey," I said, flatly.

He looked at me in confusion. "What do you mean, Charlie? I just told you, we've won. It's done."

"What more can we squeeze out of the hand." I said.

"Charlie," Harvey said in exasperation, "it's done. It's two years minimum security; it's a walk in the park. That's no problem. A guy like you can handle that without a worry."

"Not me," I said. "I need to look after some friends of mine."

"What are you talking about, Charlie," cried Harvey. "This isn't a game, here. This is real life. You just walked away from complete disaster. Leave it alone."

"I haven't walked away yet, Harvey," I said. "You're my lawyer, right? I've got the money. Let's see what we can do."

"I am your lawyer," said Harvey, more emotional than he was when he first walked in. "And as your lawyer, I'm advising you to do the deal. Do it right now before Jerry Calloway stubs his toe and changes his mind."

"Look Harvey," I beseeched him, "just hear me out. I've done a lot of things in my life I'm not proud of, and not too many things to brag about. I realize what you're telling me, and I thank you for what you've done. But something inside me is telling me I have to do this. I have to take this chance for my own sense of humanity. How can I feel right about this if I don't use this single, temporary asset to help someone who needs it?"

"I don't know what you're talking about, Charlie," complained Harvey, "but I really think you must be having a breakdown. You were doomed a week ago, and you have been given new life. What am I going to tell these guys? They will not believe what you want me to tell them."

"Tell them I'm having a breakdown if you want," I said. "Just buy a little time, enough to talk to my guys."

"Who are you talking about," whined Harvey.

I told him the story of Tomcat, and how he saved my life, and what a friend he had become, and the trouble he was in, just because the feds set him up on the cocaine deal to use him to get to Vince. Then I spoke of Marvin, of what a friend he was to me in prison, and the small time legal problems he had, which were evolving into huge financial problems threatening to collapse in on him. His problems were also indirectly caused by Vince. I waited to play the trump card.

"Charlie," cried Harvey, "Tomas Maroni is part of our hand – a substantial part. He's not the ace or the king, but maybe a six or seven. Now you want to take him out of play?"

I played my trump card. "Look," I said, feeling stronger and more justified than ever, "we got what we wanted without Bobby Wells. Maybe we involve him if we have to, but I want you to do it."

Harvey studied me silently as he weighed my argument. Then he spoke. "I ought to shoot myself for listening to you," he said. "It is crazy, but you're the client. These guys are going to freak out, but I'm going to tell them something; I'm not sure what. I'll see your friends and we'll talk after that."

With that, Harvey King walked from my office shaking his head. I rocked back in my chair. The pressure that disappeared a few minutes before, revisited me, but this time it was energizing.

A few minutes later Harvey came back in looking haggard.

"Okay," he said, "that's it for today. They'll take you back, and I'll see you in the morning, once I've seen Maroni and Dixon. I can't believe I'm doing this."

"What'd you tell them," I said, out of curiosity.

"I told them the truth," he said, trying to smile. "I said you weren't feeling well, some kind of breakdown. They're puzzled, but surprisingly patient."

Within half an hour Jon Mailer and I were rooming together again at our personal motel. The television provided white noise as Jon confronted me.

"What the hell happened back there," he asked in amazement. Evidently the few people involved in the process were abuzz with wonder.

"It looks like we're close to agreement," I told him. "There are just a few more details to work out before we finalize things."

"That's not what I heard," said Jon. "The word is they were giving you the sweetest deal in the world, and something about... you wigged out on them. They're flabbergasted, and they're not too happy about it either. You look okay to me. What's going on?"

I proceeded to repeat the same story I told Harvey earlier in the day about Tomcat and Marvin, and how I wanted to help them. "Hell," I finished saying, "Tomcat absolutely saved my life; it's as simple as that. And Marvin probably did the same thing. It's time I did something for somebody besides myself. What do you think?"

"I don't know," Jon said, allowing a hint of respect in his tone. "It's damn stupid, but at least it's noble."

"Like I said, I guess it's about time," I said, feeling more repentant than righteous.

"I guess so," he replied, impassively. I took no offense.

As the boring day moved into the boring night, the fire of my newborn conviction, which earlier burned so passionately, began flickering in the winds of idle doubts. I tossed sleeplessly to the laughter of Conan O'Brien's audience and wondered if I really had lost my mind. I had gotten past the menace of serious prison, breezed in and out of the justice system like a tourist at a resort. Harvey was right; the deal was done. Still, I couldn't get Tomcat and Marvin off my mind. For my own salvation I had to risk my freedom. It had to be done that way. I finally fell asleep to the gray light and scratchy sounds of *Spartacus,* the late movie on Jon's television.

……

Vince woke to the ring of his bedside telephone. He focused on the clock before he answered. It was almost noon, which didn't surprise him. Sleep and inertia were consuming his days while restlessness consumed his nights. Either way, most of his life was occurring in bed or on the couch. His affairs, legal and illegal, were drifting loosely at the hands of lieutenants, some more competent than others. Worse, there was no guiding strategy without his leadership. The voice on the phone was David Israel, who was oblivious to his client's deteriorating mental state.

"Vincent, it's David. The FBI picked up Tommy Maroni in Bermuda. He's back in the states. They have him on a cocaine rap; the word is they want to pressure him to give you up. I tried to get to him, but he refused to see me. I tell you Vince, the world's going crazy. Nobody has any loyalty anymore."

Vince groaned silently, thinking he heard David's complaint too often lately. It was wearing on him, even if it were true. David actually said it only once before when he was talking about me, but everything was wearing on Vince and the irritation of it all seemed magnified. Now Tomcat was his newest problem.

"I'll handle it," he growled, as he hung up before the lawyer could say another annoying word.

Vince was trying to wake up, but the fog of depression was making it impossible to think clearly. He didn't have the energy to handle the problem, so he called Frank.

"The feds collared Tomcat. He's downtown ready to roll on us," he said, irrationally. "Put a serious bug in his ear. He's a bad motherfucker, so make sure they get it right the first time. And I don't want any heat on this."

"Are you sure?" said Frank, who was becoming increasingly skeptical of his captain's decisions.

"Just do it," Vince snarled into the phone before he hung up and curled back under the covers seeking refuge from what had become his unbearable life.

....

Once the FBI got to Lance it was easy to find me impersonating Eddie Palomino as Nils Montgomery. When Steve Langtree found out about Lance, the same was true for Tomcat. The FBI agent took the big Geechee thug right off the construction site he was working, and had him in shackles and on a plane to the states within hours. The flight back was three hours of Langtree feeding his prisoner the idea that Vince was busted in the states and he and his lawyer were giving Tomcat up to save his own ass. Any objective view of the story would find more holes in it than a golf course, but Langtree sold it skillfully, and Tomcat didn't think well around handcuffs and FBI men. The fact that I was missing for over a week unsettled him, and he bought the fabrication.

Sitting in his jail cell, he became increasingly bitter that Vince would try such a thing. Hell, he fled the country to avoid turning on his boss. If Vince thought he could get away with it he'd be surprised at what old Tomcat had up his sleeve. As he was brooding he got pulled out to see a lawyer who came by to pay him a visit. The minute he spotted David in the conference room he turned around and turned down the opportunity to speak to him. He found another lawyer and requested a meeting with the Attorney's office. He would show his ungrateful boss who had the goods on whom, and save his own ass in the process.

There was a glitch in his plan. When he and his attorney met with Calloway and Reo to lay their cards on the table, the feds weren't impressed. They already had someone providing them with what Tomcat had to offer and much more. They offered to consider him for corroborating testimony, but he was looking at serious time.

Langtree stopped by when Tomcat was in the building. "Should have done this last year when I gave you the chance," he taunted.

Tomcat glowered at the man who was his nemesis. It was obvious Vince hadn't cut any deals. The bastard lied to encourage Tomcat to roll. When he got back to the states and found out his colleagues had a better informant, Langtree had the gall to come by and mock him.

Back in his cell, Tomcat wondered who was giving him and Vincent up at the same time. He thought of me, but evidently the information was so good they didn't need his input. Charlie couldn't possibly know the quality of information he did, he thought to himself. He resolved to find out who it was, and make them pay. Before dinner he was summoned to the attorney-inmate conference area. He was sure it was David Israel back to reach out to him again. He was wrong.

....

I awoke the next morning with knots in my belly. The little sleep I got was dominated by dreams of prison. When Jon Mailer rousted me into consciousness it was a welcome gesture. As I showered and dressed and listened to my roommate chomp on his cereal to the beat of the *Today Show*, I was anxious to get back downtown. There, at least something would be progressing – whether or not it was in my best interest.

Harvey was waiting for me in my adopted office. He was calm and resigned to our new strategy, but he looked tired. "I spoke with Marvin Dixon yesterday evening," he said. "Marvin said to say hi. He's quite a character, *and* he's appreciative of what you're trying to do. He's grateful to have me working on his behalf."

"What about Tomcat," I said. "Did you see him?"

"Oh yeah," said Harvey. "The meeting with him was a different story. He was pretty ornery during our brief meeting. He said to tell you to mind your own business and he could take care of himself, and you were crazy if you thought you could deliver Vince and him and everybody else to the feds. I tried to explain that we actually could do just that, but after his rant he stood up and walked away. I called to him that we were on his side, but he stormed out without a reply."

"Shit," I exclaimed, "so he won't even listen to us?"

"That's what I thought as I left the jail, yesterday," explained Harvey. "But last night I got a call from Mr. Maroni. It seems Vincent dispatched one of the guards to issue a threat against him. Tommy didn't take the threat well. That's when he called me. I explained our position to him, and he listened. He seems placated, but I think he's pretty confused. He's given me permission to negotiate for him, anyway. Based on what I know, I'm ready to go back in and do battle. We will need to be tactful enough to keep Reo and Calloway from going ape shit and canceling the deal. And we will have to back off on what we can offer and let Maroni spill some of the beans. I can coordinate that with Maroni if he will work with us. What we're doing is a little out there."

Harvey did what I asked, and the die was cast. He left me to wait while he entered the fray. I did just that. I waited and wondered. I didn't eat my breakfast bun; I couldn't digest it with my nervous stomach. I had reading material, but couldn't digest the meaning of the words. The clock tortured me, moving ever slower as the long day became mired in anticipation. Eventually, the day disappeared into evening, and my untouched lunch was replaced with a fancy meal that, ironically, came from one of Vince's downtown restaurants.

As I tried to choke down part of an antipasto platter, Harvey came in to update me. The morning meeting started badly, as Harvey warned it might. Harvey finessed his opponents and they left the meeting to regroup with each other. Finally, they all sat down together and began with a fresh slate. They were making progress, but Harvey was forced to back off of our claims a little to give Tomcat a chance to deal. They were going back to the table after dinner. They all agreed to see it through no matter what the conclusion would be. It promised to be a long night, and I was there with the rest of them for the duration.

As wrung out as I was, sleep eventually began to overtake me, and I found myself being awakened by the very tired Harvey King.

"What time is it," I asked groggily.

"Ten after two," he told me with a handshake.

"Charlie, we're almost done," said Harvey, with a breath of apprehension "We're where we were the other day, with a couple of variations – some good and some not too bad."

"What are the changes," I asked with a yawn.

"The good thing is that Marvin Dixon is taken care of," Harvey explained. "His charges will be dropped, and he will be released tomorrow. Thomas Maroni is in the deal, too. He has agreed to testify against Vincent, but it will steal some of our thunder. He will plead out to certain racketeering charges and be granted immunity in all other aspects of the case against him. With Tommy present, I negotiated a ten year prison sentence for which he should serve five. He then goes to a halfway house and gets probation. They will set him up in a new location. He will be under the witness protection program.

"That brings us to you. When things first blew up this morning, Reo and Calloway accused us of negotiating in bad faith. I had to put out some things Tommy Maroni had to offer. That creates a slightly less desirable outcome for you.

"If you agree to the deal, you will be obligated to testify against Vince, and you will plead guilty to manslaughter and be granted immunity in all other aspects of your case. That will earn you a sentence of six years in a minimum security prison, for which you will probably serve three, maybe less, and then five years probation. You will be relocated according to the witness protection program.

"Charlie, it's not as good for you as we previously agreed, but remember, we're talking some easy time for some serious charges. Minimum security is a good deal. It's a country club. All we need to ink the deal is your agreement, and it's done."

I looked at him. He didn't say another word, but I knew he thought it was good. I nodded, glad to have the ordeal come to a close.

Soon Agent Reo walked in and said, "I think you did the right thing, Charlie. What you're going to give us is invaluable information in our investigation of mob activities from here to New York and beyond. If I didn't believe that, I couldn't endorse the deal. Congratulations on getting it behind you."

She shook my hand again, and I was speechless. I never expected to hear those conciliatory words coming from the one who manhandled and shackled me before I could get on my plane to New York. Suddenly, it was as if I were on the side of the good guys – and I actually was.

Sure, I was going to some sort of freshman prison for a time, but I had made my comeback. I hadn't felt so free since I pulled the gun on Hugh McDowell. Even though my days in Bermuda were a respite from my situation, it was only an empty anesthesia to my troubles back in the states, which I failed to recognize until that moment in the presence of my lawyer and my captors.

Harvey returned with Marvin and Tomcat and Calloway in tow. Marvin was the first to speak.

"Well if it ain't the federal man, come and rescue me out of jail," he said, beaming with relief as he offered his handshake.

"Cholly," said Tomcat, as he had spoken it many times on the island. "Look like we goin' in da same direction agin. Maybe mah journey'll be a leetle longer'n yos, but wee'll be okay." His meaty paw, which would never again be used to do Vincent's corrupt bidding, squeezed mine in a kinship born out of our common experience on the lam in Bermuda.

There was a surreal celebration among everyone in the room – criminals, defense attorneys, U.S. Attorneys, law officers. We all sealed a deal that seemed to serve everyone's best interest. My convicted cohorts and I won our futures back, our lawyer earned his fee, and the feds were eagerly anticipating satisfying their obsession with Vincent Palomino.

XXIII. CLUB FED, A REUNION AND A UNION

Bobby Wells was living his lifelong dream and enjoying it more than ever since his move from catching criminals to prosecuting them. Since my return from the dead, he was getting high marks inside the justice department for his role in initiating the process that would strike a blow against high value targets in the racketeering division of the FBI. He had been prepared when Lawrenceville Lance provided the luck of stumbling upon me instead of our dead friend Eddie.

He was able to drop in on me from time to time while I worked beside one of Harvey's associates, paging through documents, relating facts of Vincent's activities to Agents Langtree and Reo, facts I had only learned and memorized from the same documents we were all reviewing. We were even able to have lunch together occasionally. It was odd, just how normal our relationship was, even though he was a U.S. Attorney and I was a criminal in the U.S. justice system. We shared the normal things any suburban neighbors might discuss. His daughter, Courtney, was a year from kindergarten, and she already needed glasses. Eileen was four months pregnant with a second child. They just had a sonogram, and it looked like it would be another girl. Everything in Bobby's life was on track.

He was concerned about me, though. While he appreciated the fact I dodged a bullet that would have pierced the heart of my existence, he worried about what lay ahead for me. I would be a blank page with a new name in a new town with no prospects. My parole officer would force me into some sort of basic vocation, but Bobby wanted more for his lifelong friend. One night, Eileen suggested something to him that piqued his interest and changed the course of my life. He placed a phone call to Gracie.

……..

While I produced documents that provided a telling outline of Vince's organization and activities and his ties to the New York mob, Tommy Maroni, who stated he no longer wished to be called Tomcat, was able to enhance the information in the documents, offering explanations for why things were structured a certain way, or how a particular individual fit into the story. The people we worked with were satisfied with our contributions. The main investigators involved were Agents Reo and Langtree. While they both carried the cavalier attitude that was prevalent around those offices, Reo was more pleasant to be around than Langtree. I didn't have a problem with either one, but Tommy held a mutual, open grudge with Langtree, which made things unpleasant when the two were together.

There was no doubt that the Justice Department personnel were in charge and we were lucky to be there helping. They tried to be discreet while we were around, but I was attentive, and I picked up on what they were after, and the strategy of their overall mission. What became clear was that Vince was but another stepping stone in a much broader, more sweeping investigation of the top echelon of the New York Mob. The plan was to pick-off people all the way up the ladder and force them to roll until they were able to cut off the head of the monster the government had been fighting since the days of Al Capone. I wondered if Vince actually would give up his bosses in New York.

Once it became clear that my presence was no longer needed, I was told to prepare for my eviction from the motel room I shared with Jon Mailer and settle my affairs. Once the last payment was made to Harvey, much of the money I saved as Charlie Lofton was gone.

As I walked out of the FBI offices for the last time, there was almost a going away party atmosphere. Harvey gave me instructions for my next stop. Bobby stopped by, and Jon Mailer hung around the whole day. They all wished me well, even Langtree. Tommy shook my hand knowing we would never again cross paths. It was another fantastic sensation. After we said our goodbyes, Jon and his team gathered for one last journey with their charge. That was to Eglin Federal Prison Camp.

Eglin FPC was a minimum security facility in Fort Walton Beach, Florida. Its nickname, Club Fed, was appropriate, as far as prisons go. Life there was not horrible – not pleasant, by any measure, but tolerable. I have to admit, there were amenities, including a beach to look at, tennis courts, a bocce ball area, and there were no fences. There were clearly delineated boundaries you are not allowed to cross unless you have a pass to work on the adjoining air force base.

Most of the inmates were intelligent, non-violent offenders. There was never a threatening atmosphere, and everyone, including the guards, was exceedingly civil. The main thrust of the experience was structure. In that sense, the prison was sort of a lightweight military boot camp. Everyone was expected to be up by seven a.m., do a job, eat the meals, recreate, and go to bed at the same time every night. Everyone did as expected.

My sentence was for three years, but if I had to, I could have done twice the time. We were allowed visitors at specified times, but I couldn't think who would visit me down in Florida. I figured I was on my own for the duration. That's why I was surprised when visiting hours came one Saturday, and I was told I had a guest.

When I walked outside to the immaculately maintained reception lawn, there sat Gracie. It had been too long since I had seen her, except for the brief glimpse in Bermuda, but there was no mistaking my best friend. I was ashamed that she had to come to a prison to visit me, but she was so natural and obviously happy to see me, my embarrassment quickly waned.

"Charlie," she cried as she hugged me, and then held me at arms length to study my face. "I'm so happy to see you. You know, I attended your funeral."

I wondered how many times anyone had said that to another human being.

"You did?" I said, feeling more at ease with every breath. I looked at her while she looked at me, and I couldn't believe how happy I suddenly felt in her presence. Her inner beauty shone through and encompassed me.

"I'm so glad to see you," I said with utter joy. "How are you?"

"You were there weren't you?" Gracie said. "You saw me in Bermuda, and you left me that note."

"Yes, I did," I tried to explain, "but I couldn't speak to you. It would have put you in a compromised position. It would have made you an accessory."

"Well, it scared the shit out of me," she complained. "You shouldn't have done that to me. I thought I was either crazy, or I was hearing from the great beyond. That really affected me, Charlie."

I was sorry for what I did. I just wanted to touch her in some way, but it was stupid, and I didn't consider what it would do to her. But it was Gracie I was talking to, and there was no use trying to explain; she didn't suffer bullshit gladly.

"You're right," I said. "I am really sorry.

"And what the hell did you do, anyway," she said. "You lied about yourself; you *killed* your friend Eddie."

I almost corrected her to say "brother Eddie," but I didn't think she would find the humor in the heinous irony.

"I know, I know," I said, "I admit it; I have been a terrible friend. I'm so sorry, but I don't know how to make it up to you."

"Oh God, Charlie," she said, collecting herself, "you can't make it up to me, and I don't need you to. I just had to tell you how hurtful it was – just get it off my chest. Now I'll tell you, when Eileen had Bobby call with the shocking news you were still among the living, I was ecstatic. It is like I regained something valuable I thought was lost forever. Once everything was settled with your sentence Bobby told me where you were and how to get in to see you."

The reality of my circumstances imposed itself in my mind and I brought it to words. "Yeah, I'm sorry you have to come here to see me. I did some stupid and terrible things, but I'm trying to set things right."

Gracie looked at me through clear, understanding eyes and said, "I have known you my entire life. I know who you are. The idea that you're a killer is impossible for me to believe. I'm not saying I don't believe you did what you did, but I also know you can be better than that. I know what that asshole Eddie was doing to you. It must all have been a nightmare. Not that it's an excuse."

"It's been weird," I said, at a loss for any other explanation. "What about you? How's the world treated you since your last Christmas card? I haven't been getting one lately."

"That's because you were dead," she laughed.

"What about your health?" I asked. "Are you doing okay?"

"It's pretty good, right now," she said, looking away. "So far, I'm cancer free since my treatments. I keep my fingers crossed, given my family history, but they've come a long way in treating cancer since my mother's day."

"Yeah, I'm glad about that," I said. "Last time I heard from you, you were having problems with Austin. That was after you found out about the cancer." I was truly interested for Gracie's sake, but I can't say her answer didn't pique a selfish urge.

"Oh yeah, Austin," said Gracie. "Austin left me after the first operation; I don't know if you knew. I used to get down, you know, about relationships, or actually not having one."

"You said things weren't good. I just assumed," I said.

"It seems he wasn't up to having a wife who turned out to be a medical burden," she said quietly, looking through the strands of fine blond hair that framed her soft eyes. "He preferred the company of women who required less maintenance. It was not a good scene, so I was ready for him to go."

"Yeah, but that was awhile ago," I said. "Does it still make you sad?"

"That? No," she said. "It's just that it's been tough to date guys since then. You know, *your* gender can be real shits. Most guys don't want to get involved with someone who carries the baggage of cancer. It's not like I advertise it, but eventually it's got to come up. Sometimes it's lonely. Not that I don't have plenty of friends, and I actually have a busy social calendar, but I have this problem when it comes to dating."

That was something I understood. I hugged her tightly. "Don't worry about it," I said. "If that kind of stuff matters so much to a guy, he's not worth it. You'll find someone who's bright enough to look beyond what doesn't matter."

"You're sweet," she said with a smile. "You know, I'm less than an hour away at Daddy's place over in Seaside. If you want, I can come see you more often. I will be staying down here for awhile. I can work from here, but I may need to travel back to New York from time to time."

That was the best thing I heard since my fate was sealed with the deal at the Justice Department. I couldn't have wanted anything more than what Gracie was offering. "That would be great," I said, "but only if you have time and want to make the trip. I don't want to be a burden."

"That's okay," said Gracie. "Burdens are what we need to give life meaning."

That night I lay awake in bed amazed at the turn of events. If I had to be in prison, what better place than this Club Fed, with all its amenities and decent people. Then, to top it off, I was close to my long lost friend and looking forward to her visits. I hoped she was sincere about wanting to see me, because I sincerely wanted to see her. I was afraid to go to sleep, lest I wake up to find out it wasn't real.

Gracie was true to her word. The following weekend she was there waiting for me in the reception hall as I walked in wearing my denim blue inmate's shirt over jeans. We hugged hello.

"I brought some cookies I baked for you this morning," Gracie said, handing me the pre-inspected tin of chocolate chips. "Actually, they were the kind in the dairy case. I just had to cut them up and put them on a baking sheet. I thought you might enjoy something that at least seems like it's home made."

"Thanks," I said. "These will be great." I didn't have the

heart to tell her that the food at the camp, and at the naval base, was pretty good. The one thing we didn't get much of was dessert, so this was a welcome addition, even if I wasn't the biggest sweets eater.

Gracie got serious, and, as she always did when she was serious, she looked deeply into my eyes. "Charlie, what happened with all of this," she said, arms unfolding before us. "I'm not being judgmental, I swear. I just want to hear the whole truth, as they say, from the horse's mouth. Nothing has changed since last weekend."

I was tired of telling the story. It was as if it been told a thousand times before.

"I do want to know," she said, emphatically, "because I know you, Charlie, and I know you're a good person. So what could have happened to put you where you are right now?"

I relived it so many times, there was nothing special about it in my mind, but much of it would be new to Gracie. The press on my story had been local to Atlanta, sketchy, and not always accurate. There were many details that never got into the news in Atlanta, much less in the national press. My relationship to my victim never even came to light. I *did* tell her that I found out from Vince Eddie was my brother.

"Whoa," Gracie said, her dancing eyes growing wide. "So for a long time, Vincent Palomino thought he was your father, but he wasn't. And even though he was Eddie's adopted father, he thought of both of you as his sons. And Eddie was your real brother, but you never knew it? That means you…" She trailed off, afraid I didn't want to hear what she was about to say.

"Yes," I finished it for her, "I killed my own brother. But it really doesn't matter who it was; murder is murder."

"Yeah, but Charlie, you've got to admit, it's all so coincidental," said Gracie with a far away look. Either way, I stand behind you as my friend."

Her simple statement made me feel secure, but then Gracie was my security blanket when I was growing up, and even after she moved away she kept me covered with her letters. In the days that followed, I couldn't get that feeling of unconditional friendship out of my mind. Gracie and Bobby both believed in me, and they were the foundation that helped me rebuild self-respect. After all, there weren't two people I had more respect for, and if they thought I was worthwhile I trusted their opinions. My worst fear was the possibility of losing touch with them once I was given a new identity and moved off to parts unknown to start a new life.

The next time Gracie returned she carried with her an intensity, and she seemed anxious to get down to serious conversation with me. "You know what this is?" she asked, rhetorically.

"Yeah, it's a tape recorder," I said.

"Yeah, but you know what we're going to do with it?" she said, allowing only a nod from me. "You know I'm an editor," said Gracie. "I think your experience is interesting. It would make for good reading. If we can get it down on tape I know I can turn it into a book. If it turns out to be good enough I'll take it to my company to try to get it published. You might have a book on your hands."

At first I didn't have an opinion about the idea, but if Gracie wanted to work on it, I was willing to give it a try. "I'll do it if you will," I said. I spoke those same words long ago before our first trip to the garage, and I hadn't forgotten them since. "How do we go about it?"

"We just talk about your whole life," she said. "You should start telling me about your earliest memories, the things that stick in your mind as important. Tell me, even if I already know some of it, as if I were an interviewer. I'll stop you and ask questions, and I might add stuff I know about."

That's when I told her about my father, and how much he meant to me – how he used to teach me things while he was in school. I told her about Father's chaos theory, and my interpretation of the butterfly that disturbed the winds of my fate, and how devastated I was when I lost him. Those things she already knew, but there were things that were new to her. I told her for the first time that Vince was responsible for his death.

She stopped me. She was shocked. "How do you deal with that?" she asked.

"Apparently not very well," I said, looking around, indicating my surroundings.

"Do you ever think about the way things might have turned out if Vincent hadn't murdered your father; if you had grown up with him as a role model instead of a drug addicted mother and a criminal dominant male figure?"

"Sure, I used to," I said, "but it doesn't matter, because that's not reality. What if, instead of Eddie, I had been adopted by Vince; would you be here talking to him right now, instead of me? Would I have tortured him, like he did me? It's hard to say, but that's not what happened. The world is the way it is, and there is no changing what has happened."

"But Charlie, you never really had a chance, did you," she said, sounding a little like an amateur sociologist. I had learned from Jonathan Mailer and from my counselor at Club Fed, and I wanted to nip that kind of "victim rationalization" in the bud.

"I think I did," I argued. "I had my father for six years. And I had a nice house to grow up in and a good school. And I had you and your family. Look at Bobby; he was in the same boat as I was, in fact he didn't have the advantages I had, but see how he turned out?"

"Yeah, that's true, but you know what he told me," she said, lowering her voice. "He always felt responsible for your problems, because you took the shoplifting rap when Eddie was the one who stole the stuff. He said they left you holding the bag, and when you got nailed by the policeman he never spoke up to help you. He said he believes things might have been different for you if you hadn't had that first blot on your record. Of course, it didn't help when you had the incident with the gun in school."

It was true. I didn't take the shoes; it was Eddie who took them, but he handed them off to me. Gracie was trying to make me feel better about myself, but I wasn't about to go back and assign blame for things that happened so many years ago. That would be the wrong turn to take on my road to redemption.

"No matter, whatever happened back then is done," I said. "All I can do is accept reality and try to get it right in the future."

"You're right," said Gracie, affectionately. "I know…well you know…killing someone is one hell of an extreme reaction to the any situation…," she trailed off, unable to articulate her thoughts, and then she tried to clarify herself. "I believe it was an irrational response to a problem beyond your capacity to handle. I hope you believe what I tell you. I want you to survive this."

The language she chose again sounded too intellectual, trying to defend the indefensible, but the fact that she wanted me to overcome my problems made me want it even more. I renewed my vow to make the rest of my life worthwhile.

Over the next weeks, Gracie paid her weekend visits, and we talked while she recorded. She interjected her questions and opinions and the process became cathartic as it followed a natural path toward what someday would become a story. As our story moved along, she brought in the beginnings of the manuscript she started from our recordings, and I read them in between visits.

"How did you feel when I moved away," she asked me one day.

"It was terrible news," I said. "You were my best friend. First my father was taken from me, then your mother. Then, when you and your father left, two more important people in my life were gone. At least I got to hear from you from time to time."

"You were the biggest reason I didn't want to leave," Gracie confessed. "I used to think about you in New York when I was alone, and well, you know…"

I was embarrassed and titillated at the same time. I couldn't remember feeling so hopefully aroused since we were children fooling around in the old garage.

"So why did you take that gun to school that day," she said, the blood clearing from her flushed cheeks as she straightened herself in her chair. "Were you ever going to use it on Hugh?"

"I did use it on him," I said, slightly sarcastically. "I didn't shoot him with it, but he was hit with the bullet of shame. I hear he never regained his stature after he wet his pants that day. To answer your question, I never would have shot Hugh. I wish I hadn't taken the gun to school in the first place. I stupidly thought of it as a big joke on him. I don't think anyone in the school had the same sense of humor about it."

"There's no doubt about that," she said.

Gracie had a quality about her that was bluntly honest, yet not offensive. That made it therapeutic for me to be around her.

....

The next time Gracie came to see me we talked about my decision to become a renegade dentist.

"Why did you decide to do that?" she asked.

"I had a lot of time on my hands, not being in school, and all," I said. "The books were there in my grandfather's study. It just presented itself to me."

"But why did you feel like you *could* do it?" she pressed. "I mean, how did you know, without going through the formal curriculum that you would be able to succeed?"

"Hey, it's just being a dentist. It's not oral surgery," I joked. "If my grandfather could do it, anybody could. But seriously, I went to a lot of classes, and worked for a dentist before I went on my own. I didn't ever doubt I could do it. You know me. I'm learning that I have always been kind of impulsive, just doing things without thinking. Too bad for Eddie he didn't know that about me."

Gracie studied me in silence for a moment before she said, "Well, you don't suffer from low self esteem or lack of confidence, and you're not lazy. You're not a typical criminal."

When we got to my mother's death Gracie learned Vince was responsible for the loss of both my parents.

"This is unbelievable," she cried. "This man first killed your father years ago, and now you're telling me he took your mother's life, too?"

"Hard to fathom, isn't it?" I said.

"But you thought she committed suicide," she delved.

"Well, so did everybody else, and it surely wasn't beyond comprehension," I said. "The drugs and alcohol did their worst work on her, and she alluded to suicide more than once, so I accepted the wisdom of the investigators."

"How did you feel when you found out it wasn't suicide?" she asked. "Were you relieved?"

"It seems so long ago, and I was so fucked up when Tommy told me," I said. "I don't remember being relieved. I was shocked, and I just needed answers. Vince was the only one who knew the truth, so I thought I had to see him."

"But you didn't really have any animosity toward him?" she prodded. "Or did you?"

"Not really," I said. "Vince was so pitiful when I caught up with him, I almost felt sorry for him. And to be honest, I saw Vince in the same boat with my mother that I was in with Eddie. From that perspective, he was no worse than I was. In a way, maybe Mother did commit suicide. Maybe she pushed Vince so far, she knew he would finally do something about it and save her from having to do it to herself. And maybe Eddie did the same thing with me."

"So you think Eddie deserved what he got?" Gracie asked me when we picked up from where we left off the previous weekend.

"I didn't say that; I said he may have been asking for it. I have to admit one thing, though," I confessed. "Don't get me wrong, what I did to him was reprehensible, and I would give anything if it could be undone. That said, he was headed for trouble with or without me." That's when I told her about the Russians he crossed and the episode in Bermuda when, by incomprehensible luck, Tomcat arrived from nowhere to save my life.

"Eddie probably would have survived only a little longer if I hadn't beaten the Russians to the punch. If I'd realized they were going to solve my problem, we wouldn't be sitting here right now." I didn't tell Gracie that I couldn't imagine wanting to do anything other than sitting there talking to her. That's when the previous, trying months began to make sense. In spite of all the bad things I did, and all the things that happened to me, it was all worth it to be reunited with the only girl I ever loved. Perhaps if life had taken different turns, I might still have gotten back together with Gracie anyway, but there was no way of knowing. Life took the path it took, and I was back with her.

"I love you," I blurted.

"What?" said Gracie, her cheeks growing warm red.

"I said I love you," I cried. "I know it's ridiculous. I know I'm a convict, and a killer, but I had to tell you what I've known for a long time. I've always loved you, and if you can ever see past the rotten person I was, maybe you'll give me a chance to be better and share my love with you."

"Whoa Charlie," she said. "Did you just say you love me, like *in love* with me?"

"I know it sounds crazy," I insisted, "but you've never been one to follow convention, Gracie. You never know how things will work, but that shouldn't keep us from at least exploring the idea."

"I don't know," she said. "That's way beyond conventional."

"Gracie, you've been anything but conventional your whole life," I said. "Tell me you haven't at least thought about it," I urged. "If you have, that means you think it just might be a good thing. There's no way to know until we give it a chance."

"I didn't even think you had any interest," she said.

"I know," I said. "I don't do well expressing my feelings. That's one of many things I need to work on. But I *do* have an interest, so you should seriously consider it."

"Charlie, you don't know what's motivating you," Gracie submitted. "You're in prison. I guess I represent the best part of your week here. I'm afraid this is just another one of your impulsive reactions to your situation."

"Gracie, I have never in my life said such things to any other woman," I said. "This is hard for you to understand, but I feel like I have been in self-imposed incarceration all my life when it comes to relationships. To be honest, you do represent a break from imprisonment, but not from the four walls of this place. I know how good I can be, and with you in my life, I can be even better."

"Charlie, it's not fair to put me in this spot. Give me a break, will you," she complained, her face twisting in frustration.

I couldn't deny her appeal for sanity. She was right; I hit her with this weighty proposal out of the blue. She had the good sense to diffuse the situation and give us both a cooling off period. When she was gone and I lay awake that night. I wished I could take back everything I said. It wasn't that I didn't love her – I absolutely did – but I should have taken it slower and approached her differently.

I spent the entire week on pins and needles, praying I hadn't ruined the good thing I had with her. Every day seemed to drag by, and Saturday teased my impatience by refusing to arrive. When it finally did, I was crushed after I waited the entire day without any sign of Gracie. I regretted what I did. Whatever possessed me to blurt such a bold declaration of my private thoughts threatened to cost me a treasure. I cursed my impulsiveness. Those spasms of bad judgment usually reaped bad results, as in the case of the Hugh McDowell incident, the handling of the Eddie situation and my rash, impaired mission back to the U.S. to confront Vince – and now this. I sank into a lovelorn funk.

The plan to recover from the mistake was to write Gracie and make things right. It was the only avenue available, but what words would accomplish the purpose? During the next week I started an e-mail five times without finishing. There was nothing that could change the facts contained in my outburst, and I finally gave up, realizing I was hopelessly in love. It was a love I feared would go unfulfilled.

When the next Saturday morning dawned, I lay awake, waiting for our wake-up call, hoping against the odds that Gracie would at least come to see me. Her silent absence had me in limbo. I needed to hear from her, no matter what her feelings were. Not knowing what was on her mind was as bad as knowing I blew it with her.

Visiting hours came, and an elated panic consumed me when I learned she was waiting for me in the reception area. She stood there and formed a beautiful smile almost as encouraging as her warm embrace when I got to her.

"I'm so glad you came," I started, "I'm sorry about…"

"No, don't," Gracie interrupted. "Let me talk. I'm sorry for my reaction, and I'm sorry I abandoned you last week without any word. But I really had to go back to New York last weekend. You know Daddy's been sick for a long time. He seemed pretty stable for awhile, but now I'm afraid he's nearing the end, and I am going to need to be there for him a lot more, now."

Suddenly I felt selfish for being so absorbed in my own silly trauma. It was the same feeling I had when she came back from being with her mother at the hospital after my mother caught us fooling around in the garage. "Oh, I'm so sorry," I began, but she interrupted me again.

"I'll tell you something else crazy, Charlie. I thought about it for two weeks, and you and me together sounds crazy. You know me, though; you said it yourself. I was never one to follow convention. Actually, I was always one to flout it. That's why I want to ask you one question. Did you really mean what you said, about loving me – about always loving me?"

I was frozen. For the past fourteen days in prison I tried in vain to figure out how to soft pedal that irresistible emotion. But there she was asking me to give her the hard sell. If I followed the plan, and downplayed it, I might lose the moment she was seeking to reciprocate. If I was honest, she might be driven away for another two weeks – or worse. My road to redemption finally led me to an honest response.

"Are you kidding," I said. "I spent the last two weeks agonizing over our last conversation. I was so afraid I scared you off forever. All that time you were all I could think about. Nothing else mattered. I love you. If the two of us aren't meant to be a couple, I will adjust. Just please don't abandon me as a friend."

"I won't abandon you, I promise," said Gracie. "I agonized for two weeks, too. I freaked because you scared me."

I was confused. I had never known Gracie to be scared of anything. "I didn't try to scare you," I said.

"I was scared because I was thinking about myself," she confessed. "I was scared because I don't want to be hurt again. I tell you, Charlie, I am so afraid to invest myself in someone who will abandon me at the first sign of difficulty. As you probably know, I've had more than my share of relationships with a lot of men. Some were mere dalliances. A few were more serious for me. But you know what? I don't think any of those guys ever took me seriously – not even Austin. I endured all of that, but I'm not sure I could survive if you didn't take me seriously, Charlie. You are my oldest and dearest friend, and I do love you, but I don't want to screw that up."

"Well, there you go then," I said, trying to avoid another spell of reckless abandon. "I couldn't ever not take you seriously." At that point I shut up, afraid of sounding more and more inept. Gracie giggled nervously.

"Well, like I was saying, talk about crazy," she said. "I brought this ring with me if you want to wear it. It's supposed to be a wedding ring, that is, if you *are* serious."

I was floored. I wasn't contemplating marriage when I was spouting off, confessing my love, but I realized I might as well have proposed. There is no telling how long I sat, agape in the face of the astonishing turn of events, but it was long enough to watch Gracie's glowing expression ebb toward horror before I could speak.

"Gracie, there is nothing I wanted more than to hear you say that," I said. "I want to marry you so badly, it hurts. You say when, and I'll be there, assuming you can wait for my release from this place."

Her face brightened again. "Really Charlie?" she said in a breathless whisper.

"Really, I love you," I said, realizing Gracie was the only person I had spoken those words to since I had said them to my father. Suddenly I felt like a new person. For the first time in my life I felt like a man. From that moment on, I gained a deeper purpose, and I was more determined than ever to make good with what remained of my life.

……..

For the next few months, our book project got overshadowed by two events. The first was the death of Gracie's father. His final days and his passing took Gracie back to New York for awhile. I tried to be a comfort to her when I could. I wished I could have seen Mr. Willingham and been there for him and Gracie during that tough time.

The second event was the wedding. There was no hurry, but Gracie wanted to have a prison wedding, just for the eccentricity of it. That suited me, and we got permission from the warden to hold the wedding on the prison grounds while I was still incarcerated. It couldn't have worked out better if we had hired a full blown wedding planner for a big bash.

Neither of us had any family left, and we wanted our close friends to attend. One stipulation was that every inmate would be invited to attend, so the groom would have the edge in attendance. Father Brane agreed to marry us in a Catholic wedding sans Mass. Bobby would be my best man, and Eileen would be an honorary bridesmaid. Toni Strunz was to be the Maid of honor.

Ed Whitney, who was an inmate cook, was given special ingredients, two inmate assistants, and permission to prepare hors d'oeuvres and bake a cake for the affair. Florists and party rental people from the town wore security badges to get onto the grounds to arrange flowers, erect tents, and set up tables and chairs. In the home stretch before the wedding, Club Fed became a hive of all kinds of activities concerning everything except corrections.

Not all of my fellow inmates were preoccupied with what was being referred to as the Hoosegow Hootenanny, but for most it provided a break from the routine. The event itself was becoming bigger than the reason for the occasion. The fact of an actual wedding was less evident around the prison population than the anticipation of an affair to relieve the routine. It made no difference to me; for me the thrill was finally sealing my future with the woman I loved. I did gain a certain celebrity for my part in the diversion.

Even behind my figurative bars I kept busy with the plans, working within the prison to get things ready. I spent time on the internet, making arrangements with Gracie, following her instructions, and loving it. The days became very short as activity increased and the wedding neared, and that served to accelerate the sense of time left before I could walk away a free man. If everything went according to plan the parole board would release me a few months after the nuptials.

....

The day of the of the wedding was much the same as it would be on the outside, but the honeymoon was a one night stand in a room set aside for us with a makeshift bed consisting of a mattress on the floor. Gracie was a sight to behold as she strolled down the outdoor aisle in the direction of the flowery altar and our cozy wedding party. To punctuate the unconventional rite, she wore a silk, patterned, white, mid-thigh dress which turned most of the heads sitting on the groom's side. I was flabbergasted when I first saw her, unable to believe that the bawdy creature strutting toward me would soon be my wife. Gracie handed her bouquet to Toni, and Father Brane began speaking. The ceremony was a blur for me. The good priest asked us a couple of yes questions, we both said I do, and suddenly, after all those years of irresponsible bachelorhood, I was a married convict.

There was no alcohol allowed at the wedding, so we mingled with our friends and acquaintances over sodas and Ed's hors d'oeuvres. Our wedding cake was topped by the shape of a metal file made from icing, a manifestation of Ed's imagination. I was only hours from escaping into ecstasy. A deejay played the kind of music that was always played after weddings, but there wasn't much dancing, since the women were severely outmanned. Non-alcoholic events never seem to last as long as their more spirited counterparts, but this time most of the guests had nowhere else to go. I endured the wait for the honeymoon for some time. Eventually we saw off the few friends who were allowed to leave the premises, and Gracie and I were forcefully driven back to our honeymoon suite by a birdseed throwing crowd hopped up on Coca-Cola and wedding cake.

A few prankish inmates decorated the room in lieu of a car to vandalize. Soda cans clanged above us as we opened the door to find the common corny sayings plastered on the wall around our modest mattress. Vaseline coated the doorknobs and fixtures in the tiny bathroom. The ubiquitous condoms were strewn across our bed. We brushed them aside as Gracie plopped down on the mattress, her pretty dress hiked over her still girlish hips. I was immediately turned on. I hadn't seen her naked since we were kids, and I was as eager at that moment as I had ever been.

"Why don't you take off your clothes," I said awkwardly.

"I'll do it if you will," Gracie said seductively, and we both understood the reference. She slowly pulled the dress over her head, revealing a well toned body that belied her age. I caressed her belly and ran my hands up to her surgically repaired breast. The surgeons who saved her life and the surgeons who cleaned up after them left little evidence of their handiwork. A couple of well healed scars didn't bother me; I cared only about the woman who bore them.

That night I lost the virginity that I held onto for way too many years of my life. I finally understood what was so great about sex. After all those years of abstinence, I had some catching up to do, and Gracie was willing to support me in my quest. The night was blissful, but it went by too fast and without much sleep. At seven the next morning Gracie had to leave me to resume my prison routine. Gracie and I vowed to pick-up where we left off on our wedding night. I guessed I might be the only man in the country to lose his heterosexual virginity in prison.

....

The remaining months of incarceration were cloud nine months for me. Every chore, each counseling session, every task at the naval base was a breeze as I anticipated seeing Gracie out in the real world. I was truly reformed, and Father Brane and my counselor, Joe Cline, knew it. I made a pivotal decision on a problem I had been pondering since before I knew I would spend the rest of my life with Gracie.

"I've decided not to go into the witness protection program," I said when Joe asked Father Brane to join us for our last session together.

"What brought you to that decision?" asked the good father.

"I don't know," I said. "I've changed my identity too many times in this world. It's time to just be who I am, and every day I learn more and more who that is and what that person is capable of being. I don't think there is anyone left to come after me."

Shortly after Tommy and I finished our consulting sessions with the FBI and the Attorney's office, Satin was raided and closed down. Vince was arrested and charged with a litany of crimes under the RICO statute. The shit hit the fan for him, and he was no different than the others who went before him. It wasn't long before there were other arrests – in Atlanta and other cities, including New York. A lot of the people picked up were turning on each other.

I had been the tiny little atom that, when split, released megatons of damning information. After that, though, all the heavyweights began turning against each other. I was becoming a minor footnote in the grander blame game. The mob would come after a turncoat for three reasons, I reasoned with my counselors.

"One would be to eliminate the threat," I said. "Another would be to set an example for other would-be squealers, and the third would be for revenge. I am safe from the first reason, since my damage was already wreaked upon them. As for reasons two and three, there are bigger fish spilling bigger guts of information. If whoever is left chooses to act against me, I will deal with the situation through security. I just want to be me, Charlie Lofton, ex-con, husband of Gracie Lofton."

"You know this marital bliss you are experiencing will not last forever," said Joe. "You may always love your wife, but the romance wanes, and there's quite a bit of work involved in making the relationship work."

Joe had no idea the immense work – the joyful, immense work – I would put into mine and Gracie's marriage.

The priest and the counselor agreed that I had made significant progress on the road to being a legitimate, functioning member of society. With their recommendations and the parole board's rubber stamp, I was released to make a life with Gracie.

XXIV. The Real World

Gracie and I were true to our word to pick-up where we left off on our honeymoon night. We consummated and re-consummated our relationship. I was only sorry I hadn't discovered this wonderful activity with Gracie years ago. She welcomed me into her small but swank condo in a mid-rise in the Gramercy Park area of Manhattan. The neighborhood was a little slice of solace in the otherwise frantic midtown. I moved in with the clothes on my back and a little bit of money that was left after paying my legal cost. After all those years of working and running from the law and serving time, my entire estate was a dilapidated wardrobe and a small sum of cash. That was okay with Gracie. She was doing well enough on her own, and then there was her father's sizeable estate. He spread his wealth among his favorite causes, but he left us enough to keep us quite comfortable.

Harvey King told me the story of Jason Jordan's exploits, and I knew Jason was the one I wanted to consult on matters of security. He put me in touch with the Binder Group in New York. Before long our condo was wired with the most advanced monitoring equipment available and it was retrofitted with a panic room. It was expensive, but the Binder Group kept a detail of two men in close proximity twenty-four hours a day. They provided us with pistols and trained us in their use. Technically, they were Gracie's guns, since I was not allowed to own a gun as a convicted felon. We were provided with a location system and each of us kept a small device in a pocket or on a bracelet. It could be activated from the device itself, or remotely. By the time everything was in place, we were as insulated from retribution as possible.

My parole officer, Ken Wagner, was concerned about vocational training, but it really wasn't necessary. While it may be difficult and expensive for upstanding young people to get a decent education in America today, if you are an ex-con there is a myriad of programs to provide for college enrollment and vocational and career placement. Ken set me up with a career counselor. After some discussions, an aptitude test, and some entrance exams, I was accepted to CCNY where I chose English as a major.

After one semester of courses focusing on clerical skills I began my second term with my core freshman classes. I secured a job with Craft Publishing, working as an assistant in the marketing department two floors below Gracie. By then our life together was in full, routine bliss. I didn't see much of her during work, but we usually had lunch together. After work, I went to classes three evenings each week. Gracie waited for me to have a late dinner. Every night we worked a little bit on our book, even on the late nights after school. Gracie said the trick to getting such an ambitious project completed was to get something down on paper every day. No matter how tired we were, or how much schoolwork I had, we spent some amount of time on the book. Some nights we got our self-imposed assignments done so late, we were too drowsy to do any consummating.

I was truly happy. It was the first time in my life I felt like I wasn't an imposter of some kind. I was Charlie Lofton, getting a formal education, working a legitimate job, thriving in a meaningful relationship. There was a long road ahead, and I was content to proceed along, one heavenly step at a time.

Gracie's economic status and occupation as an editor affiliated us with an eclectic circle. We attended affairs defined by the crowd – the well heeled, so-called enlightened liberal society types, and the literati elite. I became a curiosity if not a minor celebrity, and I got bored with the meddlesome grilling from pseudo-intellectual busybodies about my experience. Condescending comments like, "Fascinating! You really must write a book about your experiences," or, "It must have been interesting being involved with such criminals," grew tiresome. The naïve coterie shared a fascination for organized crime and the mobsters involved that I couldn't understand. The few thugs I knew were mostly insignificant, uneducated, immoral oafs trying to get over on the system, willing to do almost anything to accomplish their aims. There was nothing romantic about the lifestyle, and I was doing my best to remove myself from it.

I tried to avoid such gatherings, but occupational and social obligations required our attendance at many of them. When we had a chance we got together with Bobby and Eileen. Sometimes Eileen accompanied Bobby on business trips and we would spend a night on the town with them. On vacations and some holidays I got permission from Ken Wagner to travel to Atlanta, where they put us up in the Hotel Wells. I'm not sure why, but Eileen's and Gracie's personalities just clicked, making it easy for me and my best friend to find opportunities to get together.

Once in awhile we got to see Marvin Dixon and his wife, Janita. He had stayed out of trouble since the deal we struck with the government, and he was working for the same company. When his daughter, Kisha, graduated from Georgia Southern we made the trip to Atlanta, and rode down to Statesboro for the ceremony. I got a little misty eyed observing Marvin's pride when Kisha was handed her diploma.

After everything I had been and done, and after my conversion to humankind, I was feeling a legitimate part of Americana, and a day didn't pass that I didn't stop to recognize the genuine joy from within for the good people and good things that happened to me.

Less than a year after Kisha graduated it was my turn to accept my sheepskin, which came complete with honors and a full year ahead of schedule, thanks to my father's genes, some hard work on my part, and Gracie's support. Craft offered me a job as an associate editor. My book was moving along slowly, but once school was past me I looked forward to spending more time on the project I was determined to complete. Gracie and I were even encouraged to spend time at work on it by our boss, Cy Leonhardt.

We were able to make some improvements to the condo, and

when the place next door went on the market we bought it and doubled our space. One night we were at Alfredo's, a cozy Italian restaurant in Little Italy, having a pasta bonanza. Gracie was radiant, and I was eating up the experience along with my pasta.

"You better watch all that pasta," Gracie said to me. "It's starting to show down there in the belly."

I looked down in amusement. I always thought of myself as too thin, but I had to admit my pants were feeling a bit tight. Gracie's plate was nearly empty, and I couldn't resist the riposte.

"You're taking care of your dinner pretty well, yourself," I said.

"Yeah, but I think I have an excuse," she said.

I looked straight into her dancing eyes, unable to believe what I knew she was about to tell me. "What do you mean," I said, unable to conceal my excitement.

"Yeah, I think I'm pregnant," she said.

We never used contraception, and three years after our first consummation, this welcome surprise fell into my expanding lap.

"I can't believe it," I said. "Are you sure?"

"I'm pretty sure," she smiled. "But I bought a test today, and we can go home and see what it says."

All of a sudden, I had no taste for my meal. We got the bill and left what was left on the plates. The test confirmed what Gracie suspected, and just like that we were on a path to parenthood. I wanted to call all of our friends and spread the word, but Gracie told me it was too soon. Given her age and her health history, she wanted to wait until we saw a doctor and time provided more certainty. We did call Bobby and Eileen, and I know she told Toni.

……..

The next morning Gracie called her gynecologist to set up an appointment. Dr. Judy Westwood happened to have an opening that afternoon, so after lunch we both skipped out of work to see what the doctor had to say about the state of affairs in Gracie's womb. Dr. Westwood pronounced that there was indeed a fertilized egg residing within Gracie. We discussed the procedures necessary to nurture the fetus. The doctor scheduled an amniocentesis and follow-up ultra-sounds to manage Gracie's gestation process. The battery of tests was enough to keep me slightly on edge while Gracie barfed her way through the first eight weeks of pregnancy. Her nausea ended almost the day we went in for an ultra-sound. I nervously studied Dr. Westwood's concentrating face as she moved the instrument over Gracie's inflated bare belly. The darting of her eyes, the pursing of her lips, and her indiscernible murmurs made me suspect something was out of the ordinary.

"You look like something is wrong," I tried to say nonchalantly.

"Not exactly wrong," said Dr. Westwood. "Just a minute; let me see if it's what I suspect."

The doctor asked for a minute; she only needed about twenty seconds, but it seemed like an hour of agony until she spoke again.

"Yes, I believe it is," she said. "It looks like you two are going to have twins."

My heart bounced from the depths of concern to elation. Gracie looked at me as if to say, "Whoa, this is whole lot of a good thing," and she was right.

We couldn't be sure what the gender of the results of our consummating was going to be. We had to wait for a later ultra-sound to find out what was in store for us. Gracie's ever expanding abdomen contained a boy and a girl. Armed with that intelligence we did what we could to fortify ourselves for the onslaught that would be visited upon us by the birth of our babies. Our friends at work organized a baby shower for both of us to attend, and their offerings were gratifyingly complete. We mistakenly believed we were prepared for whatever challenge the twins could throw at us.

As our babies grew inside Gracie, she grew on the outside.

She grew into a hearty, radiant mother-to-be. Once she passed the nausea phase she entered into a period of feeling better than human. She had more energy than I ever witnessed, and she channeled it into nesting activities. She planned the design of our newly expanded quarters and hired architects, engineers, and contractors to bring it to fruition.

Immediately after the contractor finished the punch list Gracie set about decorating improvements. We worked all day and continued to work on the book at night. After a couple of hours I would have to get some sleep, but Gracie, in her super human condition, worked long into the night. I would drag myself out of bed in the morning, groping to get ready for work, as Gracie bounced out of bed, making a hearty breakfast and reviewing the decorating ideas that would come to her during the night. Her energy was boundless – that is until the home stretch of her pregnancy.

At some point she seemed to hit a wall, and then it was all she could do to set her rather cumbersome baby vessel in motion. The doctor proclaimed this normal and said she should try to get as much rest as possible, in spite of her relatively trouble free gestational experience. Finally, four weeks before her due date Gracie had to confine herself to our bedroom. Craft arranged for her to work at home. I kept our coworkers informed of her progress – and Gracie up to date on the office gossip.

On the Thursday, exactly two weeks before her due date, I got her call just after lunch. Her water broke, and Dr. Westwood told her to head for the hospital. By the time I got back to the condo she was practically in labor. The cab waited as we gathered our things and left our place as a childless couple for the last time.

Gracie was in labor for only a short time before it became clear to the doctor she would need a cesarean delivery. I watched and winced as a cold, impersonal instrument cut a clean, bloody wound into my love's lower regions. I marveled as first one, and then another tiny creation of our love was pulled prematurely from the cozy cocoon that had provided life support since their conception. They seemed too tiny to be real. Charlie III was four pounds, fourteen ounces, and Sara was five pounds, six ounces – not bad for twins born slightly early.

We had our initial visit, and they were whisked away to be poked, prodded, tested and incubated. Gracie was sewn back together and given a strong pain reliever. She didn't last long. I was left to make phone calls and visit the preemie ward over and over again to check on the babies. I checked with the nurses, and they said the babies were doing well. They were healthy and small and quite a phenomenon for me. They toasted themselves in incubators, dozing in and out of the world that had become theirs only hours earlier at the hand of the scalpel wielding doctor.

Gracie dozed like her new babies. She was barely able to keep her eyes open when they paid her a visit, but I could see the delight emanate from her sleepy expression when both babies cooed up against her cheeks.

This was a pattern we fell into for a couple of days until Gracie was weaned from her pain medication. Each day we could see signs of continuing development in Charlie and Sara. The most apparent progress to us was their lung development. They didn't hesitate to express themselves at any displeasure, and at least one of them seemed to always be displeased. Whenever one was affronted by some act of negligence on our part, the sibling did not hesitate to join in the plaint. It was nice to imagine that they would always support one another in time of need.

The twins were progressing to the doctors' satisfaction, and they discharged us after a few days. The time in the hospital was probably more therapeutic for Gracie than it was for the babies. The pain from her surgery was practically gone, but she was having a hard time regaining her strength. Strength and energy were our only defense against the barrage that greeted us when we arrived home, helpless and confused. We thought we were well prepared. We proudly walked in to debut the babies' new home, the keenly arranged environment that would nurture its new residents as they learned what it was to be a human being.

They reacted to their new home the same as they reacted to everything else; they bellowed from way down deep in their ever developing lungs. I looked at Gracie, hoping she wasn't too disappointed at the response to her efforts to provide the ideal home for our loud bundles of joy. She just smiled back at me and shuffled slowly to the bedroom where she took a nap while I plied my wiles to try to placate the twins.

The first four weeks of parenthood consisted of sleepless nights for Gracie and me. She still tired very easily at the slightest physical activity, and not only was I at the beck and call of our babies, but I often found myself attending to her needs, as well. During this time we tried to collaborate on some work at home, but just as we would get started one of the babies would summon. By the time I returned to business, Gracie would be too tired to continue. I was tempted to consider my wife a shirker of her responsibilities, but I kept reminding myself that she had been through quite an ordeal, and her lethargy was justified.

As time passed she did her best to pitch in on baby duty, but I could see it was taking a toll on her. Once in awhile I escaped to the office to drop off and pick-up work. Technically, I was entitled to paternity leave, but there was work to do, and besides, being at the office afforded me the opportunity to pull out pictures of our babies to anyone who made eye contact with me. Our colleagues were appropriately impressed with our new, expanded family. I was hungry for stimulation that didn't involve infants, and they were nice enough to share the office cooler news, which I reported back to Gracie.

While I was out for my short respites, Gracie managed the household, but it took all she had. I could tell she was sincerely trying. She even offered to take the twins to their first doctor's visit while I went into the office. They checked out well – both of them had gained weight, and were crawling up the percentile scale of babies their age. Life was good and busy at the Lofton household.

Shortly after the twins paid their first visit to our

pediatrician, Toni volunteered to sit for the babies so Gracie and I could get out of the house and relax for a few hours. I told her I appreciated the gesture, but I wasn't sure how game Gracie was for an evening on the town, even a short one. To my surprise, Gracie thought it would be a fine idea.

On a Friday night Toni arrived at our home. After exhaustive instructions we left for a non-home-cooked meal at Alfredo's, the place where Gracie first told me we would be parents. It seemed like years had passed since that euphoric night. So much had happened since then to change the dynamic of our life together. When we walked into the restaurant the aroma and ambiance recalled a flood of emotion from our last visit almost a year earlier.

We sat down and ordered a glass of cabernet, and I realized it was the first bit of alcohol either of us had since Gracie had become pregnant. We ordered dinner and then just sat across the table from each other, wine stems in hand. I stared at Gracie, thrilled to be there with her. I gazed into her eyes with an unconscious smile pasted above my chin. Gracie looked back, smiling at me for as long as she could.

"I love you," I said, my emotions wafting among the bouquet of the eatery.

"And I love you," said Gracie, as tears began to roll down her cheeks. At first I thought they were tears brought on by the kind of joy I was feeling, but it became apparent it was something else.

"What's wrong," I said, perplexed.

"Oh Charlie," Gracie spoke quietly as her eyes held my gaze. "I'm so sorry."

"Sorry? Sorry for what?" I asked, taking her hand.

How she found the strength to compose herself, I'll never know, but she finally spoke. "You know I took the babies to the doctor last week," she said. "You know I've been tired, and I thought it was just having the babies and everything. But I started wondering more and more, and I went to my doctor."

"Yes," I said, anxious to hear the rest of the story. "Dr. Westwood?"

"No, my oncologist, Dr. Matsui. It's back; I just know its back," she said, leaking tears through the glass in front of her face.

I went flush. I know how I would have wanted to react for her sake, but I have no idea how I did react. The tight world of togetherness and happiness and purpose that we cultivated suddenly flew apart on the wings of a bad butterfly, and I have no idea what I must have looked like sitting there, hearing such shattering words. At some point I gathered myself.

"Cancer? Oh Gracie, what did he say," I said, hungry for information.

"He ordered an MRI, and I know he thinks its back," she said. "We don't know the extent of it, and what the prognosis will be, but I'm scared."

"I know, sweetheart, but I know you can fight this thing. You're strong, and I'll be there to support you and help you through it," I said trying to be brave, sure that I wasn't.

"I don't know, Charlie," she said. "This is the second time, and I really thought I was out of the woods. Oh God, I don't want to lose you and the babies. I want to be there for you all – with you all."

"I know you do," I tried to smile at her. "And you will. We will go see the doctor, and we'll find out what we need to do and just do it, that's all. I'll be there – hell, we'll be there – and we'll do whatever it takes."

It was the thing to say, and I really believed it when I said it, but I was naïve. What happened after that, I can't say. I have no idea if we were served dinner – and if we were, whether we ate. We had been in that restaurant two times in the past year, and both times Gracie carried a secret into it that would profoundly change our lives in very different ways.

In the two days that followed, we went through the motions of doing what we trained ourselves to do; we fed and changed and tended to general maintenance of Charlie and Sara. Since the moment we brought them home with us the responsibility was taxing, but the subconscious happiness I previously felt became apparent by its absence after Gracie's revelation. I still felt the desire to care for them, but there was a void while I plodded along. Gracie was as much help as she could be, but she was tiring easily, and she had to rest.

We went to the cancer center for the MRI and other tests, where I spent most of my time walking one baby or another trying to protect the other visitors from the brunt of their terror. I couldn't even concentrate on the post exam consultation, which took place while Charlie was wailing due to a dirty diaper and Sara was loudly laughing at her brother's discomfort. I had to extract myself from the conversation with the doctor to tend to the poop and occupy the noisy newborns. From the other side of the room I picked up only fragments of the advice, but I didn't sense much optimism.

On the way home I waited for Gracie to fill me in, but she just sat catatonically in the cab, staring straight ahead, weighted down by her own heavy world. I slouched in the back of the cab, unconsciously doing the things I always did to entertain and mollify the kids. The driver dropped us off and the doorman greeted a somber family as we struggled into the elevator with all our accouterments.

Once we were in the privacy of our own home and the babies were content to wobble around in their playpen watching their big servants, I got up to speed on Gracie's condition. I hadn't misread the tone of the meeting. The doctor was frank, but humane when he told Gracie of her situation. Without a biopsy, he couldn't be absolutely sure, but he told her to prepare for the necessary steps if his worst suspicions were realized. There was cancer, but there was no way to know its progress. There would doubtlessly be the invasion of the scalpel and the poisonous chemotherapy, the ravages of which Gracie was intimately familiar.

"Dr. Matsui recommended I make plans for immediate surgery," Gracie said, looking deadly serious. "After asking me, he contacted the surgeon, Dr. Silverman, and arranged for it in two days. Dr. Matsui must have some pull with Dr. Silverman because Silverman's busy as hell. He generally doesn't alter his schedule like that. The fact that he did feels kind of good, and it really scares the hell out of me." Gracie's voice reached a quiet, panicked pitch.

I held her, not knowing how to feel. It was so overwhelming, I just felt nothing but the intense love I had for her as I clung, supporting her, even as she supported me at that indefinable moment. The babies lay in their playpen quietly cooing, thankfully oblivious to the very real life drama taking place right beside them. Finally, I spoke.

"You just have to do it," I said, immediately feeling inadequate and guilty for not being the sick one. "I'll do whatever it takes to help you through it. We'll get you into the hospital, and you'll have the surgery, and I'll take care of the babies, and we'll get through it."

"There's another thing I want to do, Charlie," said Gracie. "We've got to get the kids to the doctor for some tests to make sure they're alright. Dr. Matsui said that we shouldn't worry; only in very rare cases, certain types of cancer, which he feels certain I don't have, can spread to a fetus, but I want them to be thoroughly checked out," she said.

I went flush again. To lose Gracie was more than I could bear, but was there something even worse? I looked over at the innocence personified in the two little bodies squirming happily next to each other, and couldn't allow myself to imagine that the disease set it's evil upon them.

"Oh Charlie, I'm so sorry," Gracie said, almost as if it were her fault.

I was scared, but at that instant I knew I had to be strong so that Gracie could be strong, and she could have the best chance of beating the disease. I had to remain positive for her and the babies – and for myself.

"Charlie, we must have caught a really bad butterfly," she said, trying to smile through her stoic expression.

"That's okay," I said. "We don't have to let it beat us." We placed a call to a pediatric cancer specialist and set-up an appointment.

Gracie called Toni and updated her on the situation. We would need her best friend's help, and from that moment on

Toni would prove worthy of that designation.

After a quiet dinner we put the babies to bed and collapsed on the bed early, huddled together, lost in our shared thoughts. The stress had a draining effect, and we both fell quickly asleep. It was a fitful night of bad dreams, and I will never forget the painful dream that punctuated the horrible nocturnal experience. God came to our home. He was a no-nonsense God. He came to take Gracie and Charlie and Sara away from me, and he meant to do it.

At first I begged him to please let them stay, saying, "Please, I love them so much. I can't get by without them. Please, I beg you," I cried sobbing as he went about collecting them, one by one, dragging them by the arms as they lifelessly bounced along the floor in his powerful grasp.

His omnipotent words to me were, "It's got to be done. Don't be such a pussy about it," as he toted them toward the door.

I finally gave up begging and ran into the bedroom to get my gun. I checked it for bullets and ran into the living room, afraid he might have escaped with them. I began shooting him. The bullets went straight through him, not slowing him one bit, but evidently angering him. He had all three of my cherished ones in one hand as he glared at me and said, "Now that really pisses me off. If you could have kept your hands off that thing in your previous lives I might not have to do this now. I'm not going to forget that," he threatened, and then he dragged them out, slamming the door behind him. I collapsed on the floor, sobbing, helpless to do anything to stop him. That's when I woke up, more exhausted than when I fell asleep.

Charlie was crying, and that woke up his sister who chimed in. They had been sleeping a long time. It was less than an hour before we would be getting up to start what had become our decreasingly routine, routine. Normally we resisted the temptation to respond to the first cries for attention. That morning, both Gracie and I leapt from the bed. I don't know what *she* was feeling, but I just wanted to see all of them and know they were still with me.

The terrible dream that started my morning in the doldrums soon gave way to the reality of making breakfast and preparing each of us for the day's activities. I went into the office, but I wouldn't get much done, other than to make arrangements with Toni for her to take the babies from the hospital once Gracie went in for surgery.

When Gracie called I met her and the children back at the house. We went to the doctor who would run tests to make sure our babies were okay. Charlie and Sara rested quietly and unsuspectingly in their respective car seats with Gracie in between in the back of the cab. I rode up front, unable to speak to the foreign cab driver, my heart pounding ever faster as we approached the building where our babies would be poked and prodded so the doctors could reach a weighty conclusion. It was as if life stopped while we watched the procedures that would intermittently irritate one or the other into a fit of bawling. I hated to see their little faces bunch up into a ball of tears as they let out a wail when being stuck by a needle or trapped inside a machine. Finally the ordeal was over, and we took our babies away from the unavoidable cruelty of the medical center. The cruelest thing was that we would have to wait for definitive results.

The rest of the day was occupied by preparing for Gracie's stint at the hospital. She was nearing the end of her maternity leave. She wanted to get back to work, but the surgery would delay that for awhile. After dinner Gracie packed some things and called Toni. We put the twins down and succumbed to exhaustion, ourselves.

Soon enough, wake-up time was upon us, and our beleaguered little household came to life. The kids were fed and dressed. We all made our way to the hospital where I did everything possible to protect the denizens there from the shrill noise emanating from both babies. While Gracie endured the admissions process it occurred to me that forcing patients to go through admissions was simply another test the doctors administer. If a patient can survive that, he probably would stand a better chance recovering from surgery.

After all the paperwork was complete, and routine vital signs were recorded, we were told that a room wouldn't be available for a few hours. We put the twins in their stroller and walked to Central Park. The sun glinted off the tall Manhattan buildings etched into the cloudless blue sky. It was a perfect day to stroll in the park along with the joggers and skaters if you're not waiting to go into surgery to get a verdict on your future. As beautiful as it was, we both walked silently, anxious to get back to the sterile, perfunctory atmosphere of the hospital. After a quick lunch for me and the babies, we plodded in trepidation back to the hospital. Gracie got her room at twelve-thirty, and the surgery was scheduled for four.

Toni arrived right on time to take the children as the nurses began to feed some kind of anesthetic through Gracie's intravenous tubes. She began to relax before the kids left. I could see her look at the children with such a euphoric expression that for a moment I was sure all our troubles would be behind us. Toni rolled the babies and all their paraphernalia out without my help. Dr. Silverman came in to introduce himself to me and check on Gracie before they rolled her out. Suddenly, I was alone – no Gracie, no children; I was all alone to sit and think. If the worst happened, what would I do when I finally lost the love of my life? And what about the children; I would surely die of grief if anything happened to them. I had to leave the confines of the hospital room and get into the perfect day just to maintain sanity.

When I returned there was no word from the operating room. My lack of sleep finally began to take its toll, so I sat in the chair next to where the bed used to be and was instantly out. There was no dreaming in the deep slumber that set in for almost an hour before they woke me to bring Gracie back into the room. I watched groggily as they rolled the even groggier Gracie and her bed into place. I stood on wobbly legs trying to focus as the nurses positioned her bed and set up a variety of instruments. A sheet covered a thick bandage over her torso where they cut her. The wound was obviously severe, and it snapped me into the harsh reality of where we were and why we were there. I took Gracie's hand to steady myself, but she was too deeply drugged to respond. Dr. Silverman arrived and called me out of the room.

"I don't know if Gracie is ready to discuss where we are, so I thought I would speak out here to you first," the doctor said.

As highly recognized a surgeon as the man was, it was beyond me how he couldn't recognize that Gracie wouldn't know it if a team of witch doctors were dancing and chanting over her bed at that very moment.

"The mass we removed from her lung is malignant," Dr. Silverman said in a tone that made me want to cry. "The pathology is consistent with the cancer from her medical history. We got all of the tumor, and the surrounding tissue. The fact that it has occurred in the lung is not what we would like. At this time, we don't know if it has affected other organs, but we aren't encouraged with its reappearance, anywhere."

I swallowed hard, trying to remain composed. "I see," I said, actually still in the dark. "What do you think; can we take care of it? Can you make her well?"

The doctor looked as though he wished he could tell me everything would be alright. He said, "We can treat it, Charlie. Can we cure it? I don't know. We have found it in a major organ. This is her second occurrence. With each occurrence survival rates decrease. I can't tell you with certainty how she will respond to treatment. I know you are looking for some definitive answer, but there isn't one. The only thing I would say is, you should hope for the best, but prepare for less successful results."

"...prepare for the worst," is what the doctor didn't say, but he didn't need to say it; I understood his meaning.

"How will you treat it?" I asked, amazed I was still engaged in a coherent discussion.

"I think chemotherapy is the most obvious approach," said Dr. Silverman. "There are other treatments we might consider to compliment chemo. Some combined modality therapy might be indicated once we learn more. Further surgery is a possibility, for instance if we suspect an endocrine link to her condition, we may want to remove her ovaries, probably a total hysterectomy. In the long run, she will have to weigh these radical treatments and their chances of success against the quality of her remaining life.

At that, my mind was spinning, groping for any fiber of optimism that would allow me to dare to believe Gracie would survive. When the doctor suggested she may want to forego even one possible treatment, the writing on the wall was coming into focus. I gave up trying to make the surgeon tell me what I wanted to hear.

I took a deep breath and said, “Okay, thanks for talking with me. One more thing; you may know, but my wife recently gave birth to twins. What do you think their chances are?”

Dr. Silverman looked at me compassionately as he spoke. “I know about her pregnancy. I wouldn’t worry about that. There is practically no chance that the type of cancer she has could spread to a fetus. I understand you took them in for tests. When do you get the results?”

“Tomorrow,” I said.

“I think you will be relieved when you hear the results,” he said. “I will need to talk to Gracie about our findings and her treatment. Is one time better than another?”

“The sooner the better, but not until she’s completely coherent,” I said. “Will you be here tonight?”

“I think she will continue to need pain medication for awhile,” said Dr. Silverman. “The nurses will be able to give her a sedative if she needs that, too. I’ll drop by in the morning and we can see how she’s feeling.”

I thanked the doctor and went back in to be with Gracie. She was sleeping comfortably, unaware of the challenges facing her in the future. I wished she could remain so oblivious to her situation. I called Toni to check on the babies, who were doing better than any of the adults, and then went to sleep on the cot the hospital provided me. The nurses paid regular visits to our room throughout the night, but I was so tired, I only stirred, and drifted off immediately. Gracie didn’t come to the entire night.

The morning light pierced the window above my cot, waking

me with its stifling heat and forcing the stress of reality back into my thoughts. I looked over to see Gracie still sleeping, removed from the cruel truths that emerged since she was cast into drug induced oblivion the previous day. A nurse came in, and I excused myself to stretch and clear my head. When I returned, Gracie was sleepily lolling in bed, trying unsuccessfully to capture clarity of mind.

"How'd it go," she said, unable to grasp the gravity of any answer I could provide.

"Fine Gracie; you're here talking to me aren't you," I said, trying to be lighthearted. She smiled at the name Gracie.

"How are the babies?" she slurred, slightly.

"They were fine last night. "I'll call in a little while, at a more decent hour," I said.

"Toni's probably been up all night doing their hair," Gracie giggled as her eyes closed and she dozed. Even though that made no sense I could see she was coming back into the world and would have to see the doctor and engage in the serious business at hand.

I squeezed her hand and left her to sleep while I went outside for a cup of coffee and a newspaper to try to occupy myself until the next wave of events descended upon us. At eight, I called Toni's house. She answered the phone in a raspy morning voice.

"How are you?" I said. "Was it a rough night?"

"Oh, no. They were pretty good, actually," she said. "I had to get up with them a couple of times, but it was easy. How's Gracie?"

"She's doing okay, right now," I said. "She's mostly drugged out on who knows what. She doesn't seem to be in any pain, yet."

"Did you talk to the doctor?" Toni said, stirring the cauldron of anxiety.

"Yeah," I said, knowing she would expect news. "It's hard to say for sure, but I don't think he's too optimistic, Toni. He's coming to see Gracie today. I don't know when she'll be up to it, but sometime he has to talk to her about what he found and what the plan is. It's serious; that's all I know."

"God," was all she could say. After a pause, she said, "Well, I'll wait until after lunch, and we'll all come down there and see her and be with her, unless you think we should do something else."

"No, that sounds good to me," I said. "I don't know how coherent she'll be. As much as I'd love to be with them, if you can tend to the babies, I can tend to Gracie until we get a grip on the situation."

An odd and unpleasant feeling crept upon me. I felt as if Gracie's husband and her best friend were somehow conspiring behind her back. We were already talking about her as if she were a victim – how best to handle her in the crisis. It was the way you would talk about an old relative who needed to be put into a home, and the best way of going about the process. What Toni and I discussed was legitimate, but it was at that moment I suddenly felt I was slowly losing the relationship I shared with Gracie for so long. I was right, but what I didn't realize is that I would form a new kind of bond with Gracie in the future.

I was amazed to find the head of Gracie's bed cocked slightly, giving her open eyes a view of the room, when I arrived back there. She was sipping on some water, and she gave me a disarming smile as I walked in.

"Well, you look a lot more alert than a little while ago," I said, kissing her on the forehead and taking her hand. The television pattered quietly in the background.

"Yeah, I feel more awake and more pain," she said. "Have you checked on the babies?"

I noticed how out of breath she was when she tried to speak, and how hoarse she was from the surgery.

"Yes, I spoke to Toni," I said. "They had a good night together and they're coming to see us this afternoon."

Gracie beamed as if she were a child awaiting a visit from Santa Claus, and then got serious. "When can we talk to their doctor," she asked, still a little time-disoriented.

"I'll check on that," I said. It's just a little after eight, right now. How do you feel?"

"Oh, tired. I know that it hurts, along here," she said, waving a limp wrist along a bandaged cut line above her chest, "but I can't feel the pain. Did you speak to doctor Silverman?"

"Yeah, I did," I admitted, feeling incompetent to recite anything he told me.

"How did he seem?" she asked. The question struck me as odd, and she sensed that. "I mean, does it look good, or bad, or too close to call?"

"I don't know, really," I explained. "He spoke in medical terms that I'm not sure I could repeat, verbatim. I know you're going to have to go through chemo, and there are some other treatments he may prescribe. You probably need to get it from the horse's mouth."

Gracie scrunched her face in medicated frustration as a nurse walked in with a breakfast of Jell-O to go with her water. She took a bite and succumbed to drowsiness for a little while longer. She awoke in the afternoon, ten minutes before Dr. Silverman arrived.

"How are we feeling, today," he asked, feeling her forehead and checking her pulse, probably out of some kind of habitual bedside manner. It was just what you would expect a doctor to do, and it was reassuring.

"I was telling Charlie, the pain is starting to kick in," Gracie said, as she tried to adjust herself in the bed.

"Well, we won't stand for that," he said, looking at her chart. "You've got your pain relief right there at your right hand. Just push the plunger when you need it. Meanwhile, would you like to discuss where we are with this?"

I sat, holding Gracie's hand, as the doctor settled into a professional, but grim recitation of her condition. The more he talked, the harder she squeezed my hand. He was more frank with her than he was with me the night before, and the prognosis was not good. When he started citing survival rates for her circumstances I swallowed hard and Gracie almost took my fingers off. It was hard to believe. Dr. Silverman was giving her odds of surviving more than one year. We listened in horror while the doctor spelled it out, just as Gracie asked him to do. He proposed that she may want to weigh the misery of the treatment against the quality of life she would have without it.

We couldn't believe it. He was a doctor. There should have been something he could do for her, but he insisted there were limitations. He told us there were studies, experimental programs we could look into, but you had to be the right candidate to be accepted by them. With some of them there was a chance of being given a placebo.

We didn't want the doctor to leave. We asked all the questions we could think of, and groped for more, but finally everything was said for the moment. Dr. Silverman left, promising to look into possible studies that would be a good fit for Gracie.

"Call the center about the kids," Gracie suddenly said.

"It's still a little early, Gracie," I said, as anxious as she was to find out that they were okay.

"Just call them," she said. "They may know something. I want to know before they get here."

The phone call produced the most confusing emotions I have ever experienced. The reports were in, and both babies were fine. So there I sat, so relieved that our innocent young children were going to be alright, and devastated that my wife had just been given a virtual death sentence. Gracie was so relieved about the babies; it seemed to give her a new attitude, perhaps a new resolve to fight to the bitter end.

The pain from the surgery was too much for her and she had to press the medication plunger, which made her too drowsy to stay awake until Toni and the kids arrived. I sat alone with the unconscious love of my life, trying to sort out the conflicts of the moment. I watched Gracie sleep. She seemed so healthy I couldn't bring myself to believe she wouldn't be able to overpower her familiar enemy. She did it before, and I had to tell myself she could do it this time.

XXV. GRACIE'S LOSING BATTLE

We got Gracie out of the hospital and back home to begin our new routine. I had come to rely on our routines. They offered comfort; you could trust them. Toni continued to be indispensable, constantly coming by, helping out with the babies as Gracie tried to fully recover from her surgery. Dr. Silverman tried to match Gracie up with a study using some kind of experimental treatments that might give her a better chance, but there wasn't anything that looked promising enough to try. He gave us some information on one brand new, completely unproven therapy being tested in North Carolina, but it would not allow her to follow conventional treatments simultaneously.

Early on, when we first faced the possibility of the worst case for Gracie, we vowed to do whatever it would take to fight. No experimental drug was too exotic; no location too far. But when we began to weigh all the options, our best chance seemed to lie with the tortuous, unexciting, standard chemo and radiation route. The North Carolina program offered no more hope than the conventional approach, and the logistics presented another problem. We were not going to have Gracie go there without the whole family, but we had no support there, and our lives were tied to New York. When it got down to what was best for Gracie, we put her life in the hands of the cancer center in New York, praying for the best.

The doctors hardly gave her time to recover from surgery before they began to further destroy her health with chemo. Gracie was all for it before the treatments began. Knowing her babies were healthy lifted her spirits, preparing her for the fight for her life. She had too much to live for, and she was determined to summon all that was within her to survive the treatments and beat the cancer. When the chemo began I was surprised at how well she handled it. Her energy level was as strong as her dedication to the cause. She bounced back from the actual surgery, and wanted to get back into a normal life.

Gracie dove into caring for the children. She nurtured them and tended to their every need. I indulged her tendency to spoil them, realizing she wanted to infuse them with her love and influence for as long as she could. I went back to work feeling a false sense of normalcy, while all the time a dark weight constantly nudged my conscience. Gracie wanted to work, too, to regain her own sense of the ordinary. I brought home assignments for her, but her main focus was on our family.

We took so much video of the time we all shared with each other, we filled multiple CD cases. Gracie and I wanted to make sure our kids would always know their mother and know what she was like, and what we were all like together. With the one, overriding, horrible thing going on in our life, there were so many good things, it was a strange dichotomy.

The insidious evolution of Gracie's condition crept upon us with surreptitious stealth. I can't identify a day when I woke up to the fact that Gracie had become a mere skeleton of herself, but it happened somewhere along the way. Long before that, she lost her hair to the chemo, but her physical deterioration was more dramatic; the decay that set itself upon her sweet, frail body took its toll. As positive as we started out to be, there came a time when we each, in our own way, arrived at the inevitable conclusion.

The more chemo Gracie endured, the sicker it made her. Besides that, the doctors reported very little progress from the treatment, so the disease was advancing toward its ultimate, evil purpose. The energy with which Gracie initially approached her challenge was waning, and her spirit was breaking. I saw her cry only one more time. One night, after putting the babies in their cribs, I walked into our bedroom to find Gracie in tears.

"Oh Charlie, you're going to think I'm horrible," she said, wiping tears from her drawn cheeks. "Please don't take this wrong, because you know I love you. It's just that I am jealous.

I'm jealous of you, and I don't think it's fair, that's all. You are so vital, so healthy, and we have the kids that have so much to look forward to. You will be there for them, and while that's a comfort, it makes me so jealous. I won't be there. I won't see Charlie's first loose tooth, or their first day at school, or Sara's prom dress. I want so badly to be there for them, and for you, but I feel cheated out of all that. I want it so bad…" Gracie trailed off into more tears, and there was nothing I could say or do to change the reality or make her feel better about it. She reached her weak, bony arms around me, and we both went to sleep in each others embrace. At some time during the night, we both awoke.

"Charlie, I'm sorry for what I said to you," Gracie said in a whisper. "It's just the emotion of the whole thing. I do want to be there with you all, but I'm glad you will be taking care of them. If they can't have their mother, there's no one else in the whole world who could be better for them."

The next morning Gracie announced that she was through with the chemotherapy. She just wanted to take the rest of the time she had left to enjoy her family without the ravages of the treatments. Dr. Hollis at the cancer center took the news with compassion, in full support of her decision.

Gracie had less than three weeks to enjoy the babies and me before the pain became so severe, she had to be medicated into listlessness. Eventually, no amount of drugs could ease the relentless pain, and Gracie begged me to give her more, which would be lethal.

Her excruciating agony went on for days, as her only source of comfort cruelly refused to visit itself upon her. No matter how she cried out – how much she begged for mercy, none was available to her. It was tormenting me, and I didn't know what to do about it. I tried to tell myself that Gracie was strong, and that I needed to be strong until the end, but I couldn't resolve the conflict.

Suddenly, one night, Gracie sat up and looked at me with wide, beseeching eyes and said, "Steer clear of the bad butterflies, Charlie." She raled through clenched teeth and seemingly motionless lips. Her breath came not from her ravaged lungs, but somewhere deep inside her soul. "Nothing but beautiful butterflies for you and the babies, from now on," she said as she collapsed back onto the bed. "Be strong Charlie, you have to be strong," she said and she fell back in her relentless state of pain. That's when it hit me; being strong didn't mean sitting by and watching while someone I loved suffered in such horror; it meant doing something to save her from the pain. That's when I gave her what she wanted – what she had been begging me to do for so long. Knowing the dosage would be lethal, I administered enough medication to finally take her away from the pain. I watched, tears blurring my eyes as she fell into a deep slumber. The serenity on her face washed over me. I held her slight, bony fingers between mine, already mourning what had not yet happened. Who knows how much time passed before her delicate grip fell away from my hand, and I knew if she wasn't gone, she soon would be. I lay there next to her until I knew it was time to leave her. Eventually, I garnered the presence and the energy to call Dr. Hollis. I told her what happened, and how I helped nature take its ugly course.

"Have you called anyone else," she said urgently. "Stay right there, and don't speak to anyone else until I get there."

I went in to check on the babies. They were sleeping so peacefully, and there is no doubt in my mind that the tender aura of Gracie's spirit surrounded them as they lay there that night. It emanated from them and warmed my grieving soul, encompassing the entire room. I didn't want to leave that euphoric experience, so I stayed with them until the doorman rang the phone.

Dr. Hollis pronounced Gracie dead at one forty-eight that night. I sat with the sleeping children, allowing the doctor to arrange for the funeral home to pick-up her body. Gracie's wish was to be cremated, and Dr. Hollis's wish was for her to be cremated as soon as possible. The funeral director obliged. This irritated the police coroner who caught up with us to express his displeasure over that fact.

We were gathered at the mortuary: Toni, Dr. Hollis, the funeral director Mr. Peterson, and I. We were discussing plans for the service, which Gracie had spelled out in detail, when the coroner meekly appeared beside our group, momentarily unnoticed. Mr. Peterson looked up, acknowledging the presence of the man who joined our meeting.

"Dr. Hollis?" the surprisingly young, studious man said as he scanned the group. "Mr. Peterson?"

"I'm Dr. Hollis," the doctor spoke up, prepared to take control of the situation.

"I'm Dr. Cript from the City coroner's office," said the grim man. "The young lady up front said I would find you back here. I see where you signed the death certificate for a Mrs. Ann Grace Willingham Lofton?"

"Dr. Crypt? You're kidding, right? Yes that's correct, I signed the death certificate," said Dr. Hollis.

"It's Cript with an i," he said, eyes looking downward. "We will need to take custody of the remains for examination before interment." He could sense Dr. Hollis' hostility and tried to remain respectful.

Dr. Hollis reached for Gracie's ashes. "Help yourself," she said, handing the urn to the mortician.

"But these are cremated remains. I need a body," the coroner said trying to hand back the urn as if he could receive the intact body by simply redeeming the ashes. He lost his air of morbid composure.

"Sorry, but this is Mrs. Lofton," Dr. Hollis insisted, pushing the urn back in the direction of the coroner.

"Well, how will we examine these remains?" Dr. Cript said. He turned to the mortician searching for an answer from him.

"Why do you need to examine the remains?" Dr. Hollis asked.

"You know as well as I do, when someone of Mrs. Lofton's age dies at her home, we're required to do an autopsy to determine the official cause of death," the coroner said, looking back to Dr. Hollis.

"Uh, Mrs. Lofton had stage four, terminal cancer, Doctor,"

she said. "I can assure you, she didn't slip on her kitchen floor while lying in bed in an incapacitated state. Cancer was the cause of death. I will be glad to certify and attest to that, as well as provide any medical records your office may require."

"Just the same," said the frustrated coroner, "the body shouldn't have been cremated before we had a chance to examine it. Why was it cremated so quickly?" He handed the urn back Dr. Hollis, who exhibited a smile of satisfaction.

"Because the deceased expressly stated that she wished that to be the case, and the family, here, honored her request," said Dr. Hollis, waving a hand in our direction.

"Well, that's not the proper procedure," the defeated coroner stammered. He looked like he wanted to complain further, but with respectable decorum he just said, "Dr. Hollis, my office will contact you if we have any more questions." After that, at some point, he faded away as meekly as he arrived until he was no longer in the room, but no one was sure of when he was actually gone.

I chuckled to myself, knowing Gracie would have loved the encounter – especially being the center of it – dead or alive.

....

The days after Gracie's death, before the funeral, stand vivid in my memory. I worked from home to be with the children and give myself some solace from the rigorous schedule we had all been following. There were moments of grief, but I was relieved for Gracie. The relaxation translated into every daily activity.

The babies were changed, and fed, and bathed and put to bed, all at the proper times and in the proper manner. They could sense the relief, but I hoped they missed their mother. I wanted them to somehow remember their mother, even from their infant memories. I wanted them to remember how great she had been for me and for them, and, with the best intentions, I wanted them to remember some sense of loss from her absence. They were able to spend a year with Gracie, but I looked forward to them carrying a sense of her throughout their lives.

Toni was frequently around, as she promised Gracie she would be, helping to keep the household intact in spite of me and my male deficiencies. She was eternally patient with all of us, and I would never forget what she meant to us in the days before and after we lost Gracie. She did all this in spite of the loss of her best friend – or perhaps because of it.

One day Toni and I had a different kind of conversation; one beyond who was fed or changed, and it changed the course of my life, once again. "So what's next for you, Charlie?" she said.

I had my typically opaque response. "I dunno. I guess I'll get the kids into bed, and maybe catch something on TV before turning in," I said.

"No, what are you going to do with your life?" she said.

"Well, I guess I'm about ready to get back to work," I said without much thought. "I guess I'll have to find someone to care for the children during the day, but I can work on that."

"Is that what you want to do, for sure?" she said.

"Well, I guess," I responded, realizing I was guessing throughout our conversation.

"Well I'm not so sure," said Toni. "You might want to think about it. Gracie and I did. I'm going to get home; I've got to be in the office in the morning."

Toni made me consider my future for the first time since my stay at Club Fed, and I carried my thoughts to bed with me that night. Being in New York with Gracie had been great. It was her home, and I fit in fine when I was with her. But most of my life was in the south. As I deliberated, I understood Atlanta was where I needed to be.

If I took the kids back to Atlanta, what would I do? I liked work, but the opportunities to do my job there would be more limited than in New York. I was sure I could find something similar, but it probably would not pay as much. That wasn't a major consideration, since Gracie and her father insured that the children and I would enjoy financial security. Money rarely caused a worry in my past, even when I didn't have any. Again, it looked as though I wouldn't have any problems in that area. In fact, I realized we would be quite comfortable, whether or not I worked.

As I reflected on my prospects, the ideas poured in and began to develop into a cohesive plan. I had the power and the means to control my life. Finally, I learned to not just be the pebble carried downstream with the flow of the current. I could make decisions and take myself in any direction I chose.

Gracie meant so much to me, and she was taken away. I had the children who were my joy and responsibility. I was so grateful they were healthy. Of course, there were parents and children around the world who were not as lucky. I had the means and the desire to change my focus to helping those less fortunate victims of cancer.

Also, I wanted to finish the story that Gracie and I started, which was put on the slow track for school and work and children, and finally put on hold for disease and death. It would be a tribute to Gracie, whose life and essence would be shared with anyone choosing to read about it.

And I would put my money and time toward the relief of the parents and the young victims of life threatening illnesses. When we panicked at the idea that the children might be affected by cancer, Gracie immediately began researching the best treatment centers around the country for children. If there had been a need, we could have found great care in New York, but Gracie wanted to know all the options. From her research, I knew there was a comprehensive children's cancer treatment center in Atlanta, and that would be a good place to invest in while I raised my own kids.

My epiphany lifted me out of bed and took me into the kids' room. I smiled at Sara and Charlie as I announced in a fatherly, decisive tone that we were going to Atlanta. They barely cracked their sleepy eyelids in indifference. Before I went to sleep, I called Toni to thank her for everything she had been doing for me, and especially what she had done for me that day. I kept my plans to myself that evening.

The next day I went into the office and met with Cy Leonhardt to turn in my notice and give him my reasons for wanting to move back to Atlanta. Cy was understanding as Cy always tended to be, and he offered to contact a friend of his who was the chief editor for an alternative weekly newspaper there to see if they might have a place for me. I had read *Gadabout Atlanta*, and while it was no New York Times, it was decent and entertaining. *The Gadabout* was a mixture of local entertainment news, restaurant reviews and more than a few respectable, hard hitting, in-depth articles. I wasn't desperate to get a job, but I appreciated the gesture. In return I volunteered to stay on for as long as he needed me. Craft was putting out books at quite a clip, and Cy was short staffed, so I agreed to stay on for two months, and longer if he needed me. I was in no great hurry. I had my plan in place, which included a flexible timetable.

XXVI. Finally a Decent Funeral

The day of Gracie's memorial service, it was gratifying to see the turnout of friends and acquaintances who came to pay their respects. Gracie and I had the unique privilege of attending each other's funerals, but I can attest that hers was much more uplifting. Gracie was specific about how it would go, but I insisted on one hymn, and she agreed; when it came time to sing the obligatory *Amazing Grace* I wanted to belt it out with everything I could gather from deep inside myself. I felt the song of redemption spoke directly to me on that special occasion and the words rang true in my soul. I once was lost, but now am found, thanks to my amazing Gracie. She was my life, but the service carried me into the future, and prepared me to make one more final life with my two children. When the service was over, it achieved just what those rites should. I was comforted and filled with the spirit of life Gracie left behind. I was only looking forward.

....

Our real estate agent who helped us purchase our expanded space, Mark Moss, put the condo on the market and within six weeks, I had an offer that was large enough to pay off the mortgage with plenty of profit on top. I took the deal without counter offering.

The buyers were Sam and Genie Hanson, a middle aged couple without children. Sam was an investment banker, and Genie was just retired from some kind of production position at NBC. Our condo was so well suited to accommodate a couple with infants. I wondered if that was in their plans – or if Genie might be already pregnant – but I didn't bother them with personal questions. They reminded me of Gracie and me, and I privately wished for Genie to have a long life.

Mark hooked me up with an agent, Missy Cromwell, in Atlanta. She pre-qualified some places for me before we took a weekend house hunting trip back home. It was all very easy for me and probably for Missy, too. I knew the city well, and with the attractive real estate prices in my hometown I would be able pay cash for a house that would suit our family needs and still add money to our abundant nest egg. In my only trip I identified three houses, any of which would suit our needs. When I got back to New York I discussed the pros and cons of each with Toni who helped me with the final decision. After that, Missy went to work with the offer and all the legal activity that goes along with real estate transactions. We worked it out so that the house would close a day after the New York condo.

The timing was almost impeccable, but not quite. As all the elements were coming together I was working on my last project for Craft. I was struggling with CCNY professor and author, Mitch Deavers, who seemed to want to do everything possible to delay his book's completion. It was clear he didn't like me, or at least he didn't believe I was competent to comment on – much less edit – his work product. The funny thing was, I genuinely liked his subject matter, his thorough research, and his writing style. The book was about the reign of Henry VIII. When I read of the birth of Mary, Catherine of Aragon's daughter who would later become queen of England and earn the epithet "Bloody Mary", I thought of my grandmother. That took me back to my childhood and memories of the young Gracie.

Most of my issues with Deaver's book were technical in nature, and when I began to understand *his* nature I let the least important ones slide. Still, I had been with Craft long enough to know what they expected me to do, and when it was necessary I held my ground. This earned me tantrums and insults, after which Deaver would insist Cy Leonhardt mediate our disagreements. Cy usually backed me up, and Mitch Deaver became known as Mitch "The Diva" Deaver between the boss and me. The diva's snits put us so far behind schedule we missed the planned press date. Cy realized where the problem lay, but he needed me to stay around to rescue the deal. I was true to my word, and to Cy. After I had to move out of our condo, Craft put Charlie, Sara, and me in a suite near the office until we finally put the finishing touches on *The British Crown 1509 - 1547 and the Birth of the Church of England.* Finally, Henry VIII got his divorce, the Church of England was established and Cy Leonhardt got the book he so anxiously awaited.

When it was time to leave, the office staff gave me the standard going away party. We shared fond memories of Gracie, and while I never thought I would, I got sentimental to the point of tears. The people there had been good to me. I knew I was doing what was best for the babies and me, but I did not leave without pangs of misgivings.

....

The first time the children and I lit in my hometown, I knew I made the right decision. It was familiar and inviting. There were some bad memories, but they were bottled deep in a former lifetime. Fortunately, I didn't encounter anyone with any memories of me and my escapades from years past, except for Bobby and Eileen, and Marvin and Janita Dixon, and none of them brought up that lifetime.

We moved into a house high up on a hill with a front lawn that slopes lazily down to a quiet cul-de-sac, but there is no ivy in this yard. Coincidentally, there is a lot of stonework on the house, but it is the color of warm honey, not the cold gray stone that comprised the Rock. This house had nothing in common with the Rock and its demons.

I set up a writing office that looks out onto the patio in the backyard and into the woods that stretch beyond the patio. I know when the kids get older they will enjoy exploring the abundant forest behind the house. I will eschew any discussion of butterflies and chaos theory with them for the time being. My father's well intentioned lessons gave me the impression that I was at the mercy of whatever vibrations those butterfly wings blew my way. I want my children to understand what I finally learned from my late wife.

I learned from Gracie that life is a gift that you can only lease. While you can never own it, you can damn sure manage it, and your purpose for living is to do just that. True happiness comes from self-fulfillment and finding the self-confidence and courage to do things you know you have to do. The only thing life can do to beat you is to abandon you.

People are born into countless circumstances in this country. I would venture to say that, short of arriving on this earth in a squalid, third world nation, not one circumstance is better than another. A child born with a silver spoon in his mouth has no advantage over someone born into what we call poverty here. The kid who grows up with Bloody Mary and her daughter for adult role models is no less lucky than the one with the upstanding Hugh and Andrea McDowell for parents. I can't say whether my circumstances would be considered helpful or detrimental to my development as a person. I just know they were what happened. And now I know that we all owe it to the world to find our happiness and pursue it with every fiber of our soul.

Some who read this might be put off to hear one who is a fraud and a murderer preach such high minded philosophies. Some might say I am lucky I am not rotting in a penitentiary doing the time I deserve for killing my brother. Others will say I should pay for my act of courage in releasing Gracie from her living hell. Perhaps I deserve punishment, not a future filled with promise and an abundance of love and security.

Perhaps I am lucky, but you make your own luck, and sometimes you have to grab it wherever it presents itself. While I know criminals must be punished, I am doing a lot more good with my time and my money than I would ever be doing in prison. I am finishing this story as a tribute to Gracie and to show that there is good and redemption somewhere inside the most wretched among us if someone can reach deep enough to find it. Gracie found the good in me, and she saw my optimism, and she rewarded me with herself and all she had.

So this is the end of my story, but not the end of my life. Everything I have told you I know from personal experience, or stories people told me, or interviews that my wife or my trusted friend or I performed after the fact of the events herein.

This is my latest will and testament. I am working with the brave children and their families at the cancer center, and working with the center's board of trustees to determine where their financial needs are and how I can best help meet those needs.

I will have to answer to whatever god greets me when I finish what I'm sure is this final life on earth, but for now I have to answer to myself. I will pursue my happiness, which is raising my children to be the best and happiest they can be, and spreading my good butterfly wings to blow comfort and hope to some kids who have hit the bump in the road called cancer. And when my time is at an end, I believe I will be able to look back and consider that, on balance, my life was worthwhile – and as the son of Charles Lofton Sr., the smartest man in the world, that's all I ever expected from myself.

The events and characters described in this book are fictional. Any similarity to actual events or individuals is purely coincidental.